This is a fairy tale of blood and bullets.

It is the story of two women and three men

who cannot die. Mostly.

Their names are

Andy, Nicky, Joe, Booker, and Nile.

It is a story about time, and age, and ages,

and about friendship, and love, and regret.

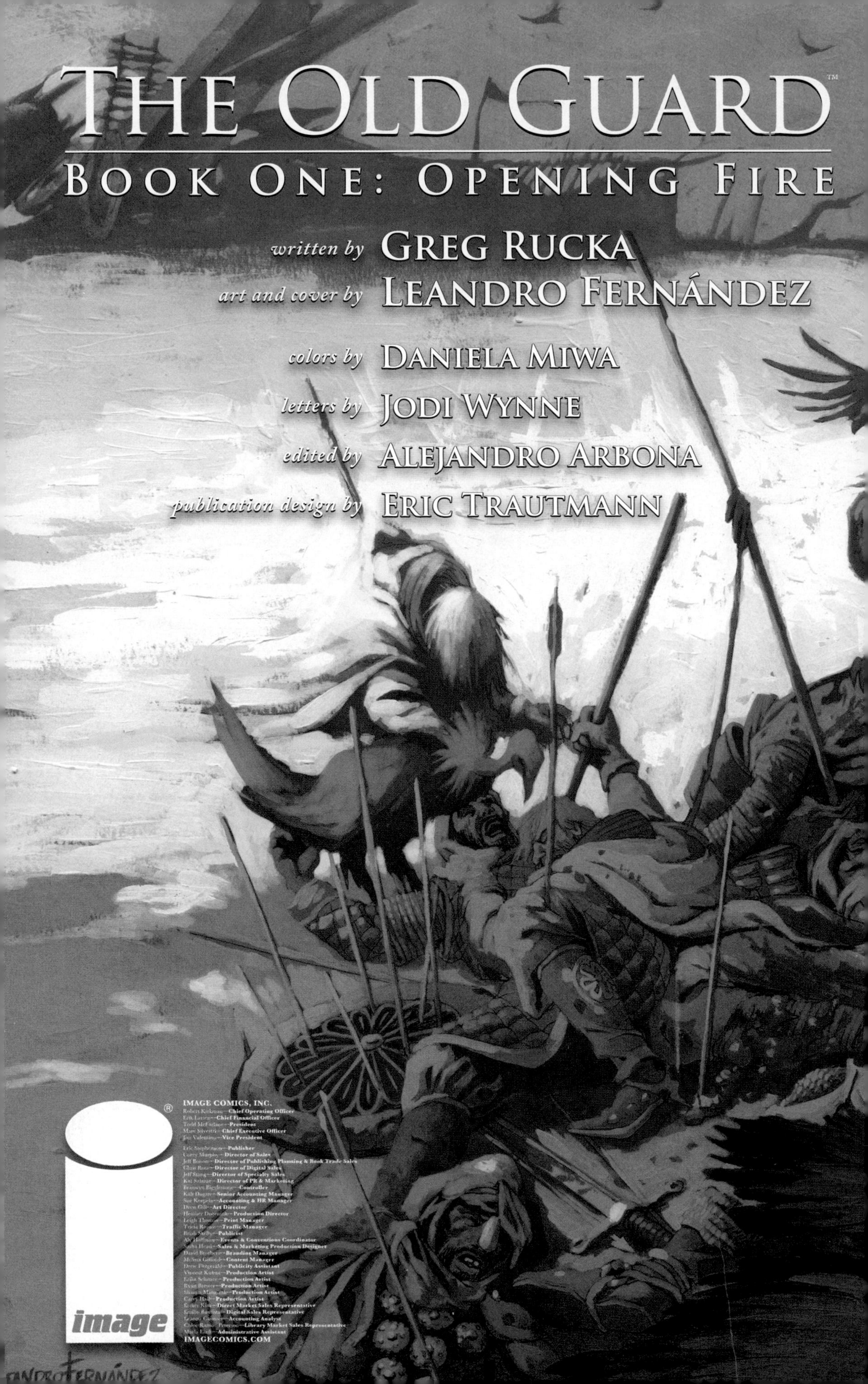

THE OLD GUARD

BOOK ONE: OPENING FIRE

written by **GREG RUCKA**

art and cover by **LEANDRO FERNÁNDEZ**

colors by **DANIELA MIWA**

letters by **JODI WYNNE**

edited by **ALEJANDRO ARBONA**

publication design by **ERIC TRAUTMANN**

IMAGE COMICS, INC.
Robert Kirkman—Chief Operating Officer
Erik Larsen—Chief Financial Officer
Todd McFarlane—President
Marc Silvestri—Chief Executive Officer
Jim Valentino—Vice President

Eric Stephenson—Publisher
Larry Marthis—Director of Sales
Jeff Boison—Director of Publishing Planning & Book Trade Sales
Chris Ross—Director of Digital Sales
Jeff Stang—Director of Specialty Sales
Kat Salazar—Director of PR & Marketing
Branwyn Bigglestone—Controller
Kelly Gray—Senior Accounting Manager
Sue Korpela—Accounting & HR Manager
Drew Gill—Art Director
Heather Doornink—Production Director
Leigh Thomas—Print Manager
Tricia Ramos—Traffic Manager
Briah Skelly—Publicist
Ali Hoffman—Events & Conventions Coordinator
Sasha Head—Sales & Marketing Production Designer
David Brothers—Branding Manager
Melissa Gifford—Content Manager
Drew Fitzgerald—Publicity Assistant
Vincent Kukua—Production Artist
Erika Schnatz—Production Artist
Ryan Brewer—Production Artist
Shanna Matuszak—Production Artist
Carey Hall—Production Artist
Esther Kim—Direct Market Sales Representative
Emilio Bautista—Digital Sales Representative
Leanna Caunter—Accounting Analyst
Chloe Ramos-Peterson—Library Market Sales Representative
Marla Eizik—Administrative Assistant
IMAGECOMICS.COM

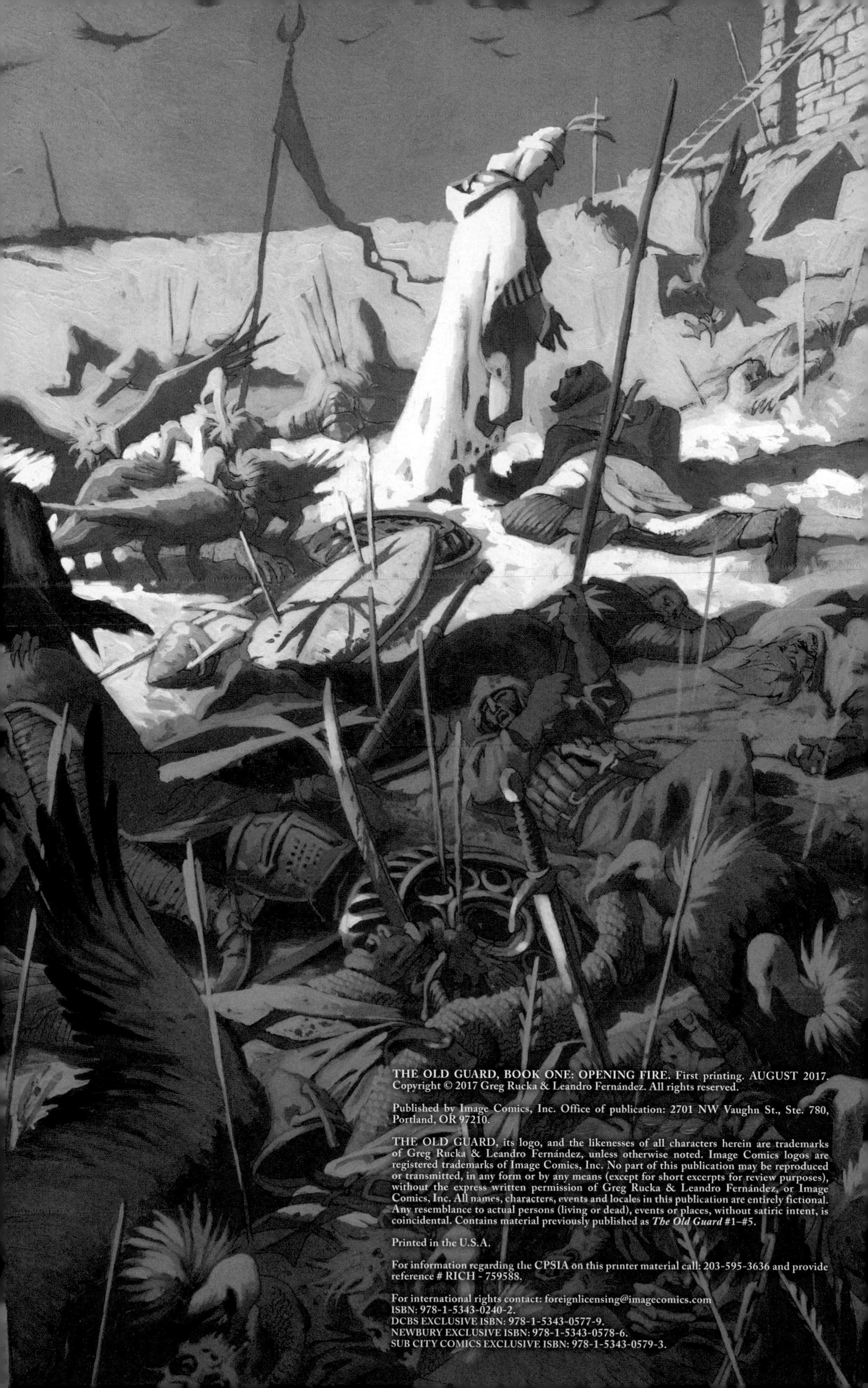

THE OLD GUARD, BOOK ONE: OPENING FIRE. First printing. AUGUST 2017.

Published by Image Comics, Inc. Office of publication: 2701 NW Vaughn St., Ste. 780, Portland, OR 97210.

Printed in the U.S.A.

For information regarding the CPSIA on this printer material call: 203-595-3636 and provide reference # RICH - 759588.

For international rights contact: foreignlicensing@imagecomics.com
ISBN: 978-1-5343-0240-2.
DCBS EXCLUSIVE ISBN: 978-1-5343-0577-9.
NEWBURY EXCLUSIVE ISBN: 978-1-5343-0578-6.
SUB CITY COMICS EXCLUSIVE ISBN: 978-1-5343-0579-3.

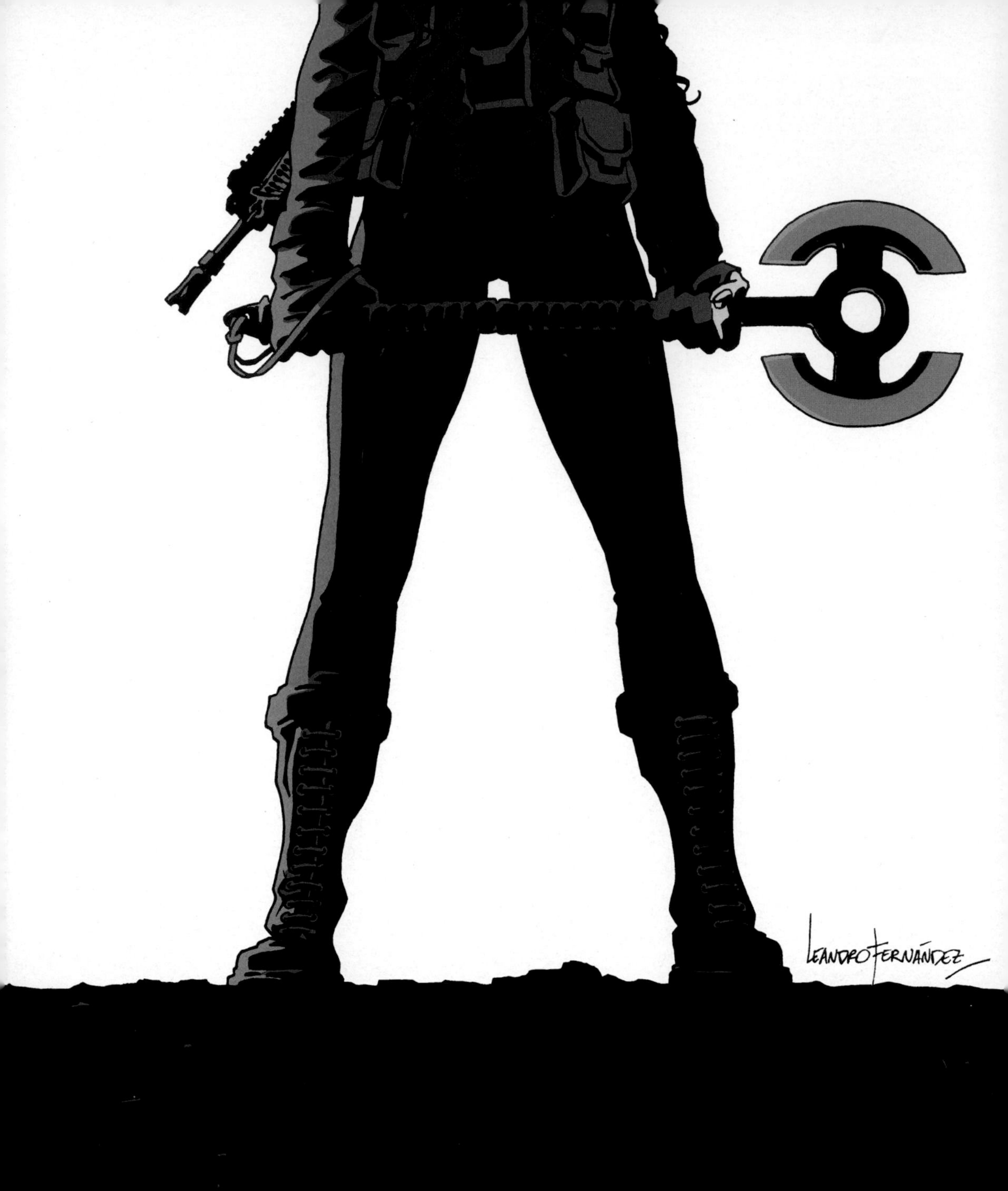
LEANDRO FERNÁNDEZ

CHAPTER ONE

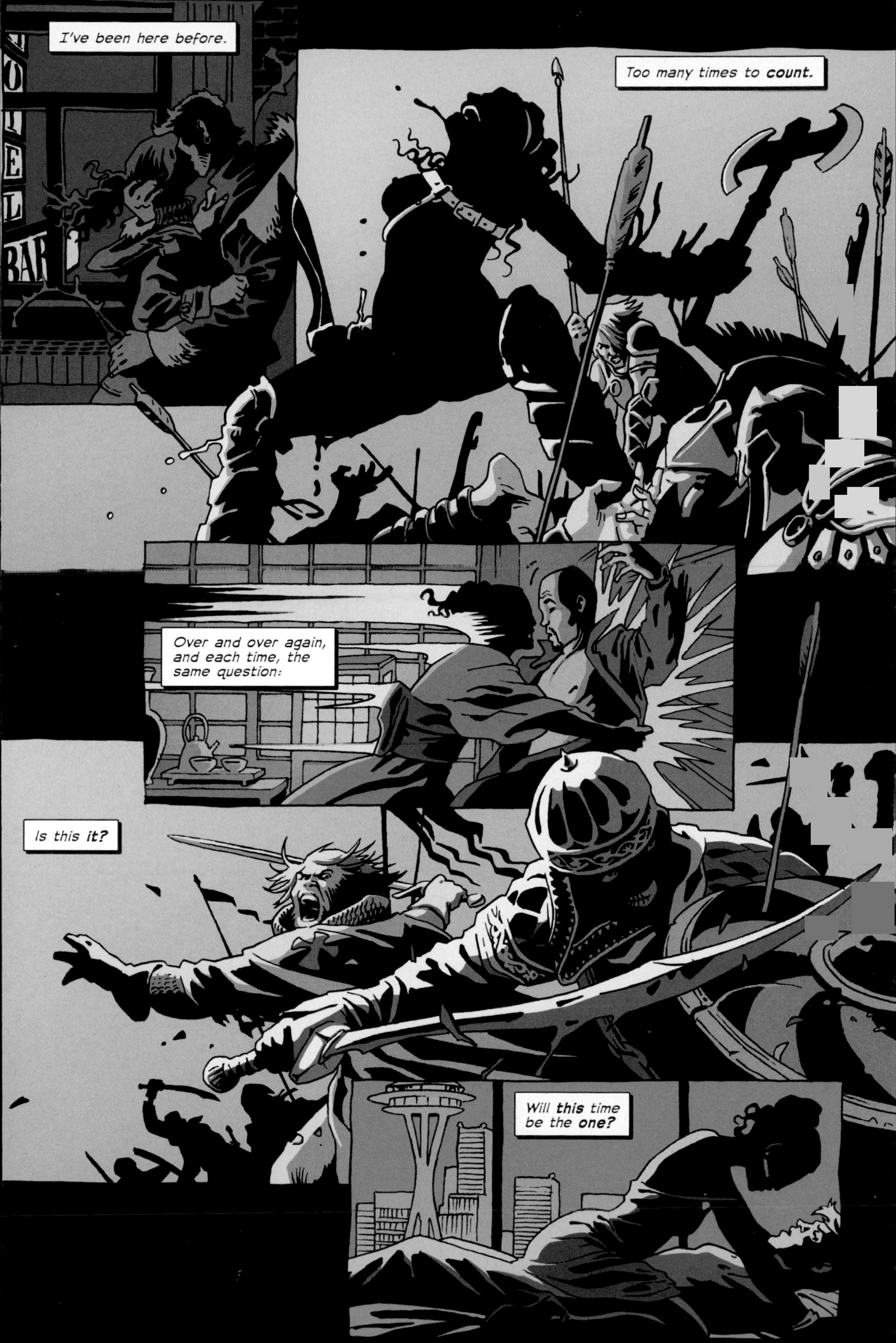
I've been here before.
BAR
Too many times to **count.**
Over and over again, and each time, the same question:
Is this **it?**
Will **this** time be the **one?**

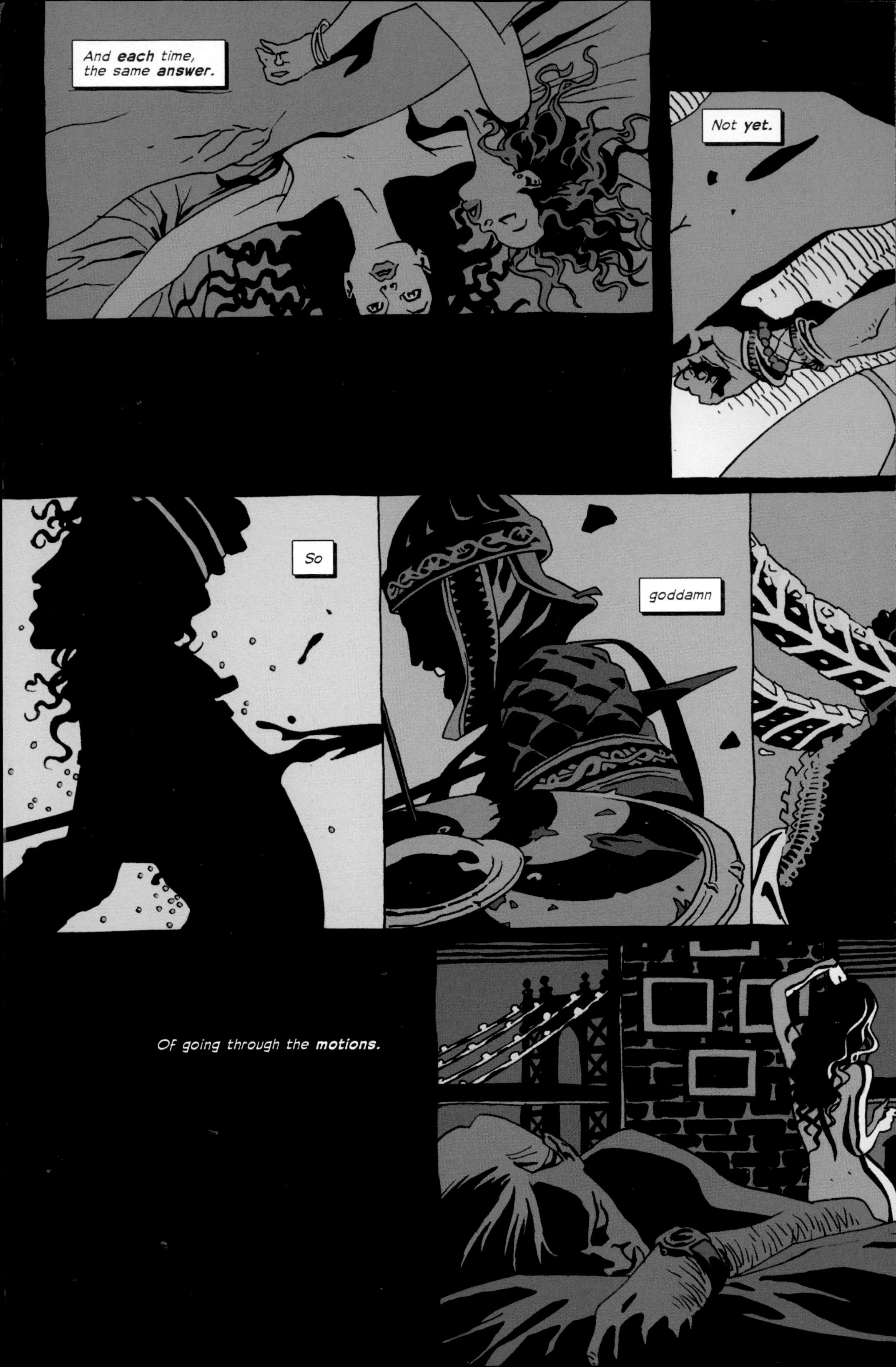
And each time,
the same answer.
Not yet.
So
goddamn
Of going through the motions.

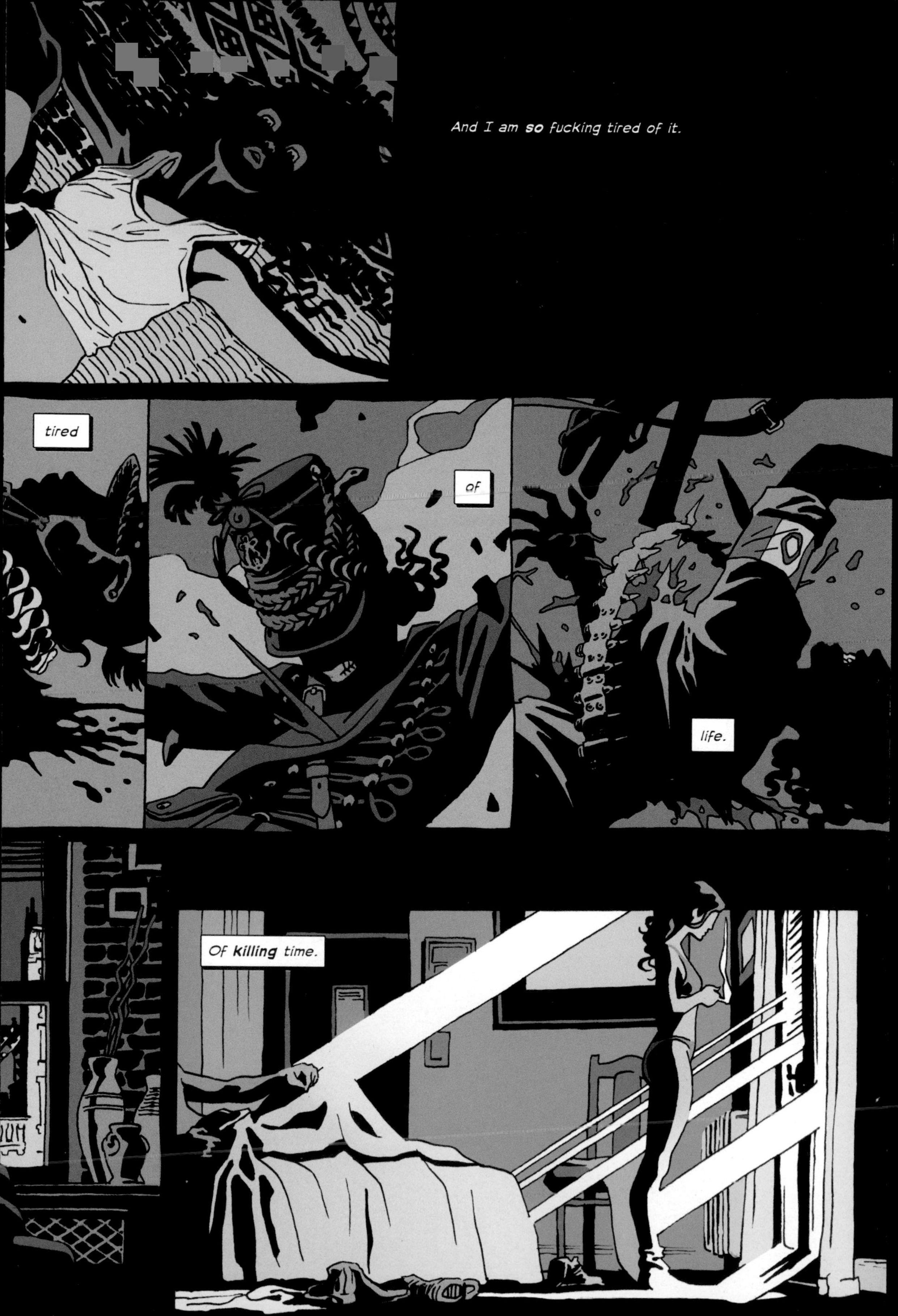
And I am **so** fucking tired of it.
tired
of
life.
Of **killing** time.

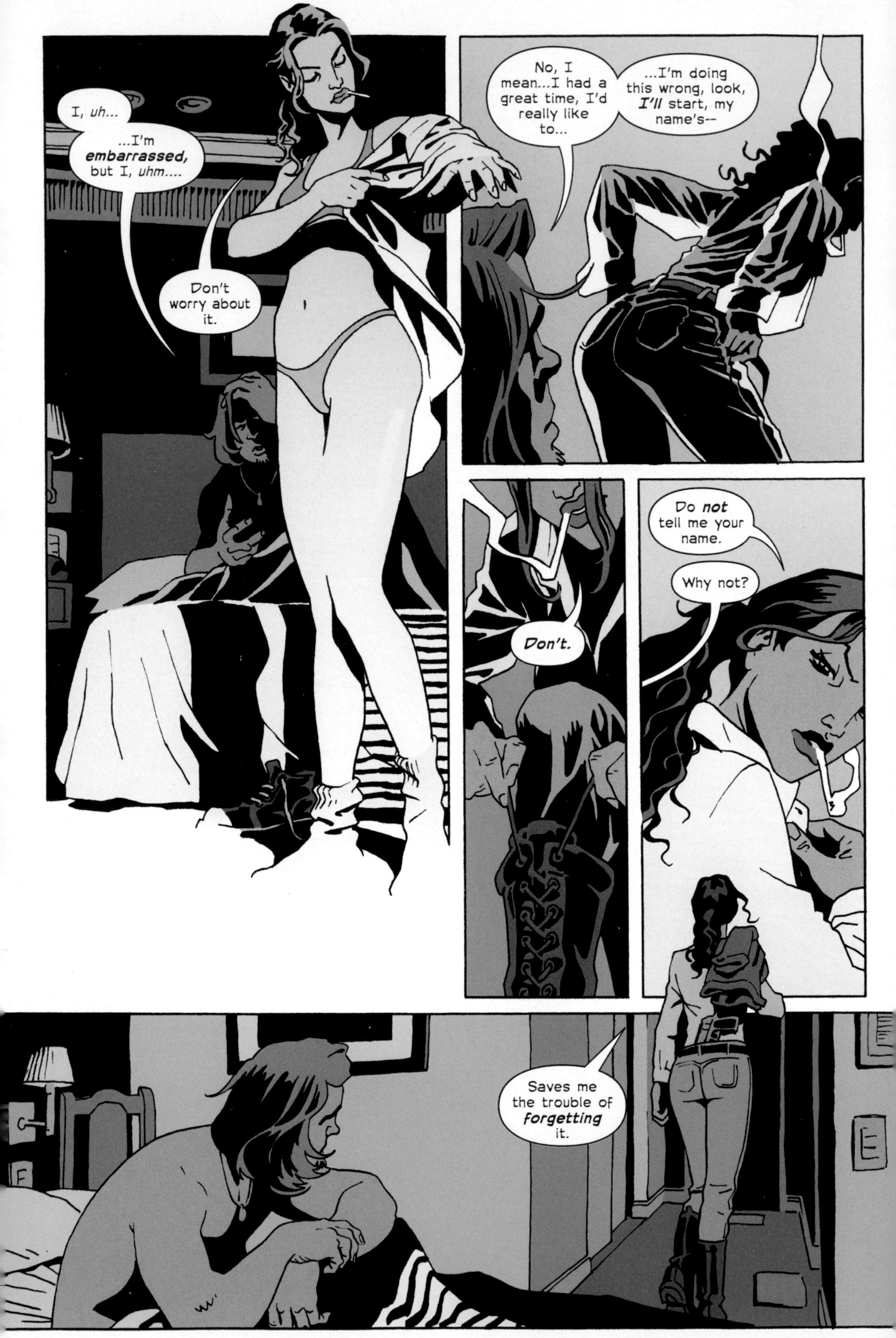

I, uh...
...I'm embarrassed, but I, uhm....
Don't worry about it.
No, I mean...I had a great time, I'd really like to...
...I'm doing this wrong, look, I'll start, my name's--
Don't.
Do not tell me your name.
Why not?
Saves me the trouble of forgetting it.

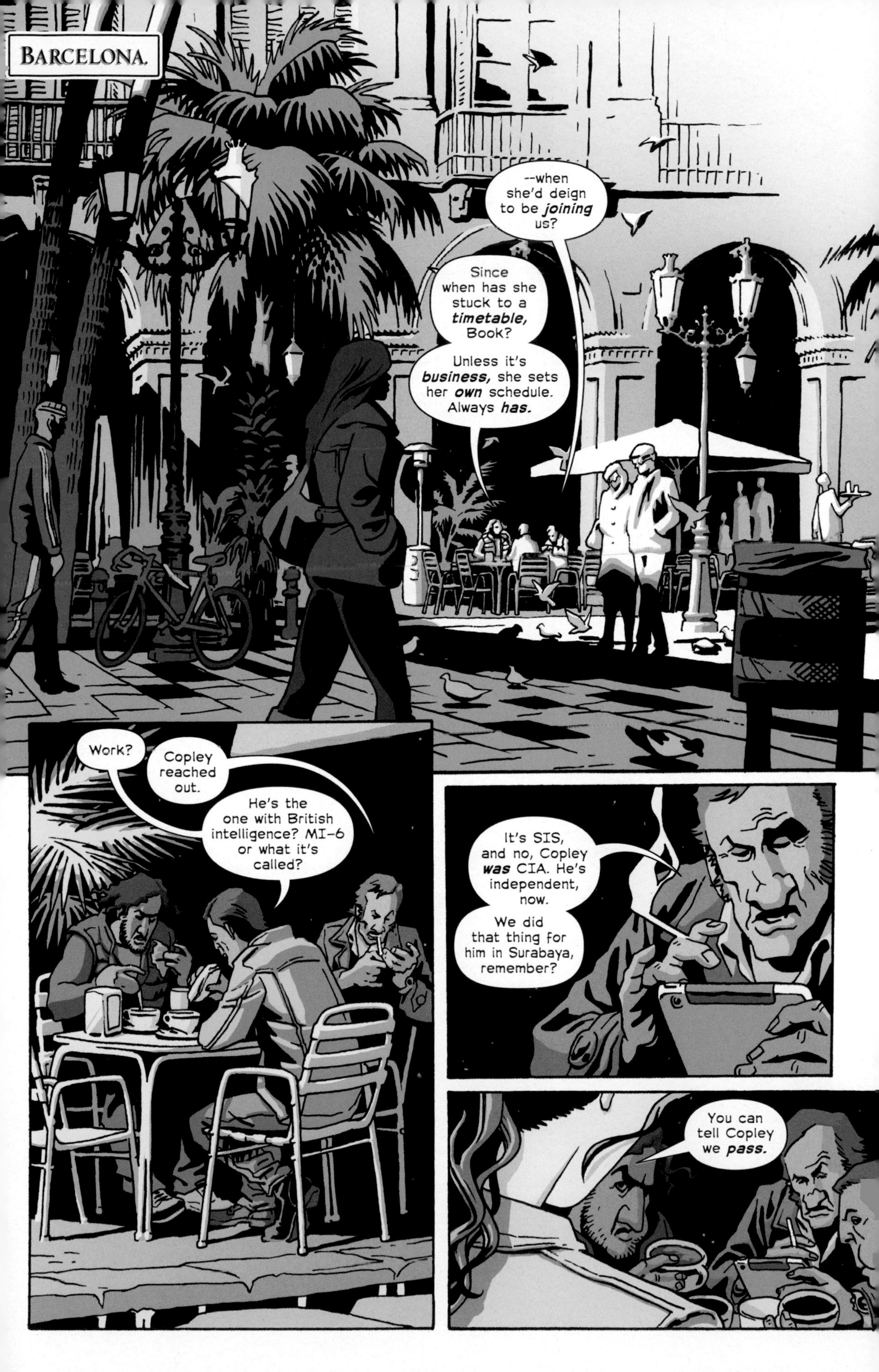
BARCELONA.
--when she'd deign to be *joining* us?
Since when has she stuck to a *timetable,* Book?
Unless it's *business,* she sets her *own* schedule. Always *has.*
Work?
Copley reached out.
He's the one with British intelligence? MI-6 or what it's called?
It's SIS, and no, Copley *was* CIA. He's independent, now.
We did that thing for him in Surabaya, remember?
You can tell Copley we *pass.*

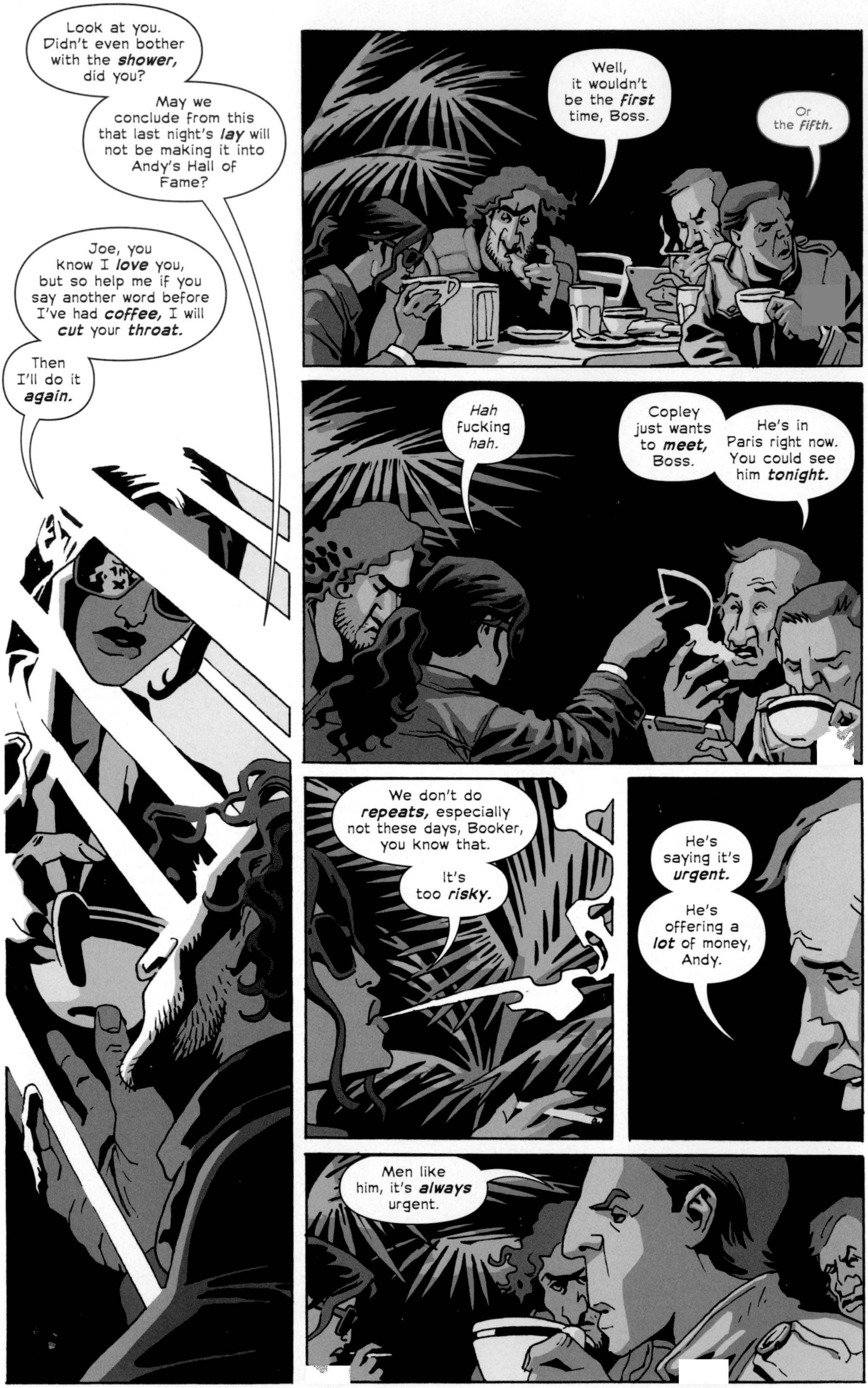
Look at you. Didn't even bother with the *shower,* did you?
May we conclude from this that last night's *lay* will not be making it into Andy's Hall of Fame?
Joe, you know I *love* you, but so help me if you say another word before I've had *coffee,* I will *cut* your *throat.*
Then I'll do it *again.*
Well, it wouldn't be the *first* time, Boss.
Or the *fifth.*
Hah fucking hah.
Copley just wants to *meet,* Boss.
He's in Paris right now. You could see him *tonight.*
We don't do *repeats,* especially not these days, Booker, you know that.
It's too *risky.*
He's saying it's *urgent.*
He's offering a *lot* of money, Andy.
Men like him, it's *always* urgent.

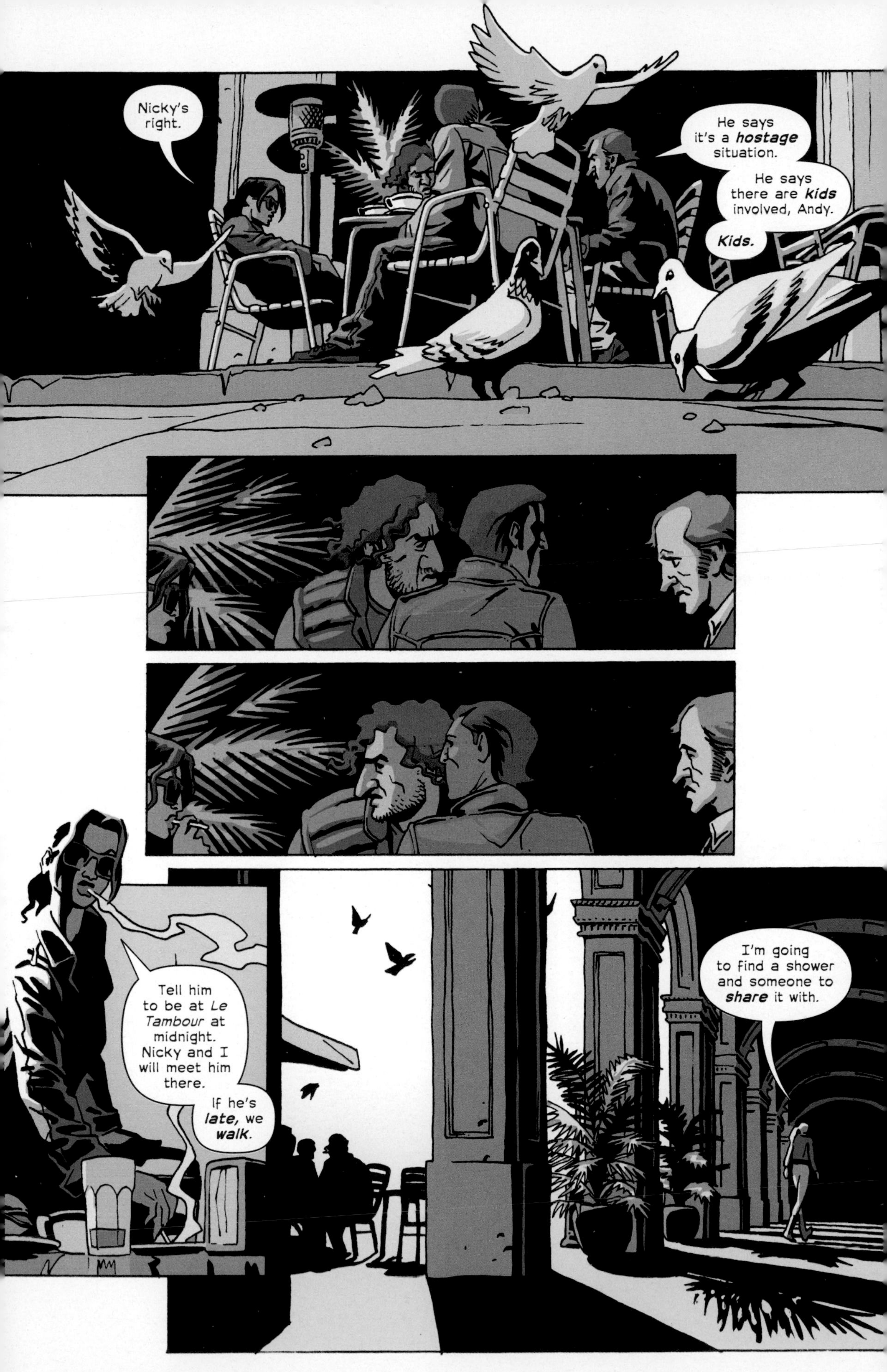
Nicky's right.
He says it's a *hostage* situation.
He says there are *kids* involved, Andy.
Kids.
Tell him to be at *Le Tambour* at midnight. Nicky and I will meet him there.
If he's *late,* we *walk*.
I'm going to find a shower and someone to *share* it with.

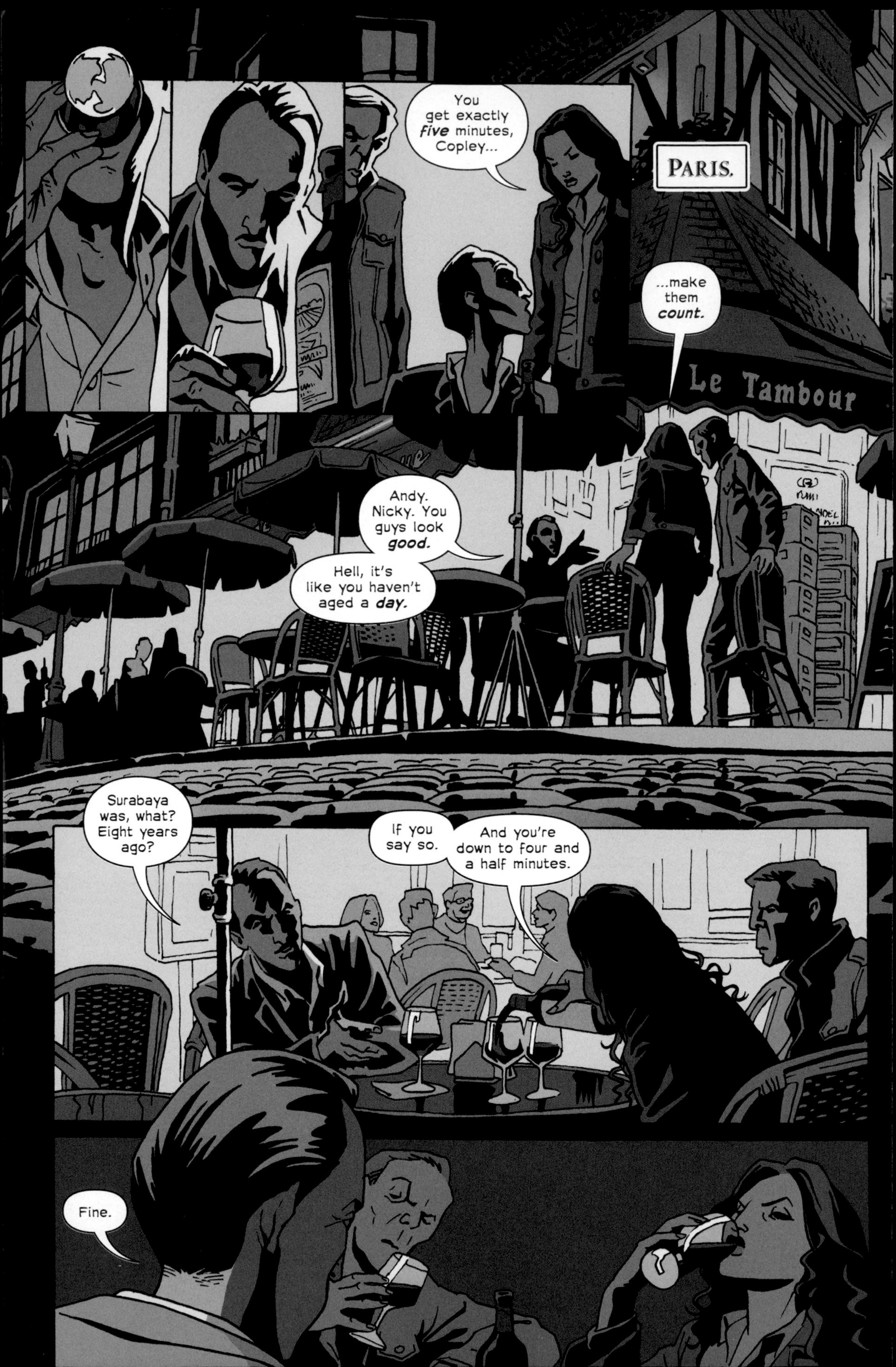
You get exactly *five* minutes, Copley...
PARIS.
...make them *count.*
Le Tambour
Andy. Nicky. You guys look *good.*
Hell, it's like you haven't aged a *day.*
Surabaya was, what? Eight years ago?
If you say so.
And you're down to four and a half minutes.
Fine.

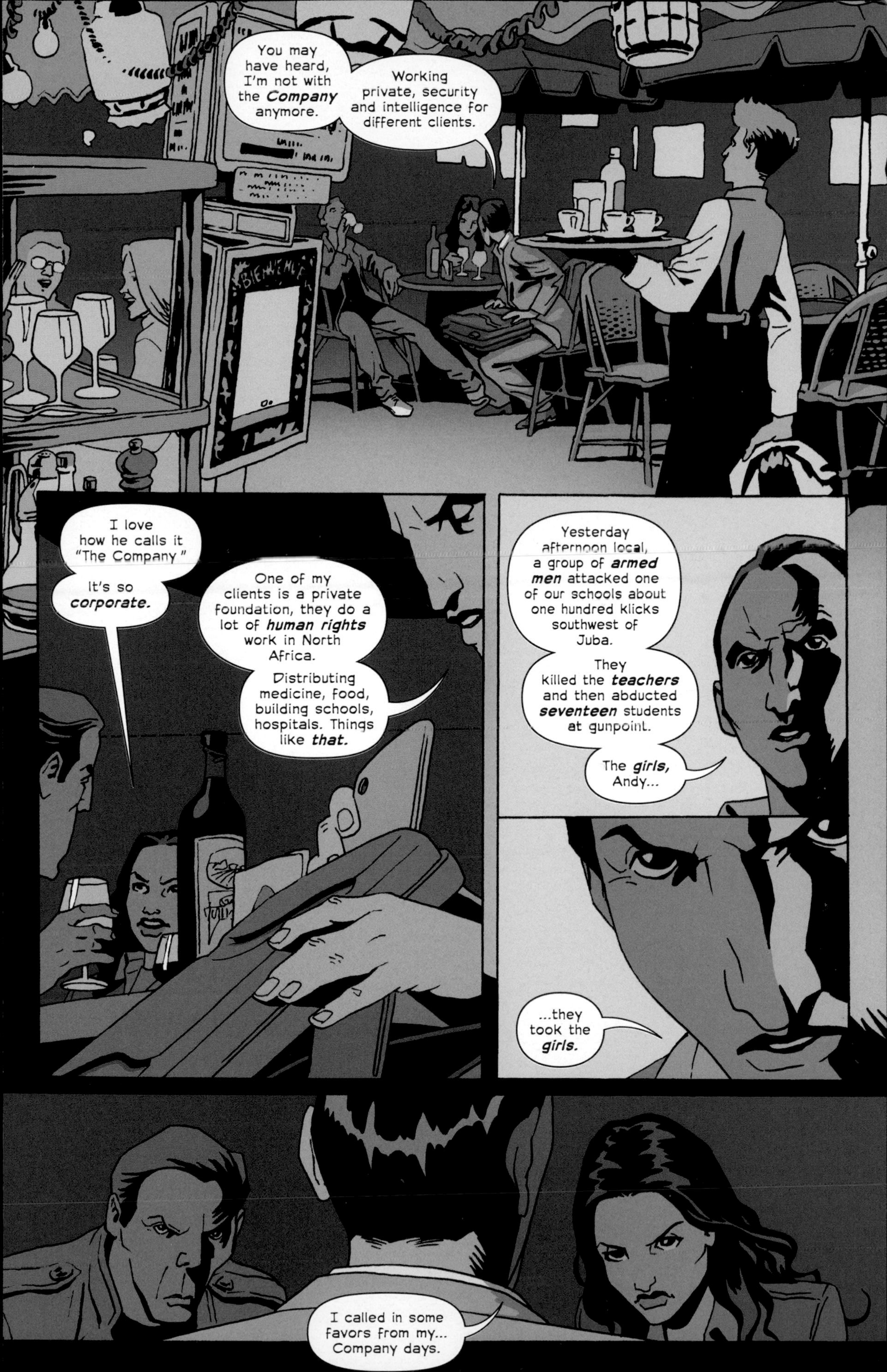
You may have heard, I'm not with the Company anymore.
Working private, security and intelligence for different clients.
I love how he calls it "The Company"
It's so corporate.
One of my clients is a private foundation, they do a lot of human rights work in North Africa.
Distributing medicine, food, building schools, hospitals. Things like that.
Yesterday afternoon local, a group of armed men attacked one of our schools about one hundred klicks southwest of Juba.
They killed the teachers and then abducted seventeen students at gunpoint.
The girls, Andy...
...they took the girls.
I called in some favors from my... Company days.

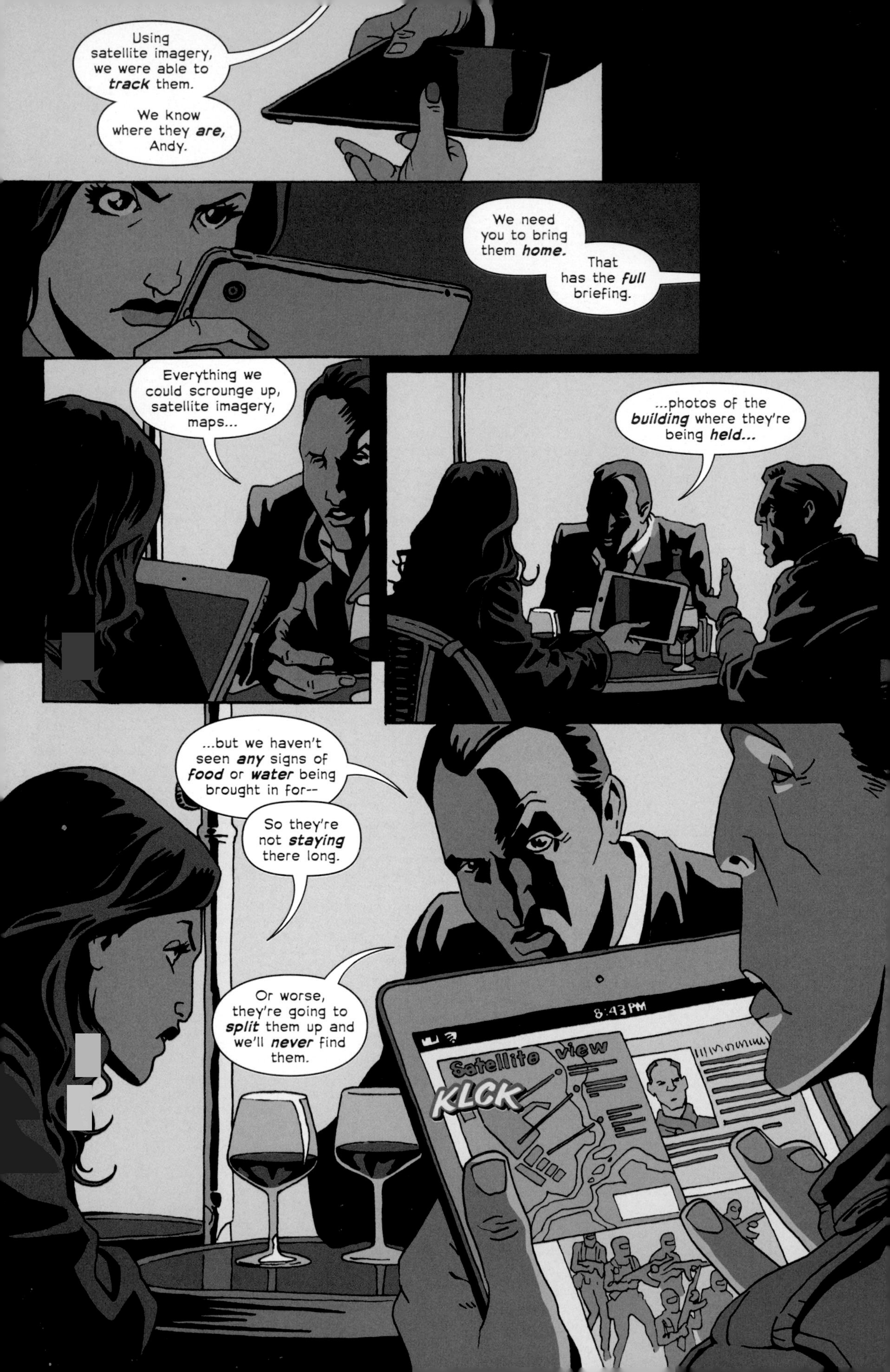
Using satellite imagery, we were able to *track* them.
We know where they *are,* Andy.
We need you to bring them *home.*
That has the *full* briefing.
Everything we could scrounge up, satellite imagery, maps...
...photos of the *building* where they're being *held...*
...but we haven't seen *any* signs of *food* or *water* being brought in for--
So they're not *staying* there long.
Or worse, they're going to *split* them up and we'll *never* find them.
8:43 PM
Satellite view
KLCK

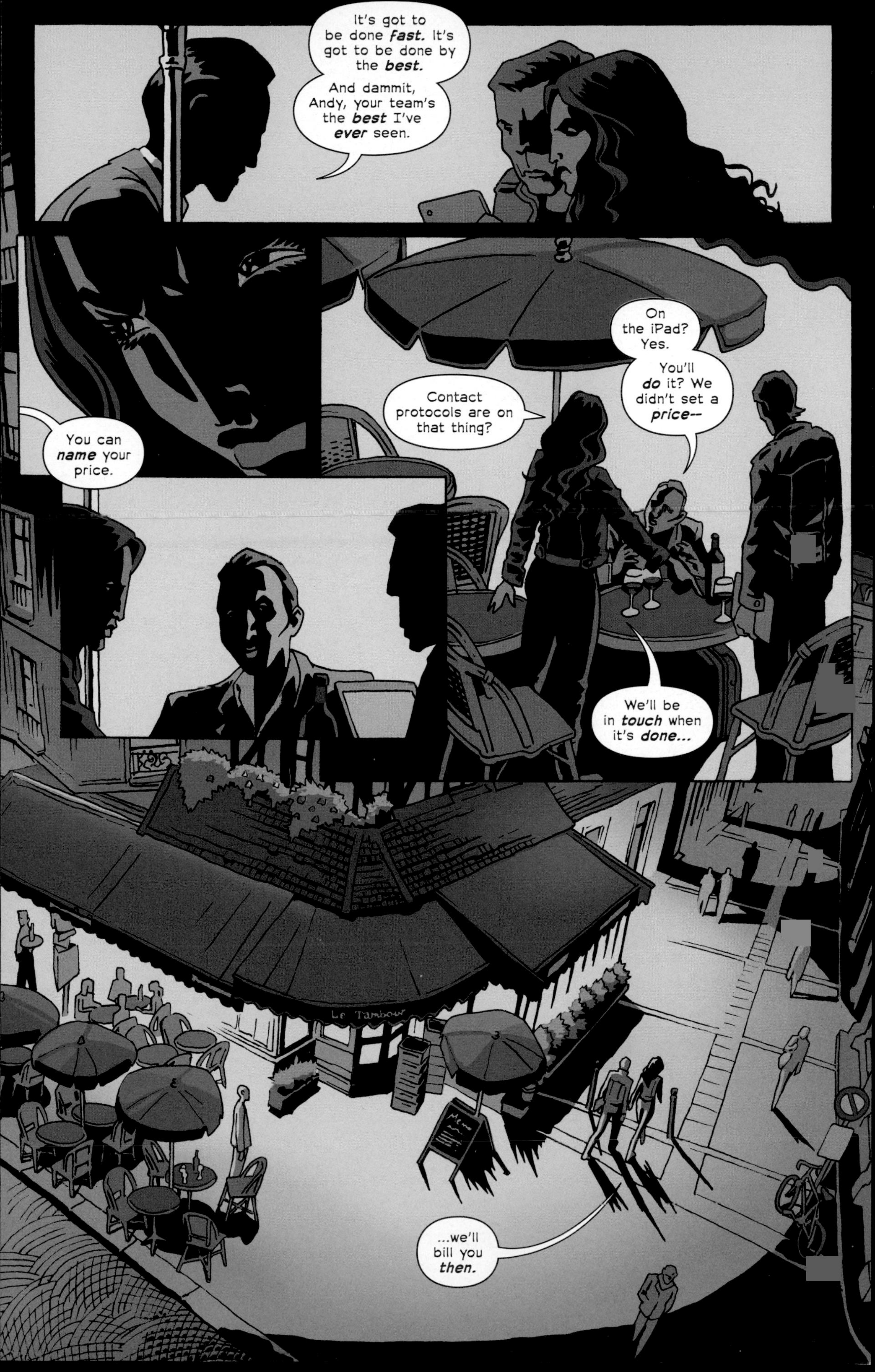
It's got to be done ***fast.*** It's got to be done by the ***best.***
And dammit, Andy, your team's the ***best*** I've ***ever*** seen.
You can ***name*** your price.
Contact protocols are on that thing?
On the iPad? Yes.
You'll ***do*** it? We didn't set a ***price--***
We'll be in ***touch*** when it's ***done...***
Le Tambour
...we'll bill you ***then.***

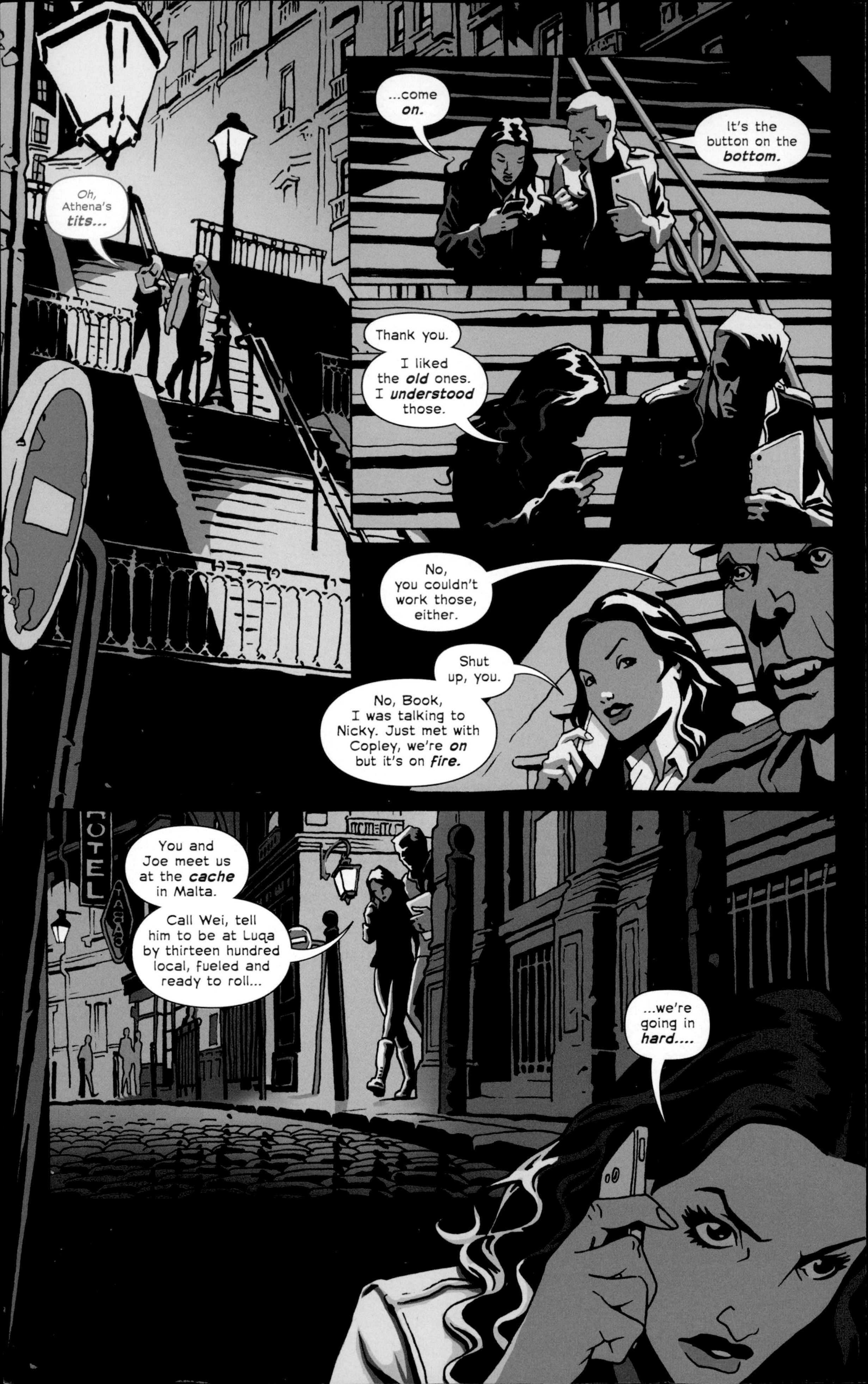
Oh, Athena's tits...
...come on.
It's the button on the bottom.
Thank you.
I liked the old ones. I understood those.
No, you couldn't work those, either.
Shut up, you.
No, Book, I was talking to Nicky. Just met with Copley, we're on but it's on fire.
You and Joe meet us at the cache in Malta.
Call Wei, tell him to be at Luqa by thirteen hundred local, fueled and ready to roll...
...we're going in hard....

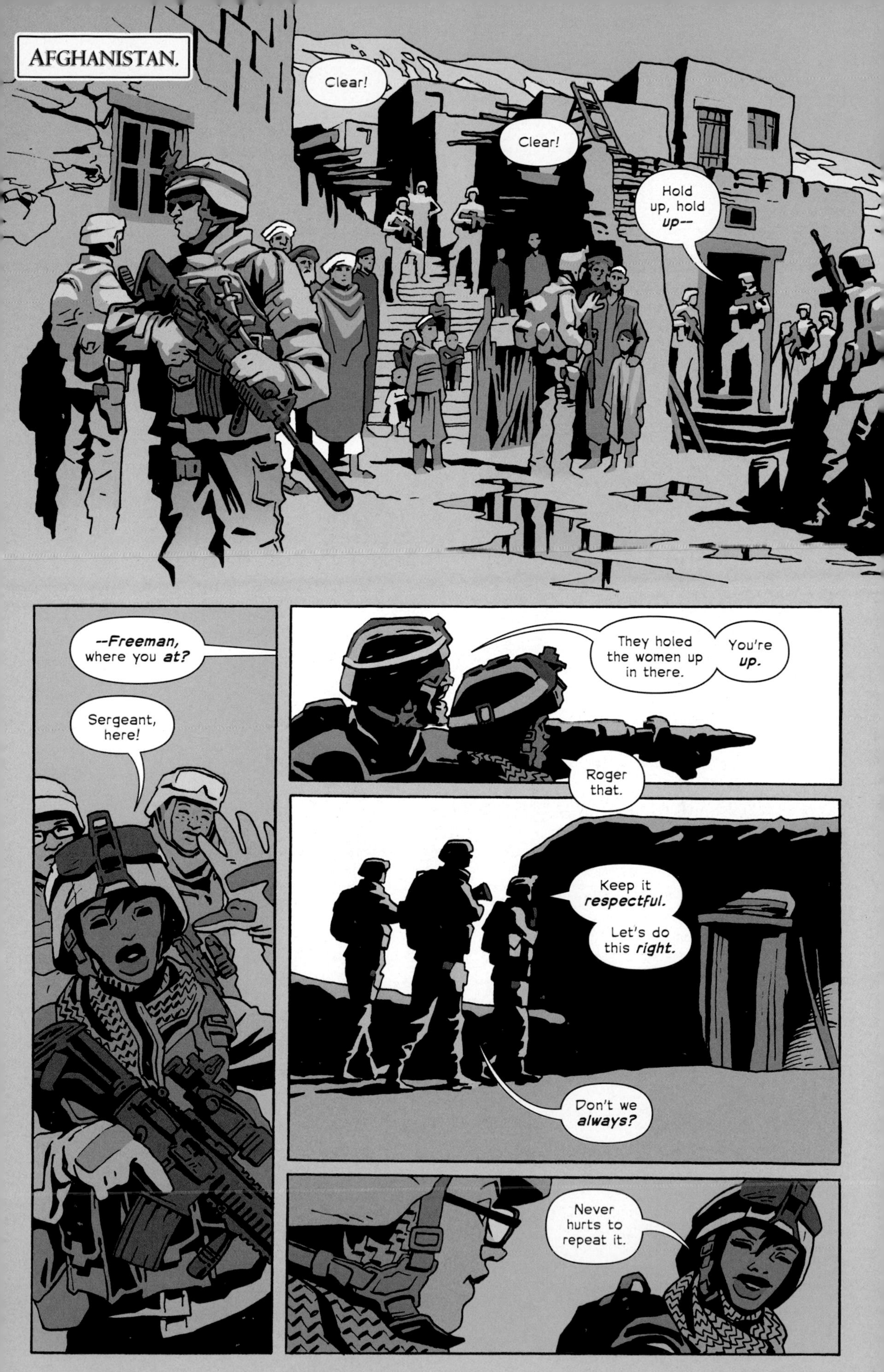
AFGHANISTAN.
Clear!
Clear!
Hold up, hold *up*--
--Freeman, where you *at?*
Sergeant, here!
They holed the women up in there.
You're *up.*
Roger that.
Keep it *respectful.*
Let's do this *right.*
Don't we *always?*
Never hurts to repeat it.

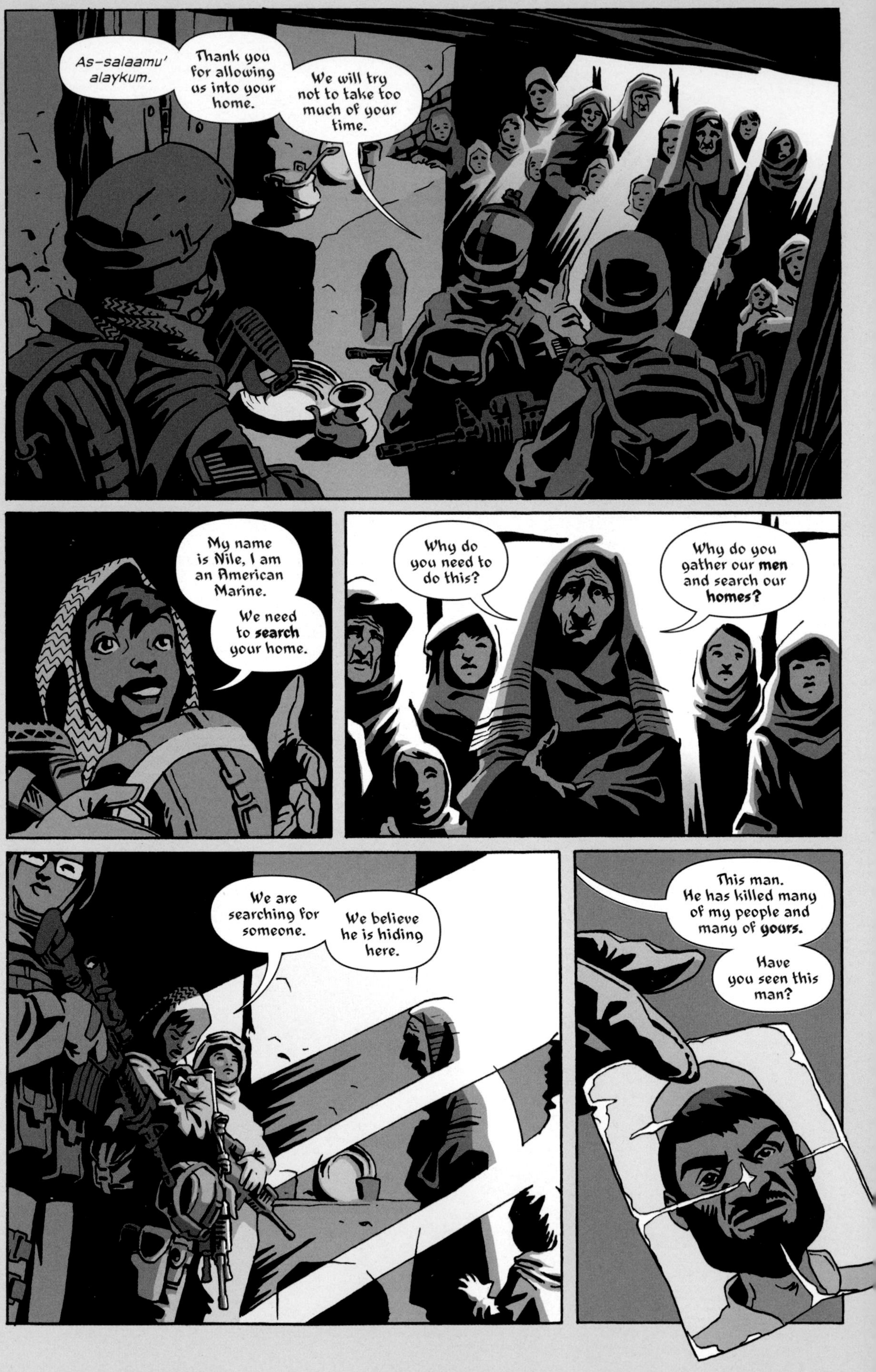
As-salaamu' alaykum.
Thank you for allowing us into your home.
We will try not to take too much of your time.
My name is Nile, I am an American Marine.
We need to **search** your home.
Why do you need to do this?
Why do you gather our **men** and search our **homes?**
We are searching for someone.
We believe he is hiding here.
This man. He has killed many of my people and many of **yours.**
Have you seen this man?

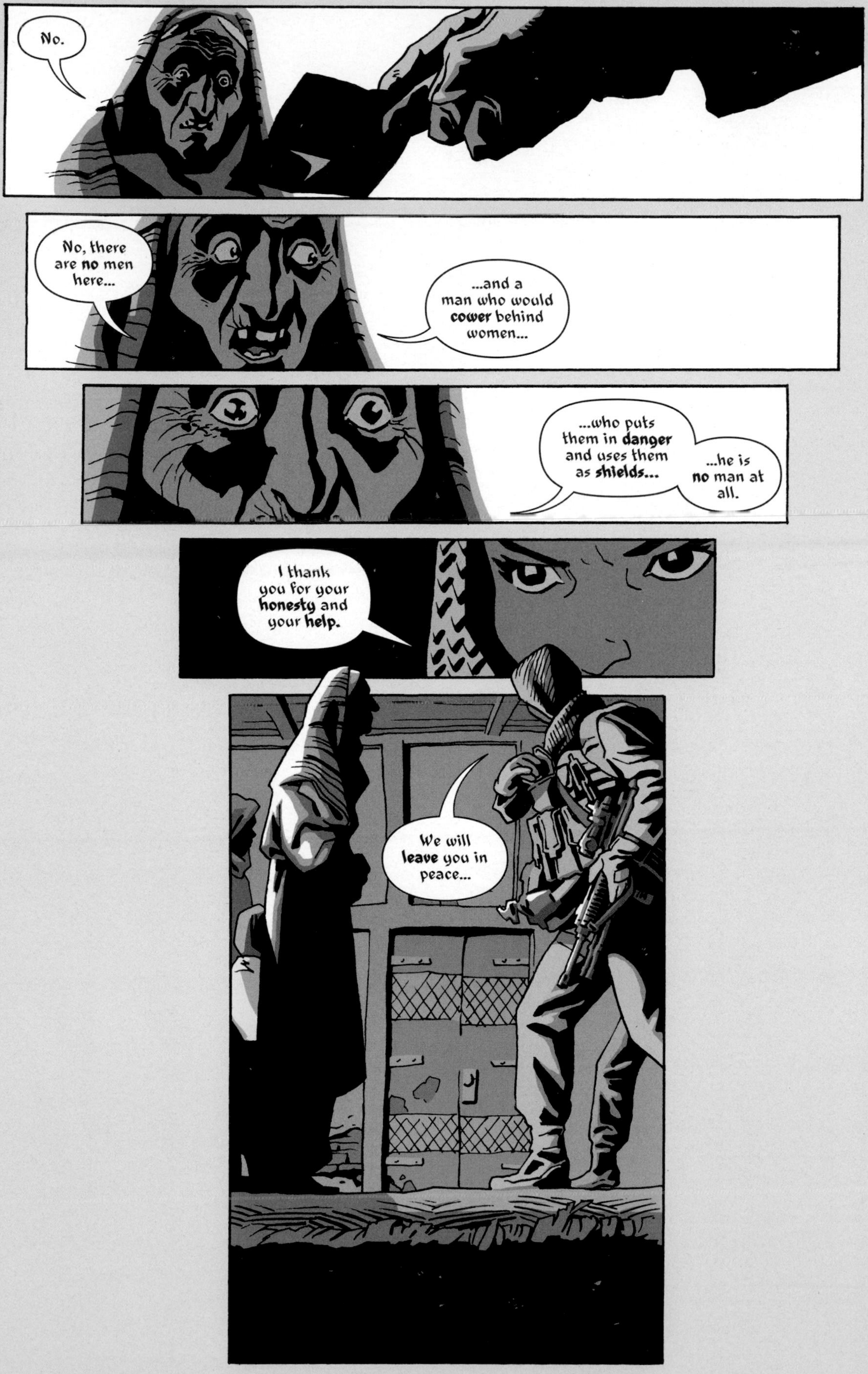
No.
No, there are no men here...
...and a man who would cower behind women...
...who puts them in danger and uses them as shields...
...he is no man at all.
I thank you for your honesty and your help.
We will leave you in peace...

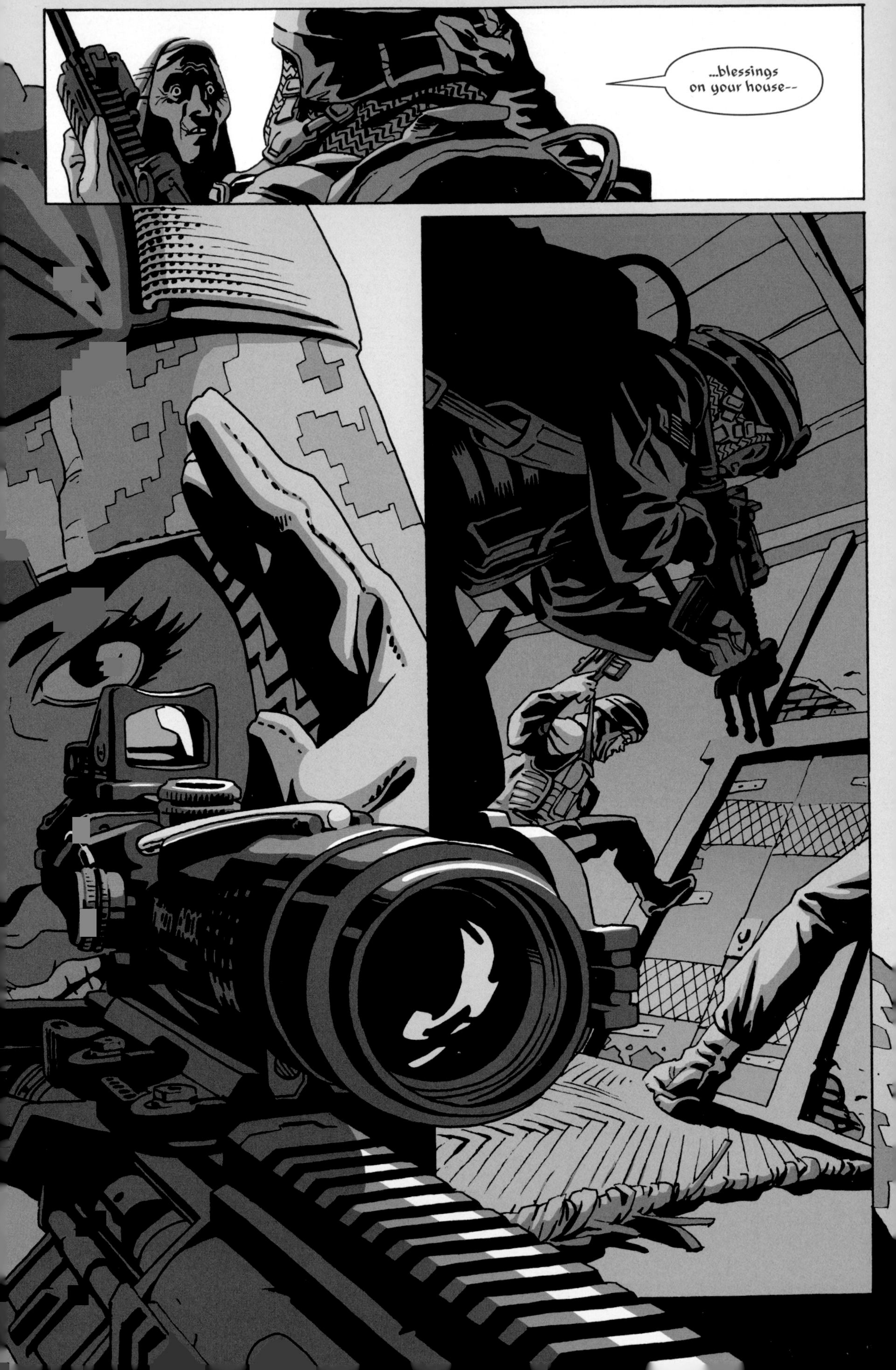
...blessings on your house--

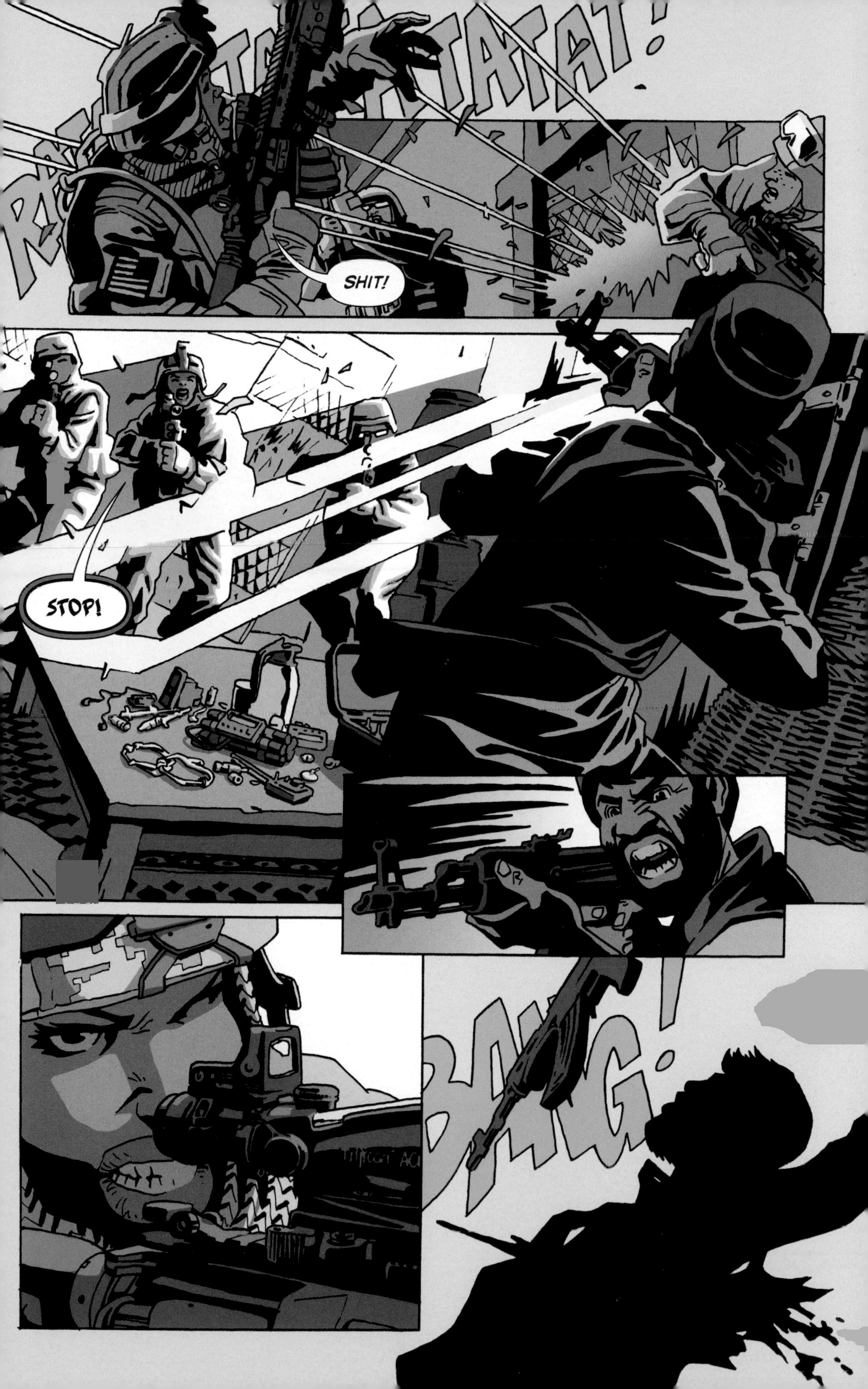
TATATAT!
SHIT!
STOP!
BANG!

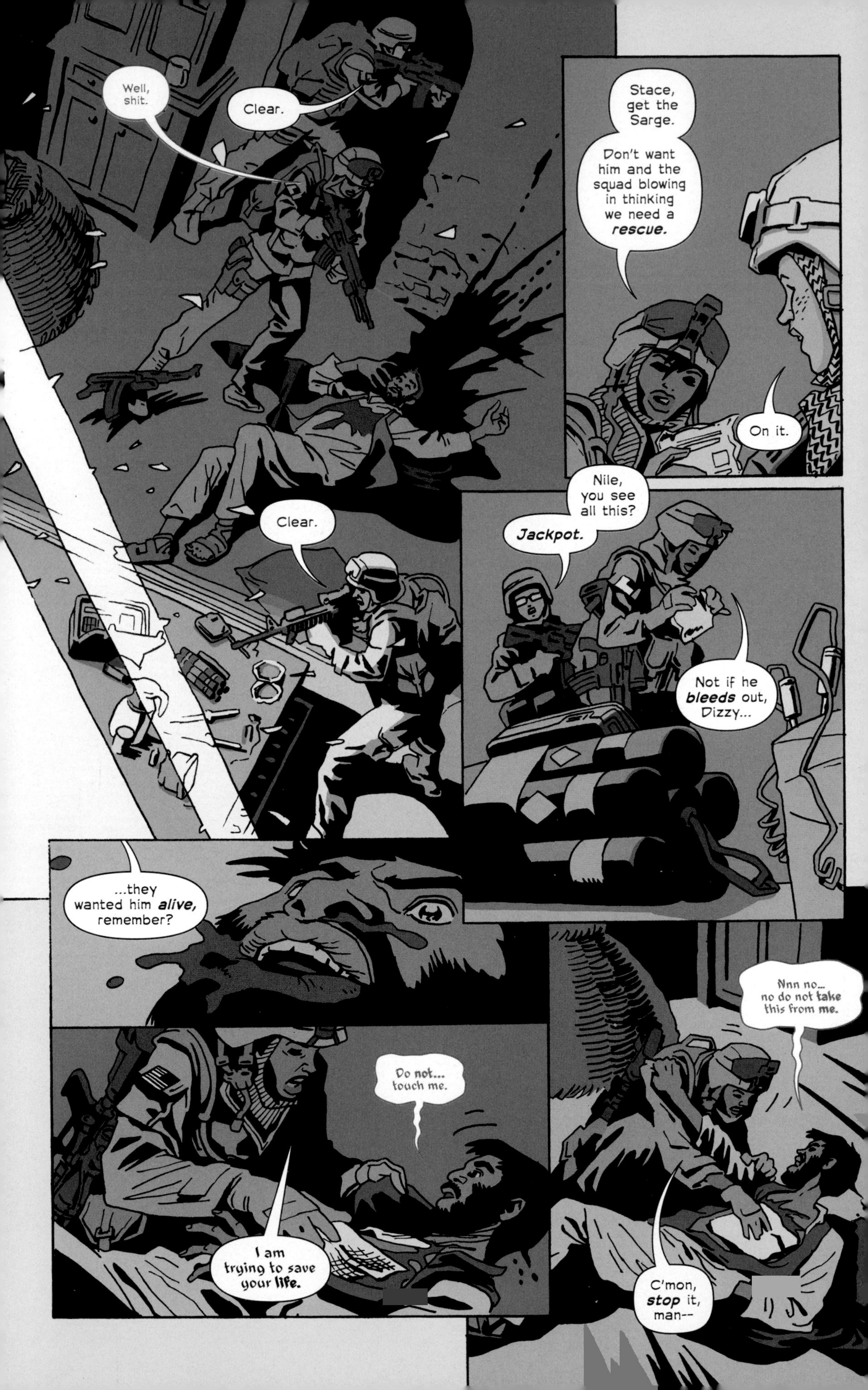
Well, shit.
Clear.
Stace, get the Sarge.
Don't want him and the squad blowing in thinking we need a ***rescue.***
On it.
Clear.
Nile, you see all this?
Jackpot.
Not if he ***bleeds*** out, Dizzy...
...they wanted him ***alive,*** remember?
Do ***not***... touch me.
I am trying to save your ***life.***
Nnn no... no do not ***take*** this from ***me.***
C'mon, ***stop*** it, man--

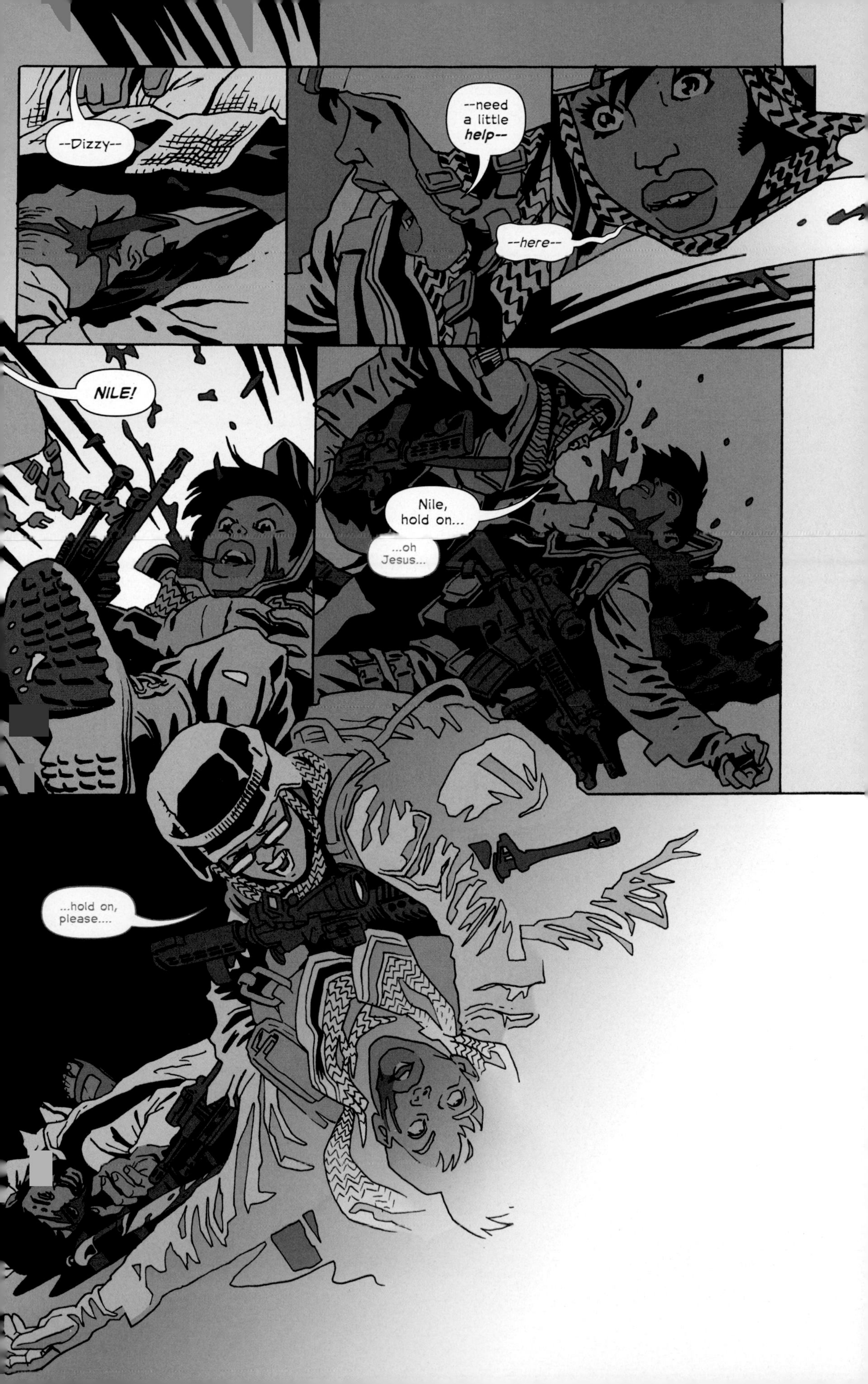
--Dizzy--
--need a little *help*--
--here--
NILE!
Nile, hold on...
...oh Jesus...
...hold on, please....

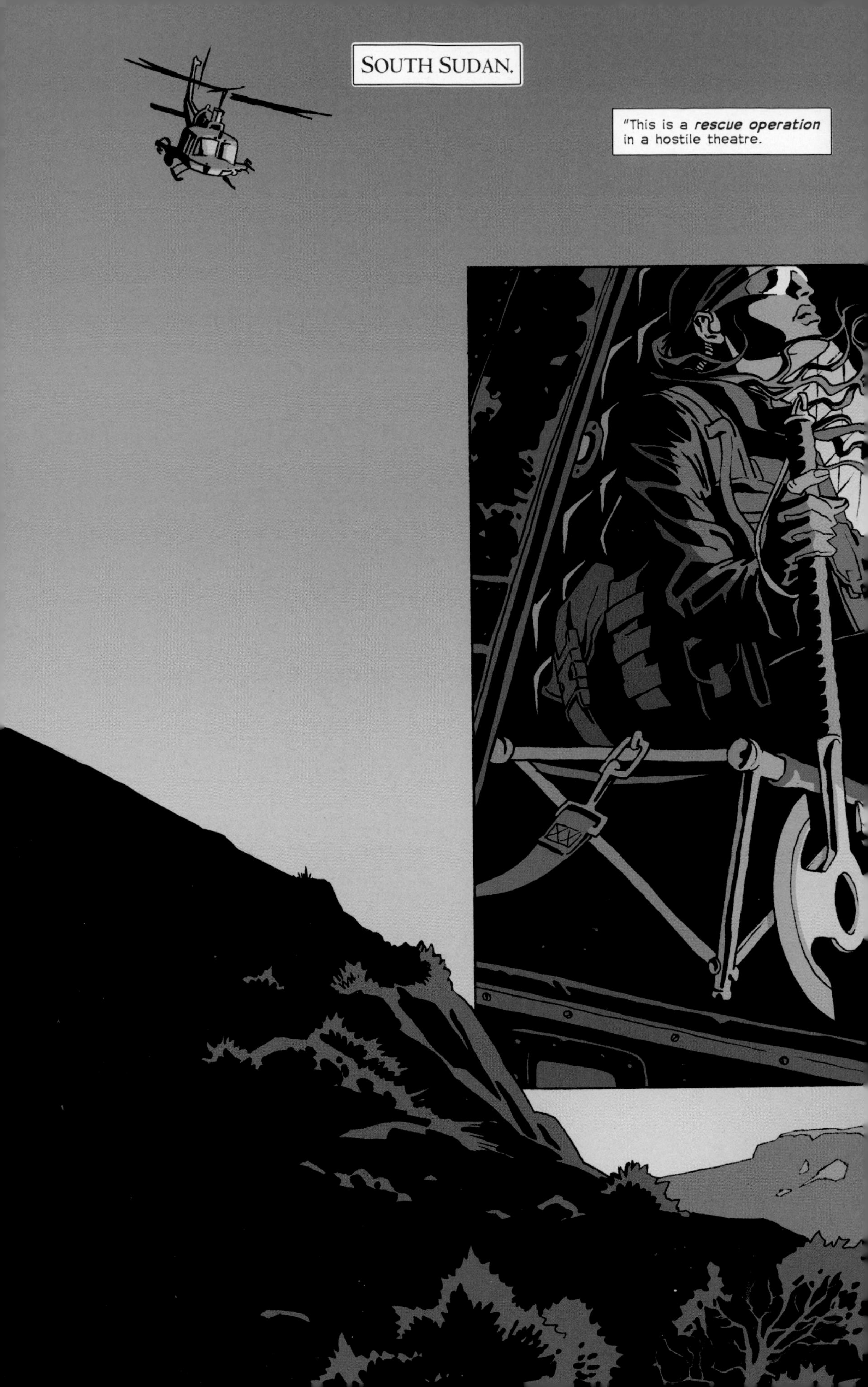
SOUTH SUDAN.
"This is a *rescue operation* in a hostile theatre.

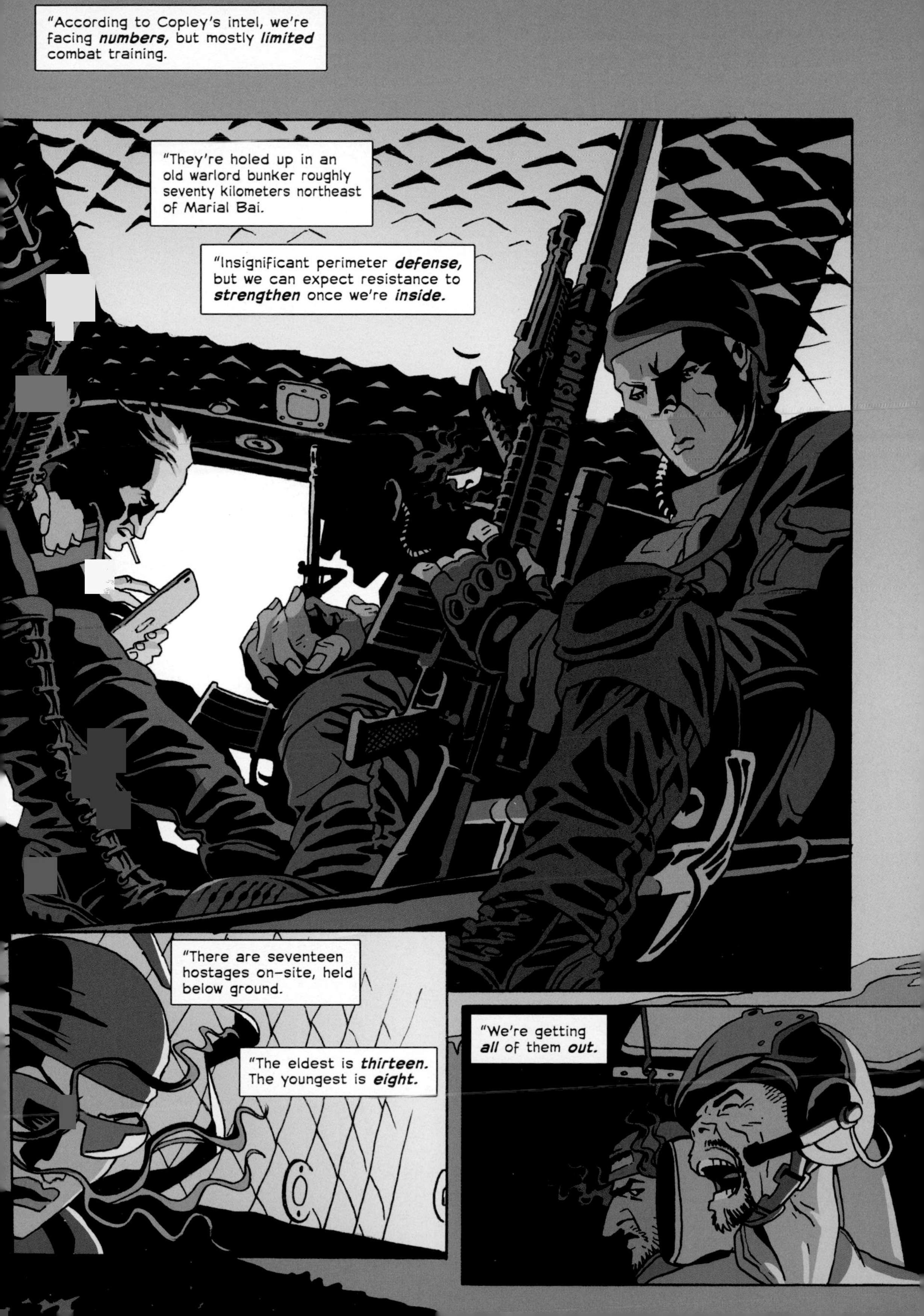
"According to Copley's intel, we're facing ***numbers,*** but mostly ***limited*** combat training.
"They're holed up in an old warlord bunker roughly seventy kilometers northeast of Marial Bai.
"Insignificant perimeter ***defense,*** but we can expect resistance to ***strengthen*** once we're ***inside.***
"There are seventeen hostages on-site, held below ground.
"The eldest is ***thirteen.*** The youngest is ***eight.***
"We're getting ***all*** of them ***out.***

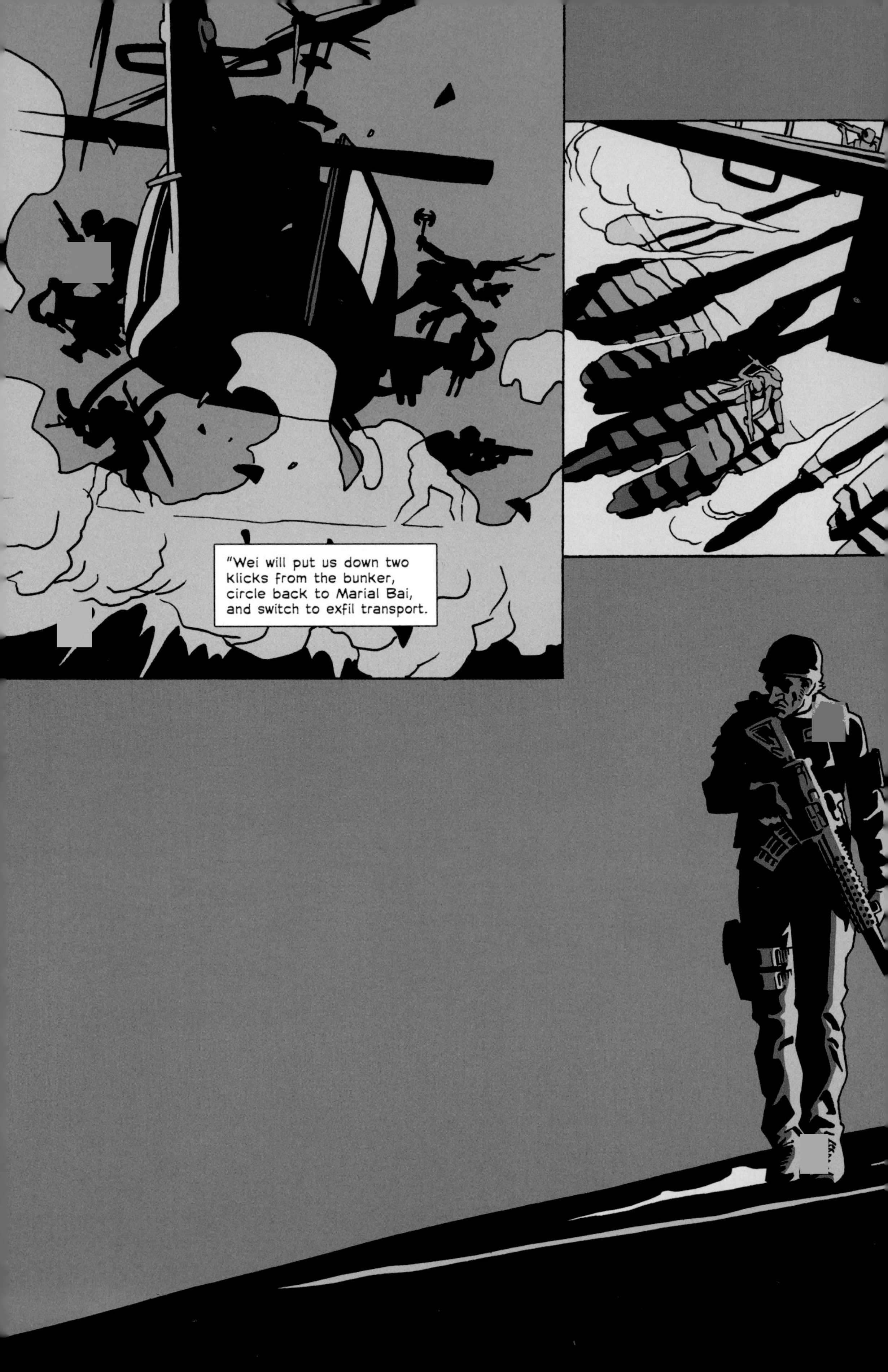
"Wei will put us down two klicks from the bunker, circle back to Marial Bai, and switch to exfil transport.

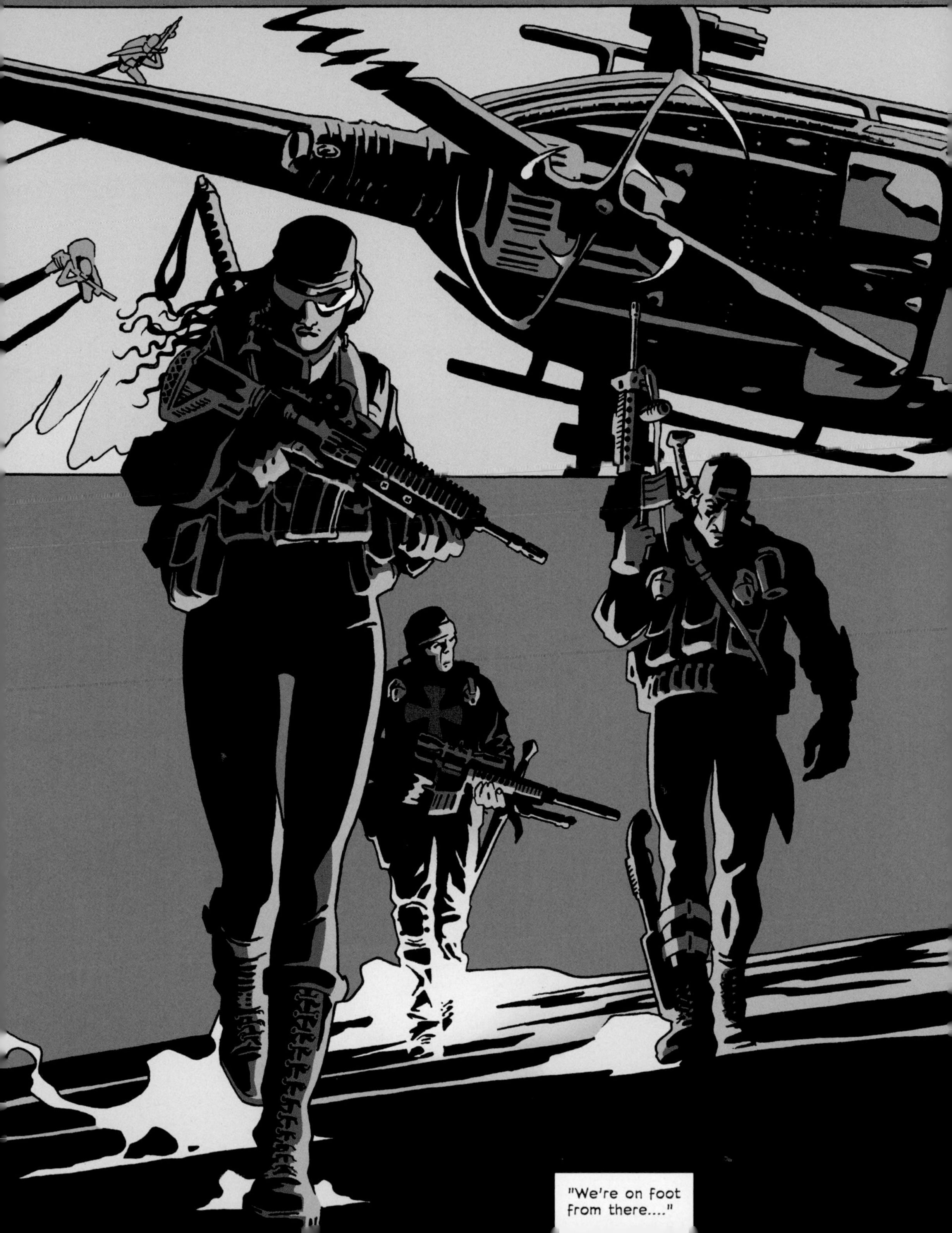
"We're on foot from there...."

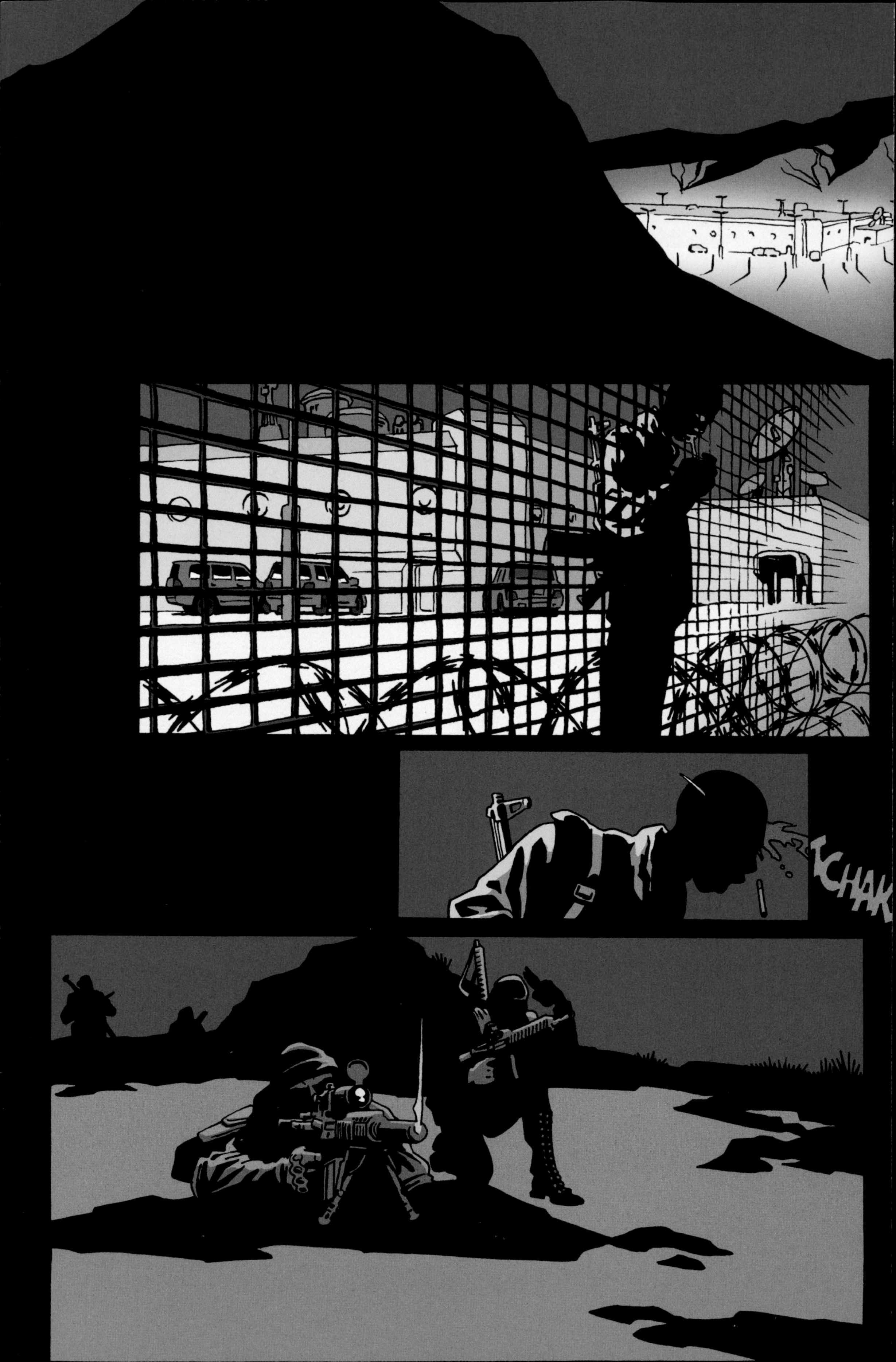
TCHAK

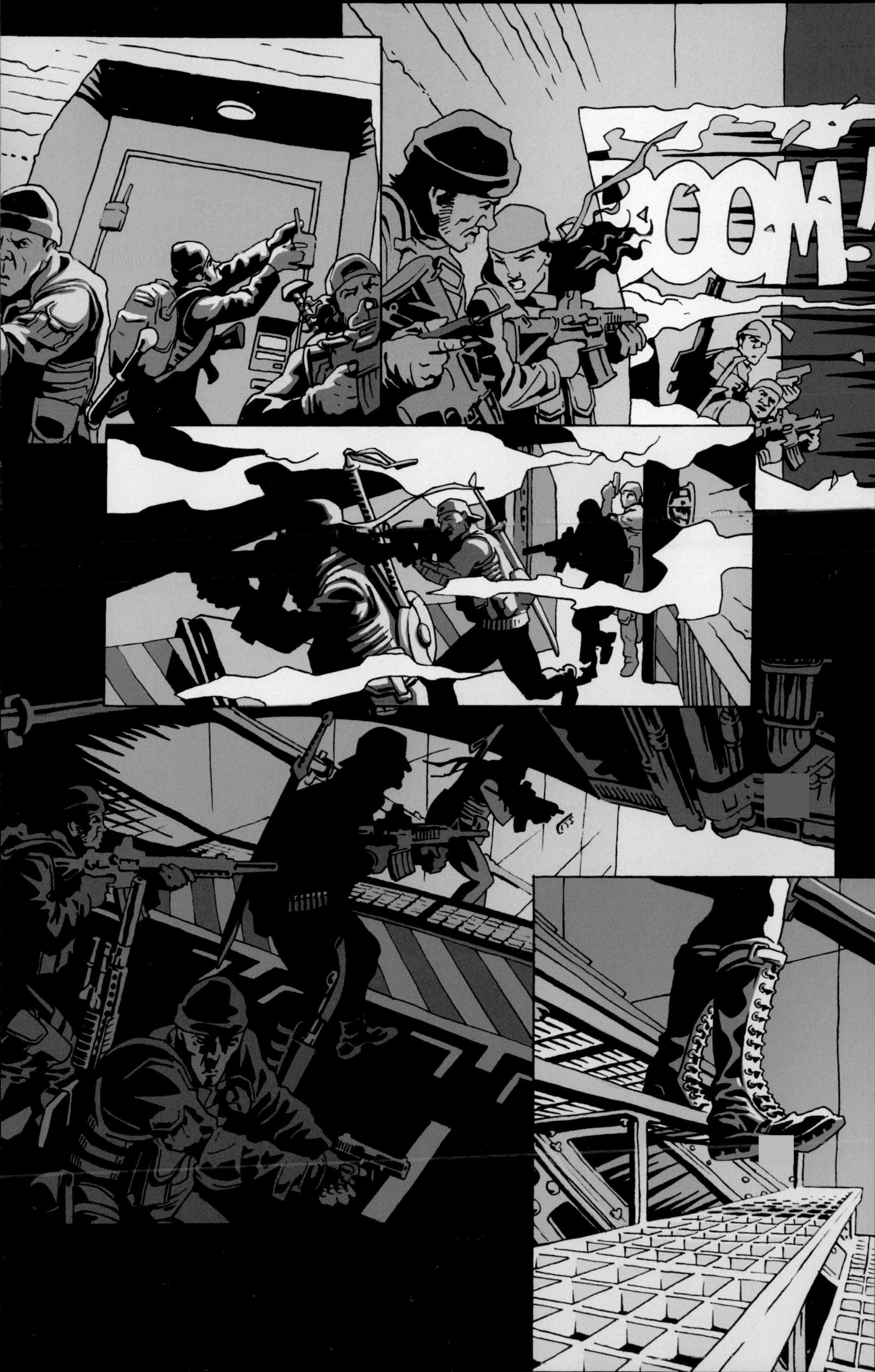
BOOM

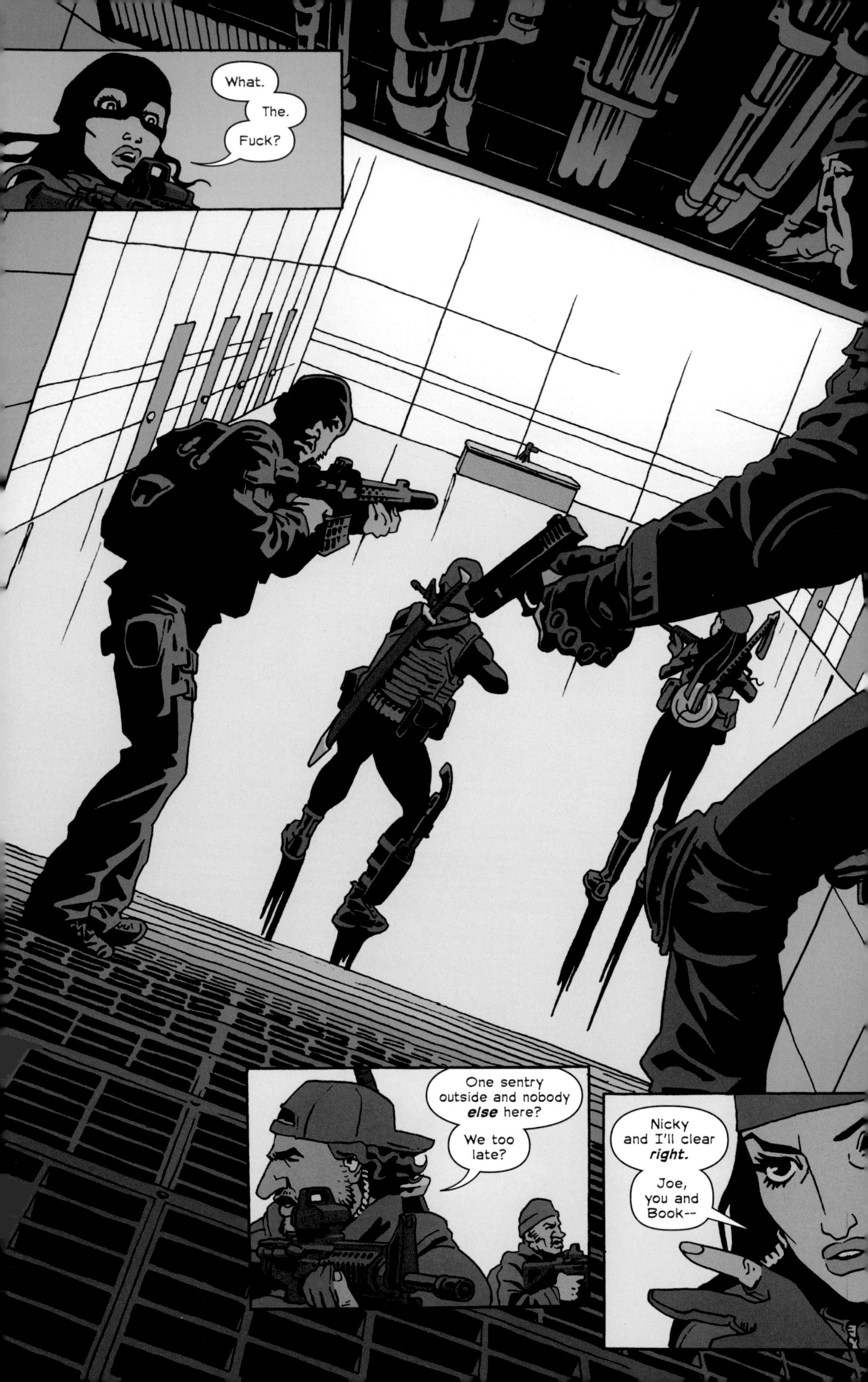
What.
The.
Fuck?
One sentry outside and nobody *else* here?
We too late?
Nicky and I'll clear *right.*
Joe, you and Book--

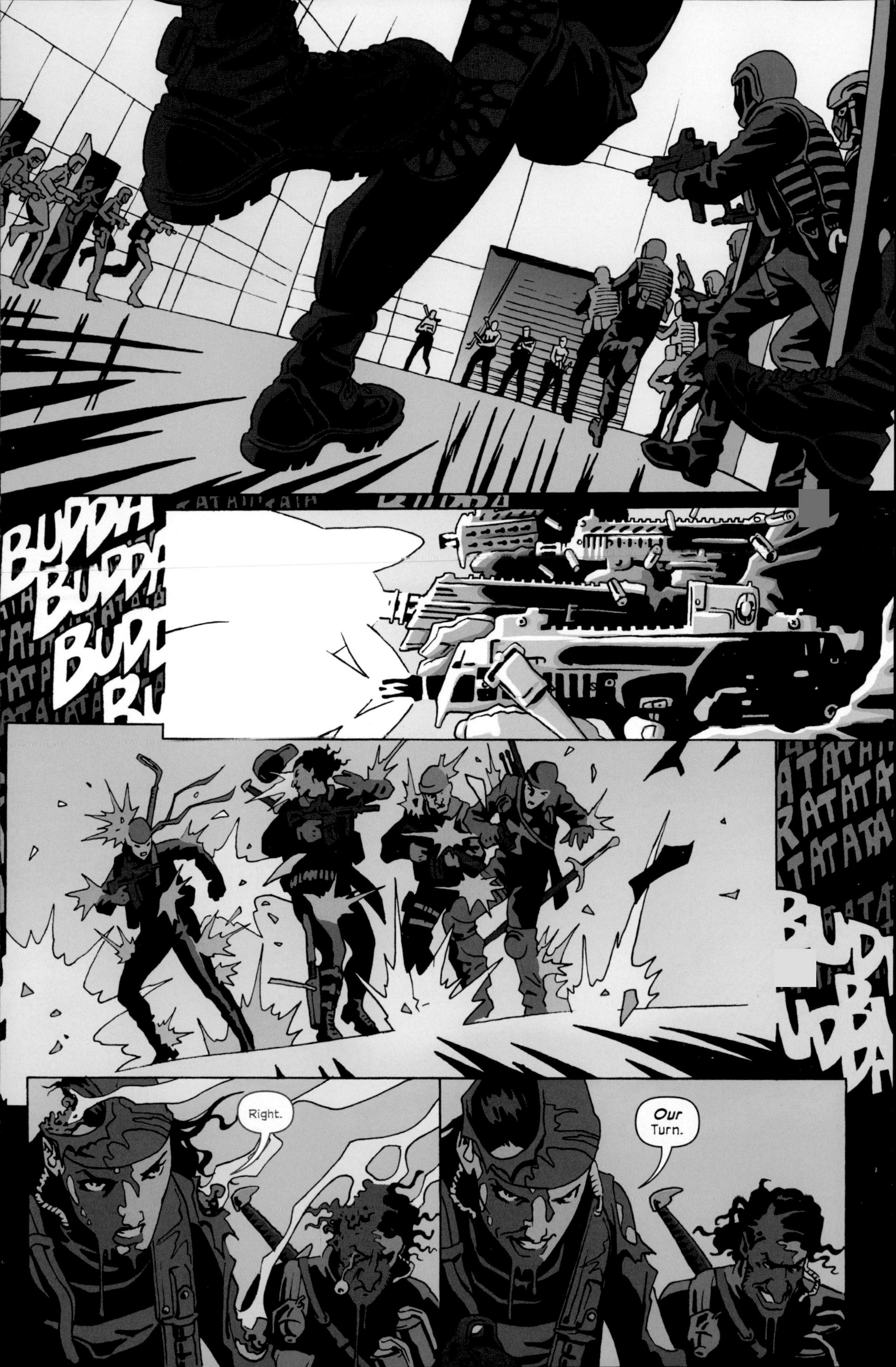
BUDDA
Right.
Our Turn.

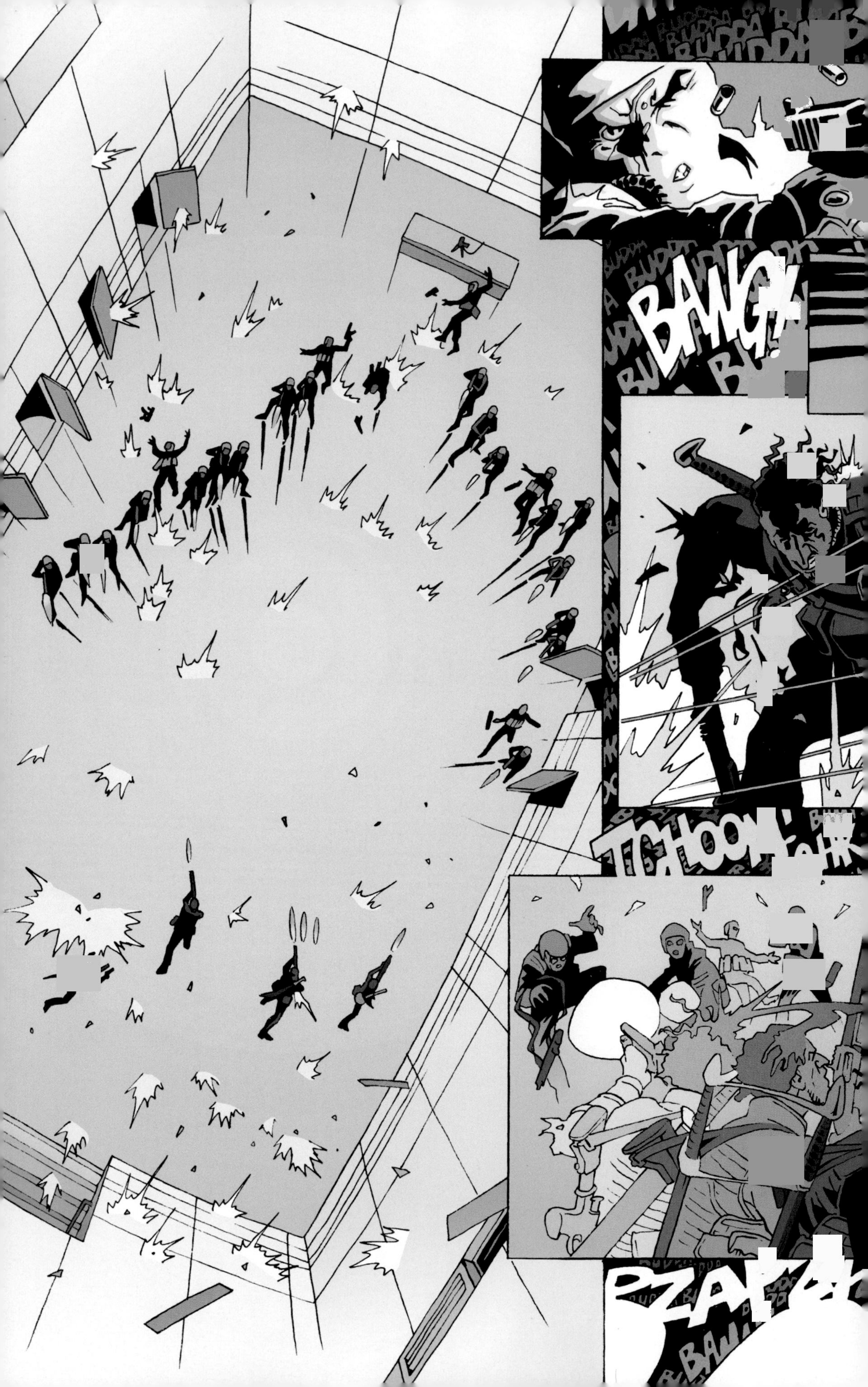

BUDDA BUDDA
BANG
TCHOOM
PZAP

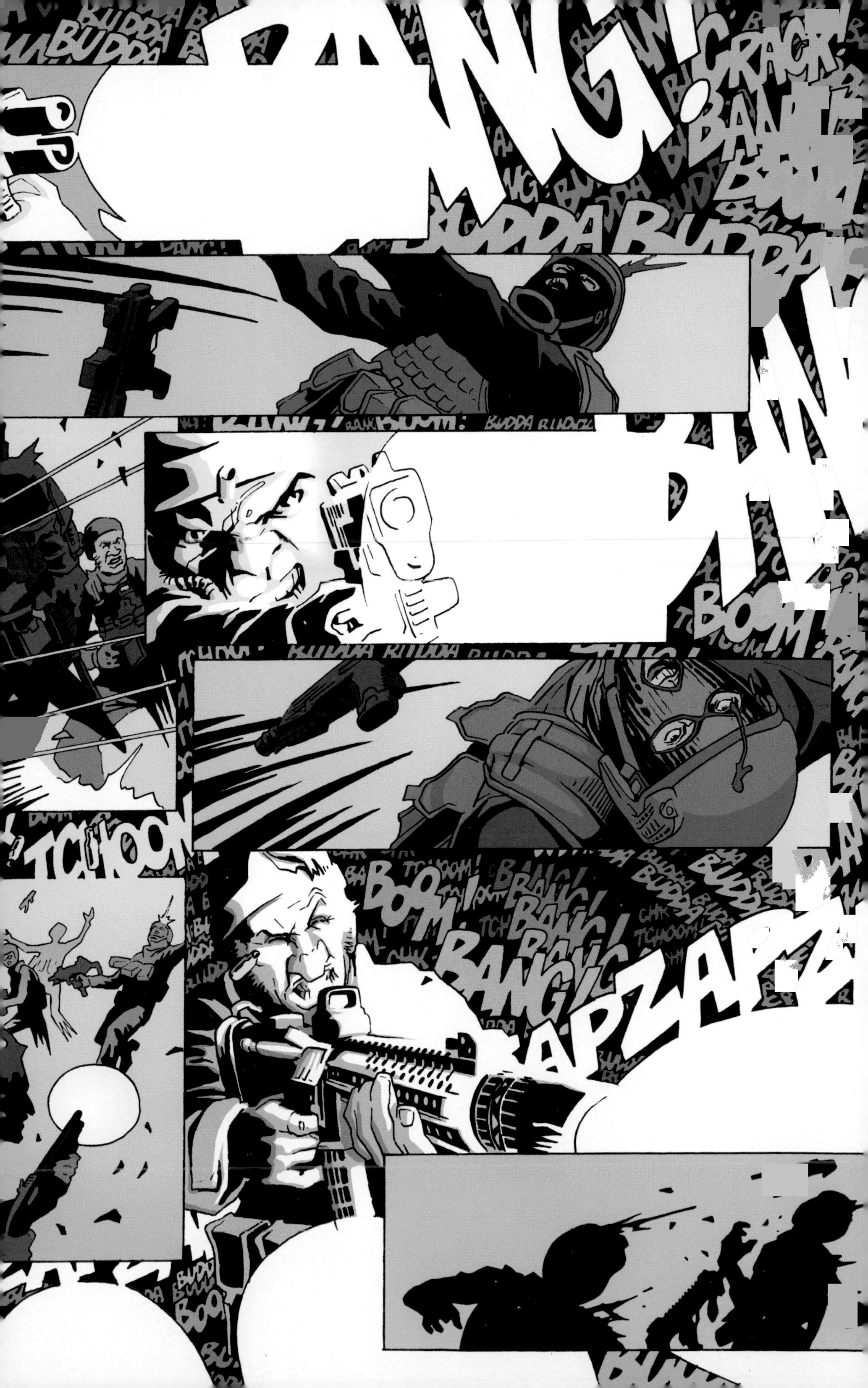
BUDDA BUDDA
BANG!
CRACK!
BUDDA BUDDA
BOOM!
TCHOOM
BOOM!
BANG!
BANG!
TCHOOM!
ZAPZAPZA

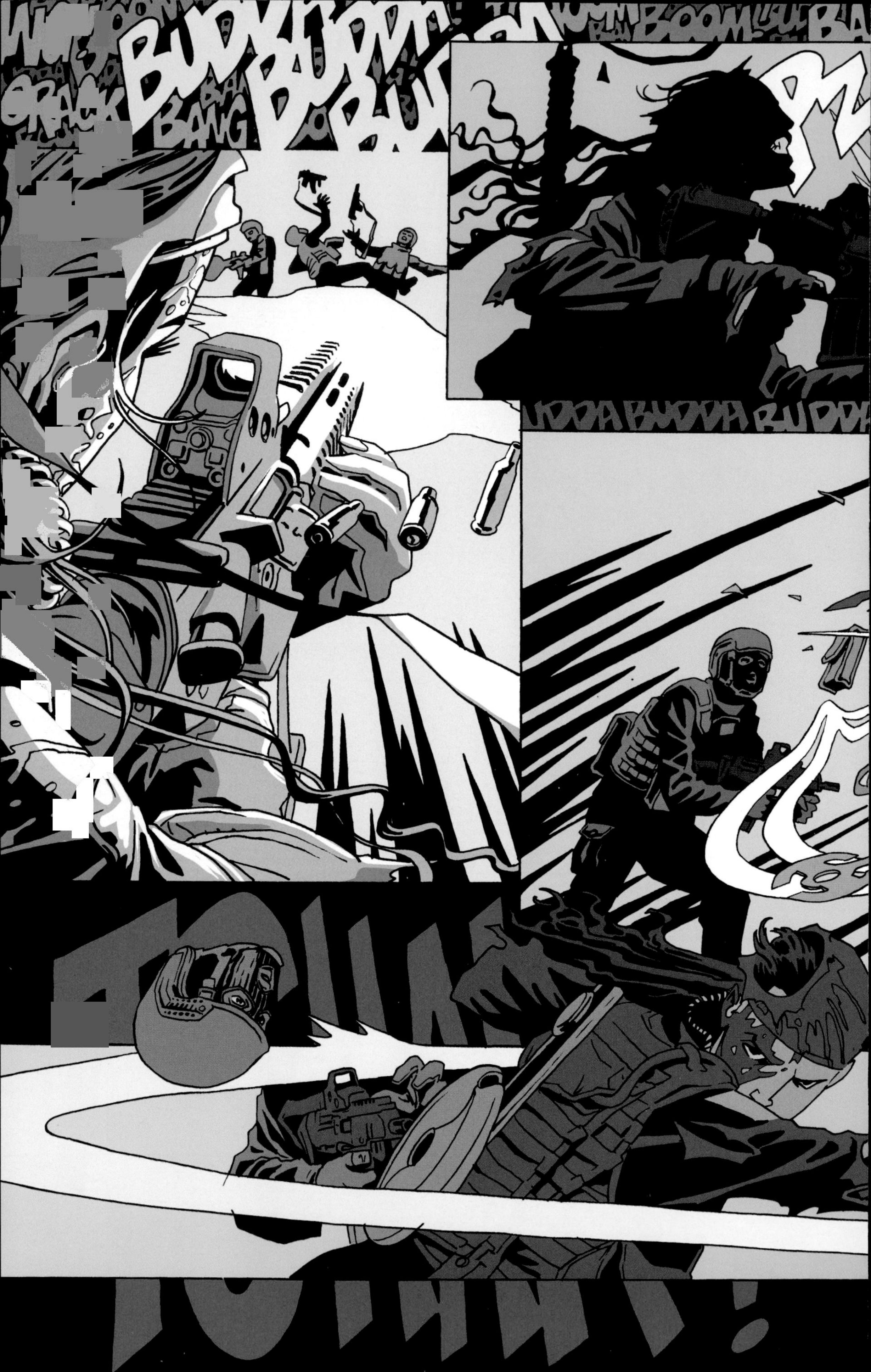
CRACK
BANG
BOOM
BUDDA BUDDA

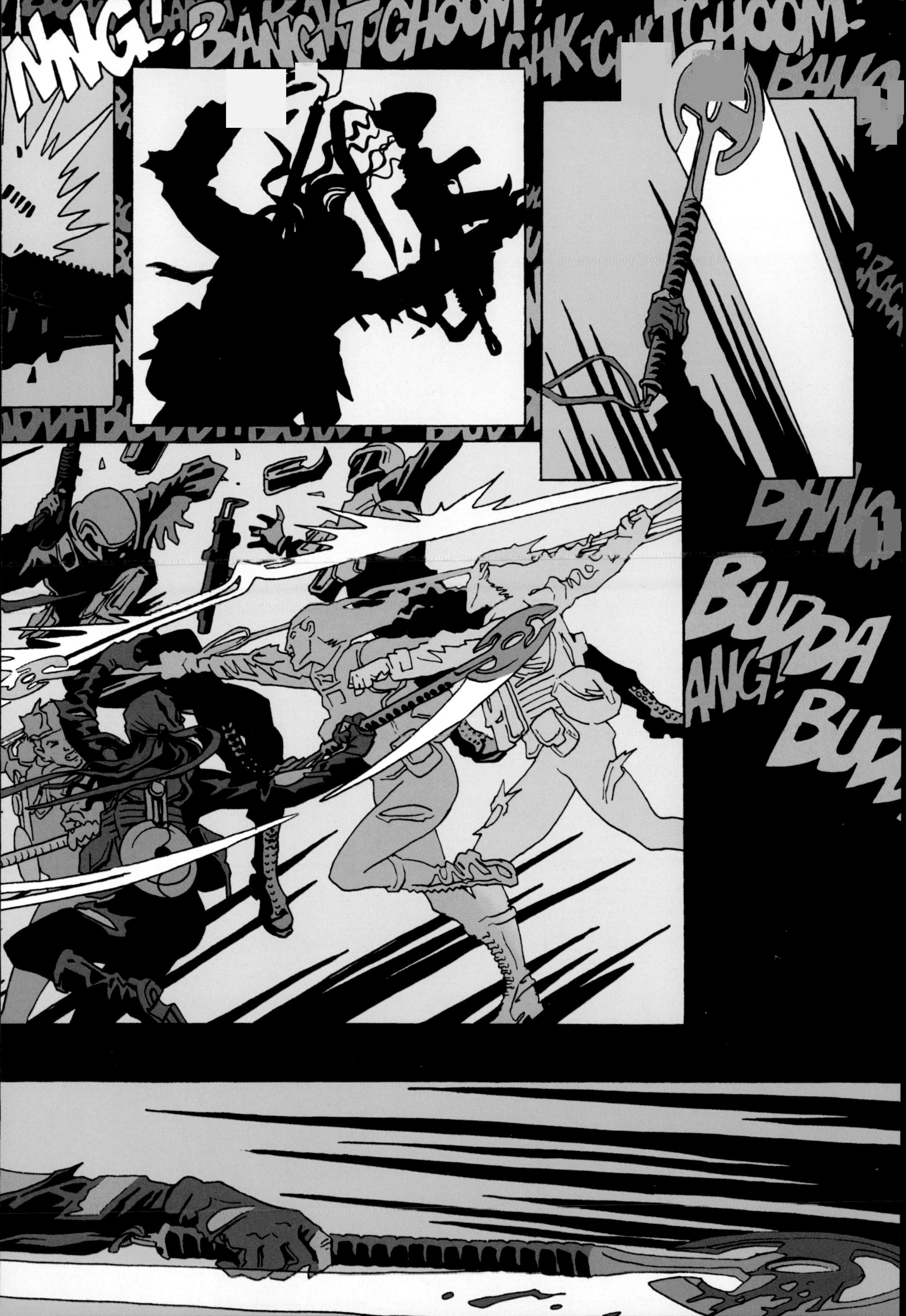
NNG!
BANG!
T-CHOOM!
CHK-CHK
T-CHOOM!
DHNG
BUDDA
BANG!
BUDDA

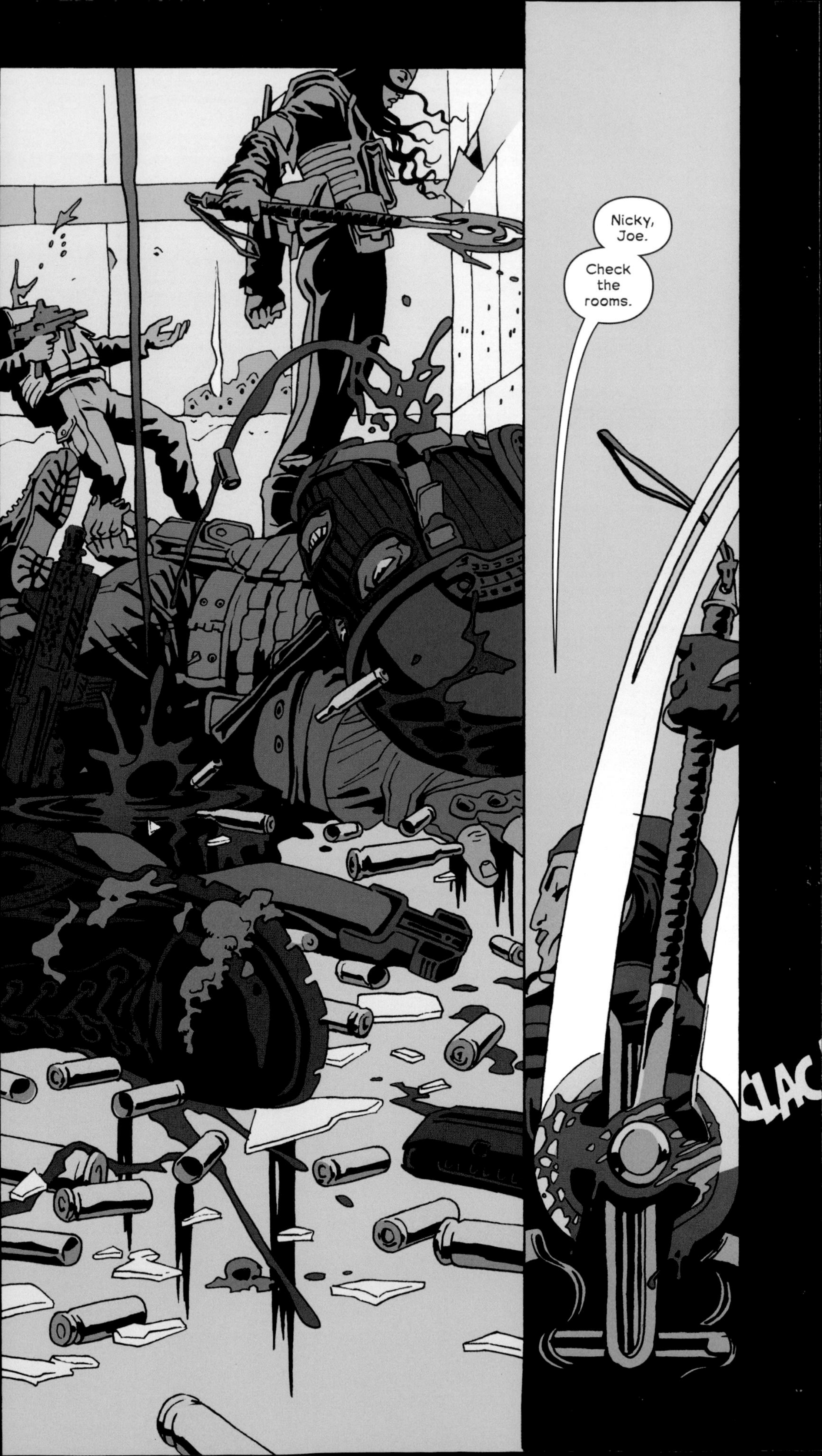
Nicky, Joe.
Check the rooms.
CLAC

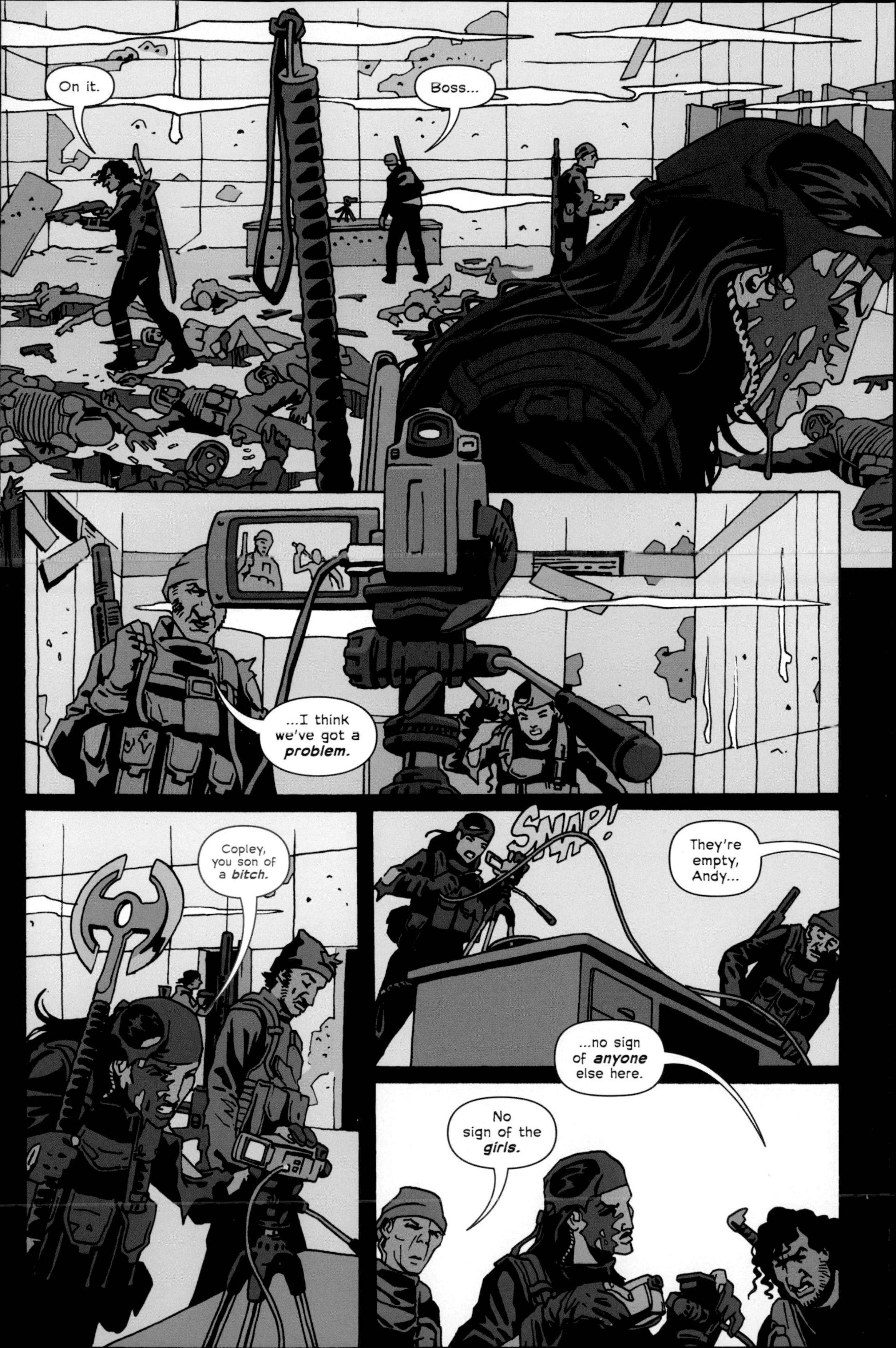
On it.
Boss...
...I think we've got a *problem.*
Copley, you son of a *bitch.*
SNAP!
They're empty, Andy...
...no sign of *anyone* else here.
No sign of the *girls.*

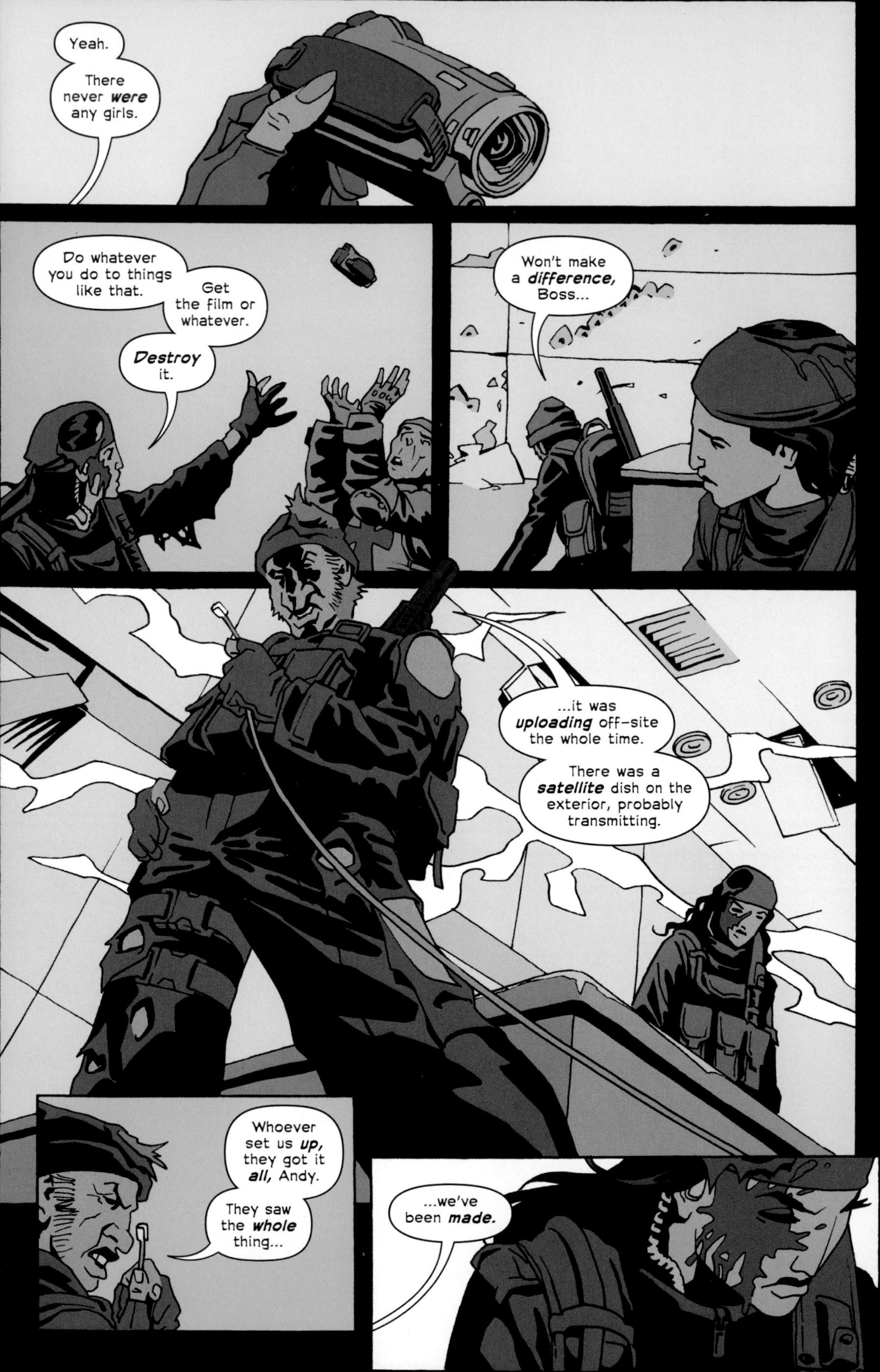
Yeah.
There never ***were*** any girls.
Do whatever you do to things like that.
Get the film or whatever.
Destroy it.
Won't make a ***difference,*** Boss...
...it was ***uploading*** off-site the whole time.
There was a ***satellite*** dish on the exterior, probably transmitting.
Whoever set us ***up,*** they got it ***all,*** Andy.
They saw the ***whole*** thing...
...we've been ***made.***

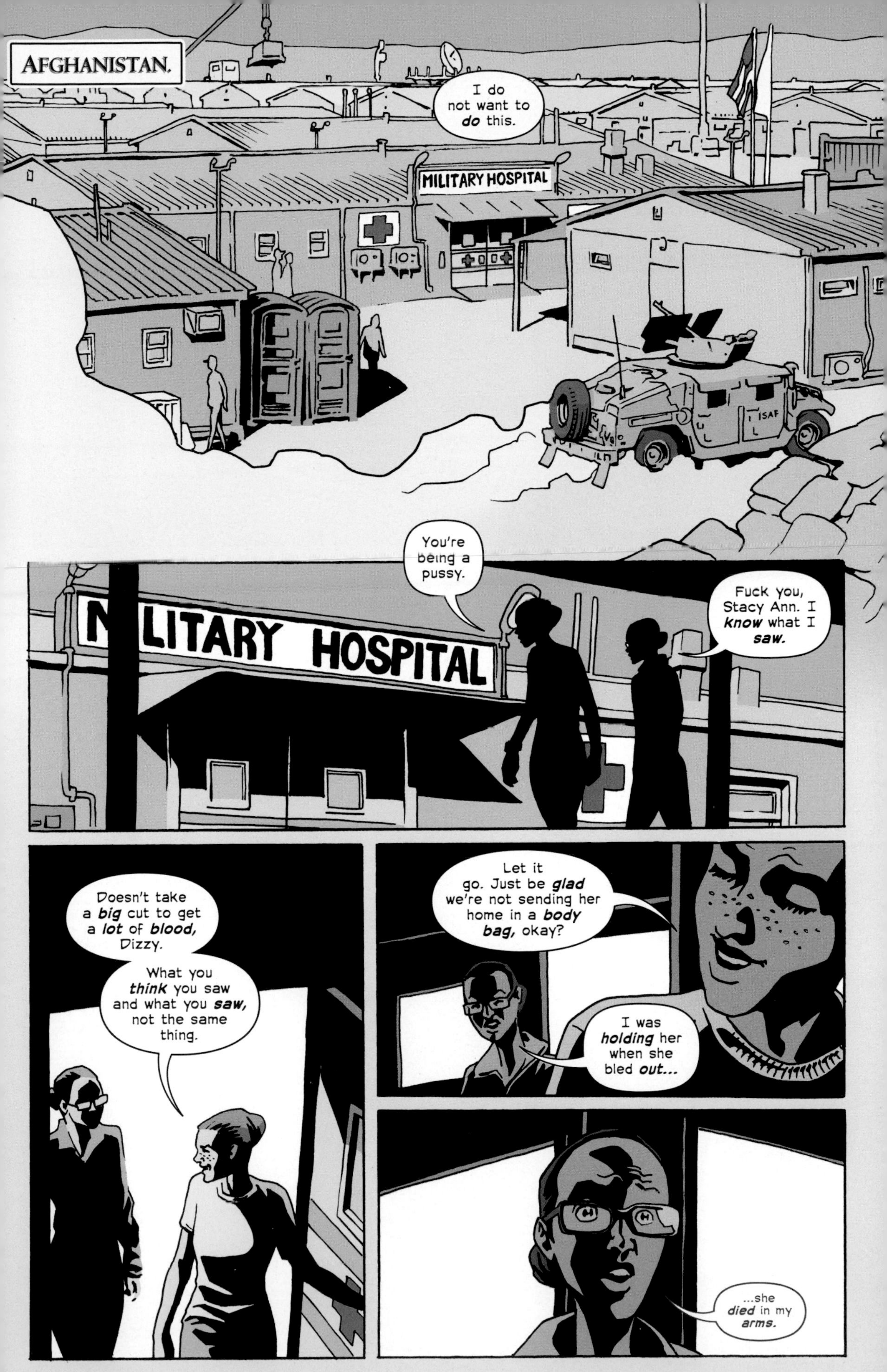
AFGHANISTAN.
I do not want to *do* this.
MILITARY HOSPITAL
ISAF
You're being a pussy.
MILITARY HOSPITAL
Fuck you, Stacy Ann. I *know* what I *saw.*
Doesn't take a *big* cut to get a *lot* of *blood,* Dizzy.
What you *think* you saw and what you *saw,* not the same thing.
Let it go. Just be *glad* we're not sending her home in a *body bag,* okay?
I was *holding* her when she bled *out...*
...she *died* in my *arms.*

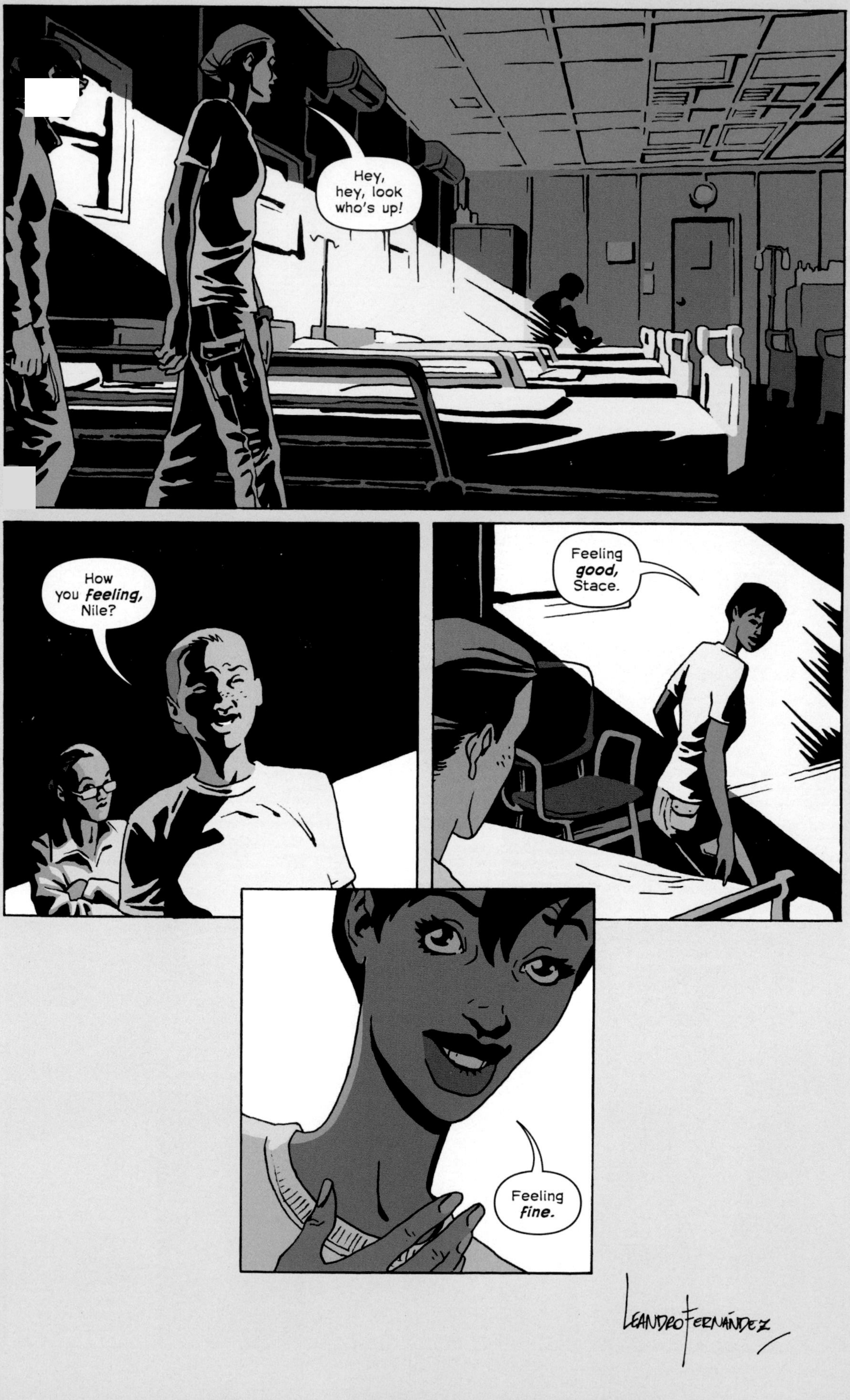
Hey, hey, look who's up!
How you *feeling,* Nile?
Feeling *good,* Stace.
Feeling *fine.*
LEANDRO FERNÁNDEZ

CHAPTER TWO

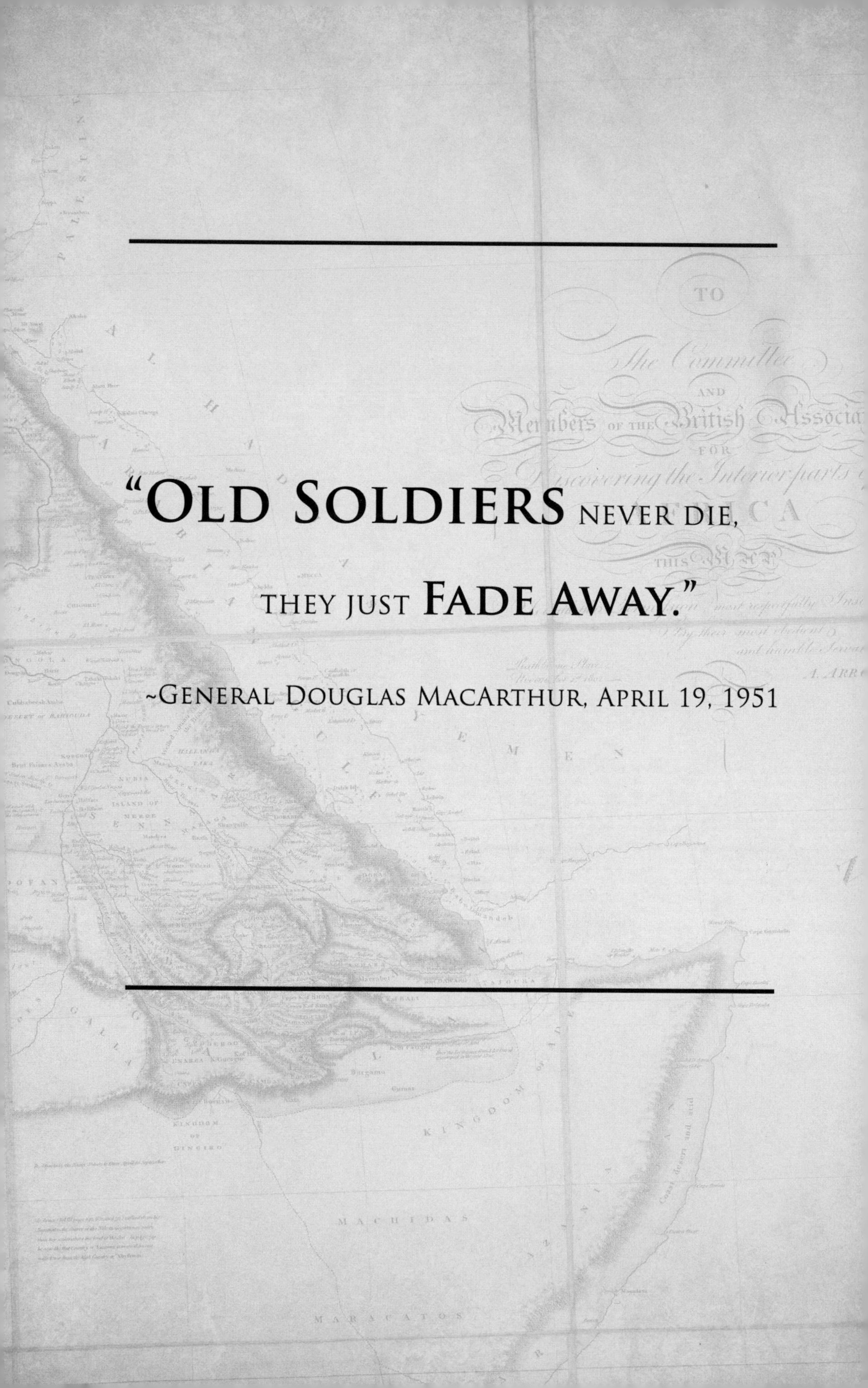

"Old Soldiers never die, they just Fade Away."

~General Douglas MacArthur, April 19, 1951

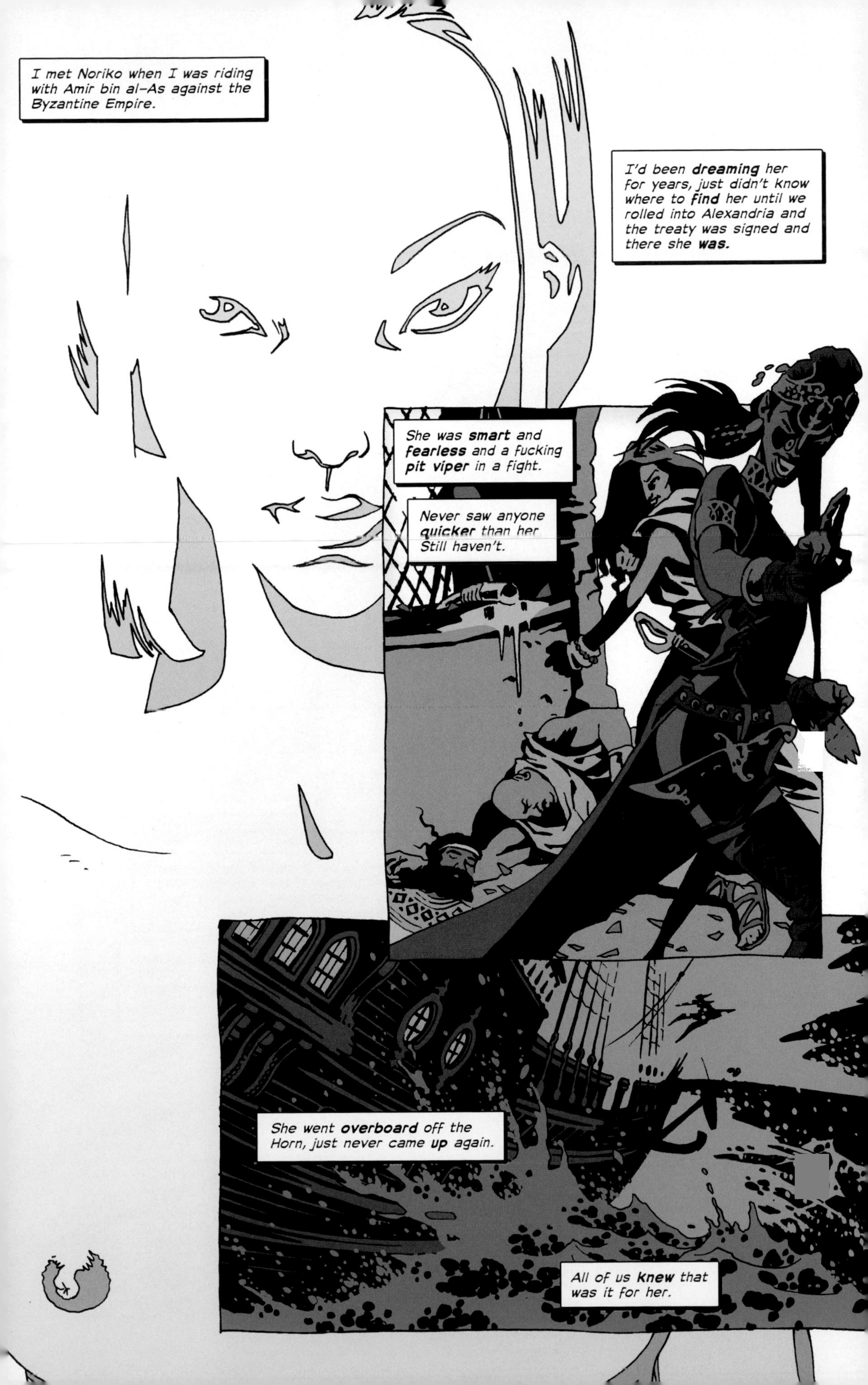
I met Noriko when I was riding with Amir bin al-As against the Byzantine Empire.
I'd been **dreaming** her for years, just didn't know where to **find** her until we rolled into Alexandria and the treaty was signed and there she **was.**
She was **smart** and **fearless** and a fucking **pit viper** in a fight.
Never saw anyone **quicker** than her. Still haven't.
She went **overboard** off the Horn, just never came **up** again.
All of us **knew** that was it for her.

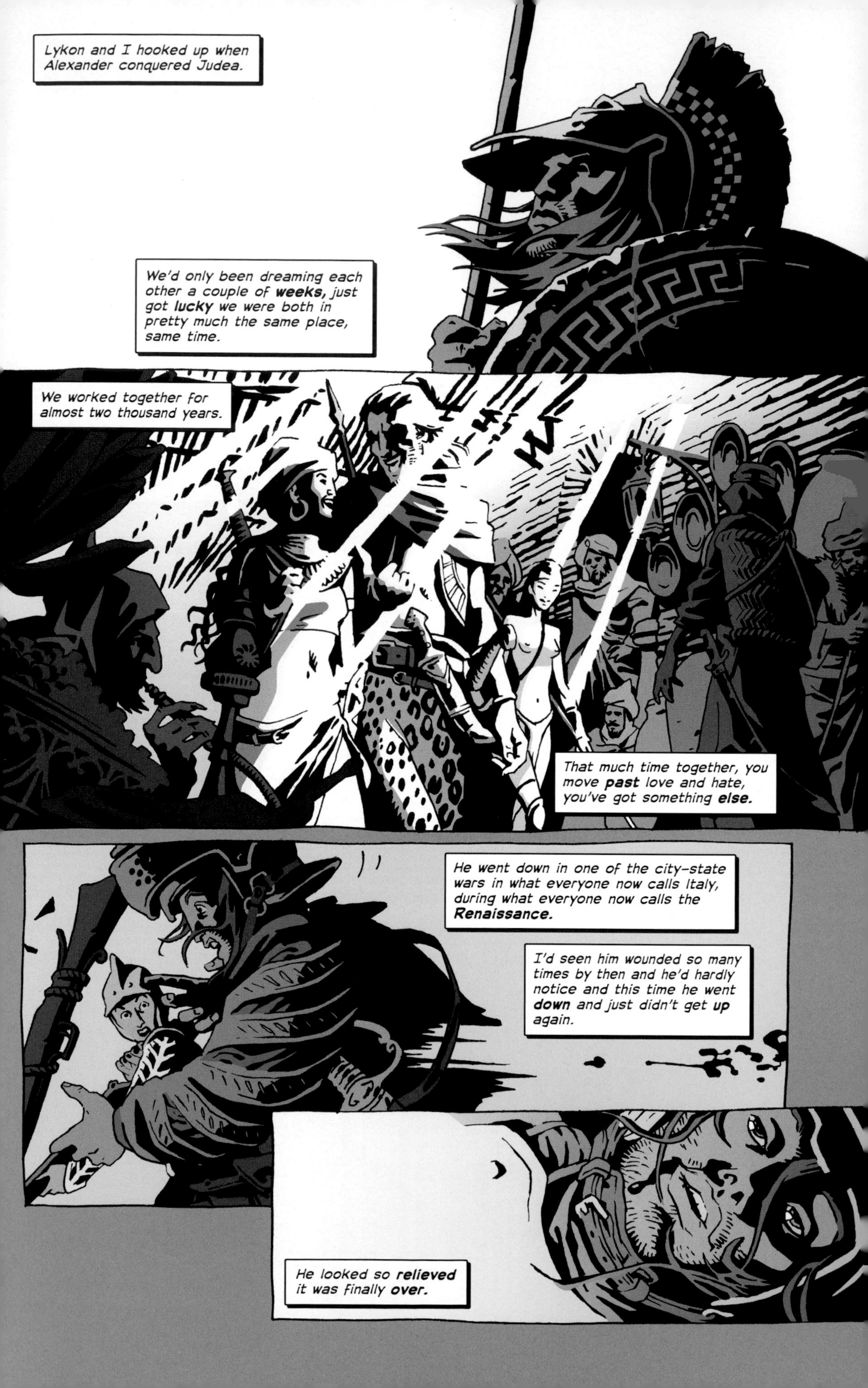
Lykon and I hooked up when Alexander conquered Judea.
We'd only been dreaming each other a couple of **weeks,** just got **lucky** we were both in pretty much the same place, same time.
We worked together for almost two thousand years.
That much time together, you move **past** love and hate, you've got something **else.**
He went down in one of the city-state wars in what everyone now calls Italy, during what everyone now calls the **Renaissance.**
I'd seen him wounded so many times by then and he'd hardly notice and this time he went **down** and just didn't get **up** again.
He looked so **relieved** it was finally **over.**

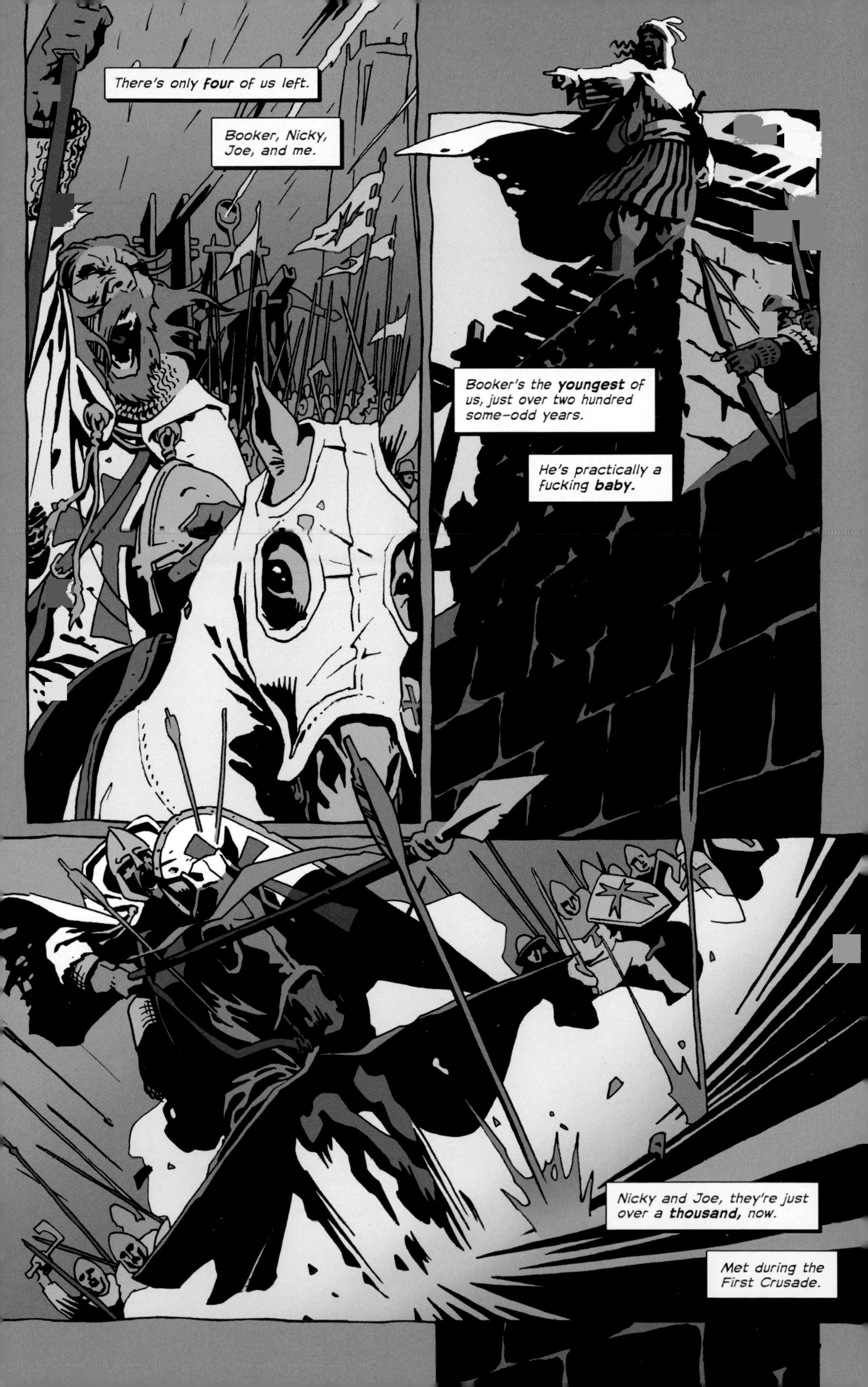
There's only **four** of us left.
Booker, Nicky, Joe, and me.
Booker's the **youngest** of us, just over two hundred some-odd years.
He's practically a fucking **baby.**
Nicky and Joe, they're just over a **thousand,** now.
Met during the First Crusade.

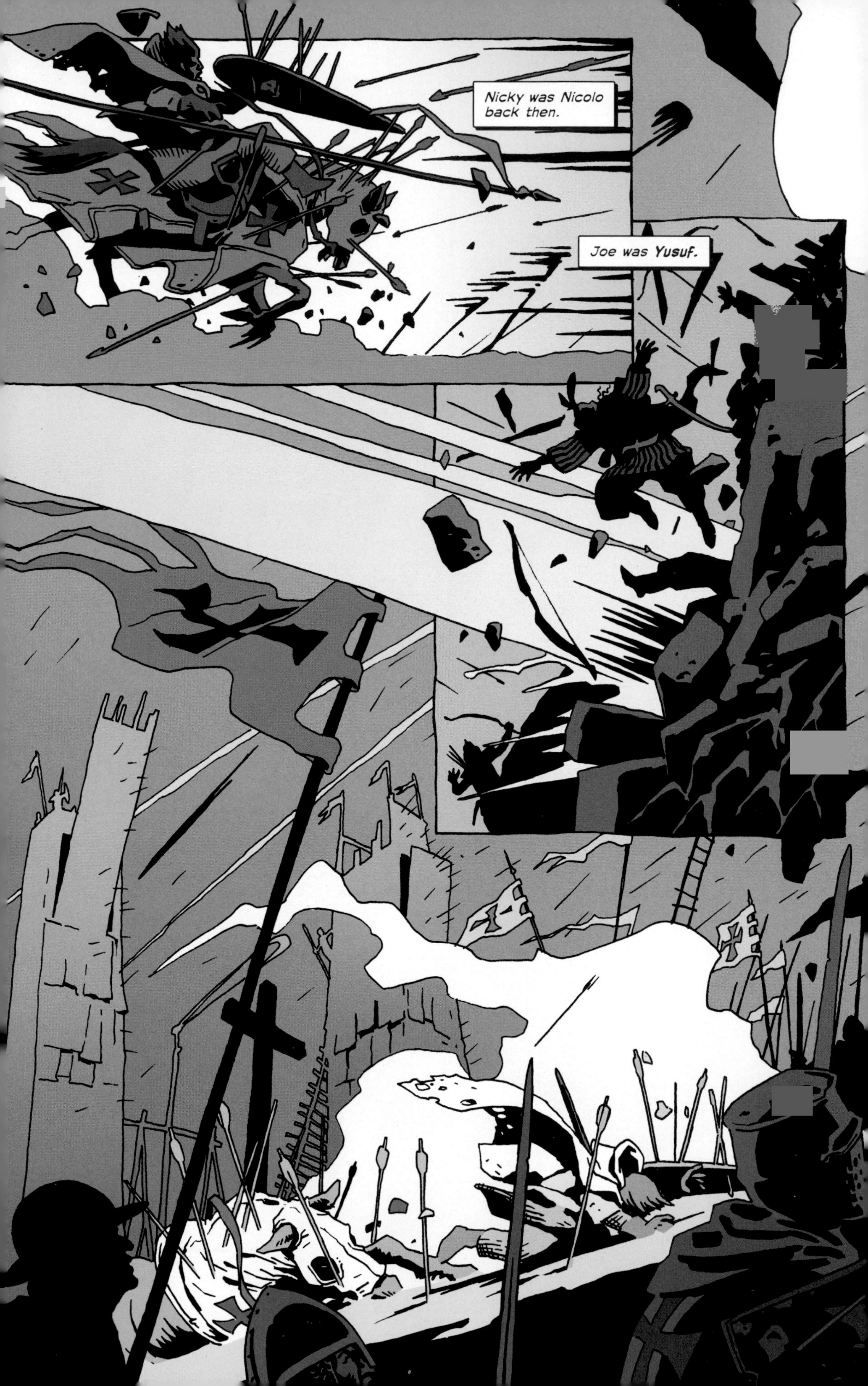
Nicky was Nicolo back then.
Joe was Yusuf.

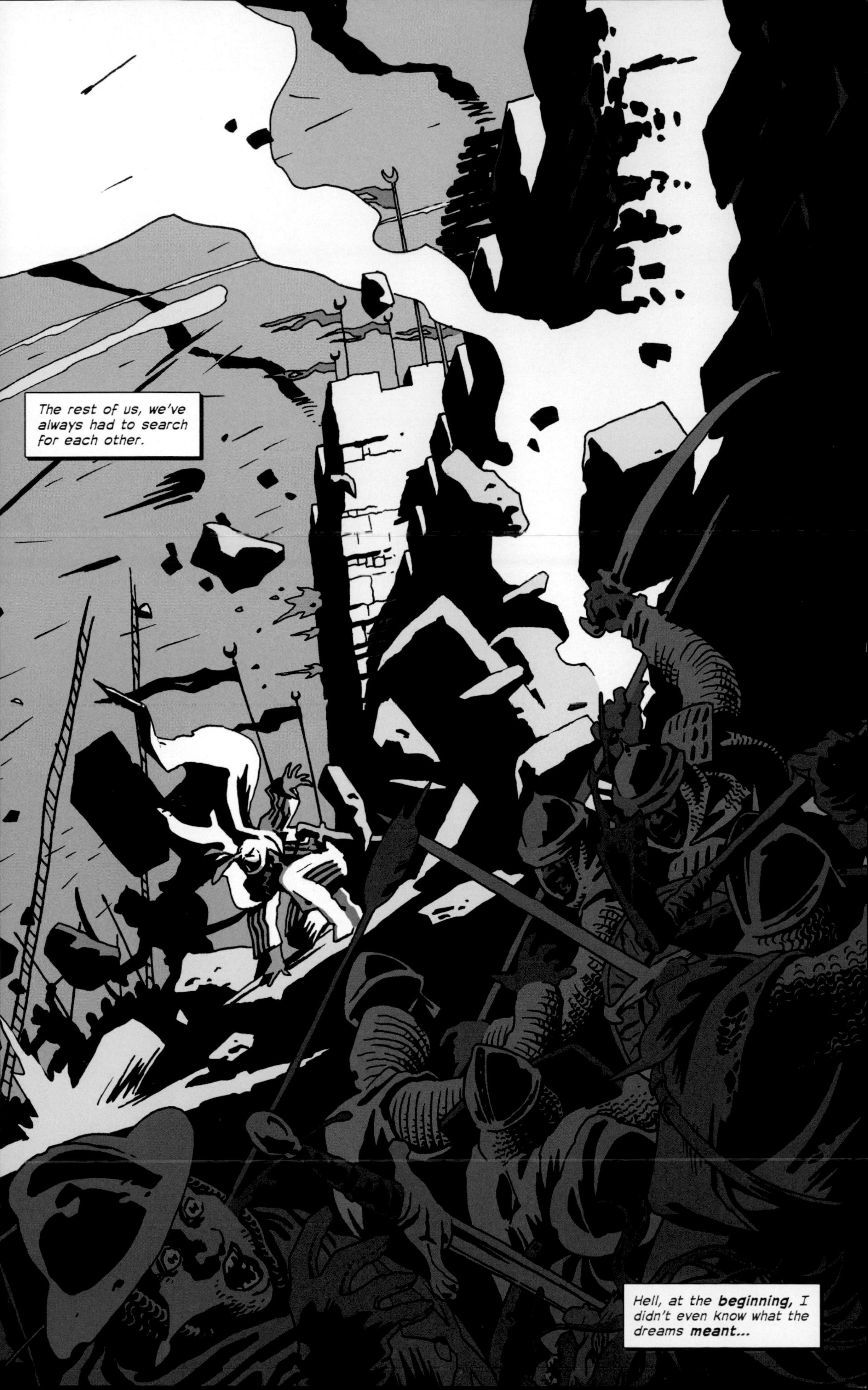
The rest of us, we've always had to search for each other.
Hell, at the **beginning,** I didn't even know what the dreams **meant...**

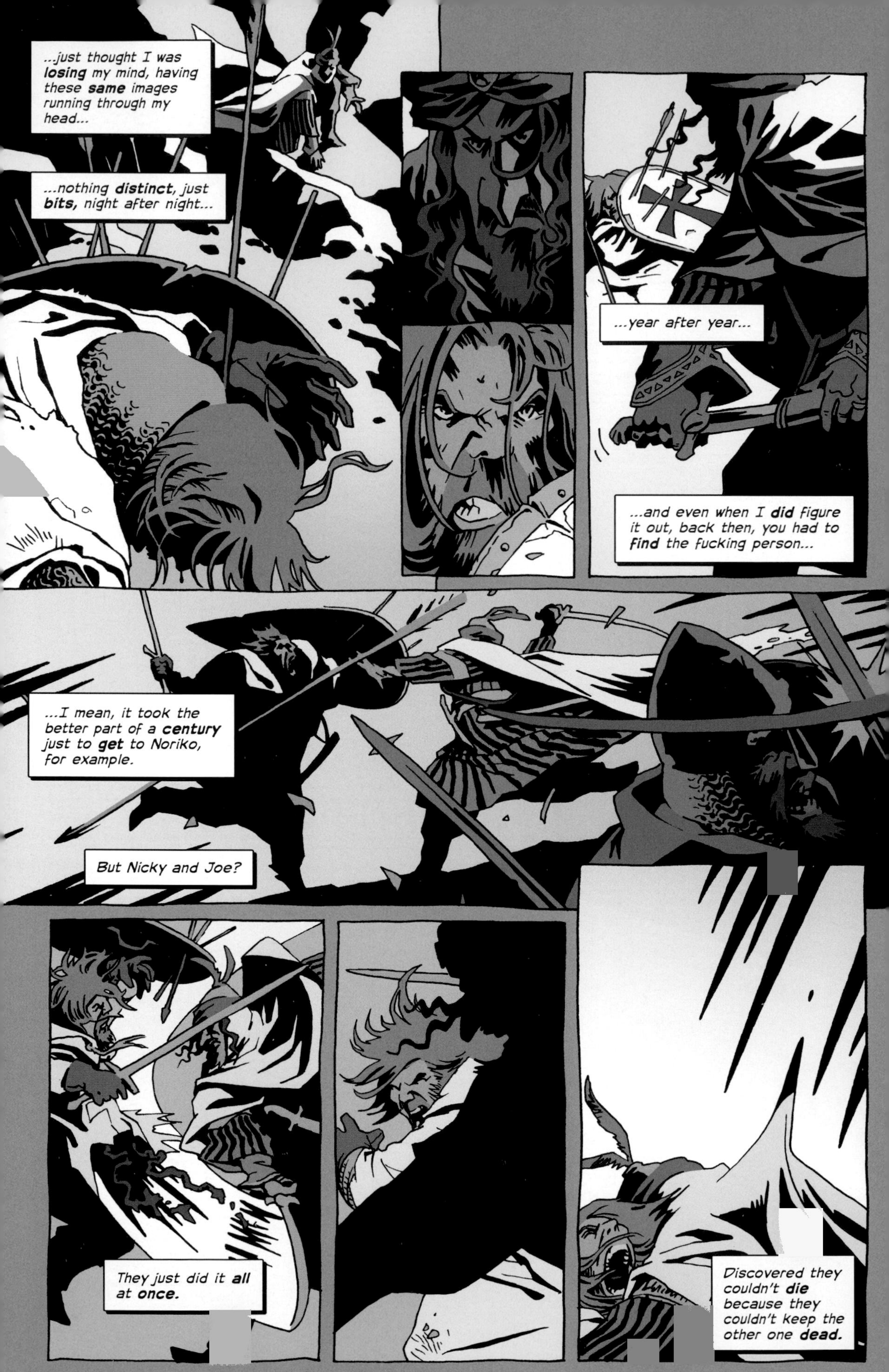
...just thought I was **losing** my mind, having these **same** images running through my head...
...nothing **distinct**, just **bits,** night after night...
...year after year...
...and even when I **did** figure it out, back then, you had to **find** the fucking person...
...I mean, it took the better part of a **century** just to **get** to Noriko, for example.
But Nicky and Joe?
They just did it **all** at **once.**
Discovered they couldn't **die** because they couldn't keep the other one **dead.**

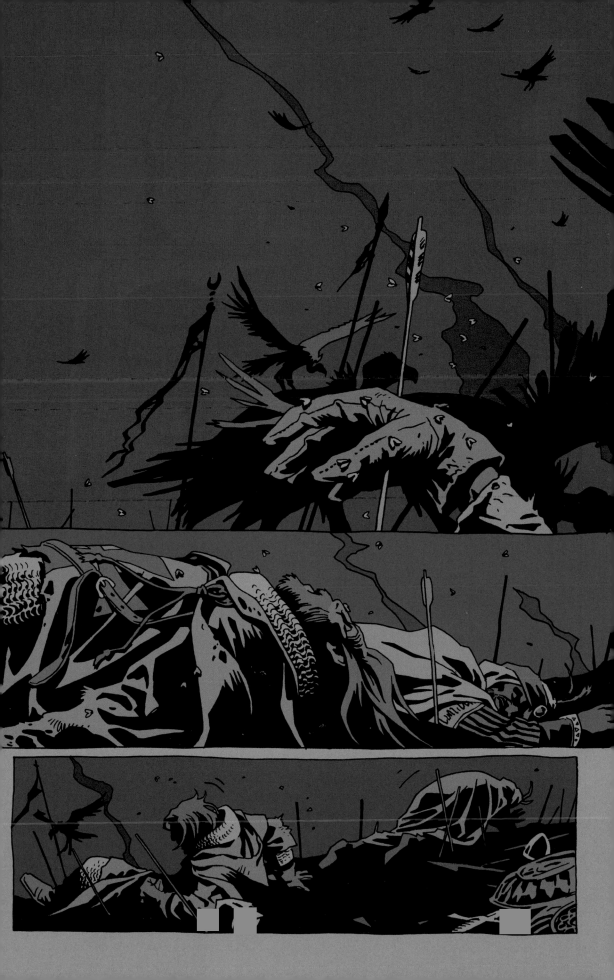

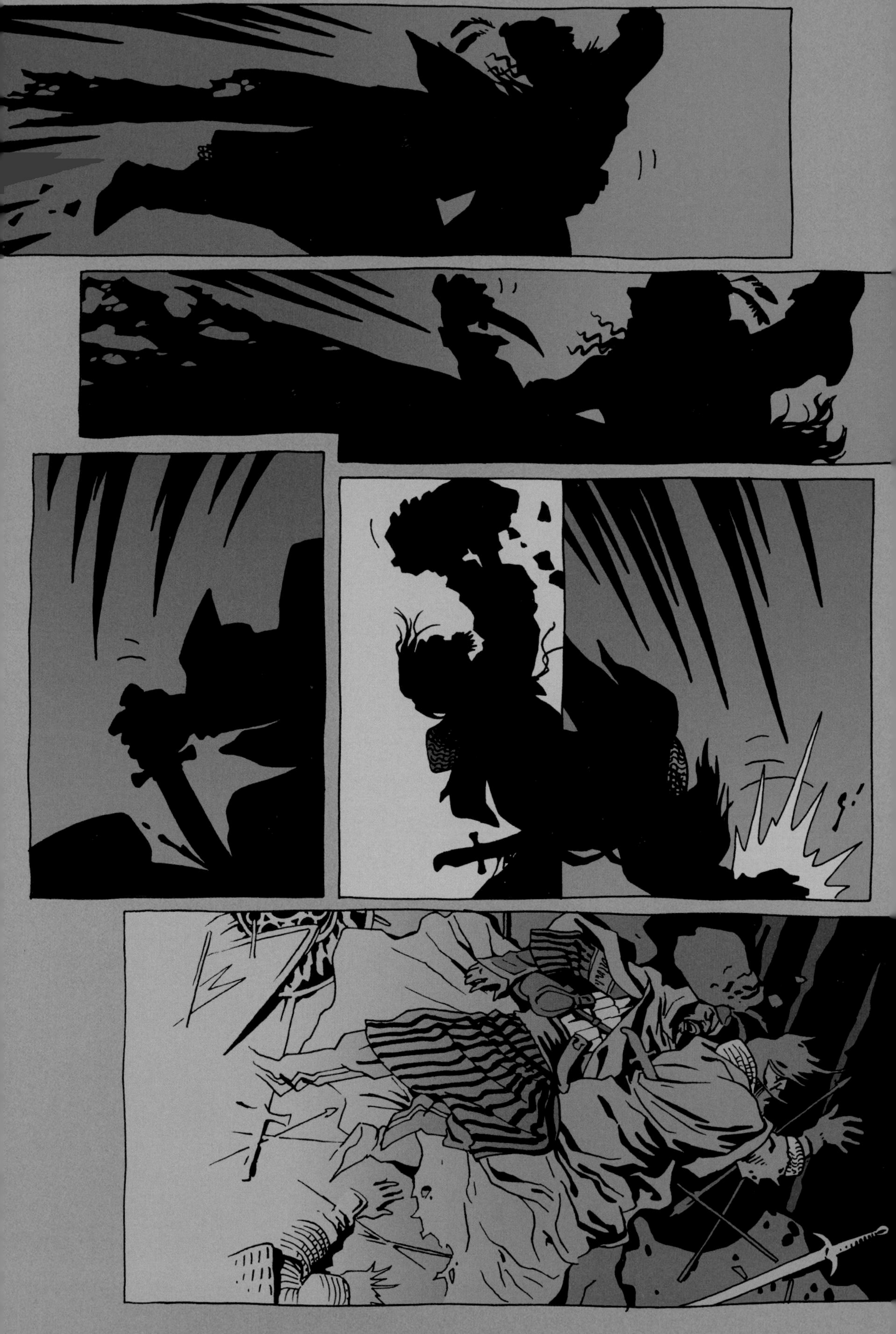

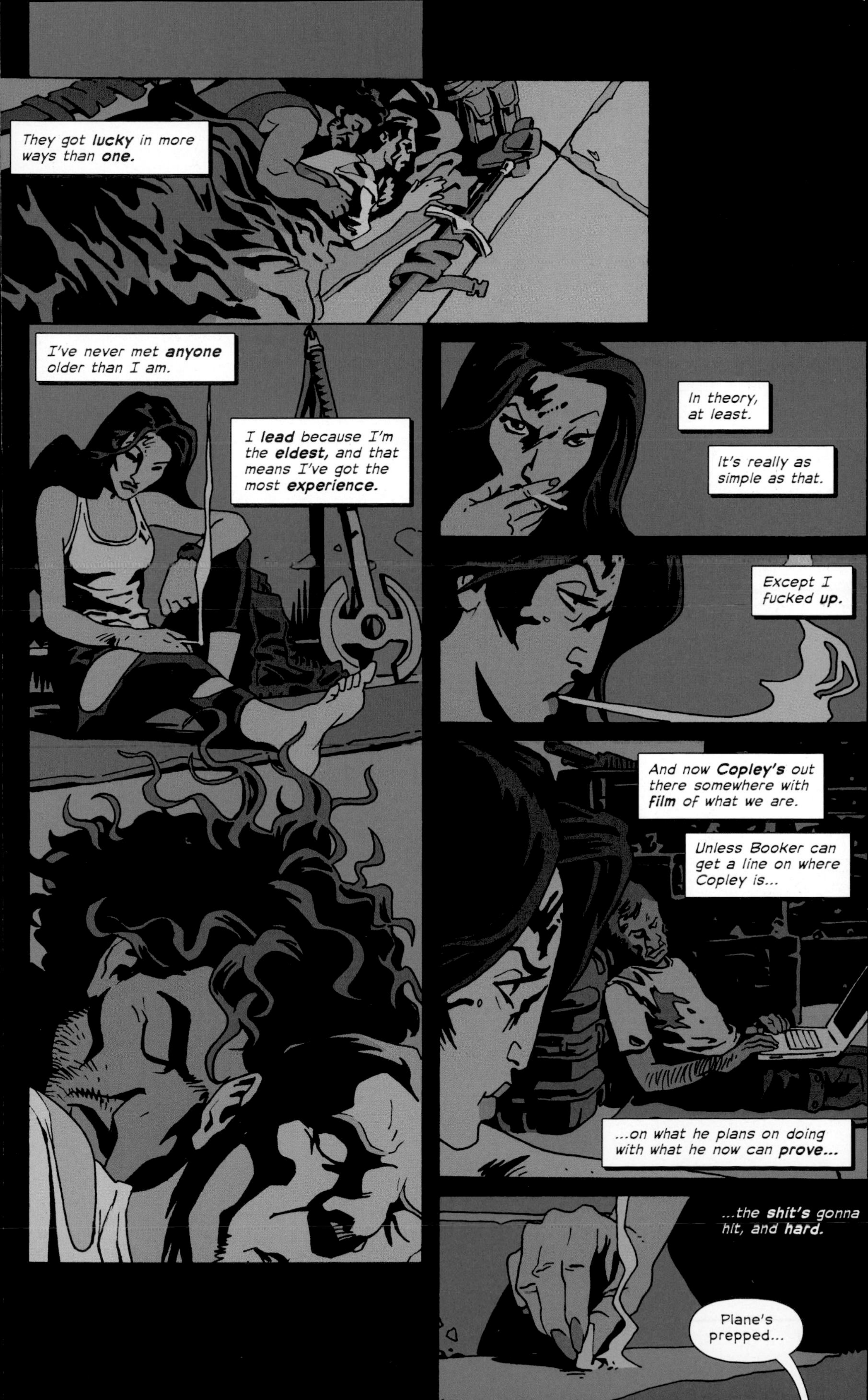
They got lucky in more ways than one.
I've never met anyone older than I am.
I lead because I'm the eldest, and that means I've got the most experience.
In theory, at least.
It's really as simple as that.
Except I fucked up.
And now Copley's out there somewhere with film of what we are.
Unless Booker can get a line on where Copley is...
...on what he plans on doing with what he now can prove...
...the shit's gonna hit, and hard.
Plane's prepped...

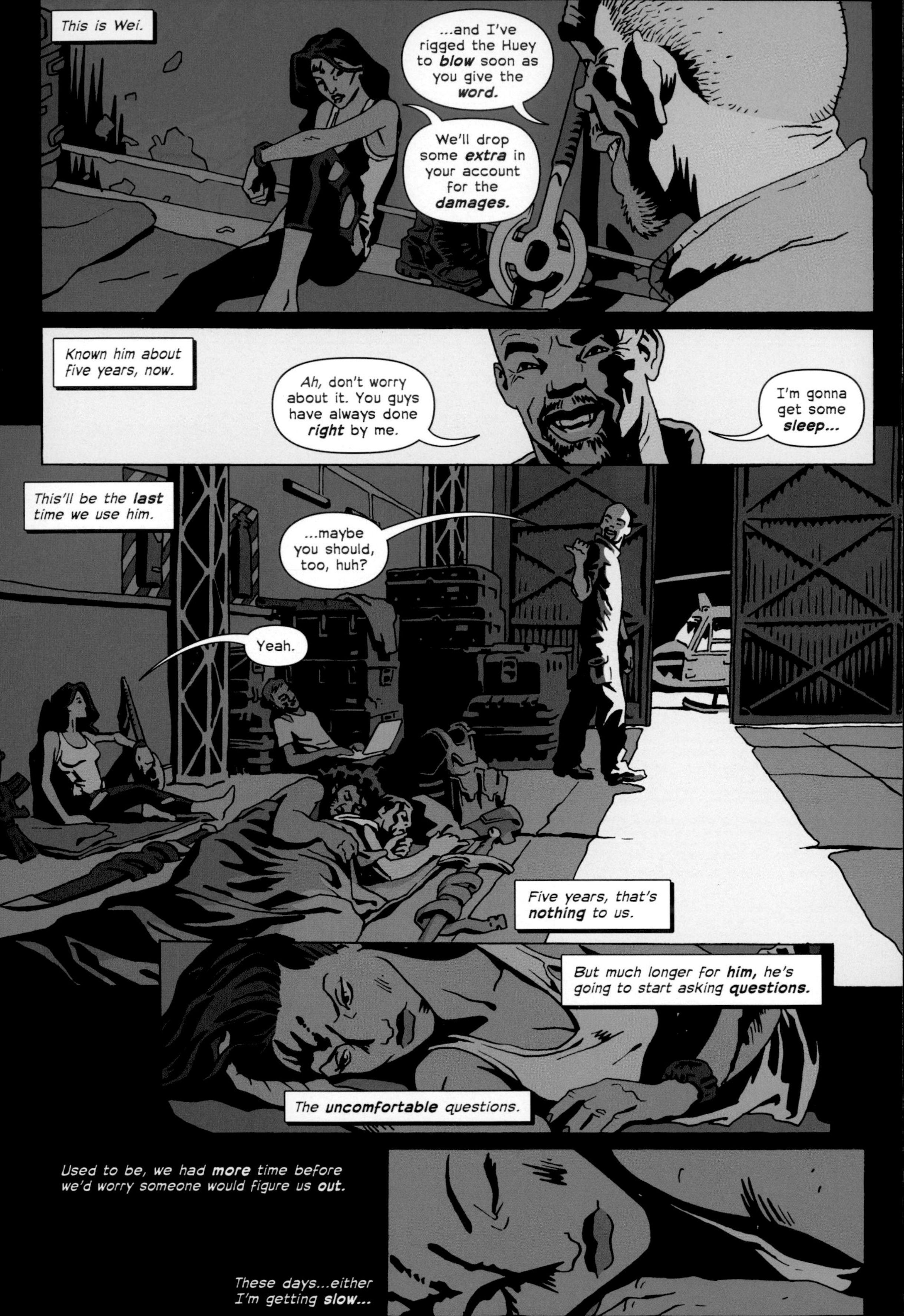
This is Wei.
...and I've rigged the Huey to **blow** soon as you give the **word.**
We'll drop some **extra** in your account for the **damages.**
Known him about five years, now.
Ah, don't worry about it. You guys have always done **right** by me.
I'm gonna get some **sleep...**
This'll be the **last** time we use him.
...maybe you should, too, huh?
Yeah.
Five years, that's **nothing** to us.
But much longer for **him,** he's going to start asking **questions.**
The **uncomfortable** questions.
Used to be, we had **more** time before we'd worry someone would figure us **out.**
These days...either I'm getting **slow...**

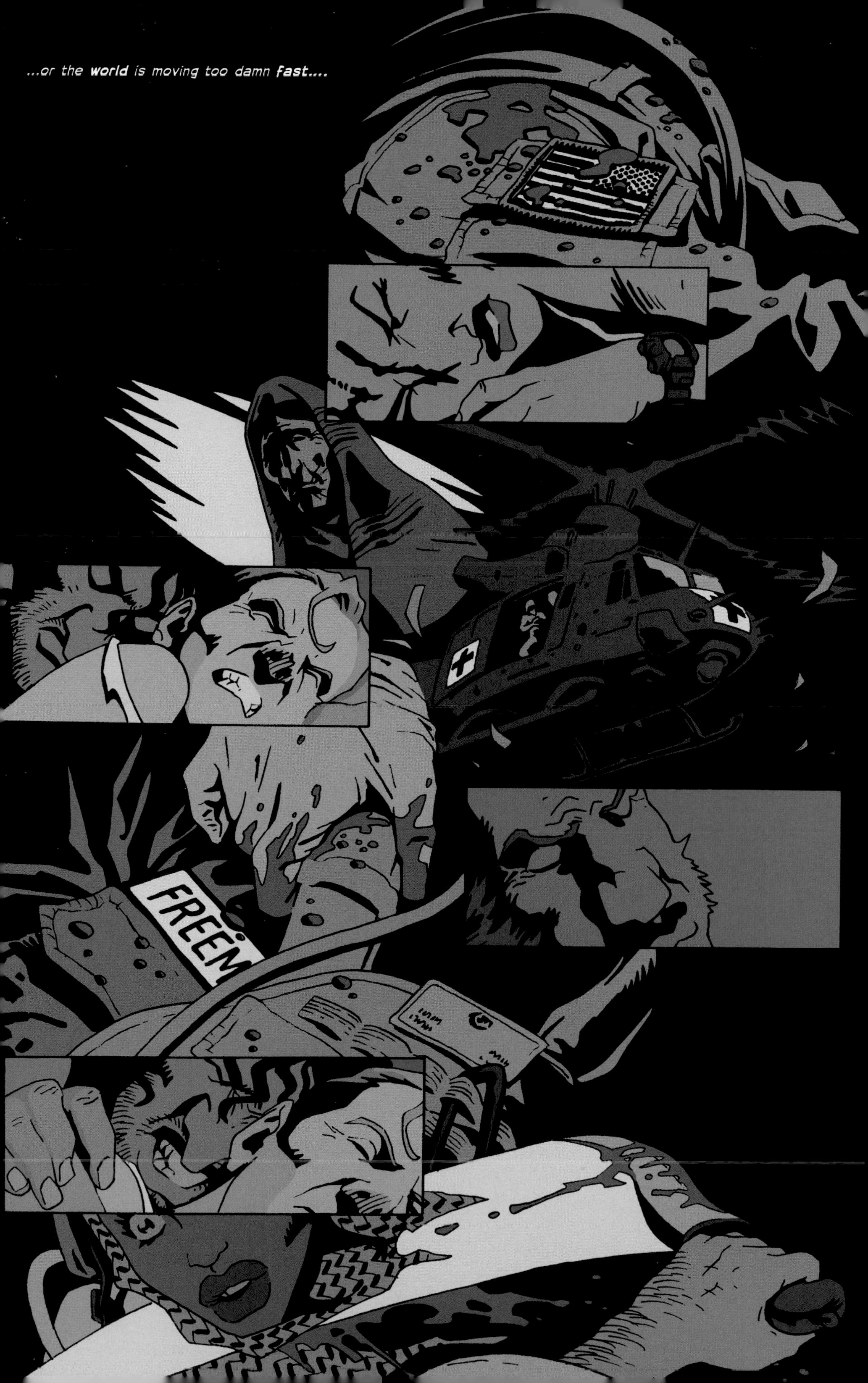
...or the **world** is moving too damn **fast....**
FREEM

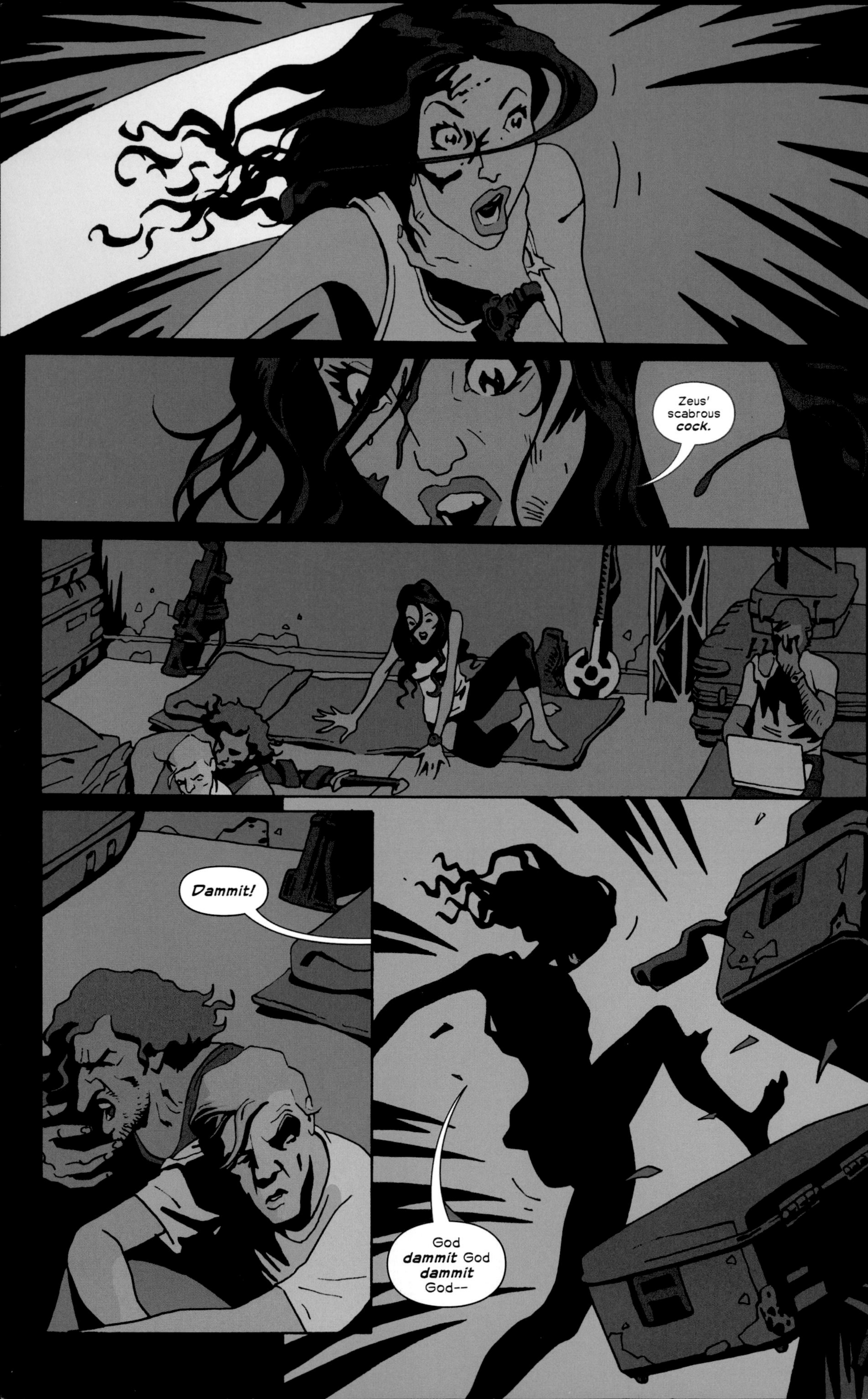
Zeus' scabrous cock.
Dammit!
God dammit God dammit God--

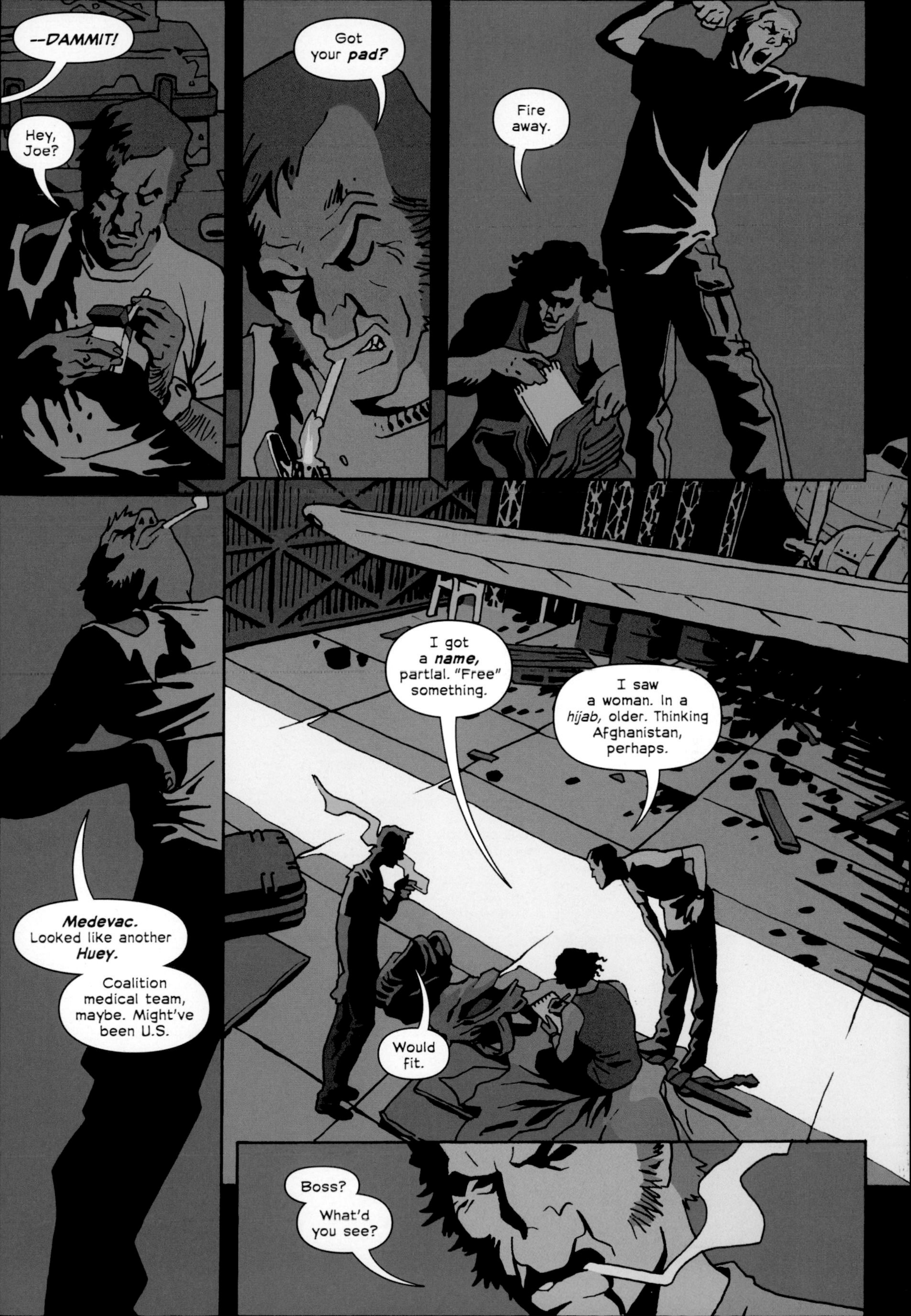

--DAMMIT!
Hey, Joe?
Got your *pad?*
Fire away.
I got a *name,* partial. "Free" something.
I saw a woman. In a *hijab,* older. Thinking Afghanistan, perhaps.
Medevac. Looked like another *Huey.*
Coalition medical team, maybe. Might've been U.S.
Would fit.
Boss?
What'd you see?

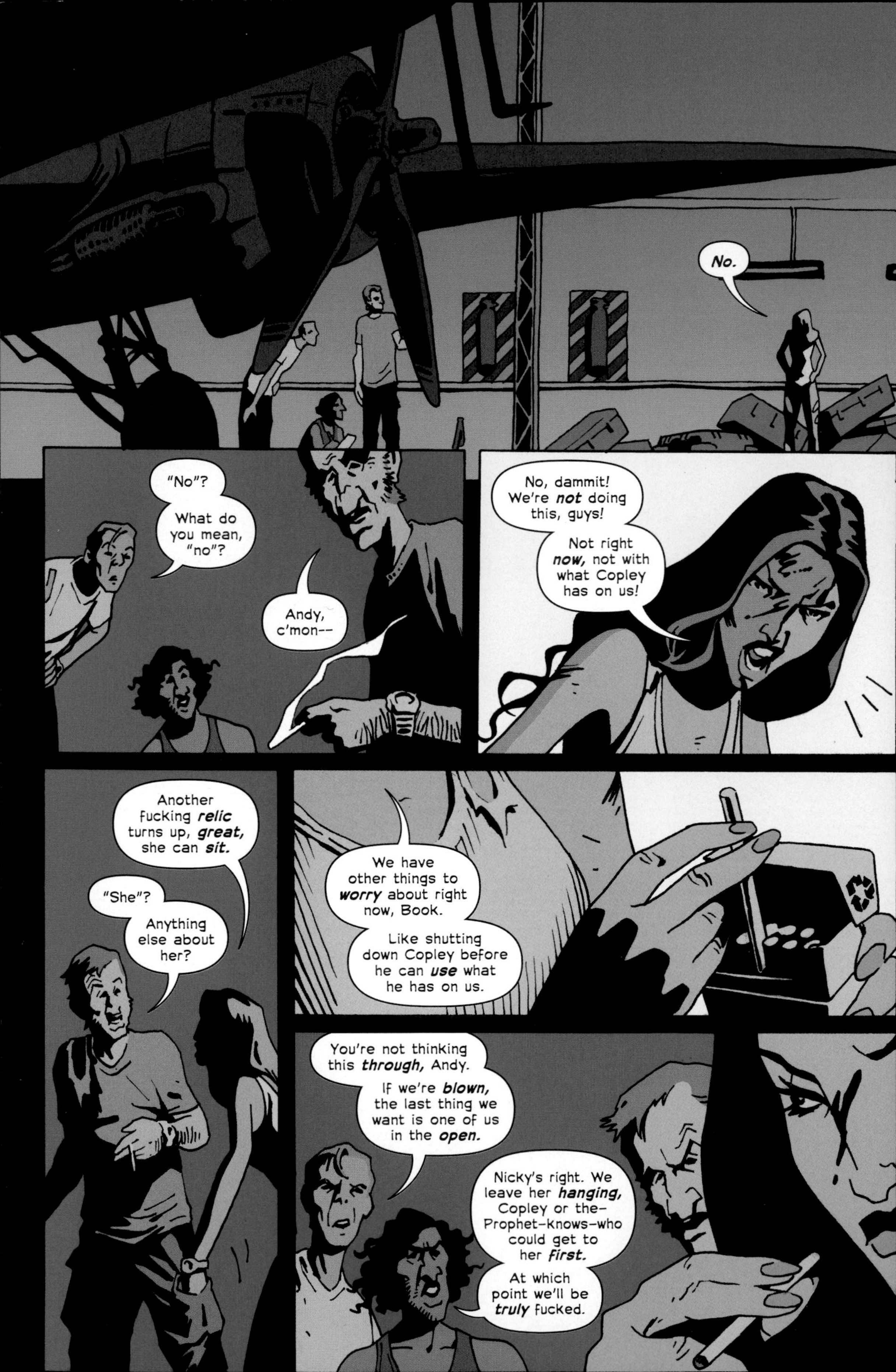
No.
"No"?
What do you mean, "no"?
Andy, c'mon--
No, dammit! We're **not** doing this, guys!
Not right **now,** not with what Copley has on us!
Another fucking **relic** turns up, **great,** she can **sit.**
"She"?
Anything else about her?
We have other things to **worry** about right now, Book.
Like shutting down Copley before he can **use** what he has on us.
You're not thinking this **through,** Andy.
If we're **blown,** the last thing we want is one of us in the **open.**
Nicky's right. We leave her **hanging,** Copley or the-Prophet-knows-who could get to her **first.**
At which point we'll be **truly** fucked.

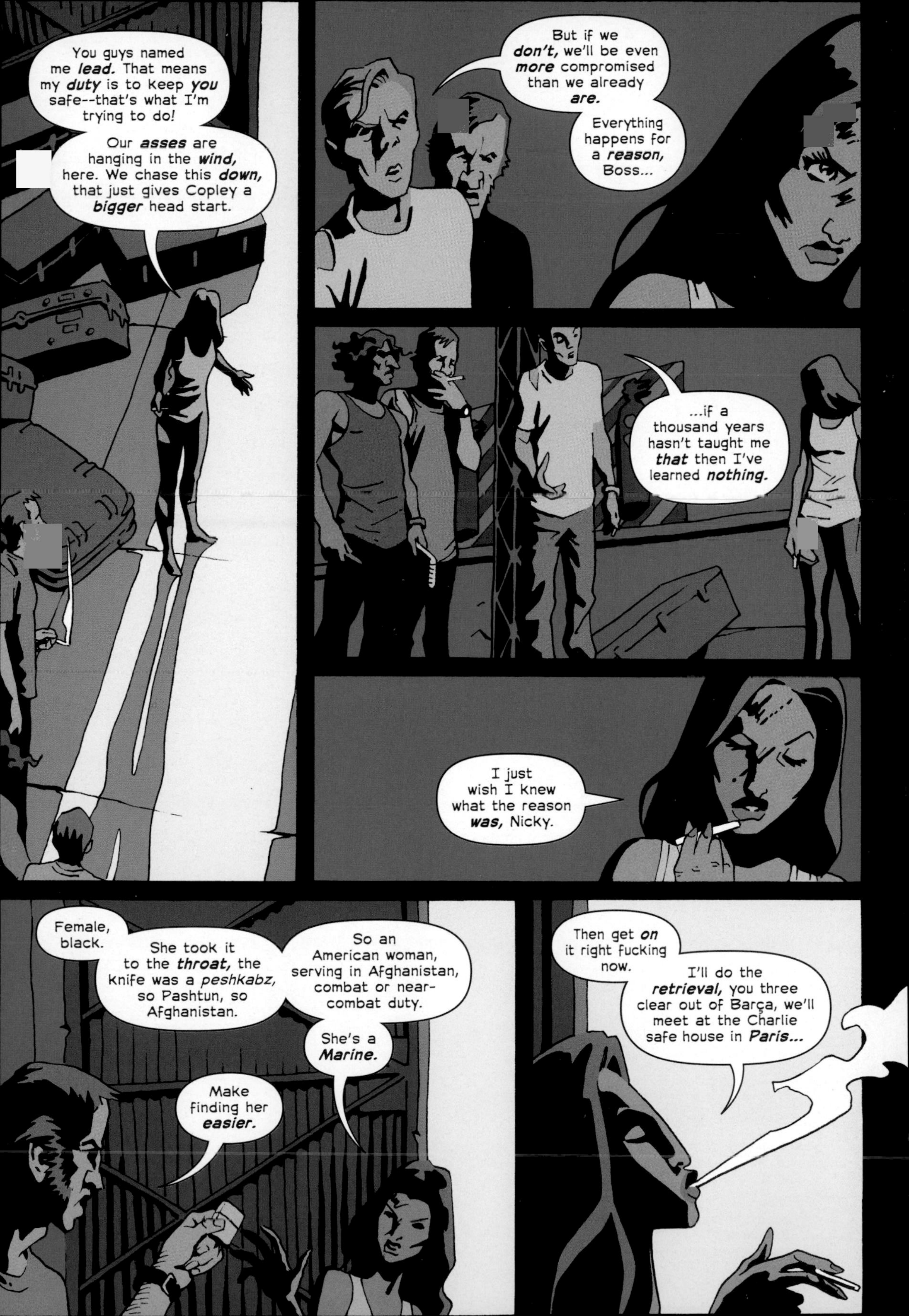
You guys named me lead. That means my duty is to keep you safe--that's what I'm trying to do!
Our asses are hanging in the wind, here. We chase this down, that just gives Copley a bigger head start.
But if we don't, we'll be even more compromised than we already are.
Everything happens for a reason, Boss...
...if a thousand years hasn't taught me that then I've learned nothing.
I just wish I knew what the reason was, Nicky.
Female, black.
She took it to the throat, the knife was a peshkabz, so Pashtun, so Afghanistan.
So an American woman, serving in Afghanistan, combat or near-combat duty.
She's a Marine.
Make finding her easier.
Then get on it right fucking now.
I'll do the retrieval, you three clear out of Barça, we'll meet at the Charlie safe house in Paris...

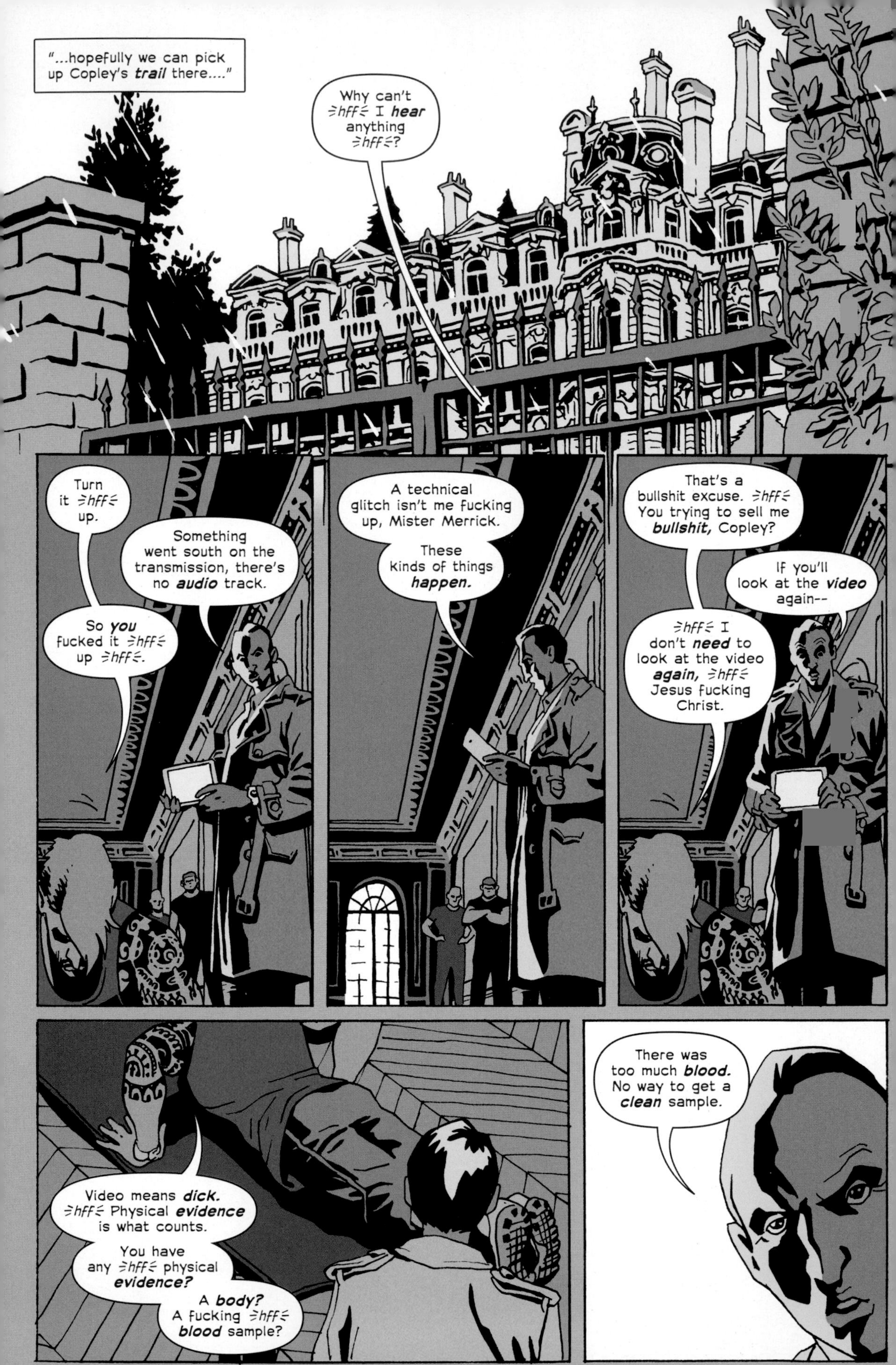
"...hopefully we can pick up Copley's *trail* there...."
Why can't ≠hff≠ I *hear* anything ≠hff≠?
Turn it ≠hff≠ up.
Something went south on the transmission, there's no *audio* track.
So *you* fucked it ≠hff≠ up ≠hff≠.
A technical glitch isn't me fucking up, Mister Merrick.
These kinds of things *happen.*
That's a bullshit excuse. ≠hff≠ You trying to sell me *bullshit,* Copley?
If you'll look at the *video* again--
≠hff≠ I don't *need* to look at the video *again,* ≠hff≠ Jesus fucking Christ.
Video means *dick.* ≠hff≠ Physical *evidence* is what counts.
You have any ≠hff≠ physical *evidence?*
A *body?* A fucking ≠hff≠ *blood* sample?
There was too much *blood.* No way to get a *clean* sample.

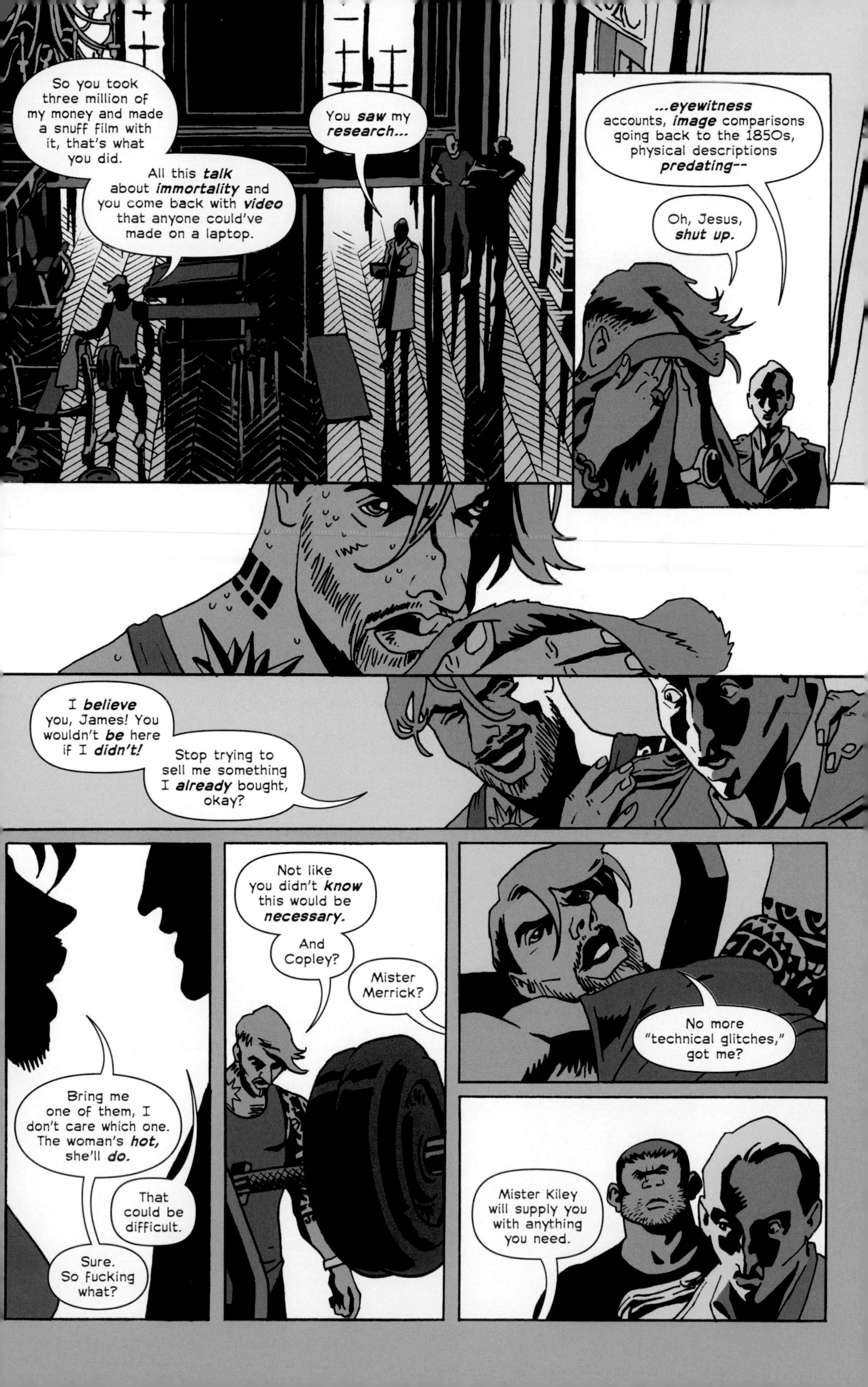
So you took three million of my money and made a snuff film with it, that's what you did.
All this *talk* about *immortality* and you come back with *video* that anyone could've made on a laptop.
You *saw* my *research...*
...eyewitness accounts, *image* comparisons going back to the 1850s, physical descriptions *predating--*
Oh, Jesus, *shut up.*
I *believe* you, James! You wouldn't *be* here if I *didn't!*
Stop trying to sell me something I *already* bought, okay?
Bring me one of them, I don't care which one. The woman's *hot,* she'll *do.*
That could be difficult.
Sure. So fucking what?
Not like you didn't *know* this would be *necessary.*
And Copley?
Mister Merrick?
No more "technical glitches," got me?
Mister Kiley will supply you with anything you need.

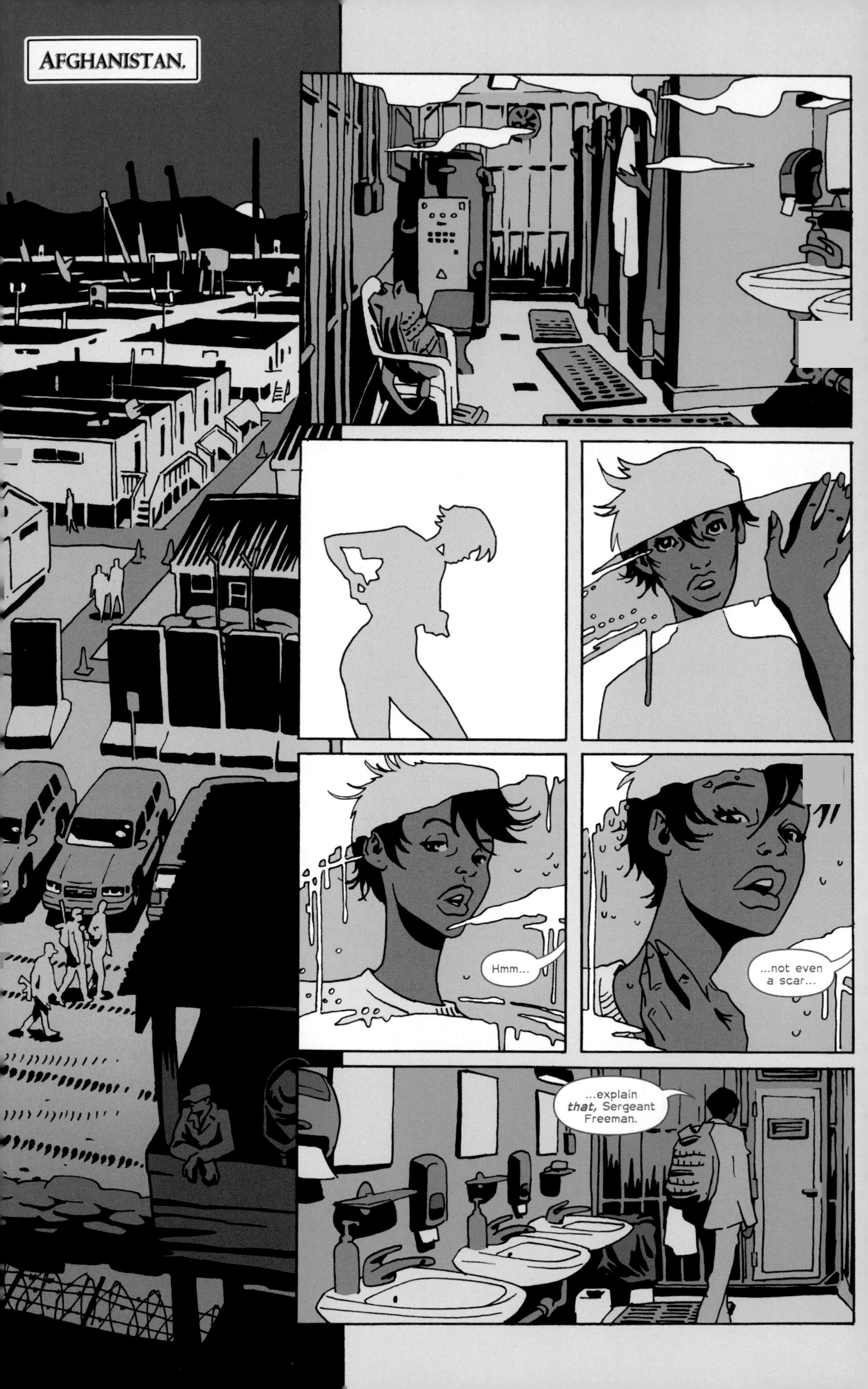
AFGHANISTAN.
Hmm...
...not even a scar...
...explain *that,* Sergeant Freeman.

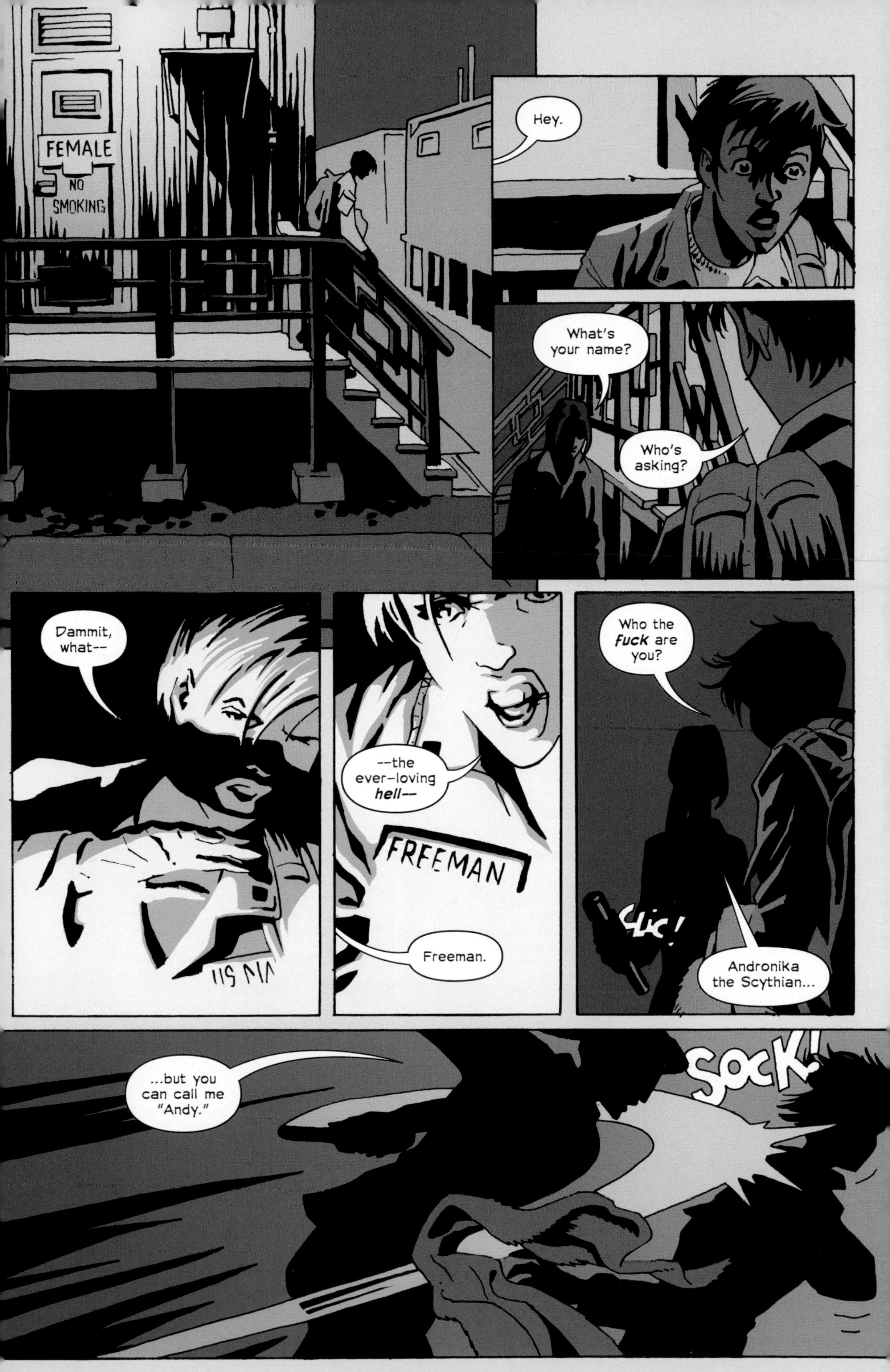
FEMALE
NO SMOKING
Hey.
What's your name?
Who's asking?
Dammit, what--
--the ever-loving hell--
FREEMAN
Freeman.
Who the fuck are you?
CLIC!
Andronika the Scythian...
...but you can call me "Andy."
SOCK!

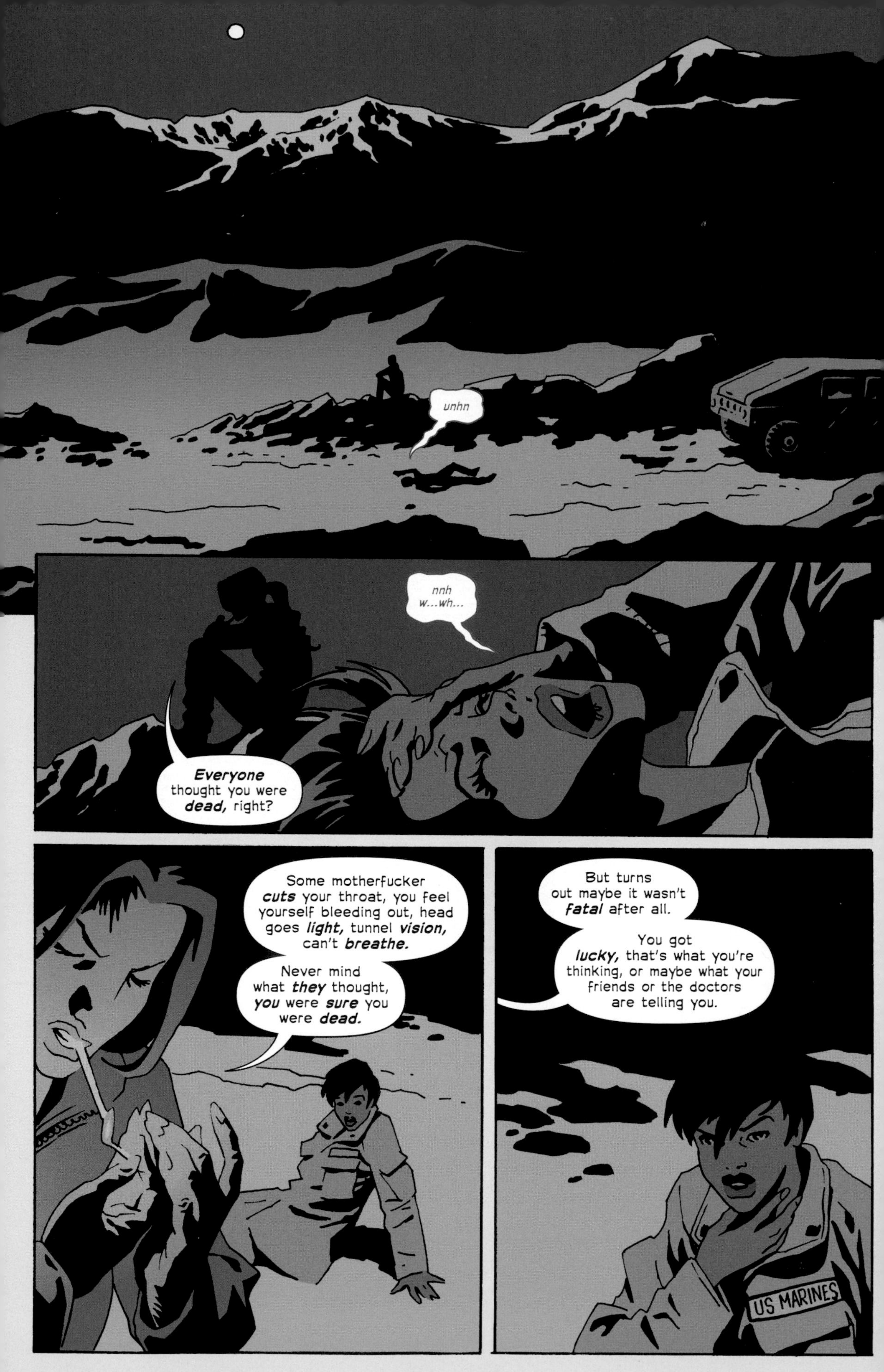
unhn
nnh w...wh...
Everyone thought you were dead, right?
Some motherfucker cuts your throat, you feel yourself bleeding out, head goes light, tunnel vision, can't breathe.
Never mind what they thought, you were sure you were dead.
But turns out maybe it wasn't fatal after all.
You got lucky, that's what you're thinking, or maybe what your friends or the doctors are telling you.
US MARINES

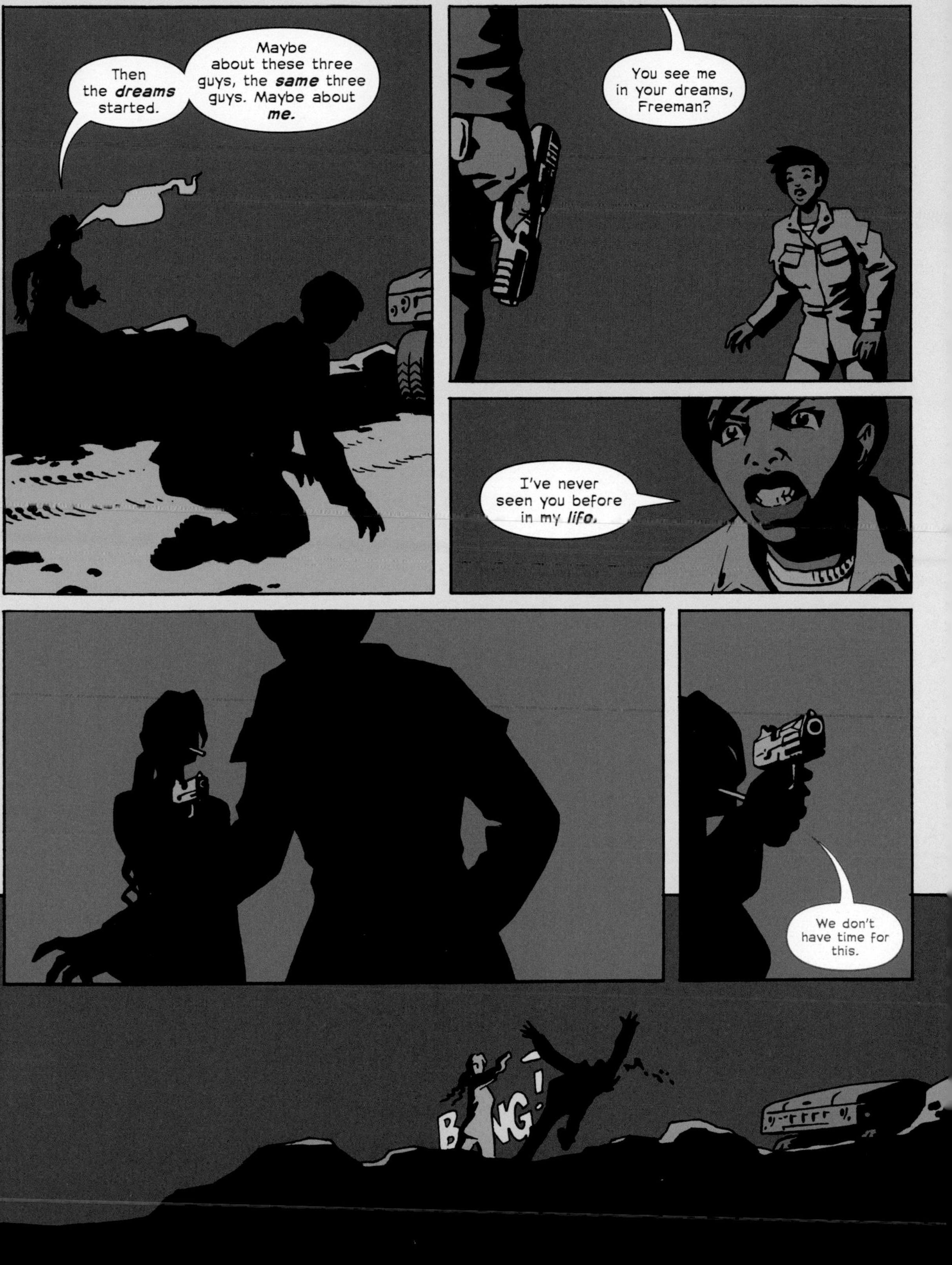
Then the dreams started.
Maybe about these three guys, the same three guys. Maybe about me.
You see me in your dreams, Freeman?
I've never seen you before in my life.
We don't have time for this.
BANG!

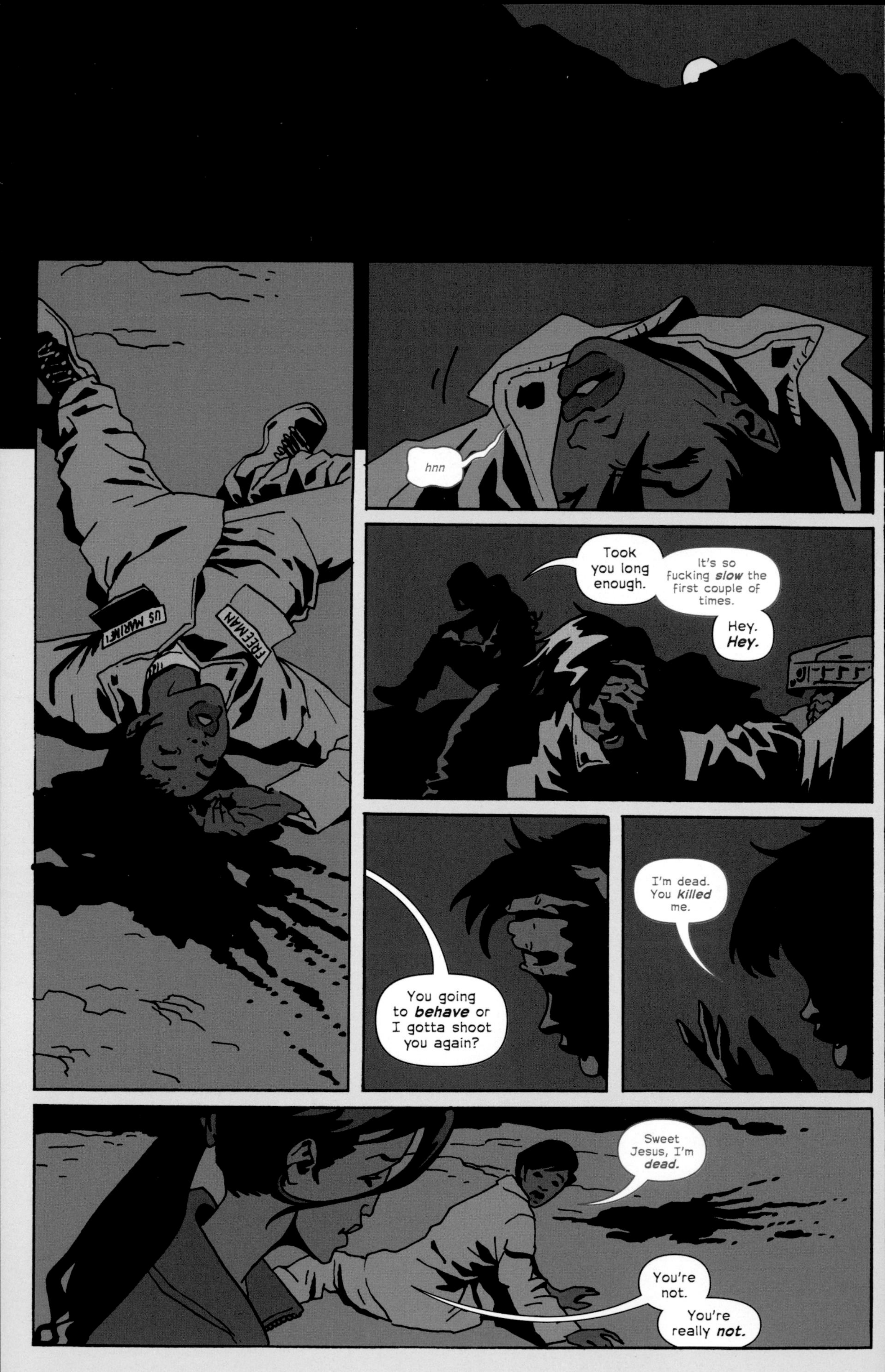
US MARINE
FREEMAN
hnn
Took you long enough.
It's so fucking *slow* the first couple of times.
Hey. **Hey.**
You going to ***behave*** or I gotta shoot you again?
I'm dead. You ***killed*** me.
Sweet Jesus, I'm ***dead.***
You're not.
You're really ***not.***

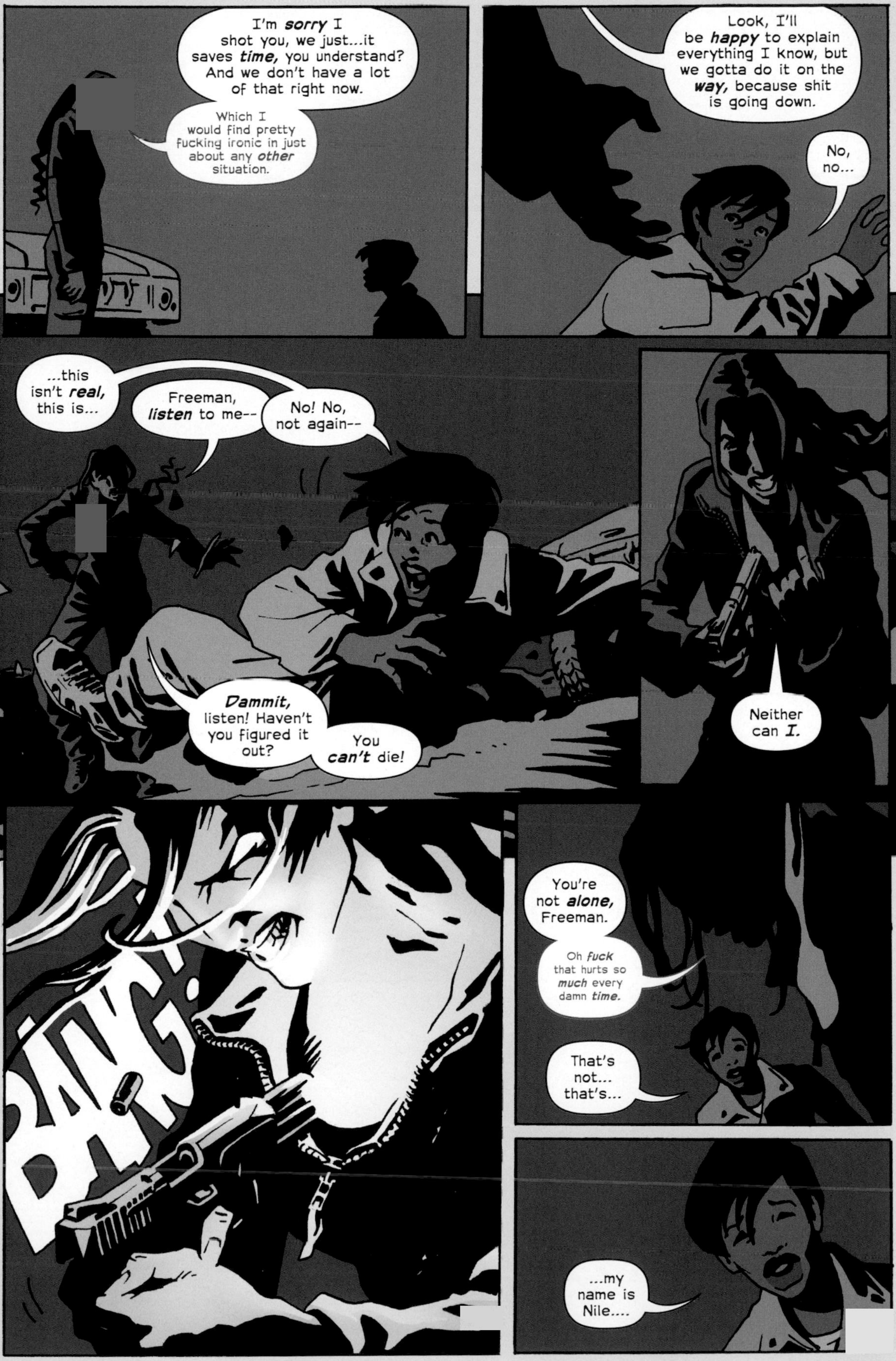
I'm *sorry* I shot you, we just...it saves *time,* you understand? And we don't have a lot of that right now.
Which I would find pretty fucking ironic in just about any *other* situation.
Look, I'll be *happy* to explain everything I know, but we gotta do it on the *way,* because shit is going down.
No, no...
...this isn't *real,* this is...
Freeman, *listen* to me--
No! No, not again--
Dammit, listen! Haven't you figured it out?
You *can't* die!
Neither can *I.*
BANG!
You're not *alone,* Freeman.
Oh *fuck* that hurts so *much* every damn *time.*
That's not... that's...
...my name is Nile....

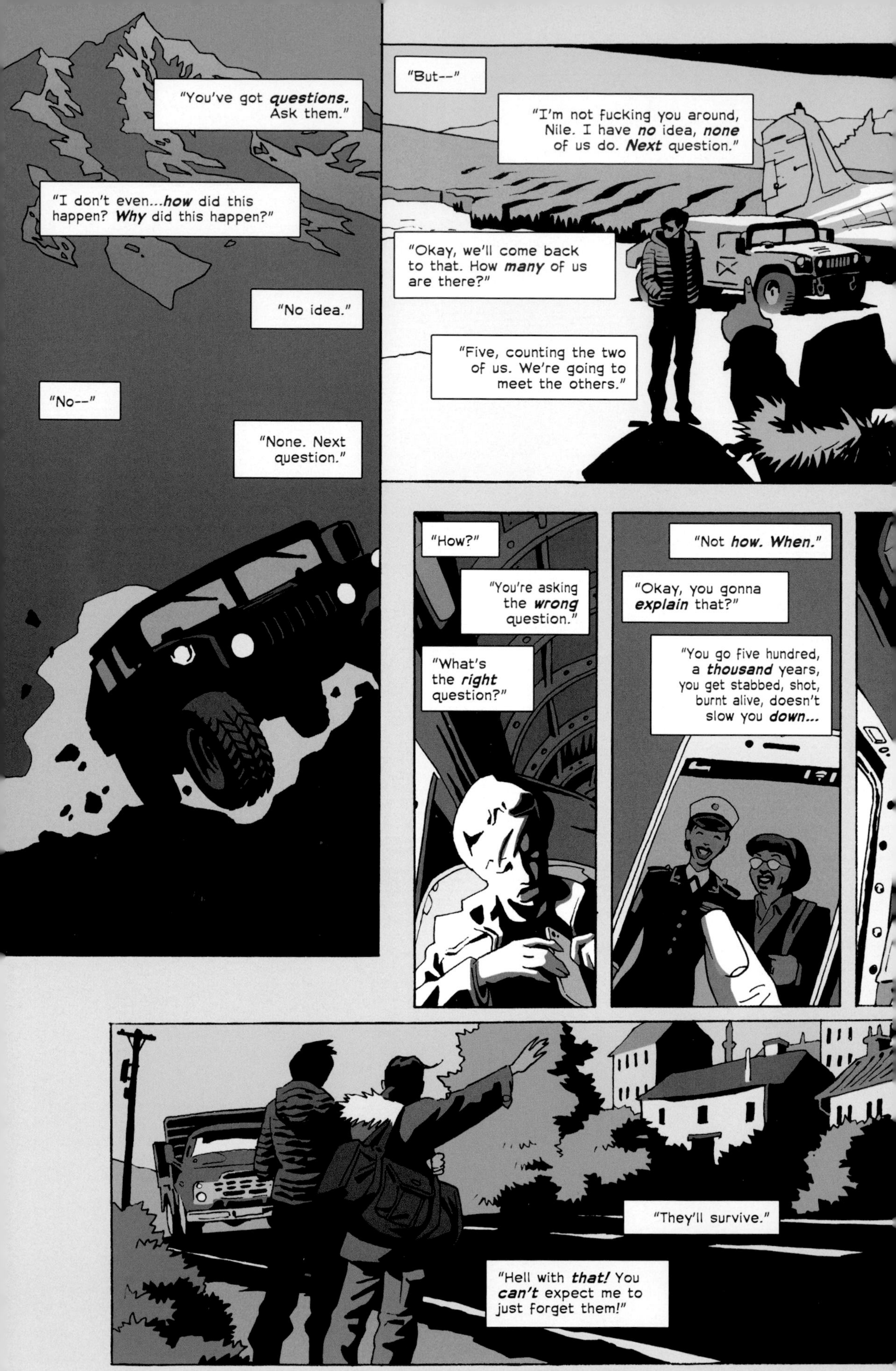
"You've got questions. Ask them."
"I don't even...how did this happen? Why did this happen?"
"No idea."
"No--"
"None. Next question."
"But--"
"I'm not fucking you around, Nile. I have no idea, none of us do. Next question."
"Okay, we'll come back to that. How many of us are there?"
"Five, counting the two of us. We're going to meet the others."
"How?"
"You're asking the wrong question."
"What's the right question?"
"Not how. When."
"Okay, you gonna explain that?"
"You go five hundred, a thousand years, you get stabbed, shot, burnt alive, doesn't slow you down..."
"They'll survive."
"Hell with that! You can't expect me to just forget them!"

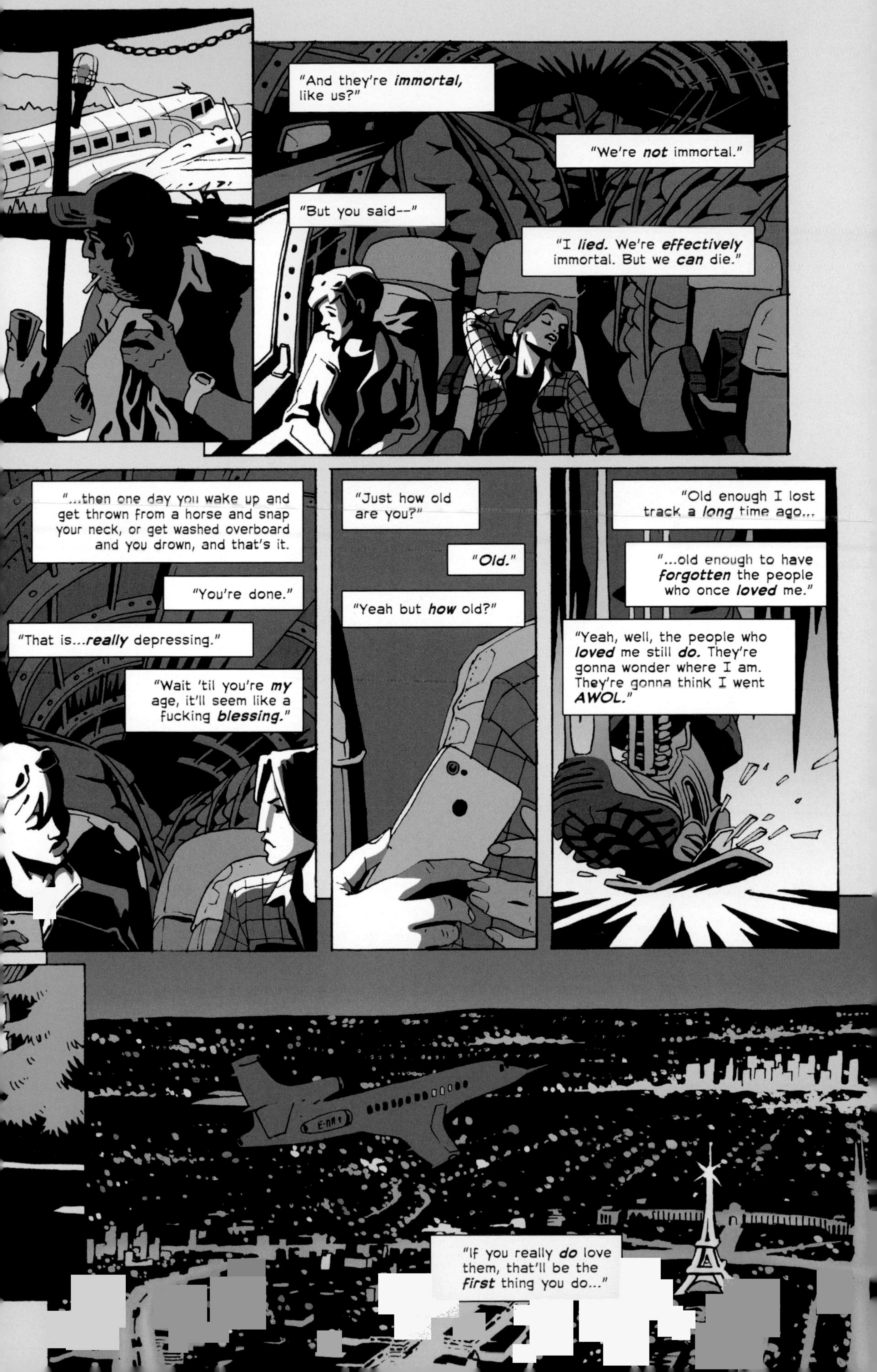
"And they're immortal, like us?"
"We're not immortal."
"But you said--"
"I lied. We're effectively immortal. But we can die."
"...then one day you wake up and get thrown from a horse and snap your neck, or get washed overboard and you drown, and that's it.
"You're done."
"That is...really depressing."
"Wait 'til you're my age, it'll seem like a fucking blessing."
"Just how old are you?"
"Old."
"Yeah but how old?"
"Old enough I lost track a long time ago...
"...old enough to have forgotten the people who once loved me."
"Yeah, well, the people who loved me still do. They're gonna wonder where I am. They're gonna think I went AWOL."
"If you really do love them, that'll be the first thing you do..."

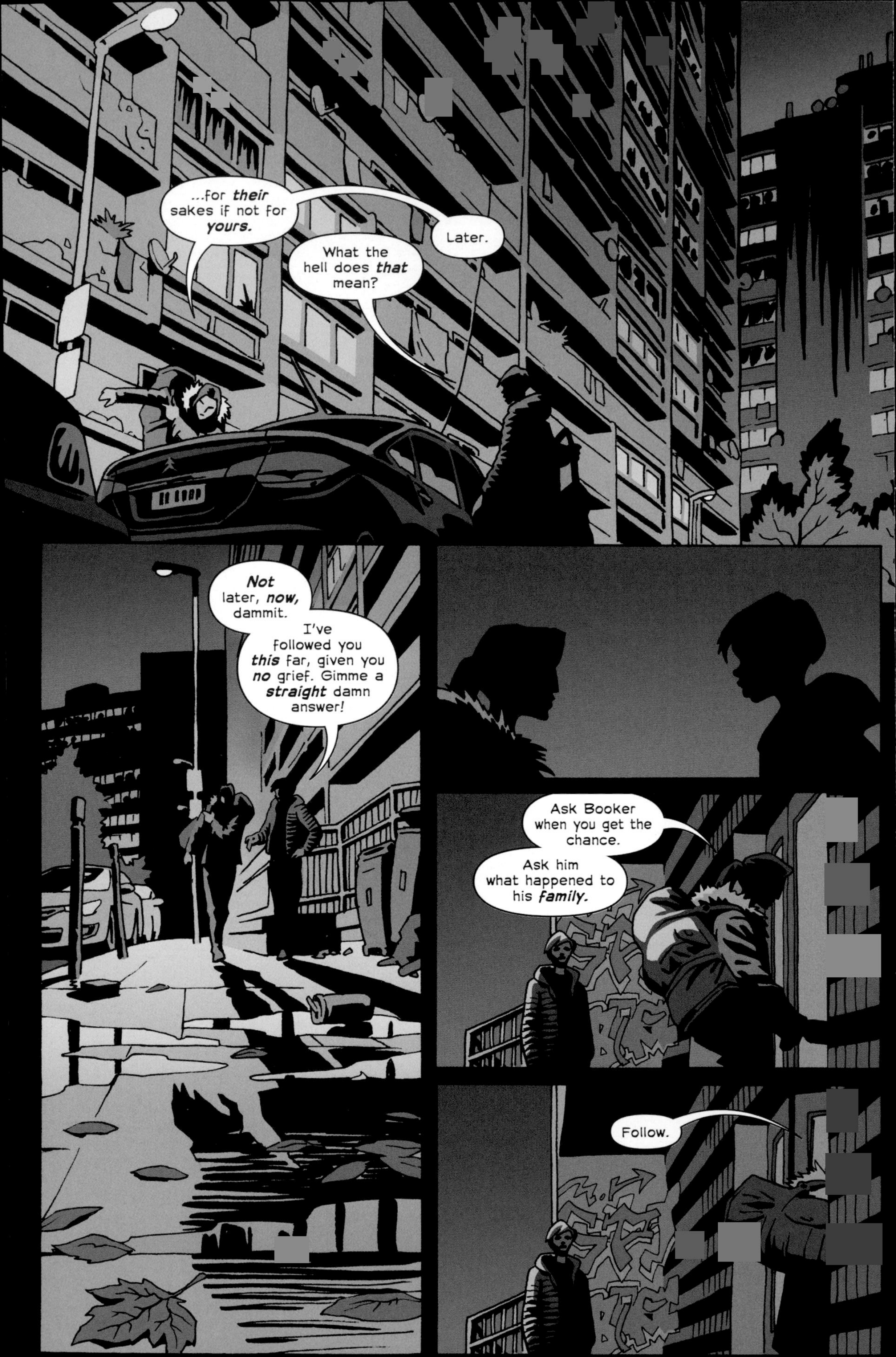
...for their sakes if not for yours.
Later.
What the hell does that mean?
Not later, now, dammit.
I've followed you this far, given you no grief. Gimme a straight damn answer!
Ask Booker when you get the chance.
Ask him what happened to his family.
Follow.

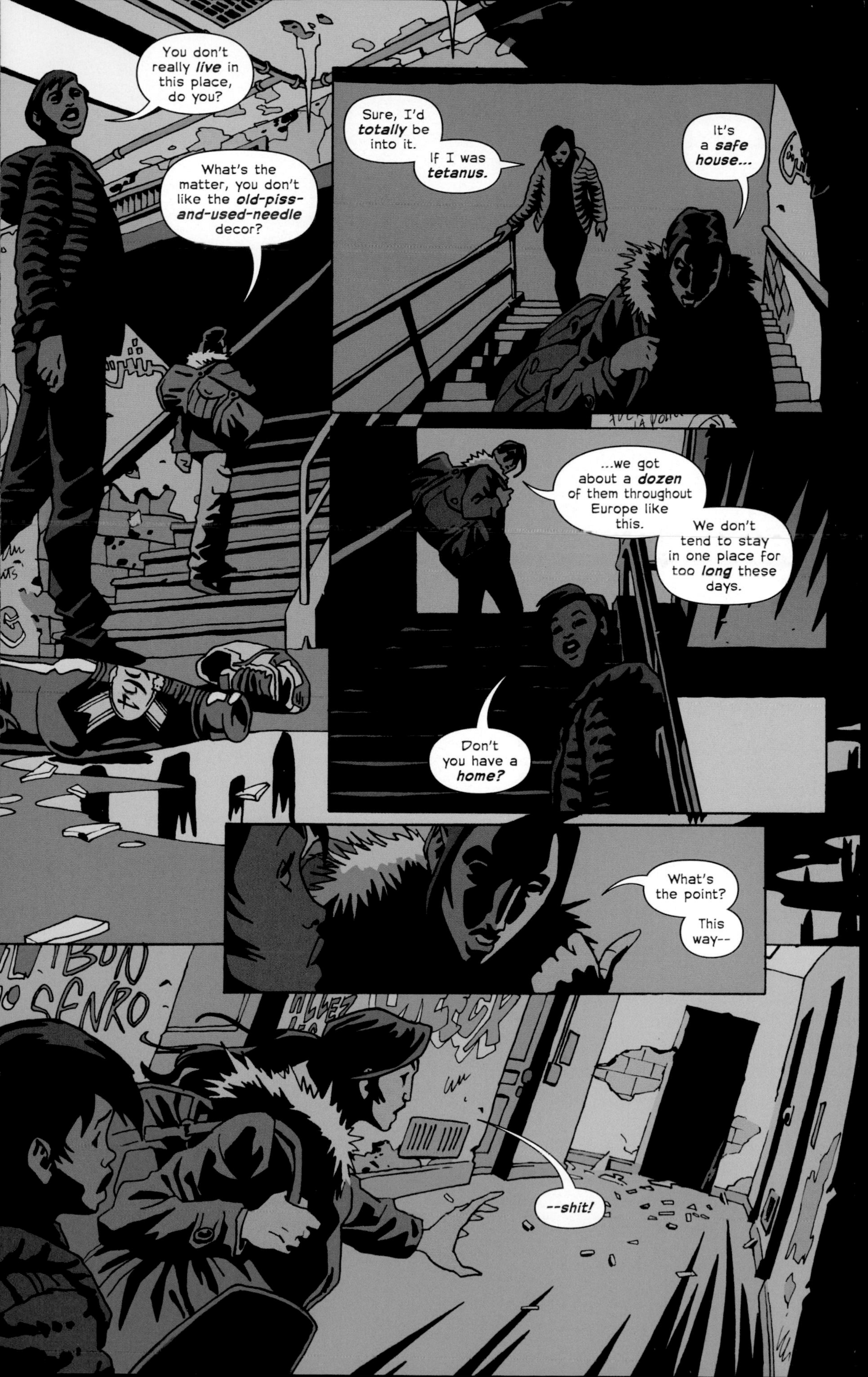
You don't really *live* in this place, do you?
What's the matter, you don't like the ***old-piss-and-used-needle*** decor?
Sure, I'd ***totally*** be into it.
If I was ***tetanus.***
It's a ***safe house...***
...we got about a ***dozen*** of them throughout Europe like this.
We don't tend to stay in one place for too ***long*** these days.
Don't you have a ***home?***
What's the point?
This way--
--shit!

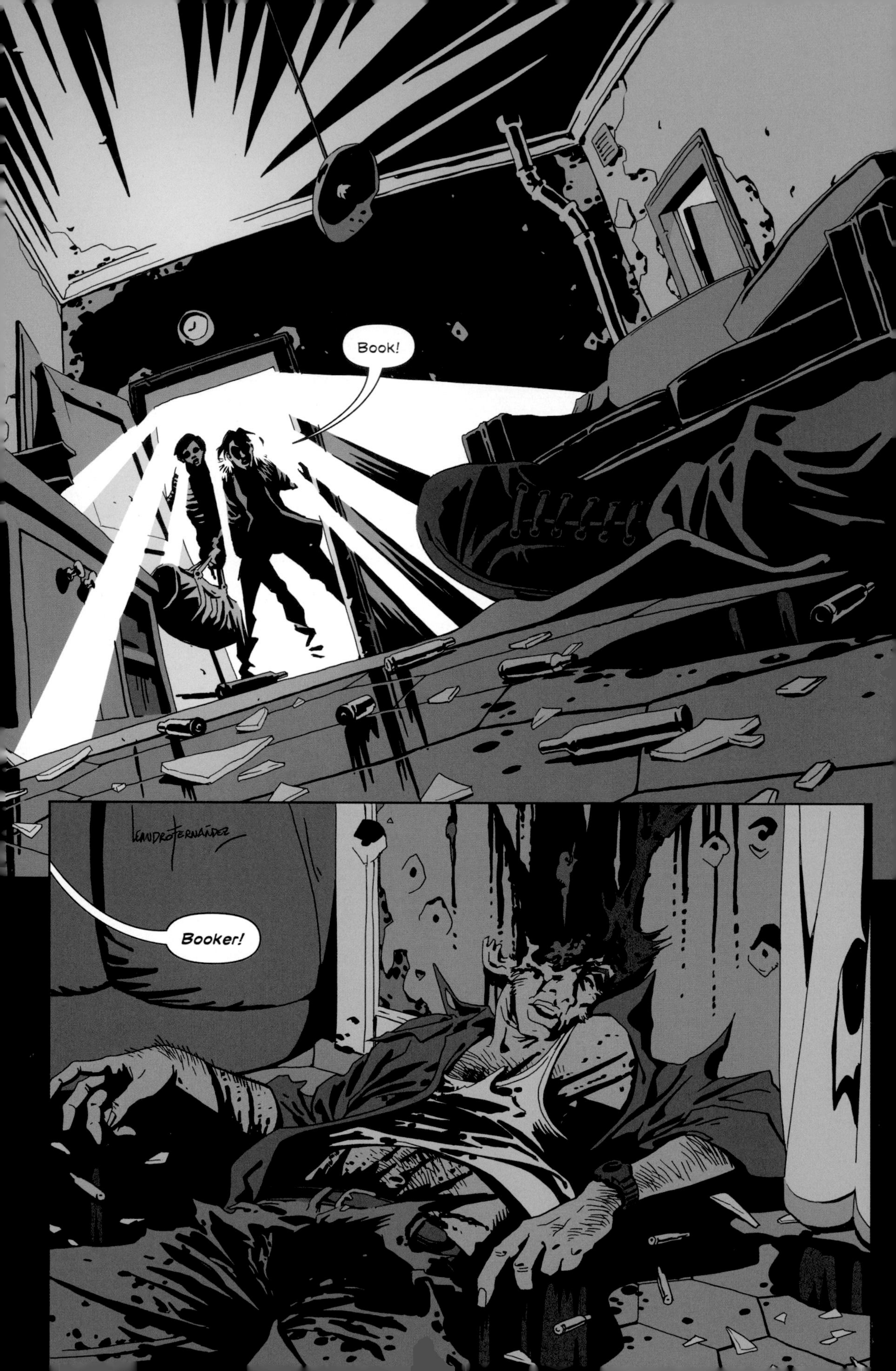
Book!
LEANDRO FERNÁNDEZ
Booker!

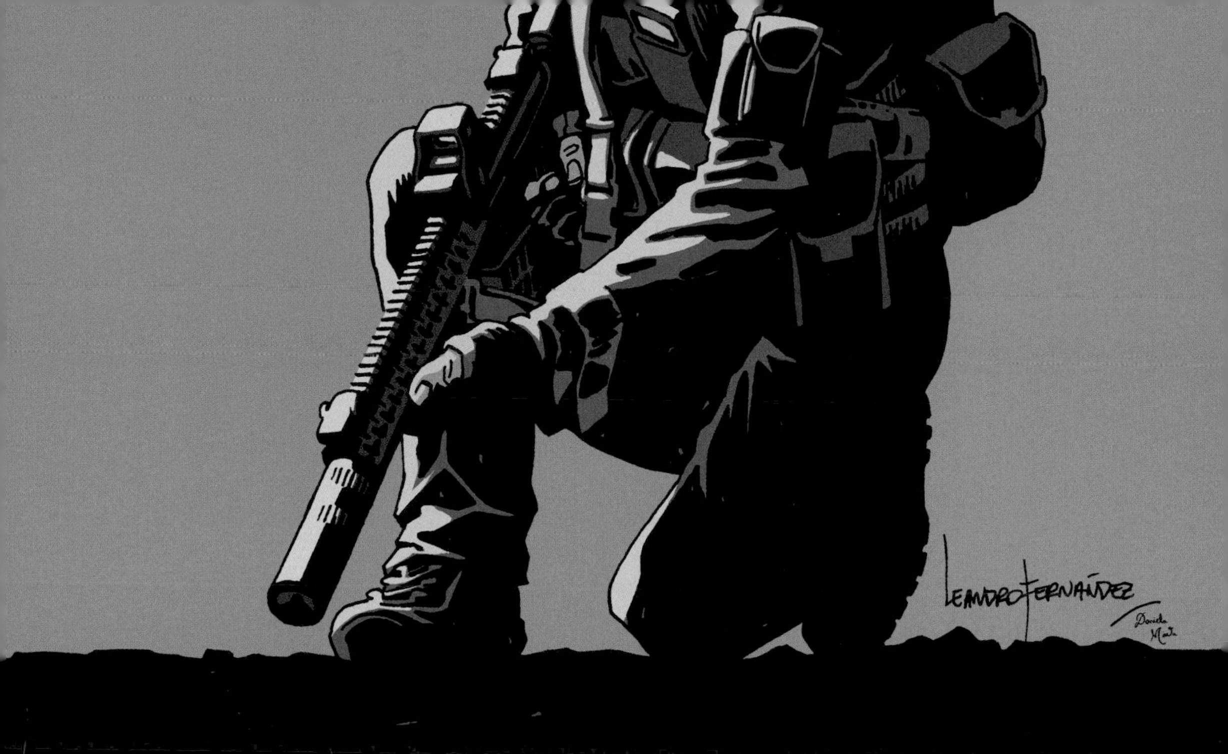
LEANDRO FERNÁNDEZ

CHAPTER THREE

"WAR NEVER TAKES A WICKED

MAN BY CHANCE, THE GOOD

MAN ALWAYS."

~SOPHOCLES, PHILOCTETES

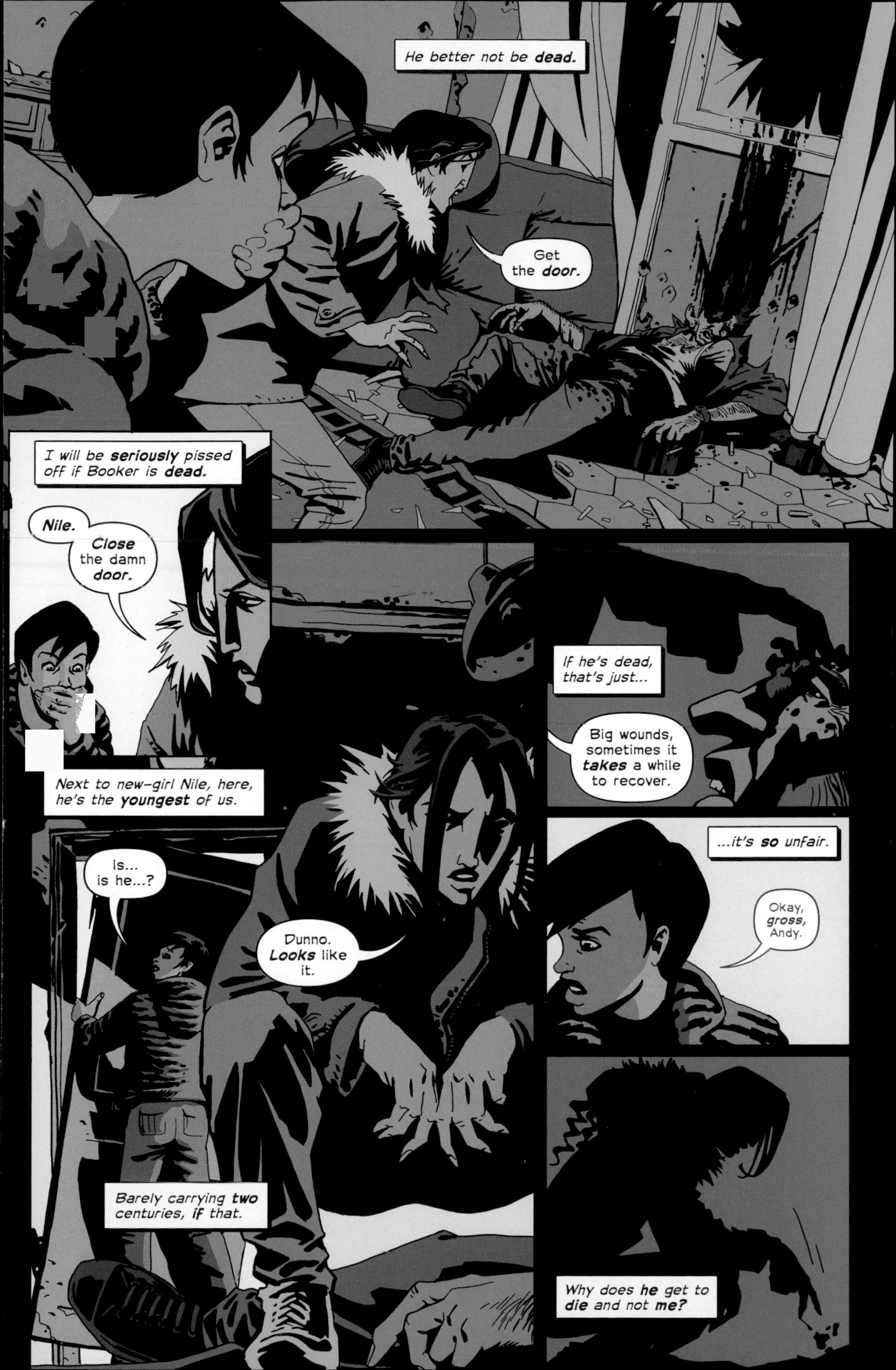
He better not be dead.
Get the door.
I will be seriously pissed off if Booker is dead.
Nile. Close the damn door.
Next to new-girl Nile, here, he's the youngest of us.
Is... is he...?
Dunno. Looks like it.
Barely carrying two centuries, if that.
If he's dead, that's just...
Big wounds, sometimes it takes a while to recover.
...it's so unfair.
Okay, gross, Andy.
Why does he get to die and not me?

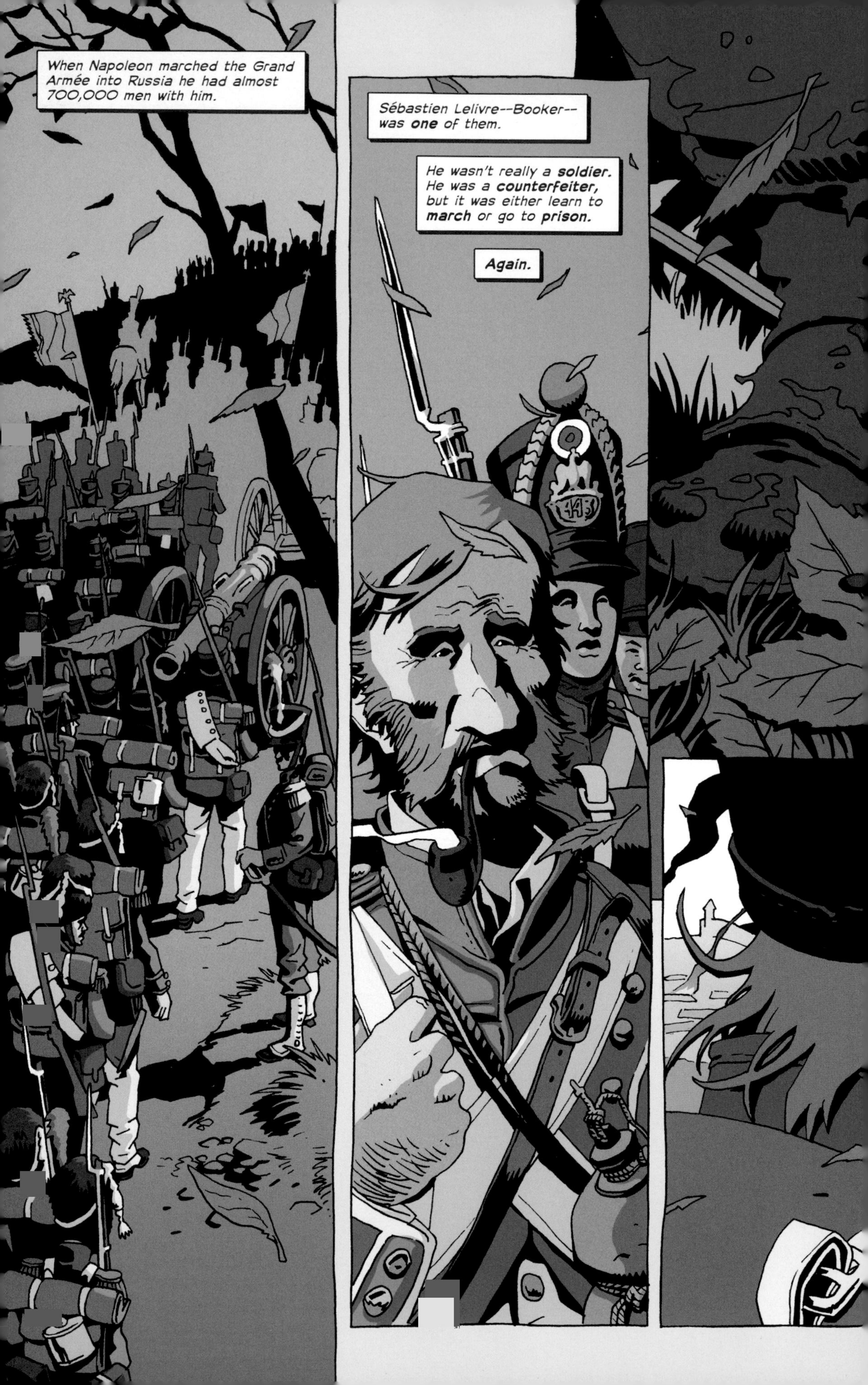
When Napoleon marched the Grand Armée into Russia he had almost 700,000 men with him.
Sébastien Lelivre--Booker--was **one** of them.
He wasn't really a **soldier**. He was a **counterfeiter**, but it was either learn to **march** or go to **prison**.
Again.

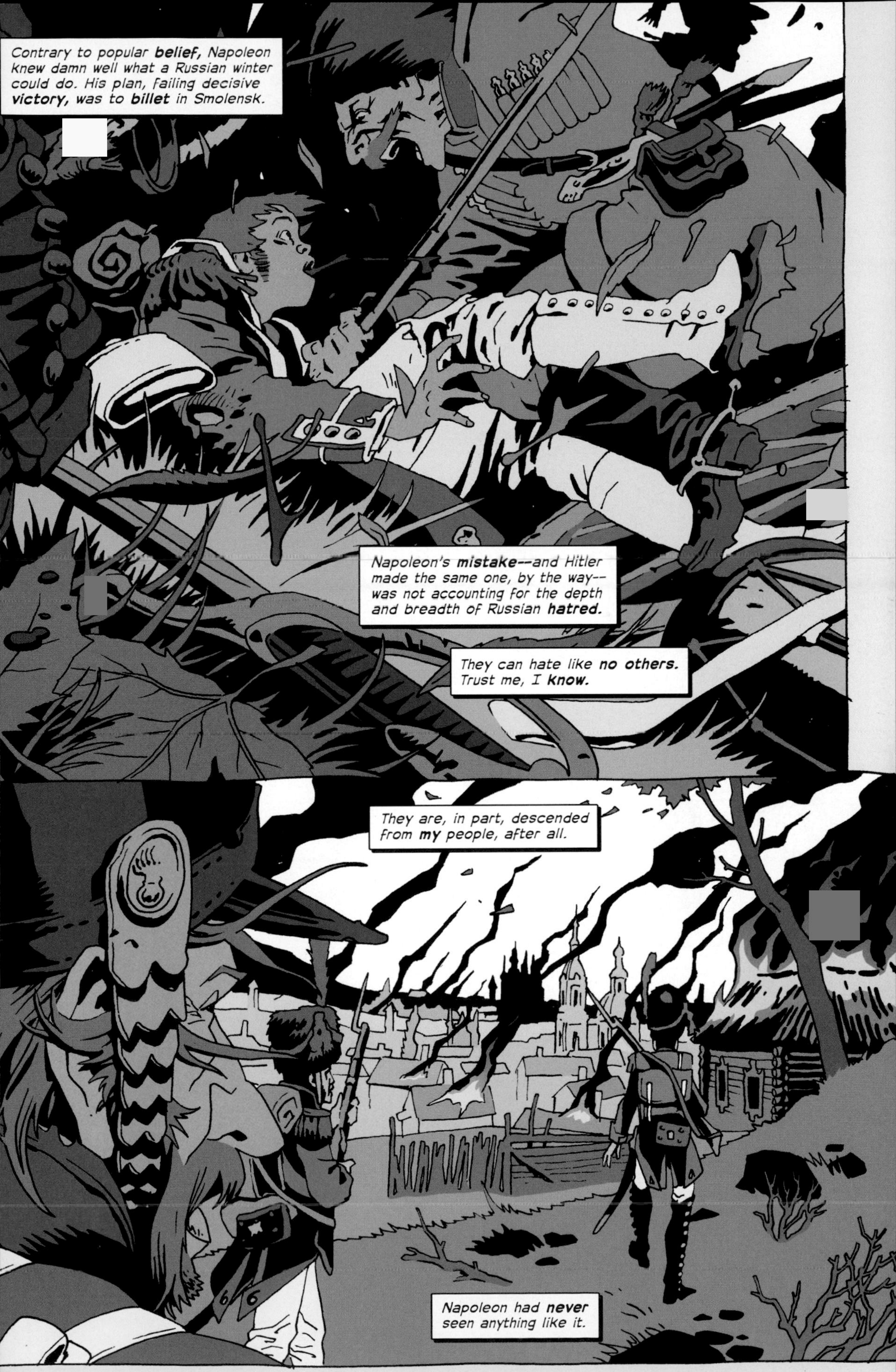
Contrary to popular belief, Napoleon knew damn well what a Russian winter could do. His plan, failing decisive victory, was to billet in Smolensk.
Napoleon's mistake--and Hitler made the same one, by the way--was not accounting for the depth and breadth of Russian hatred.
They can hate like no others. Trust me, I know.
They are, in part, descended from my people, after all.
Napoleon had never seen anything like it.

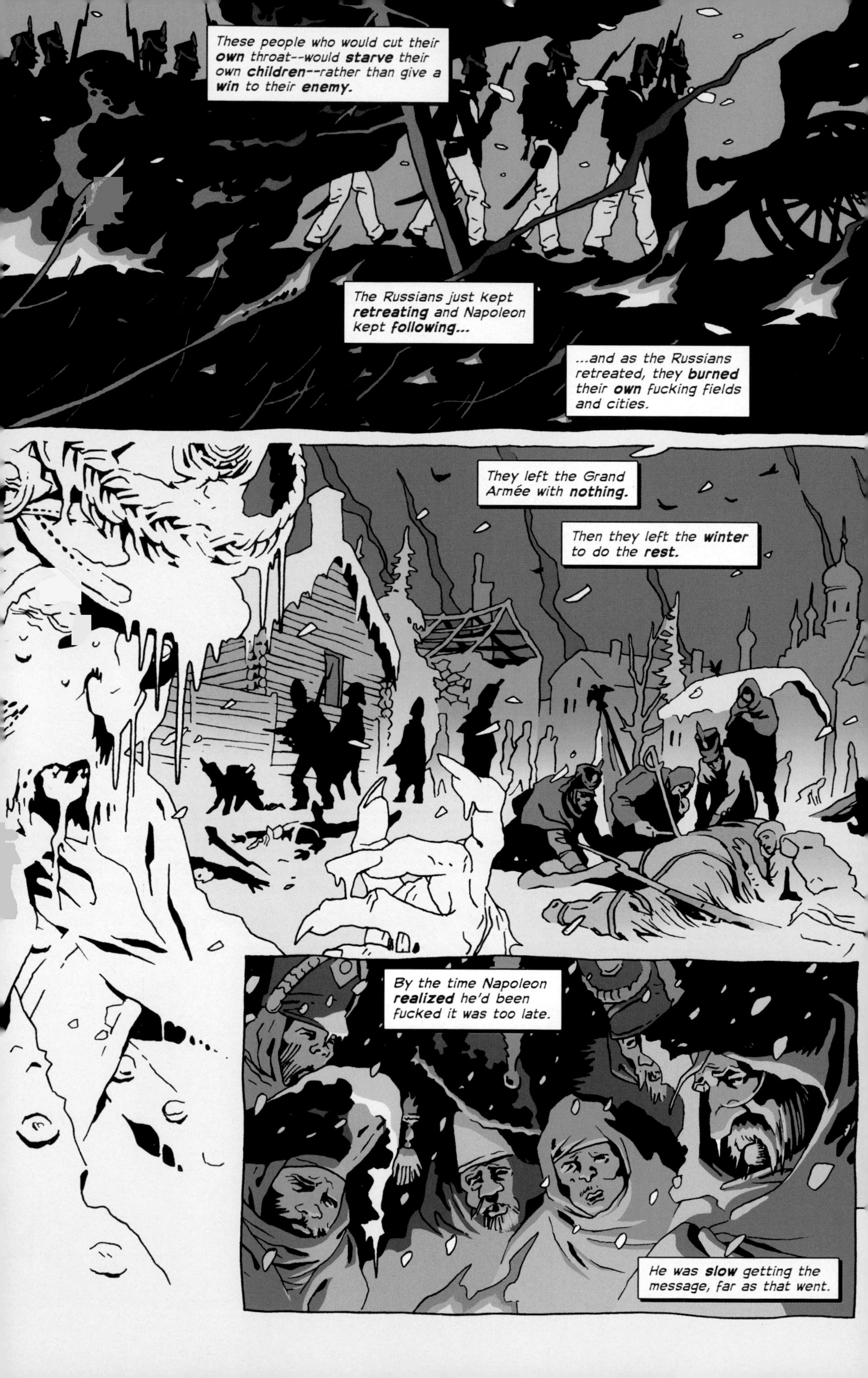

These people who would cut their own throat--would starve their own children--rather than give a win to their enemy.
The Russians just kept retreating and Napoleon kept following...
...and as the Russians retreated, they burned their own fucking fields and cities.
They left the Grand Armée with nothing.
Then they left the winter to do the rest.
By the time Napoleon realized he'd been fucked it was too late.
He was slow getting the message, far as that went.

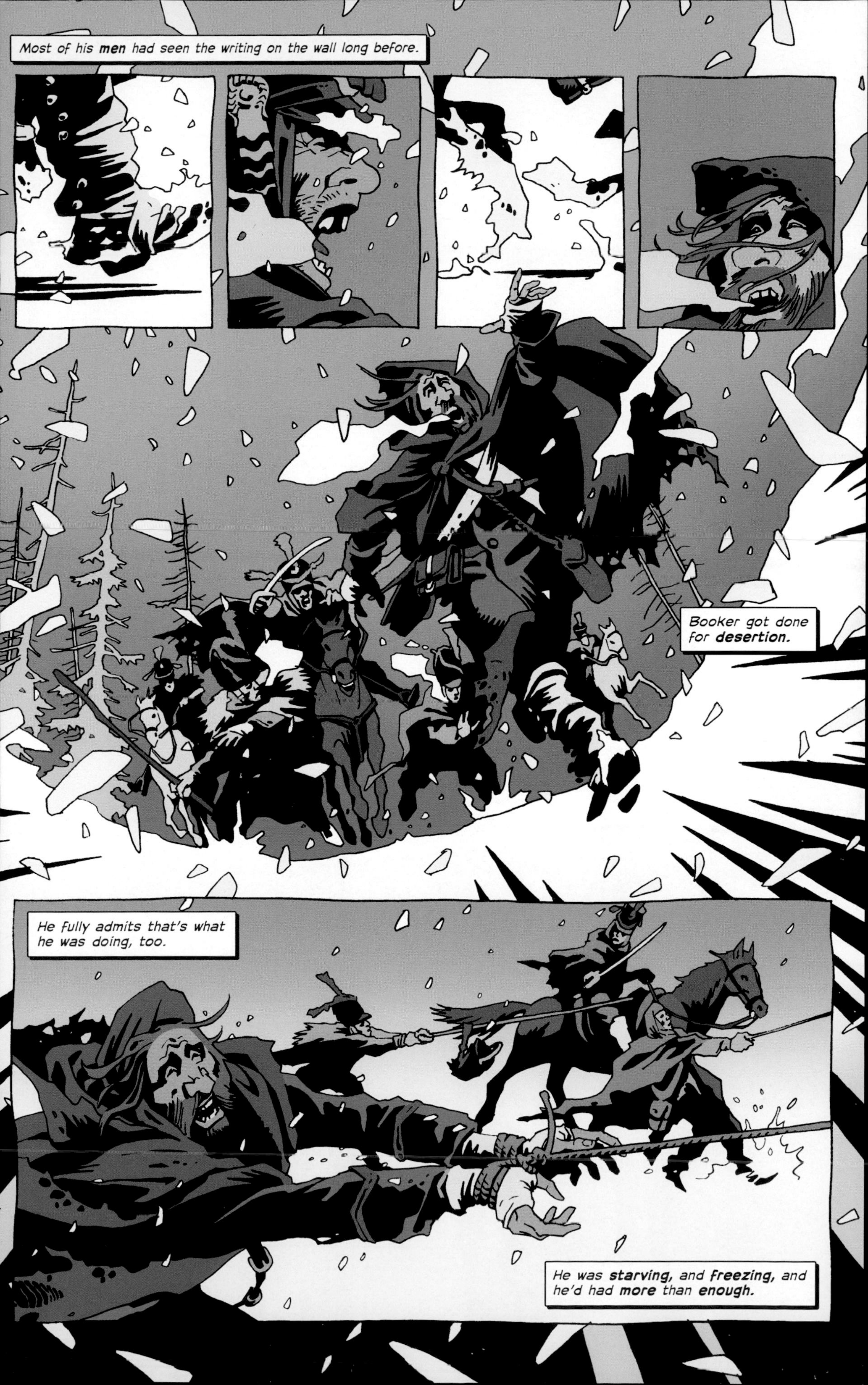
Most of his **men** had seen the writing on the wall long before.
Booker got done for **desertion.**
He fully admits that's what he was doing, too.
He was **starving,** and **freezing,** and he'd had **more** than **enough.**

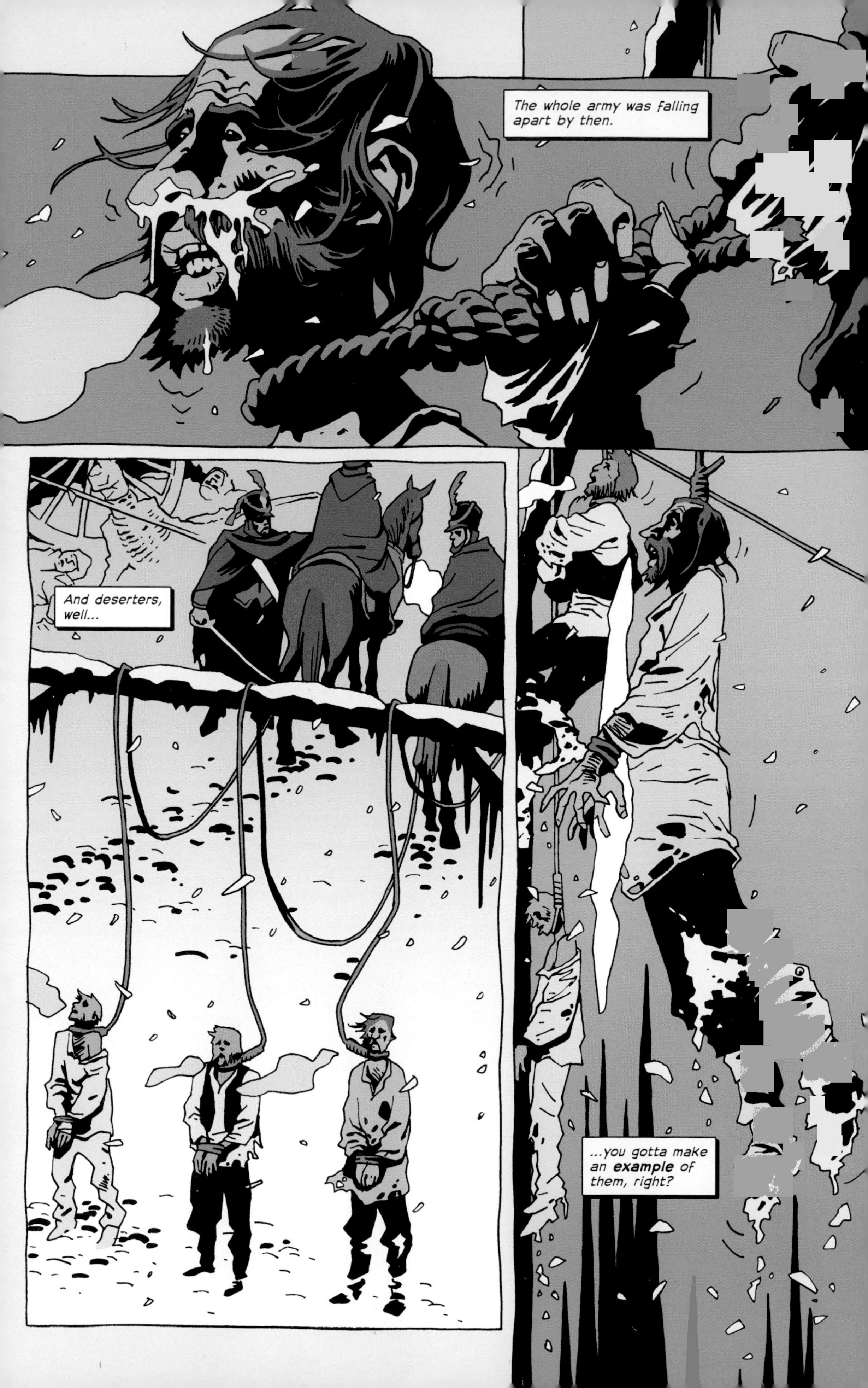
The whole army was falling apart by then.
And deserters, well...
...you gotta make an **example** of them, right?

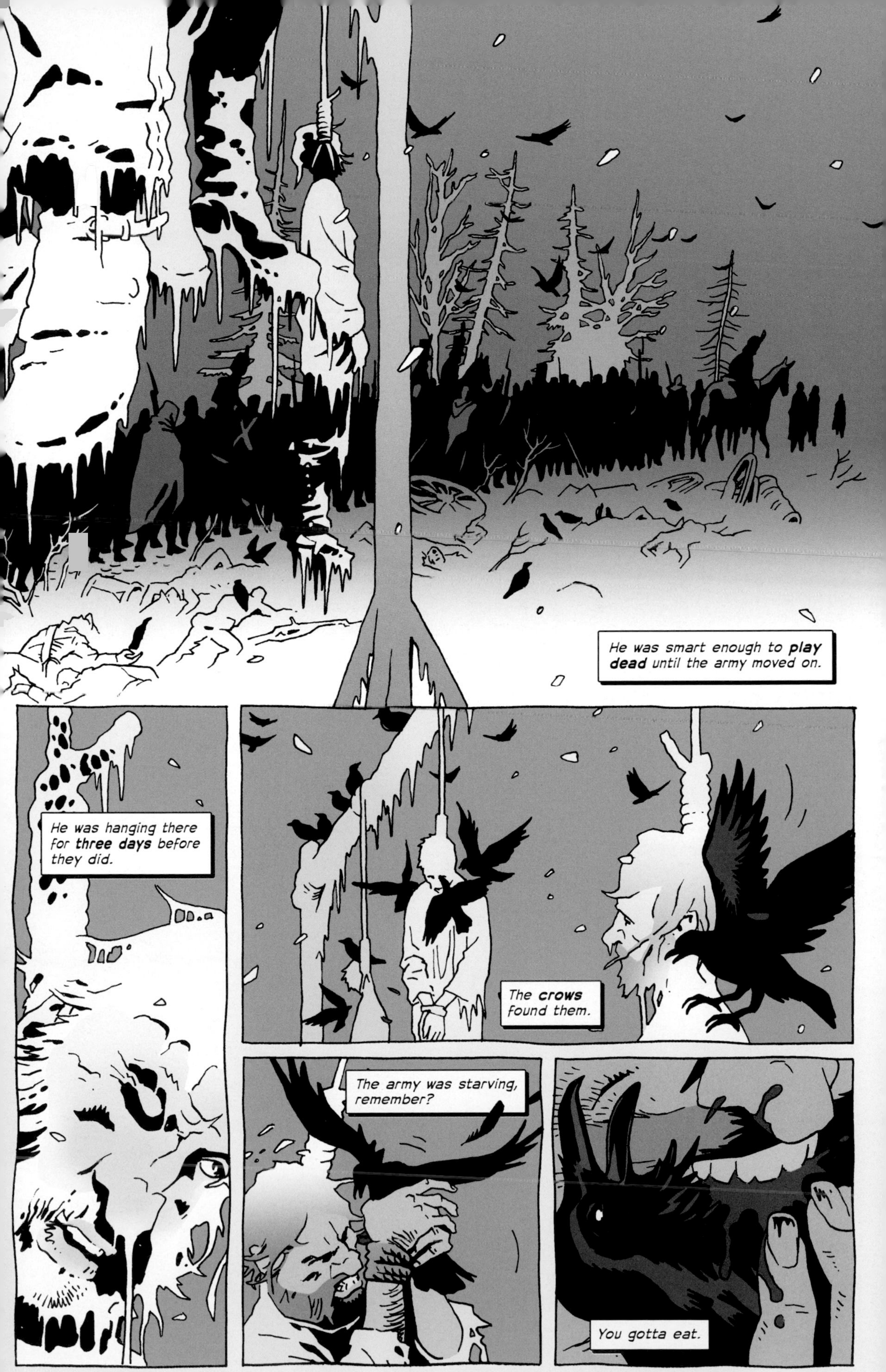
He was smart enough to **play dead** until the army moved on.
He was hanging there for **three days** before they did.
The **crows** found them.
The army was starving, remember?
You gotta eat.

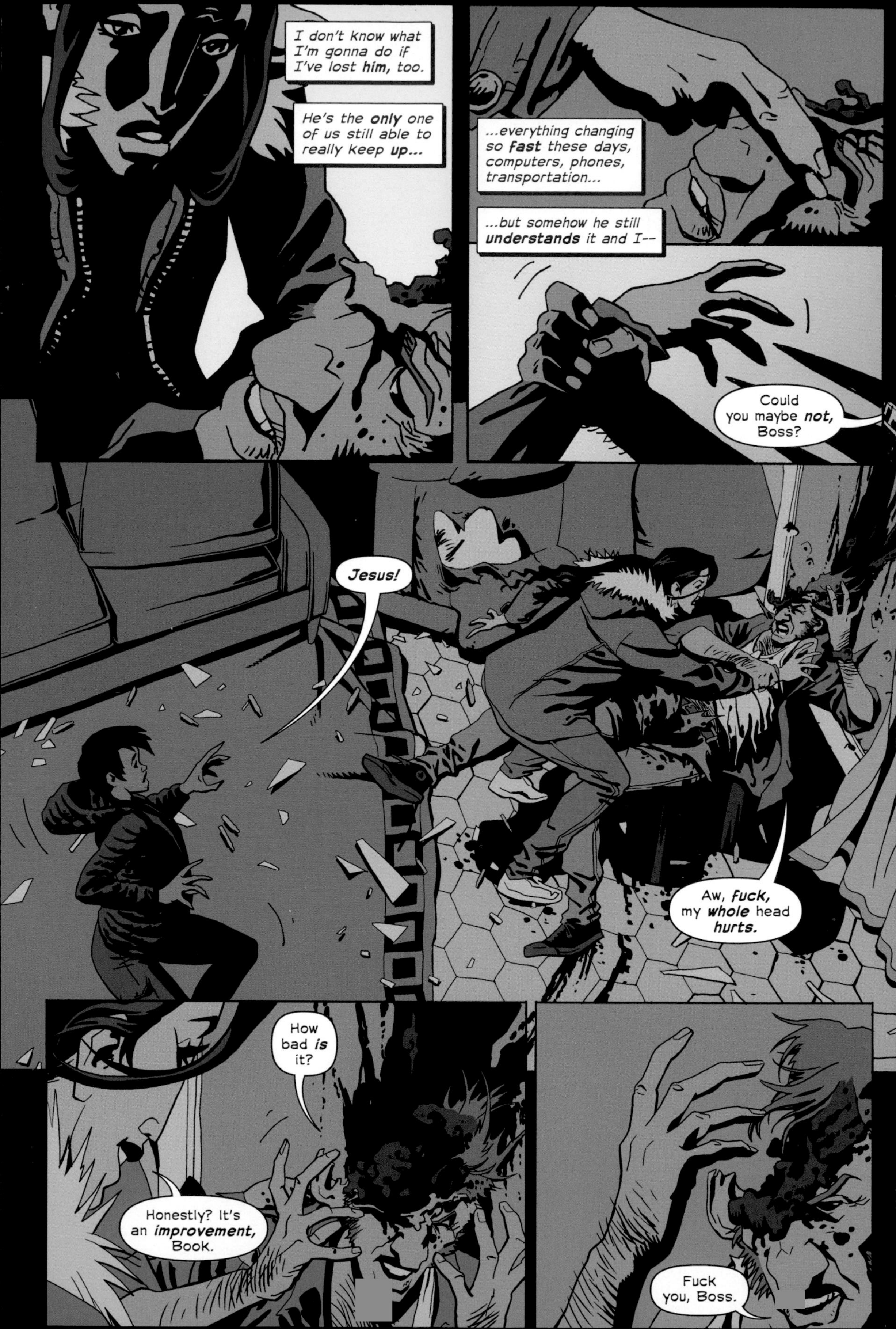

I don't know what I'm gonna do if I've lost **him,** too.
He's the **only** one of us still able to really keep **up...**
...everything changing so **fast** these days, computers, phones, transportation...
...but somehow he still **understands** it and I--
Could you maybe ***not,*** Boss?
Jesus!
Aw, ***fuck,*** my ***whole*** head ***hurts.***
How bad ***is*** it?
Honestly? It's an ***improvement,*** Book.
Fuck you, Boss.

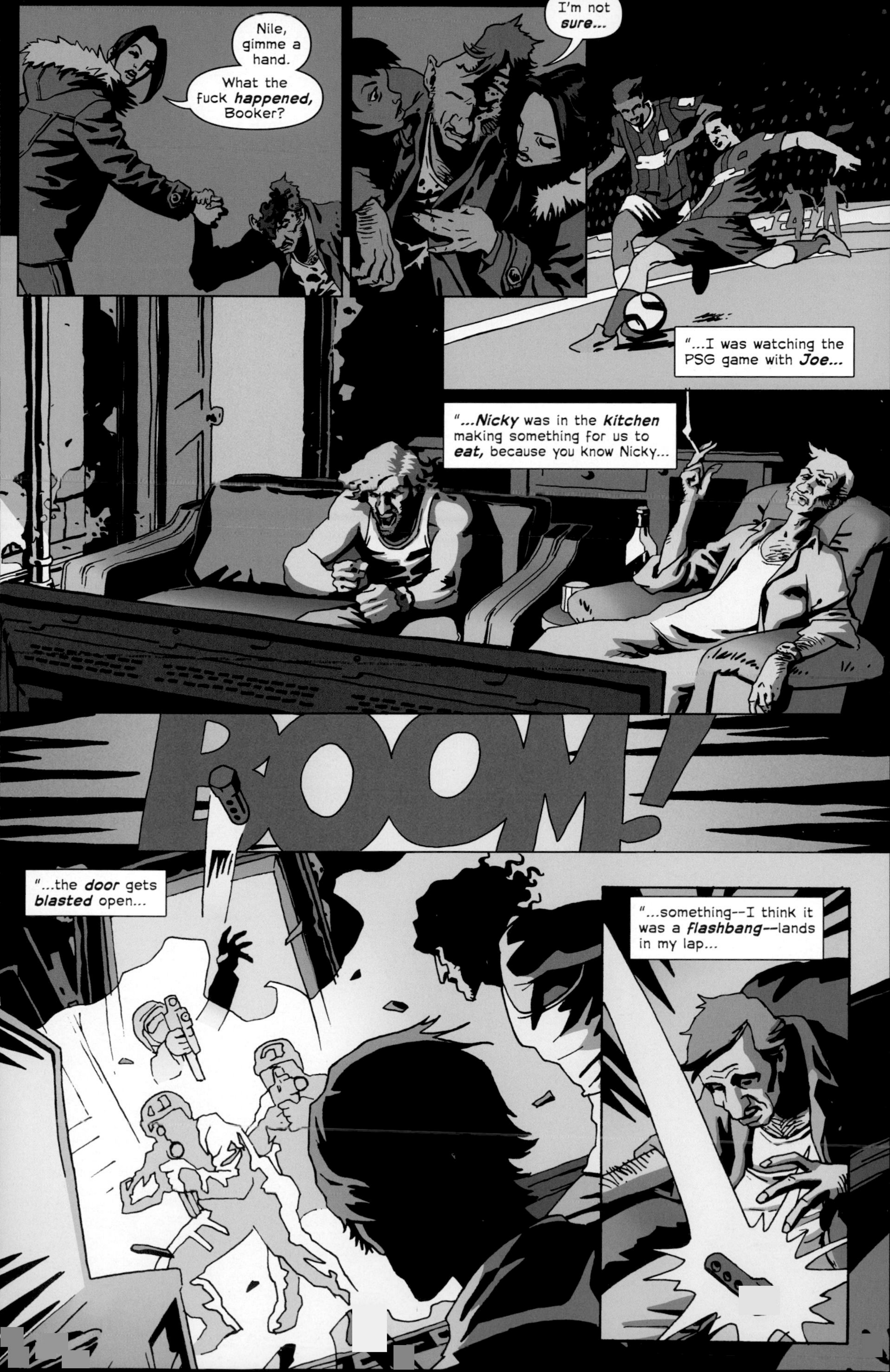
Nile, gimme a hand.
What the fuck happened, Booker?
I'm not sure...
"...I was watching the PSG game with Joe...
"...Nicky was in the kitchen making something for us to eat, because you know Nicky...
BOOM!
"...the door gets blasted open...
"...something--I think it was a flashbang--lands in my lap...

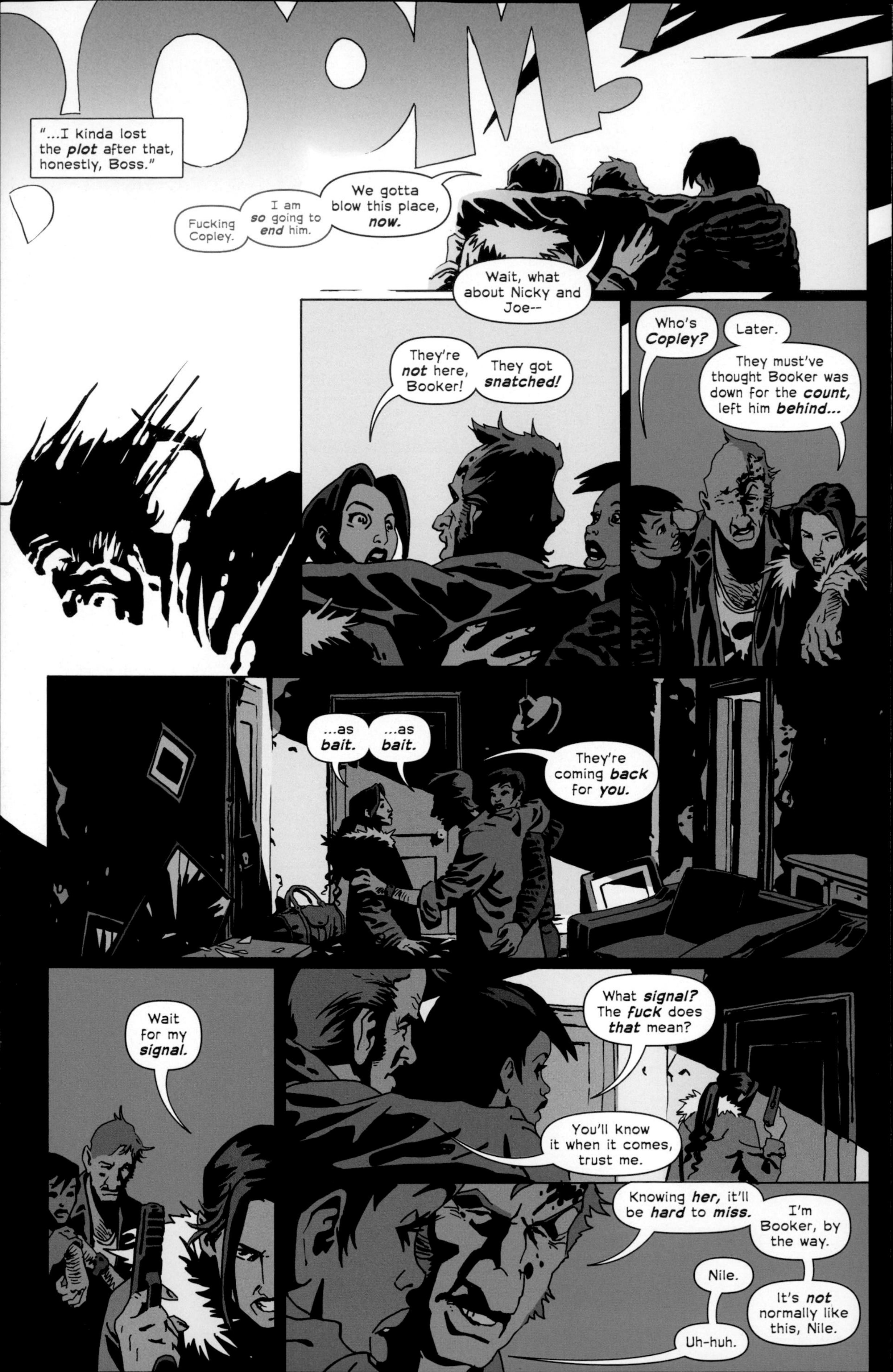
"...I kinda lost the *plot* after that, honestly, Boss."
Fucking Copley.
I am *so* going to *end* him.
We gotta blow this place, *now.*
Wait, what about Nicky and Joe--
They're *not* here, Booker!
They got *snatched!*
Who's *Copley?*
Later.
They must've thought Booker was down for the *count,* left him *behind...*
...as *bait.*
...as *bait.*
They're coming *back* for *you.*
Wait for my *signal.*
What *signal?* The *fuck* does *that* mean?
You'll know it when it comes, trust me.
Knowing *her,* it'll be *hard* to *miss.*
I'm Booker, by the way.
Nile.
It's *not* normally like this, Nile.
Uh-huh.

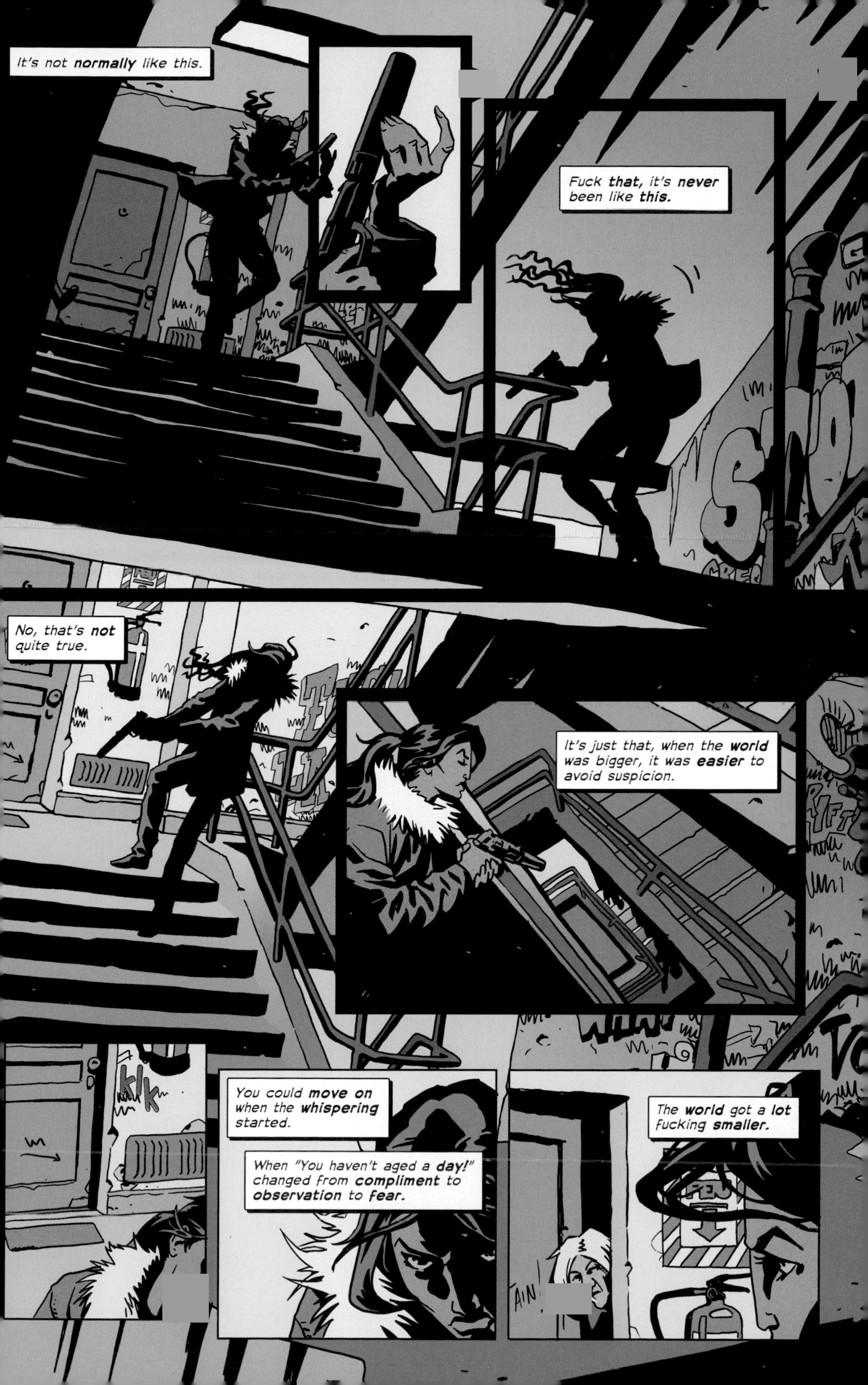
It's not **normally** like this.
Fuck **that,** it's **never** been like **this.**
No, that's **not** quite true.
It's just that, when the **world** was bigger, it was **easier** to avoid suspicion.
You could **move on** when the **whispering** started.
When **"You haven't aged a day!"** changed from **compliment** to **observation** to **fear.**
The **world** got a **lot** fucking **smaller.**

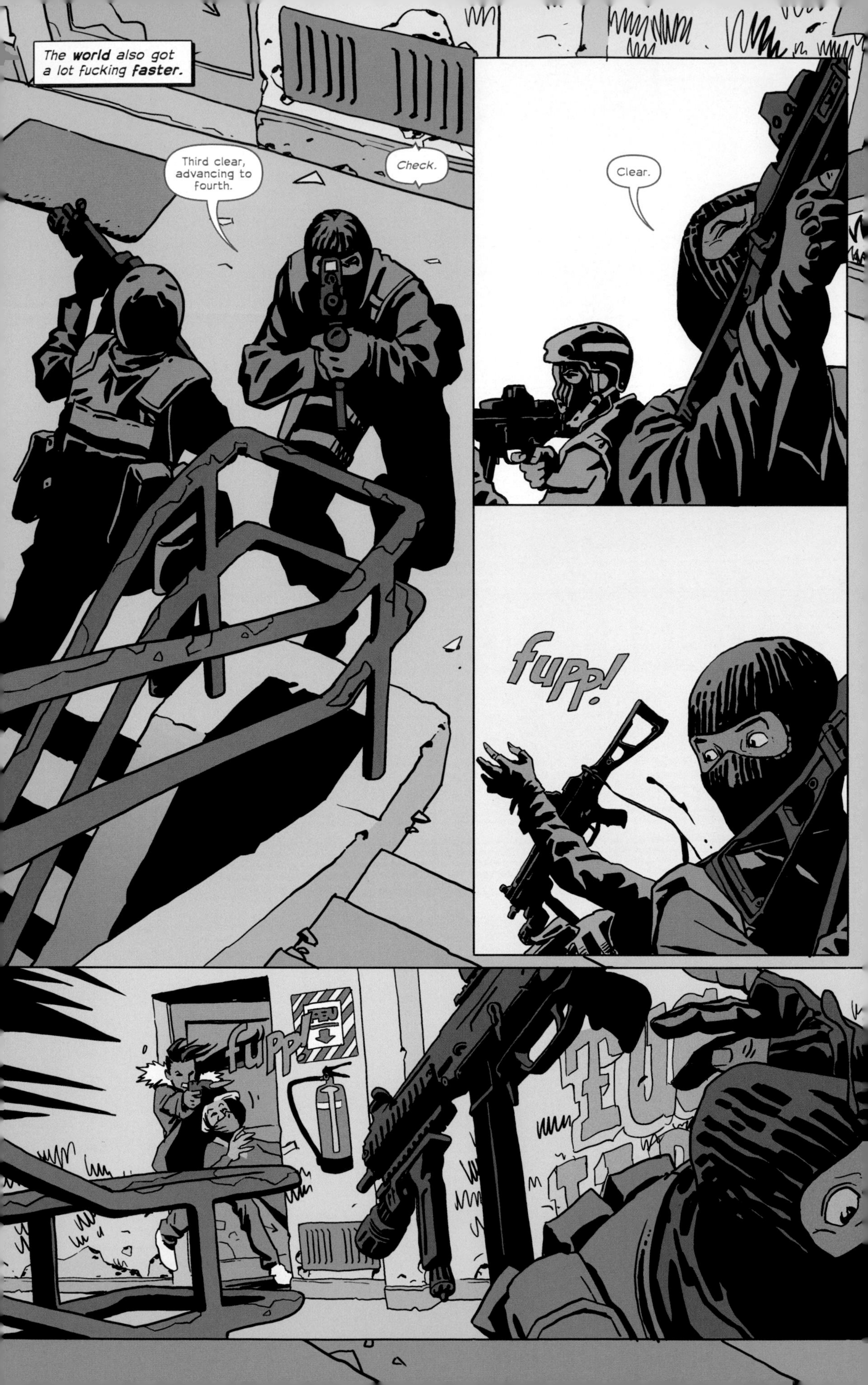
The world also got a lot fucking faster.
Third clear, advancing to fourth.
Check.
Clear.
fupp!
fupp!

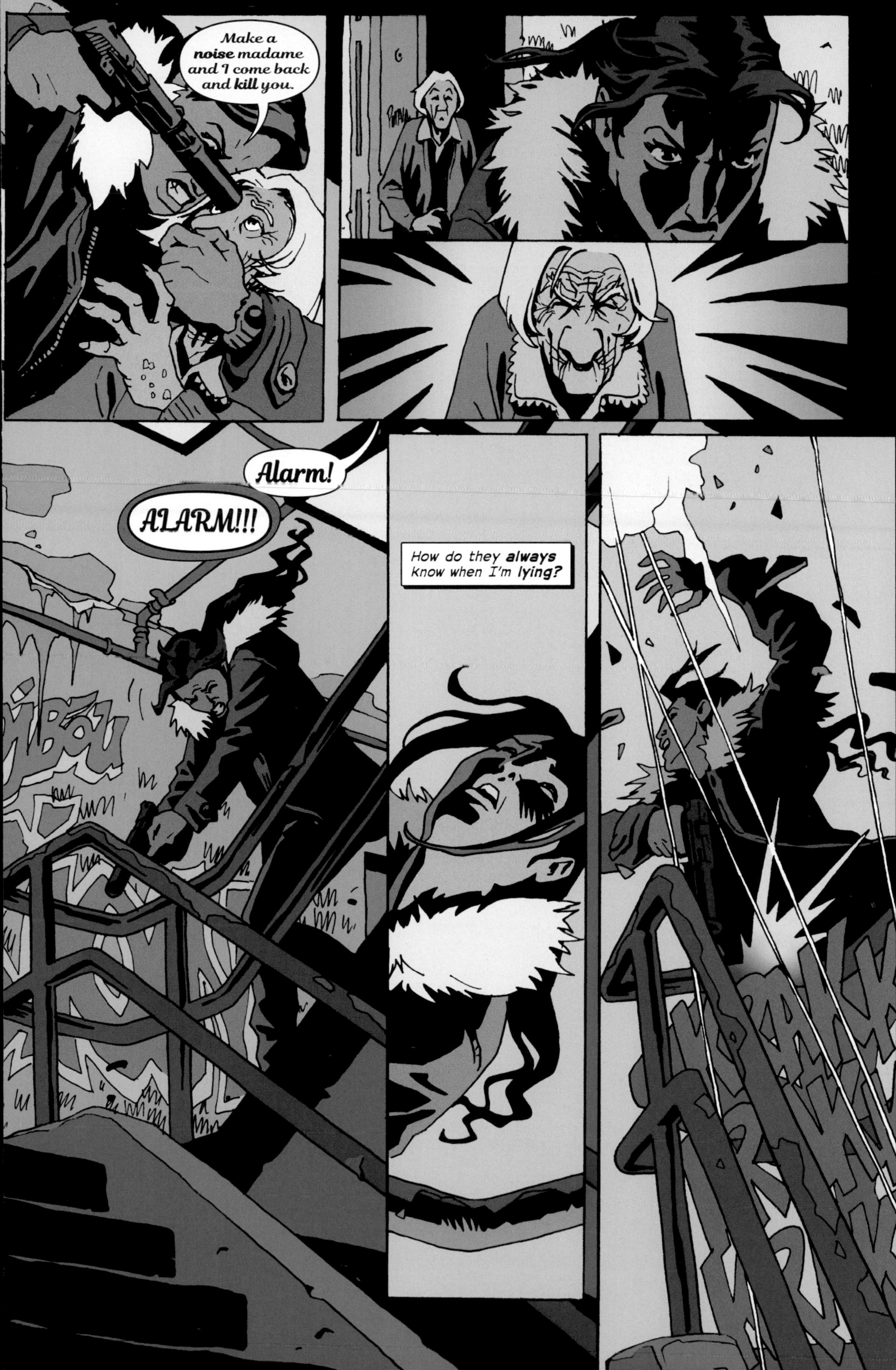

Make a noise madame and I come back and kill you.
Alarm!
ALARM!!!
How do they always know when I'm lying?

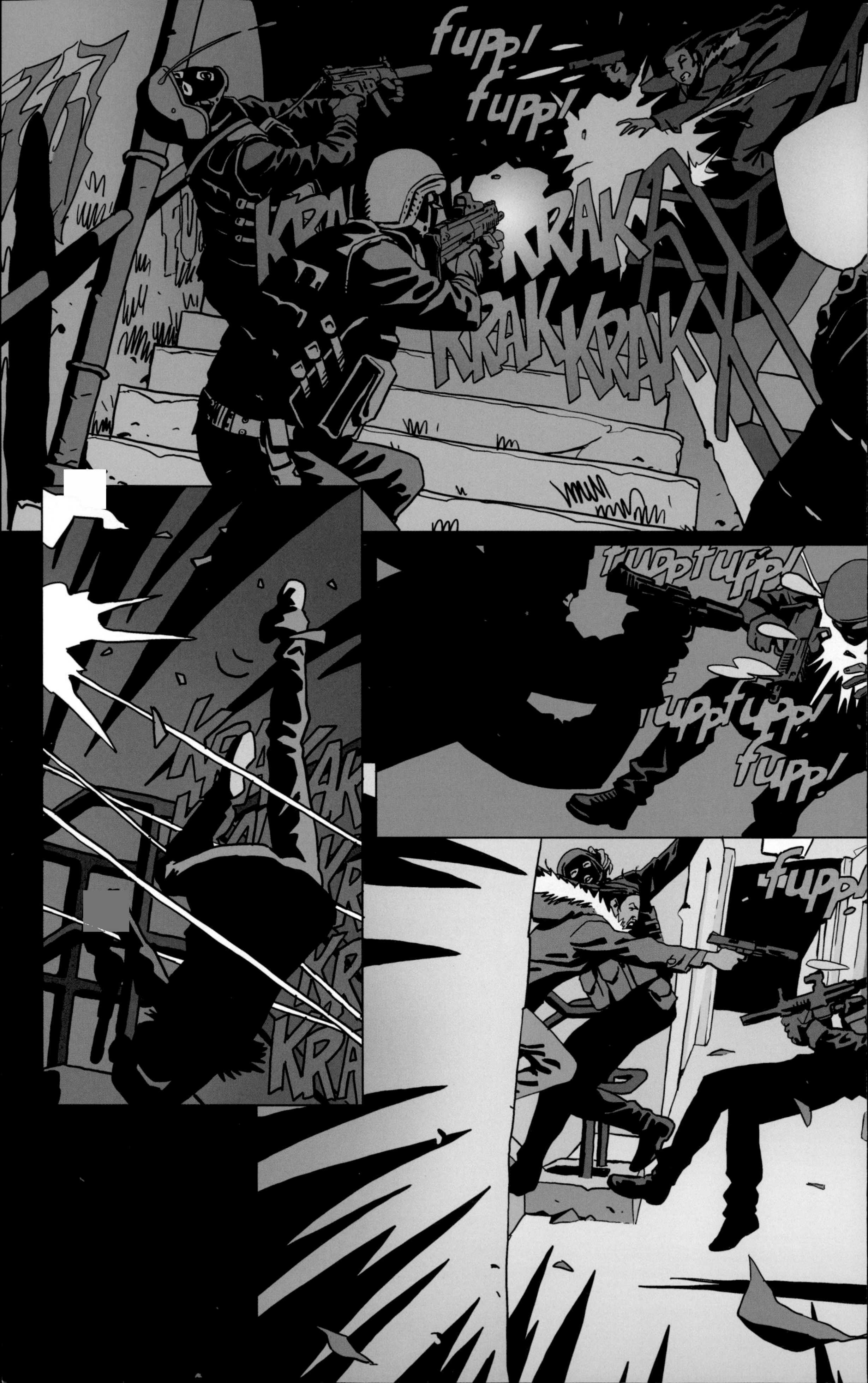

fupp!
fupp!
KRAK
KRAK KRAK
KRA
fuppfupp!
fuppfupp!
fupp!
fupp!

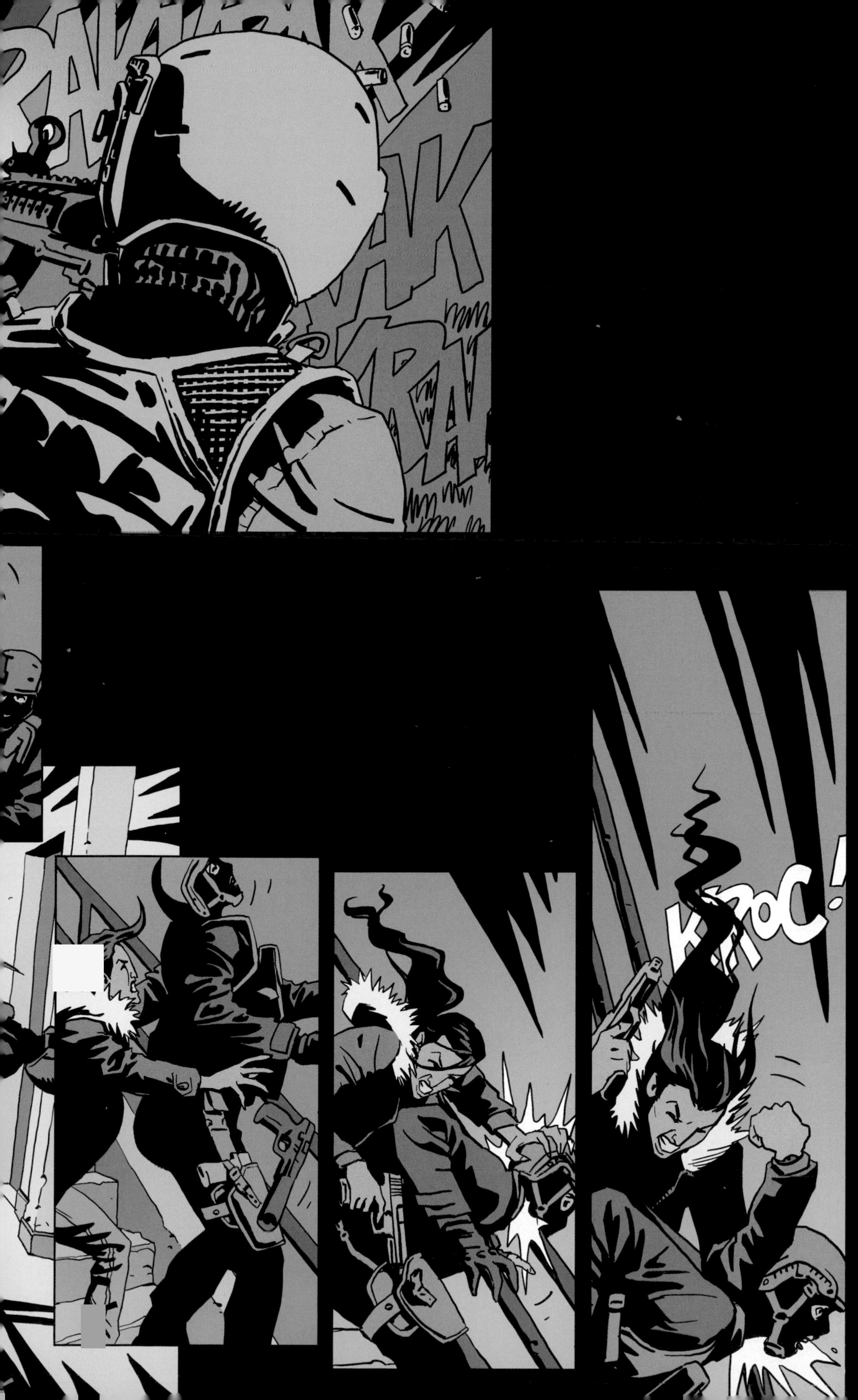
KNOC!

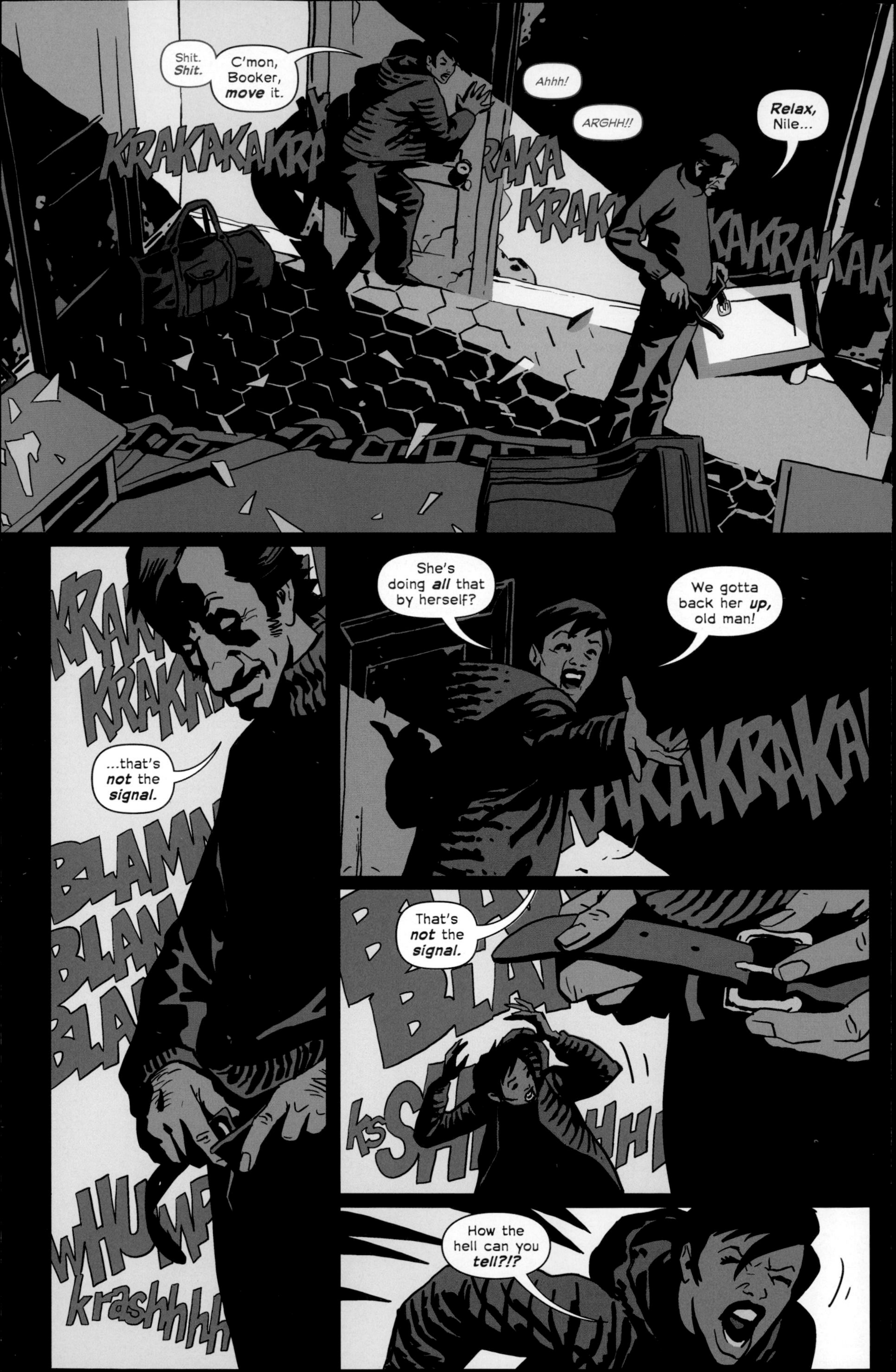

Shit. *Shit.*
C'mon, Booker, *move* it.
KRAKAKAKRA
Ahhh!
ARGHH!!
RAKA
KRAKA
Relax, Nile...
KAKRAKAK
KRAKA
KRAKK
...that's *not* the *signal.*
BLAM
BLAM
BLAM
WHUMP
krashhhh
She's doing *all* that by herself?
We gotta back her *up,* old man!
KAKRAKA
That's *not* the *signal.*
BLAM
ksSHHHH
How the hell can you *tell?!?*

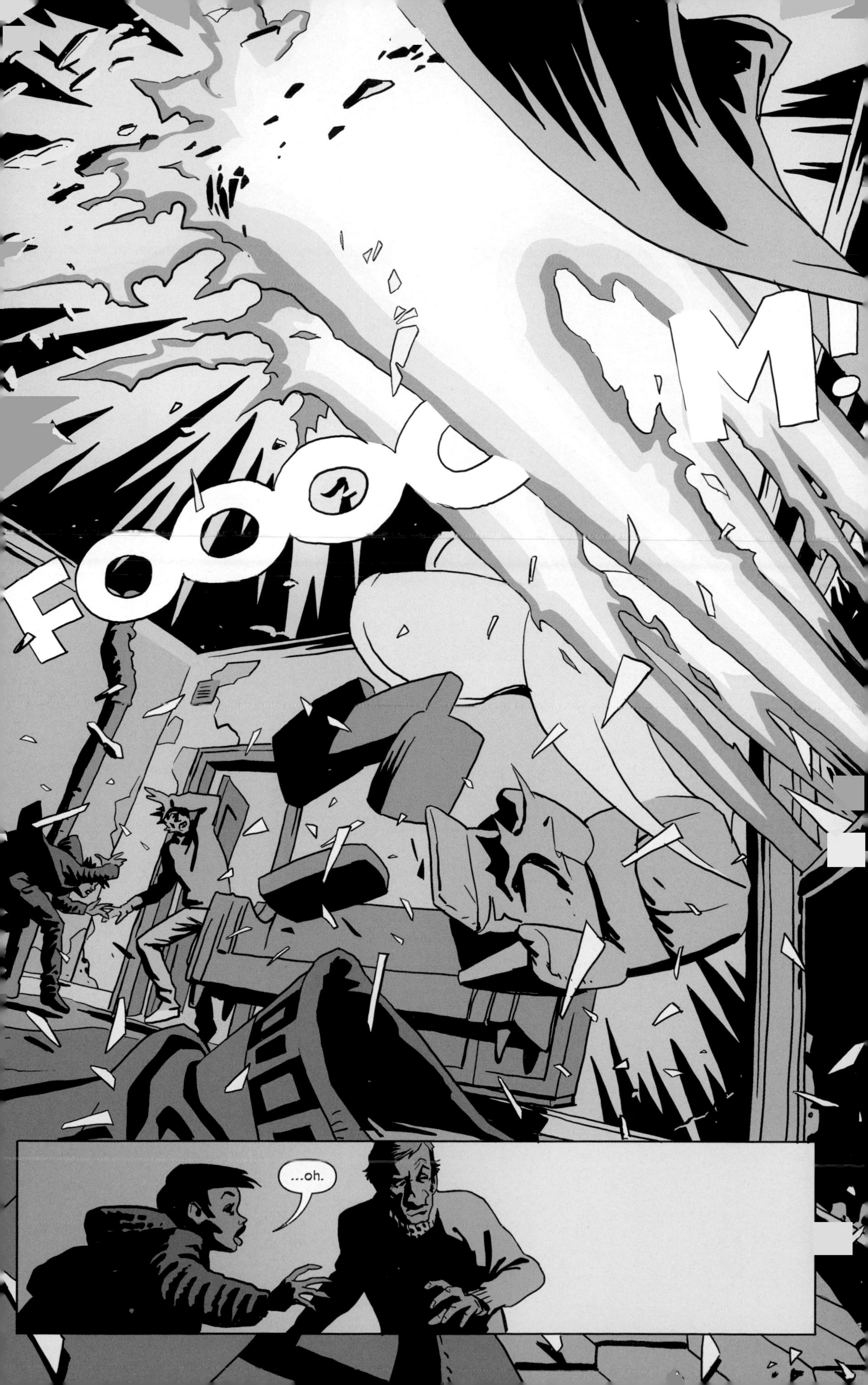
FOOOOOM!
...oh.

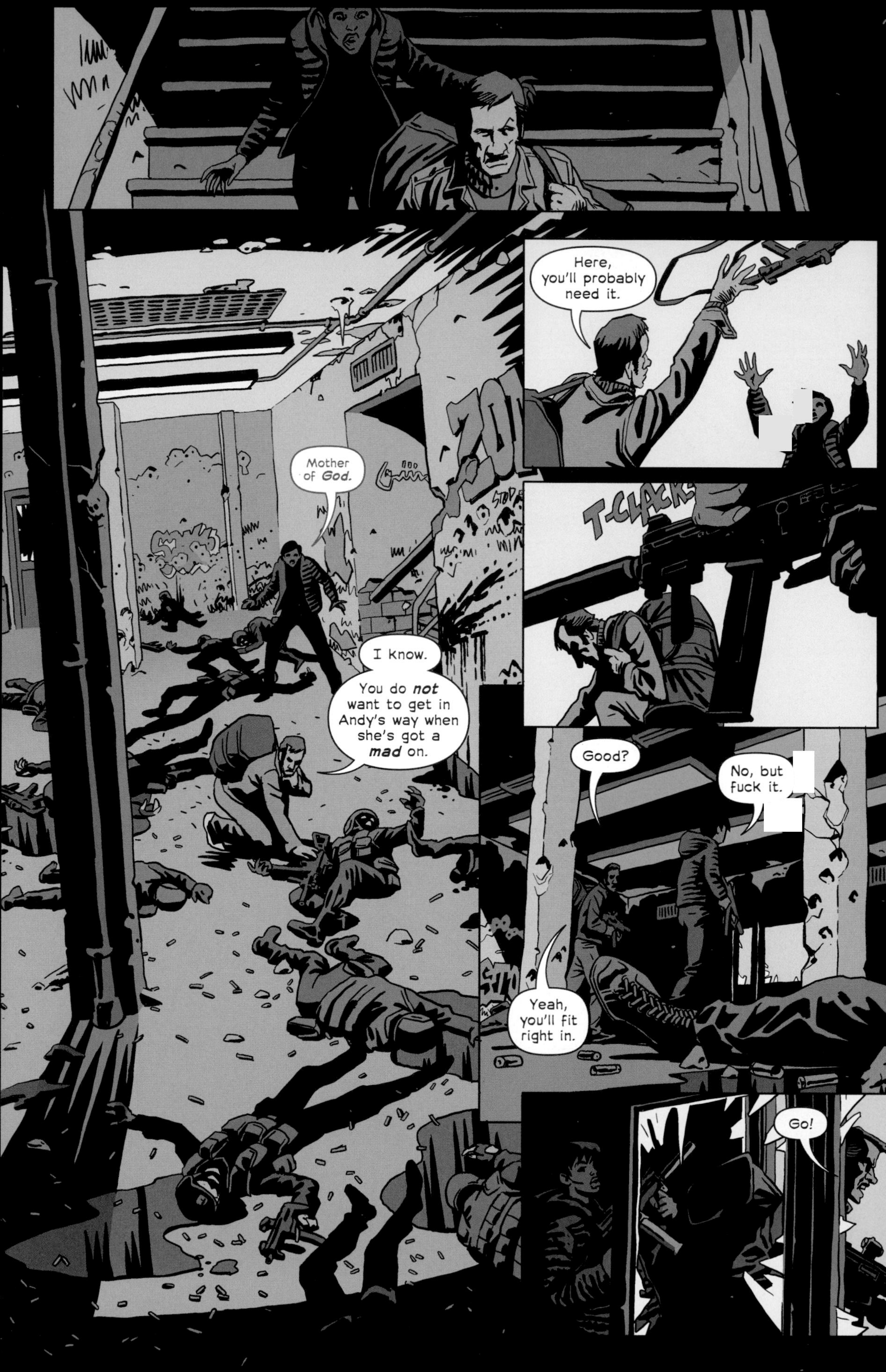
Mother of *God.*
I know.
You do *not* want to get in Andy's way when she's got a *mad* on.
Here, you'll probably need it.
T-CLACK
Good?
No, but fuck it.
Yeah, you'll fit right in.
Go!

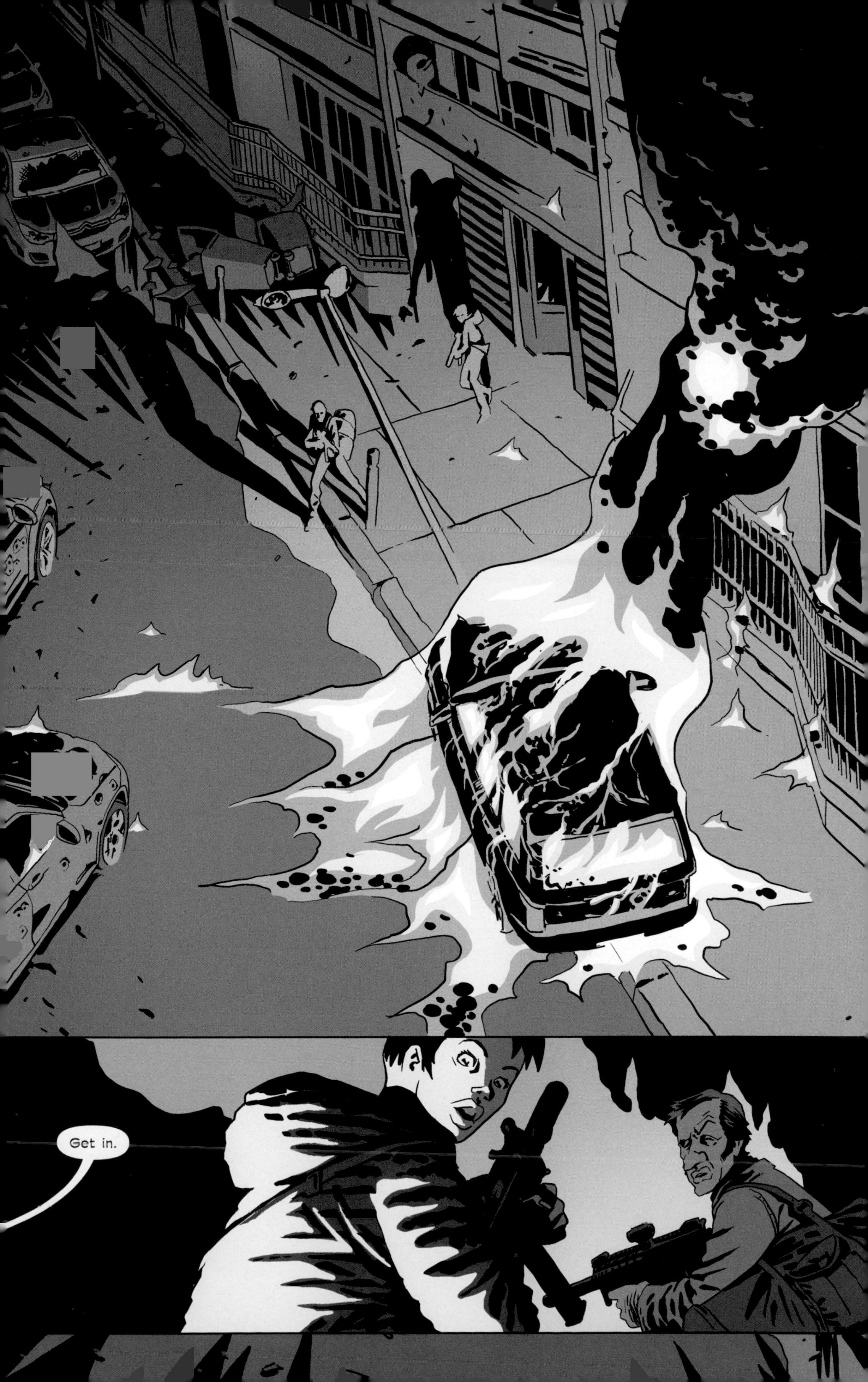
Get in.

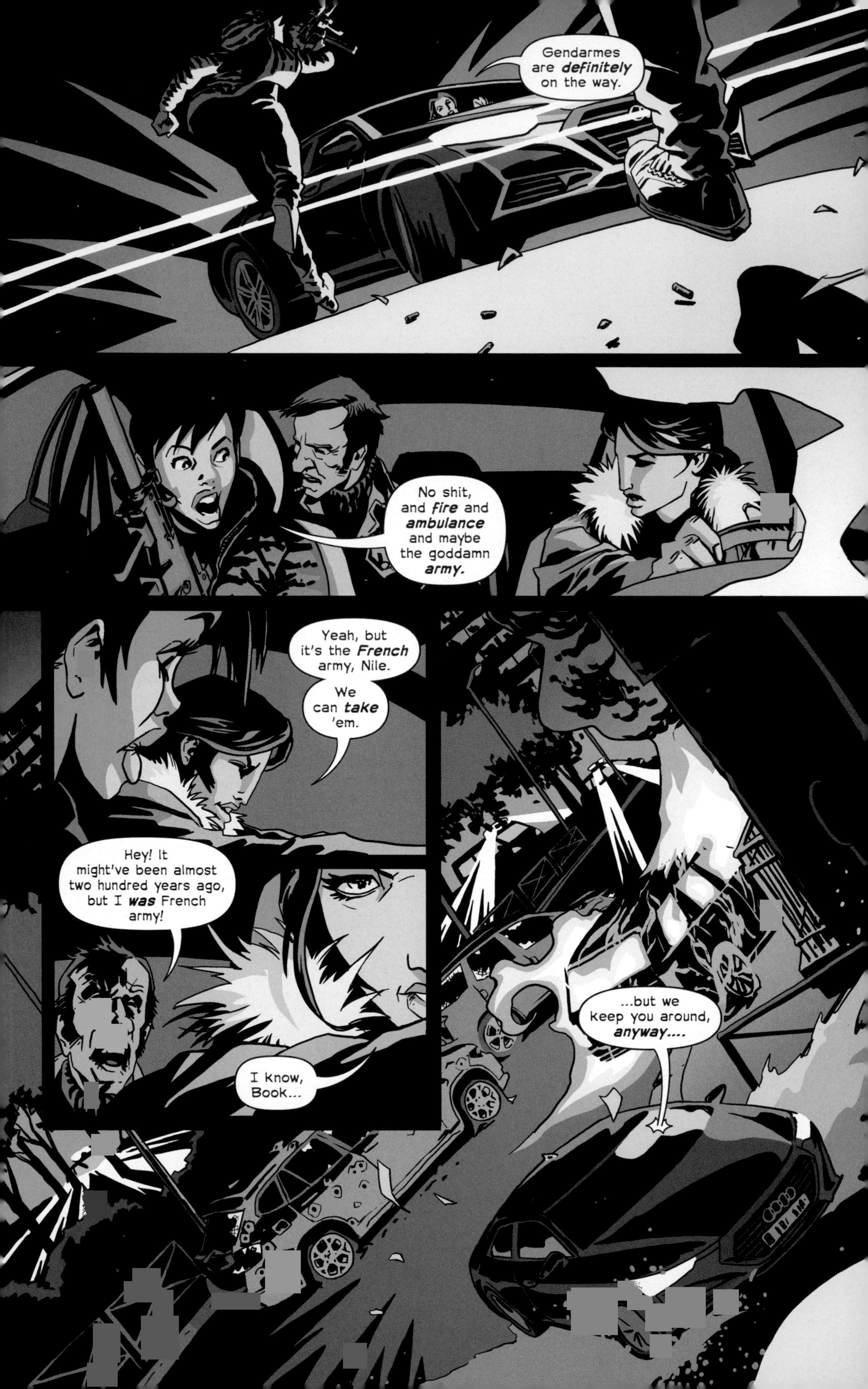
Gendarmes are *definitely* on the way.
No shit, and *fire* and *ambulance* and maybe the goddamn *army.*
Yeah, but it's the *French* army, Nile.
We can *take* 'em.
Hey! It might've been almost two hundred years ago, but I *was* French army!
I know, Book...
...but we keep you around, *anyway....*

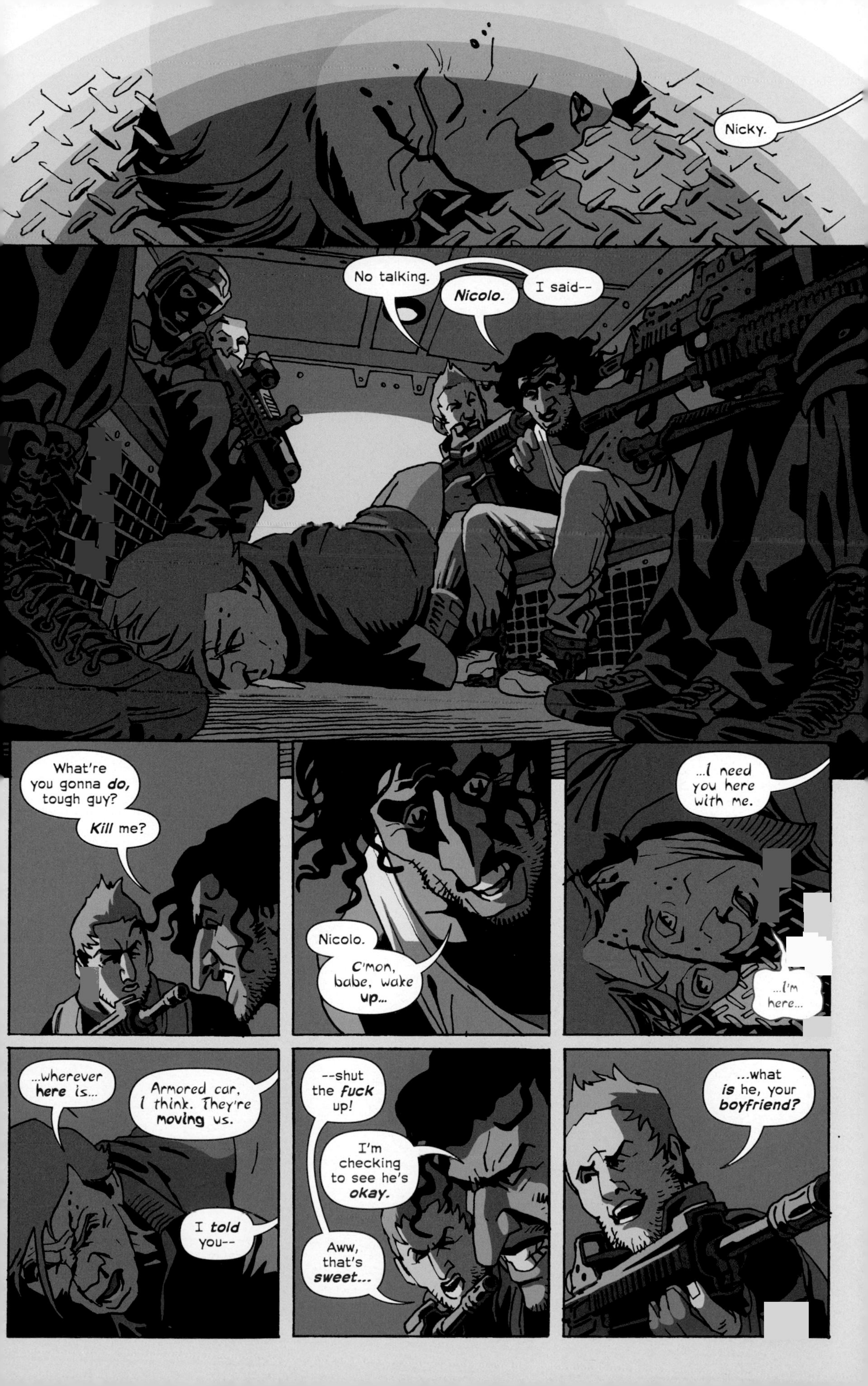
Nicky.
No talking.
Nicolo.
I said--
What're you gonna do, tough guy?
Kill me?
Nicolo.
C'mon, babe, wake up...
...I need you here with me.
...I'm here...
...wherever here is...
Armored car, I think. They're moving us.
I told you--
--shut the fuck up!
I'm checking to see he's okay.
Aww, that's sweet...
...what is he, your boyfriend?

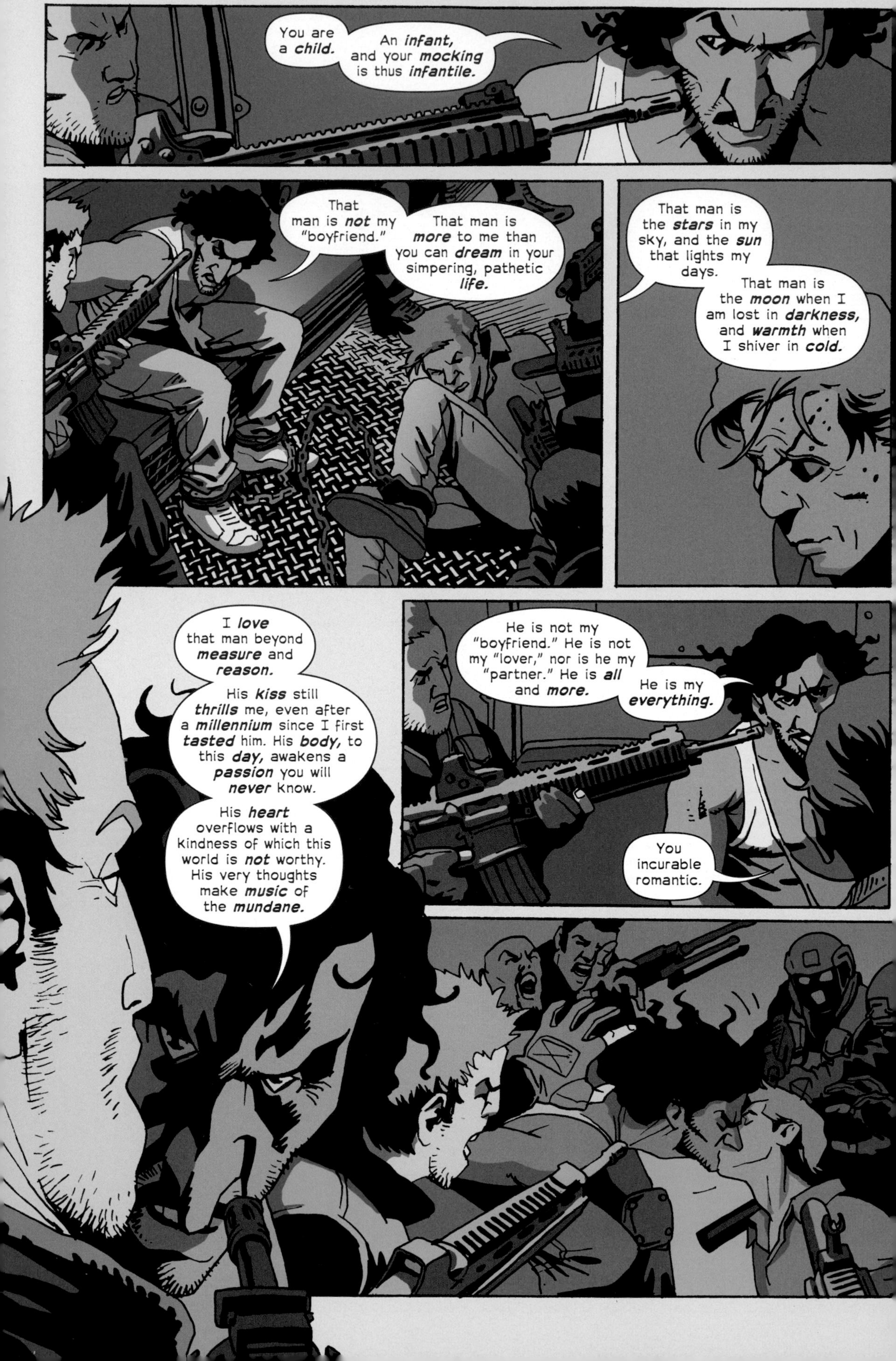
You are a child.
An infant, and your mocking is thus infantile.
That man is not my "boyfriend."
That man is more to me than you can dream in your simpering, pathetic life.
That man is the stars in my sky, and the sun that lights my days.
That man is the moon when I am lost in darkness, and warmth when I shiver in cold.
I love that man beyond measure and reason.
His kiss still thrills me, even after a millennium since I first tasted him. His body, to this day, awakens a passion you will never know.
His heart overflows with a kindness of which this world is not worthy. His very thoughts make music of the mundane.
He is not my "boyfriend." He is not my "lover," nor is he my "partner." He is all and more.
He is my everything.
You incurable romantic.

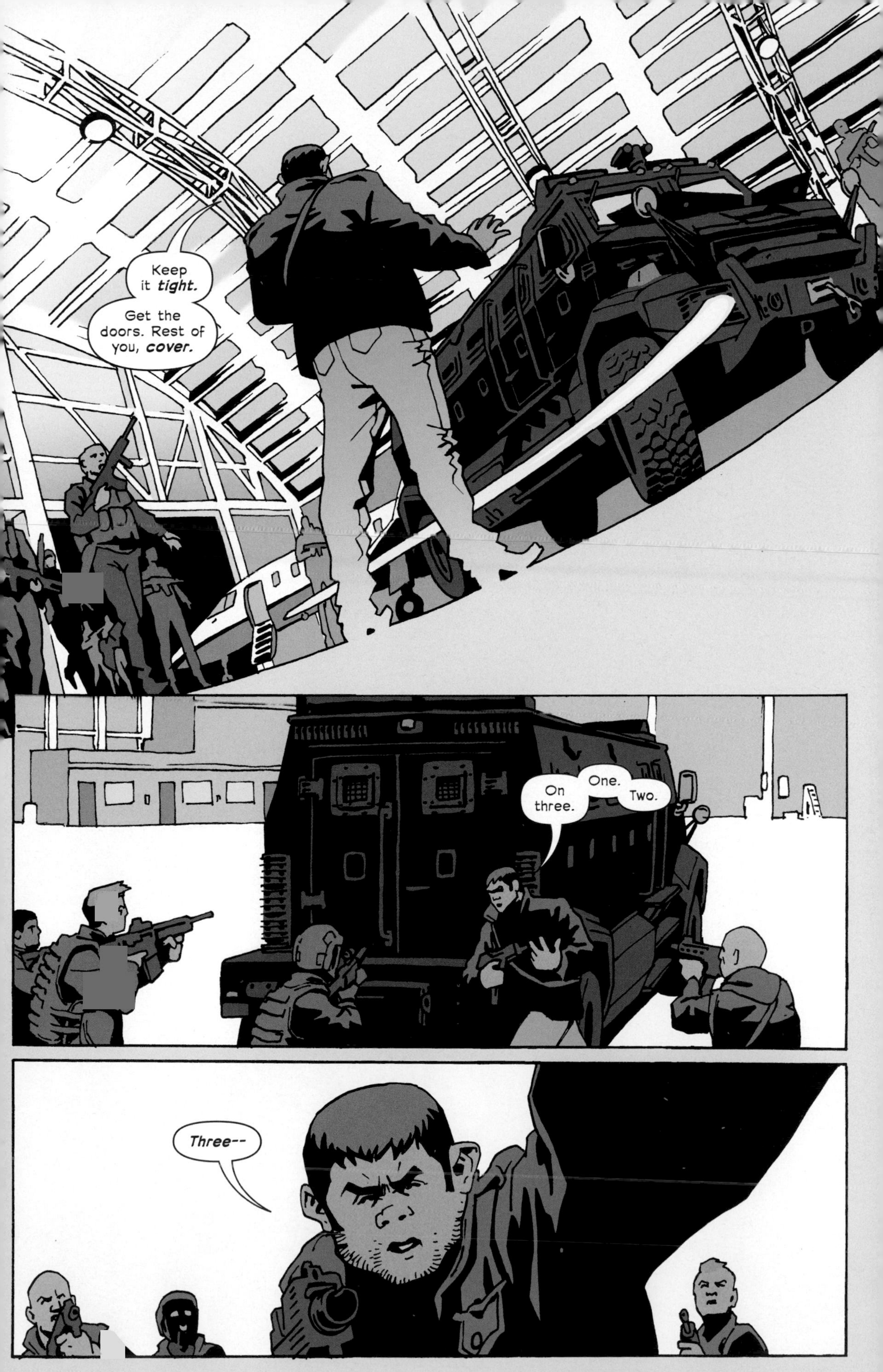
Keep it *tight.*
Get the doors. Rest of you, *cover.*
On three.
One.
Two.
Three--

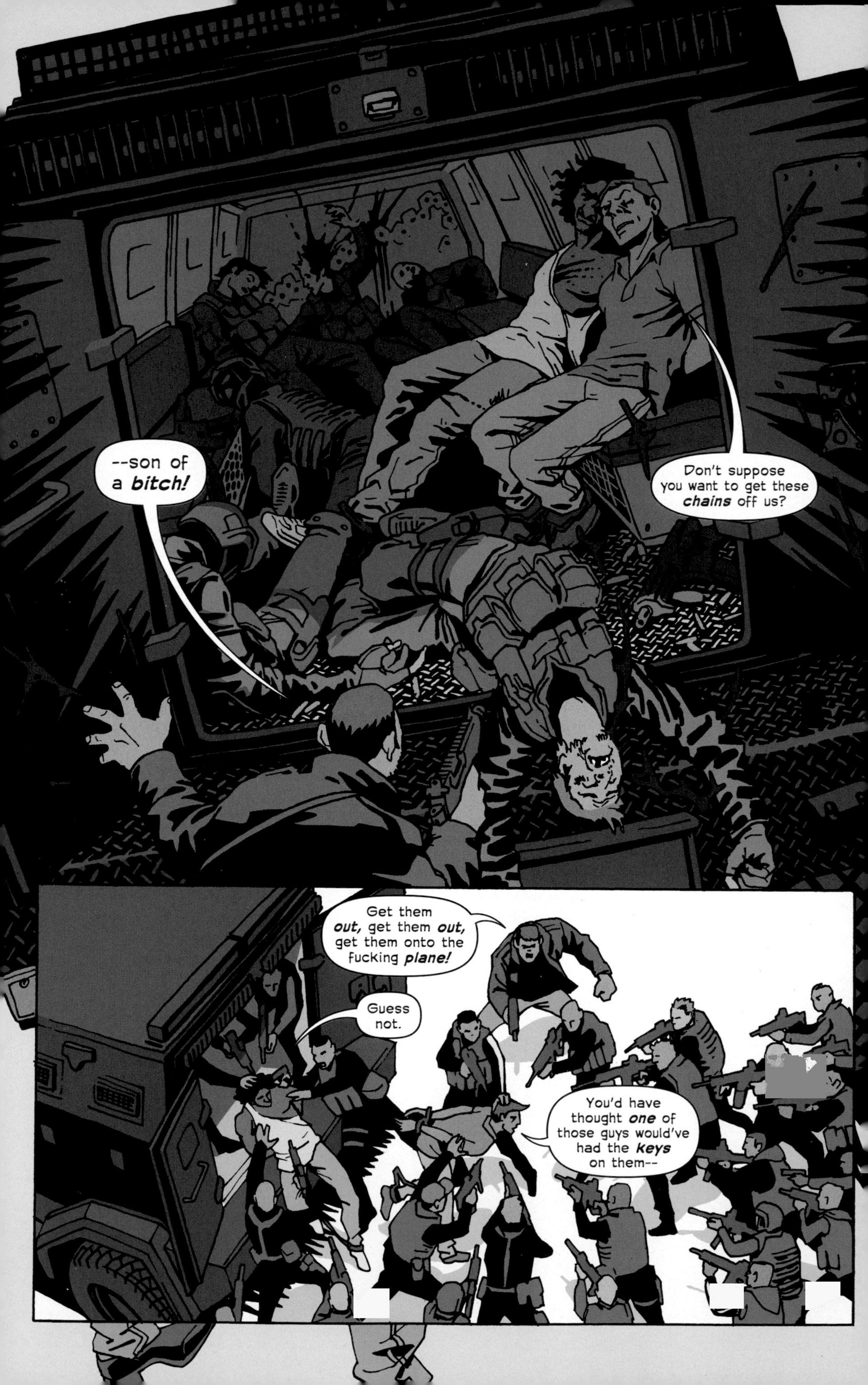
--son of a bitch!
Don't suppose you want to get these chains off us?
Get them out, get them out, get them onto the fucking plane!
Guess not.
You'd have thought one of those guys would've had the keys on them--

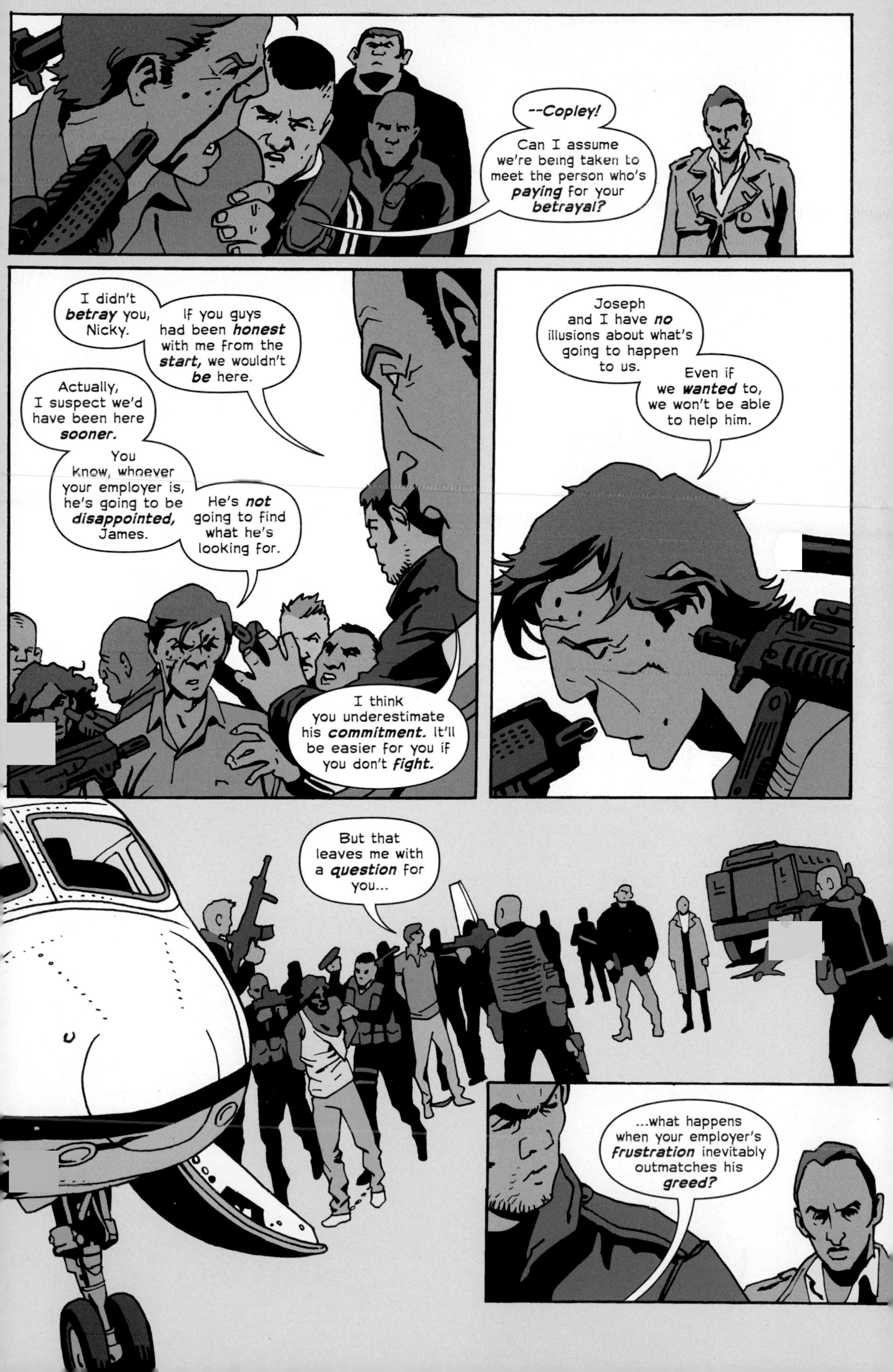
--Copley!
Can I assume we're being taken to meet the person who's *paying* for your *betrayal?*
I didn't *betray* you, Nicky.
If you guys had been *honest* with me from the *start,* we wouldn't *be* here.
Actually, I suspect we'd have been here *sooner.*
You know, whoever your employer is, he's going to be *disappointed,* James.
He's *not* going to find what he's looking for.
I think you underestimate his *commitment.* It'll be easier for you if you don't *fight.*
Joseph and I have *no* illusions about what's going to happen to us.
Even if we *wanted* to, we won't be able to help him.
But that leaves me with a *question* for you...
...what happens when your employer's *frustration* inevitably outmatches his *greed?*

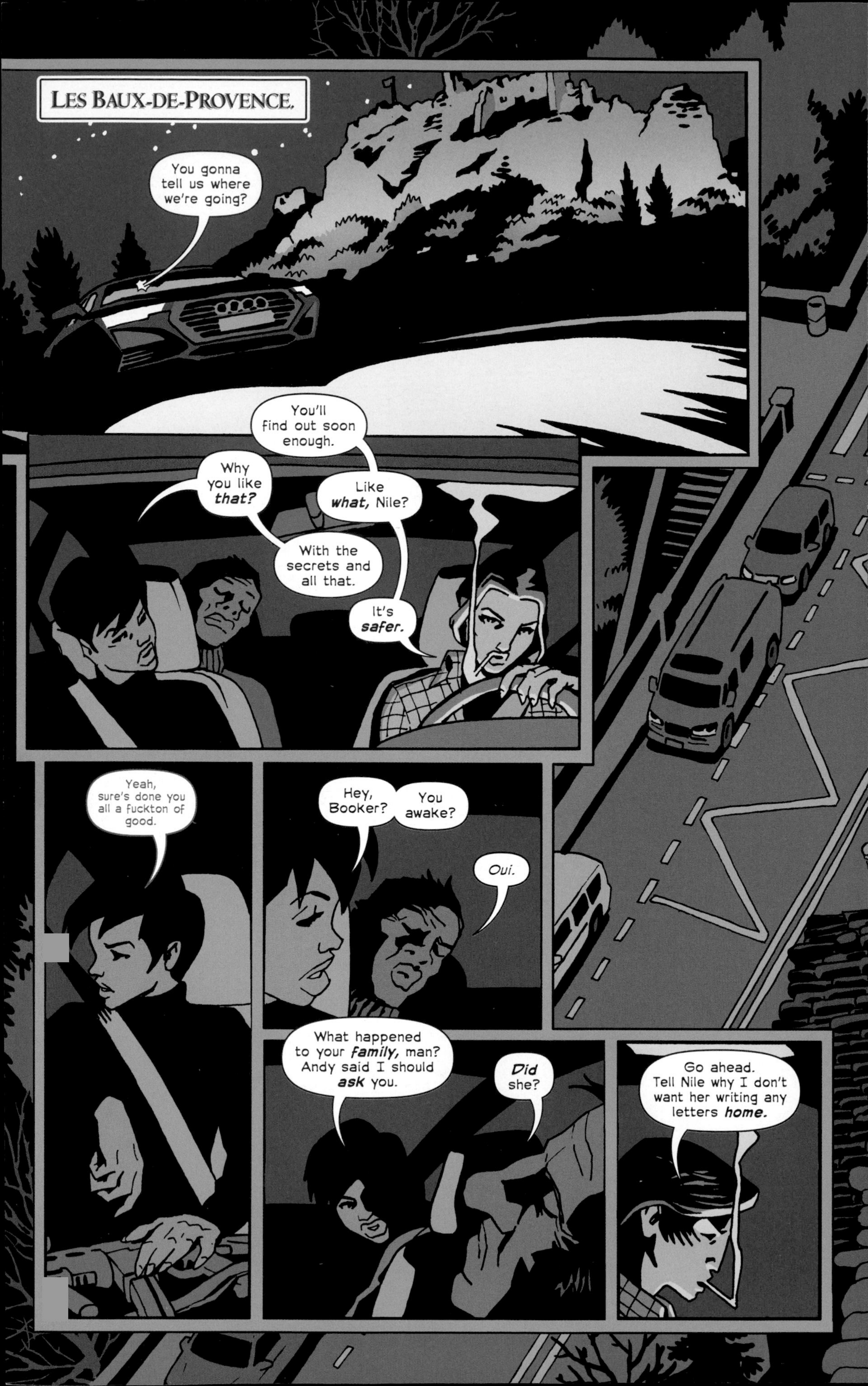

LES BAUX-DE-PROVENCE.
You gonna tell us where we're going?
You'll find out soon enough.
Why you like *that?*
Like *what,* Nile?
With the secrets and all that.
It's *safer.*
Yeah, sure's done you all a fuckton of good.
Hey, Booker?
You awake?
Oui.
What happened to your *family,* man? Andy said I should *ask* you.
Did she?
Go ahead. Tell Nile why I don't want her writing any letters *home.*

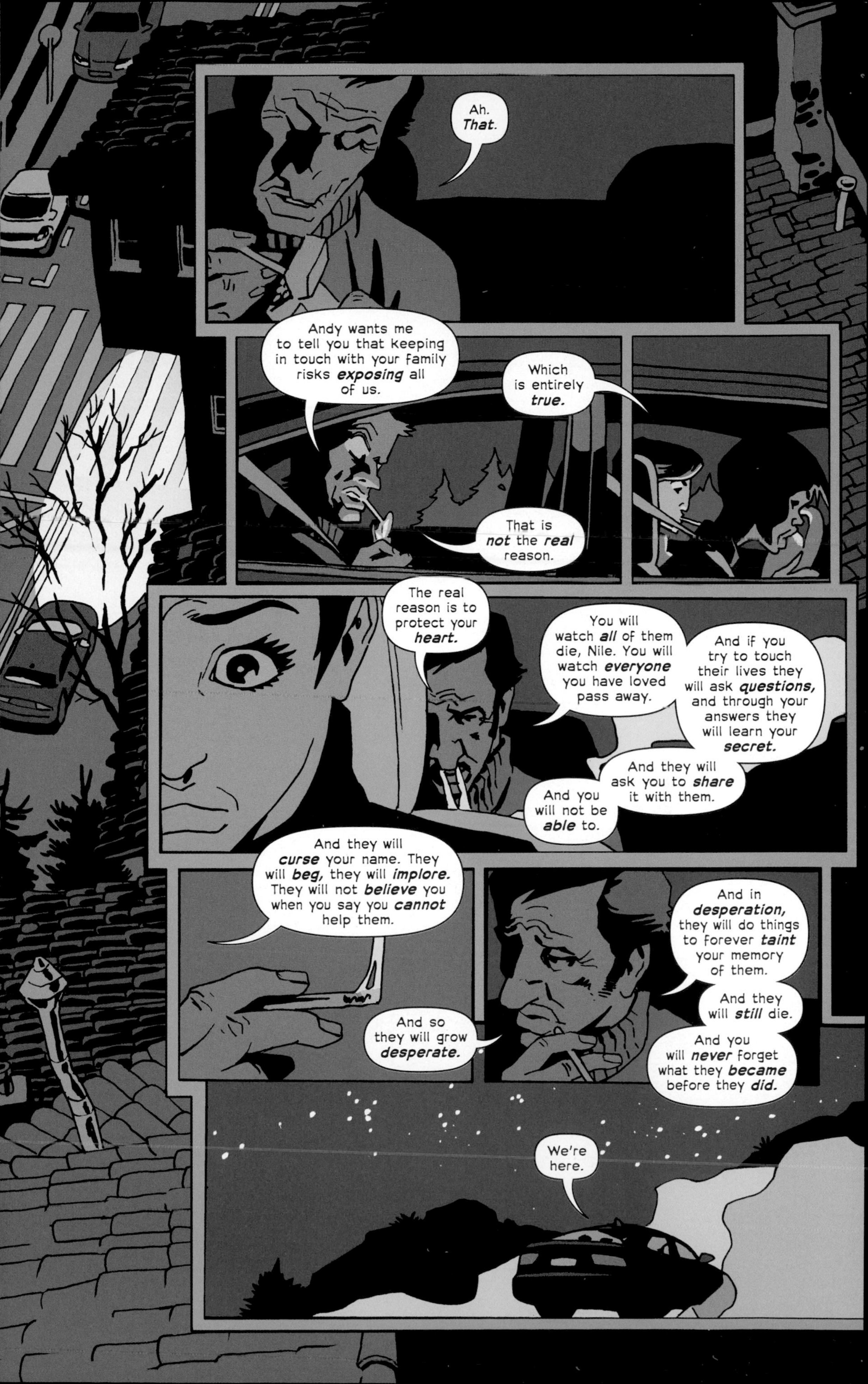
Ah. *That.*
Andy wants me to tell you that keeping in touch with your family risks ***exposing*** all of us.
Which is entirely ***true.***
That is ***not*** the ***real*** reason.
The real reason is to protect your ***heart.***
You will watch ***all*** of them die, Nile. You will watch ***everyone*** you have loved pass away.
And if you try to touch their lives they will ask ***questions,*** and through your answers they will learn your ***secret.***
And they will ask you to ***share*** it with them.
And you will not be ***able*** to.
And they will ***curse*** your name. They will ***beg,*** they will ***implore.*** They will not ***believe*** you when you say you ***cannot*** help them.
And so they will grow ***desperate.***
And in ***desperation,*** they will do things to forever ***taint*** your memory of them.
And they will ***still*** die.
And you will ***never*** forget what they ***became*** before they ***did.***
We're here.

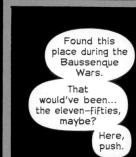

Found this place during the Baussenque Wars.

That would've been... the eleven-fifties, maybe?

Here, push.

C'mon, *push.*

Booker, get in here, you bastard!

Good.

Watch your step...

...might've left some booby traps, I can't quite remember...

Dear God.

...been a *while* since I've *stayed* here....

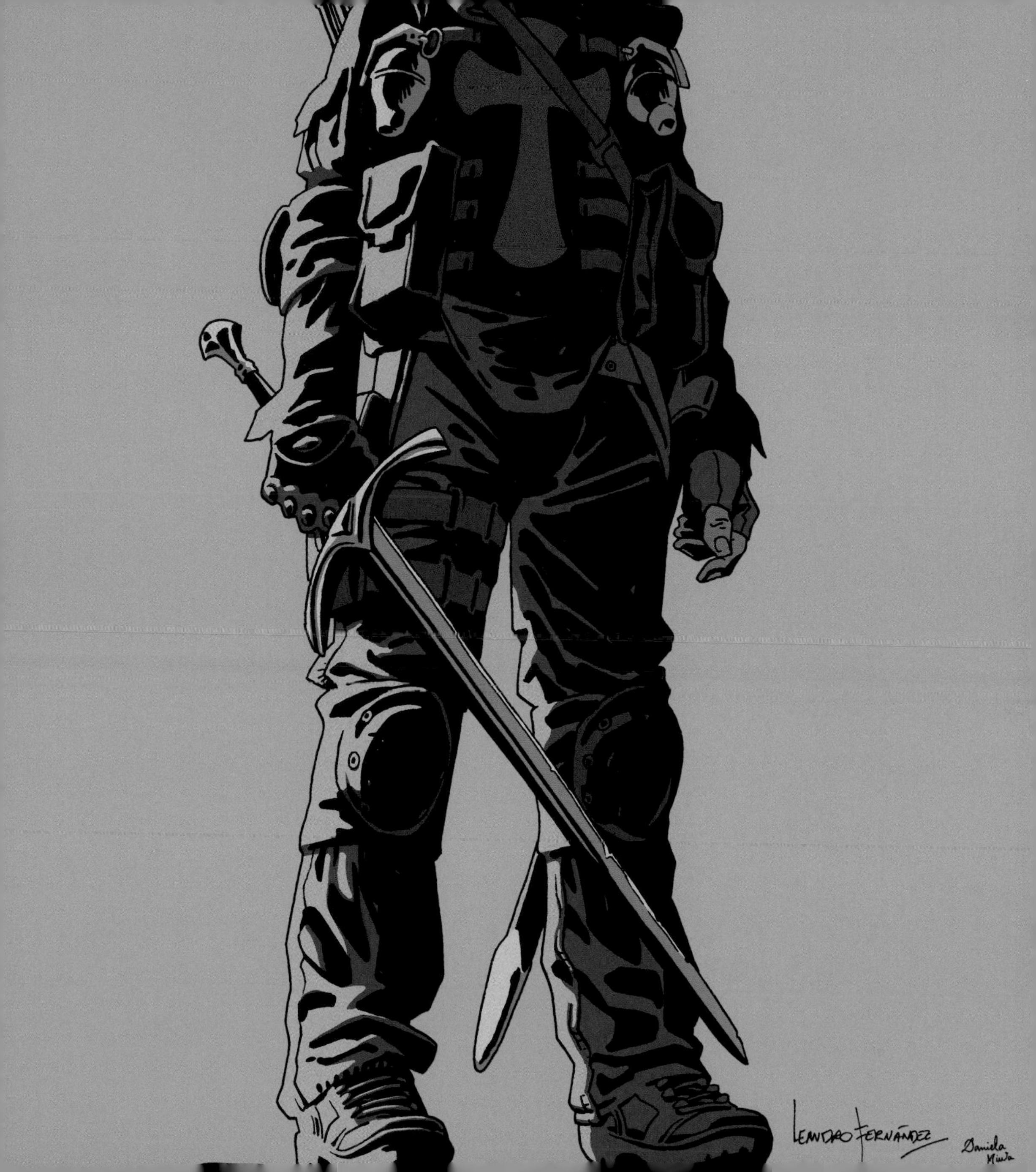
LEANDRO FERNÁNDEZ
Daniela Miwa

"LOVE IS LIKE WAR;

EASY TO BEGIN

BUT VERY HARD TO STOP."

~H.L. MENCKEN

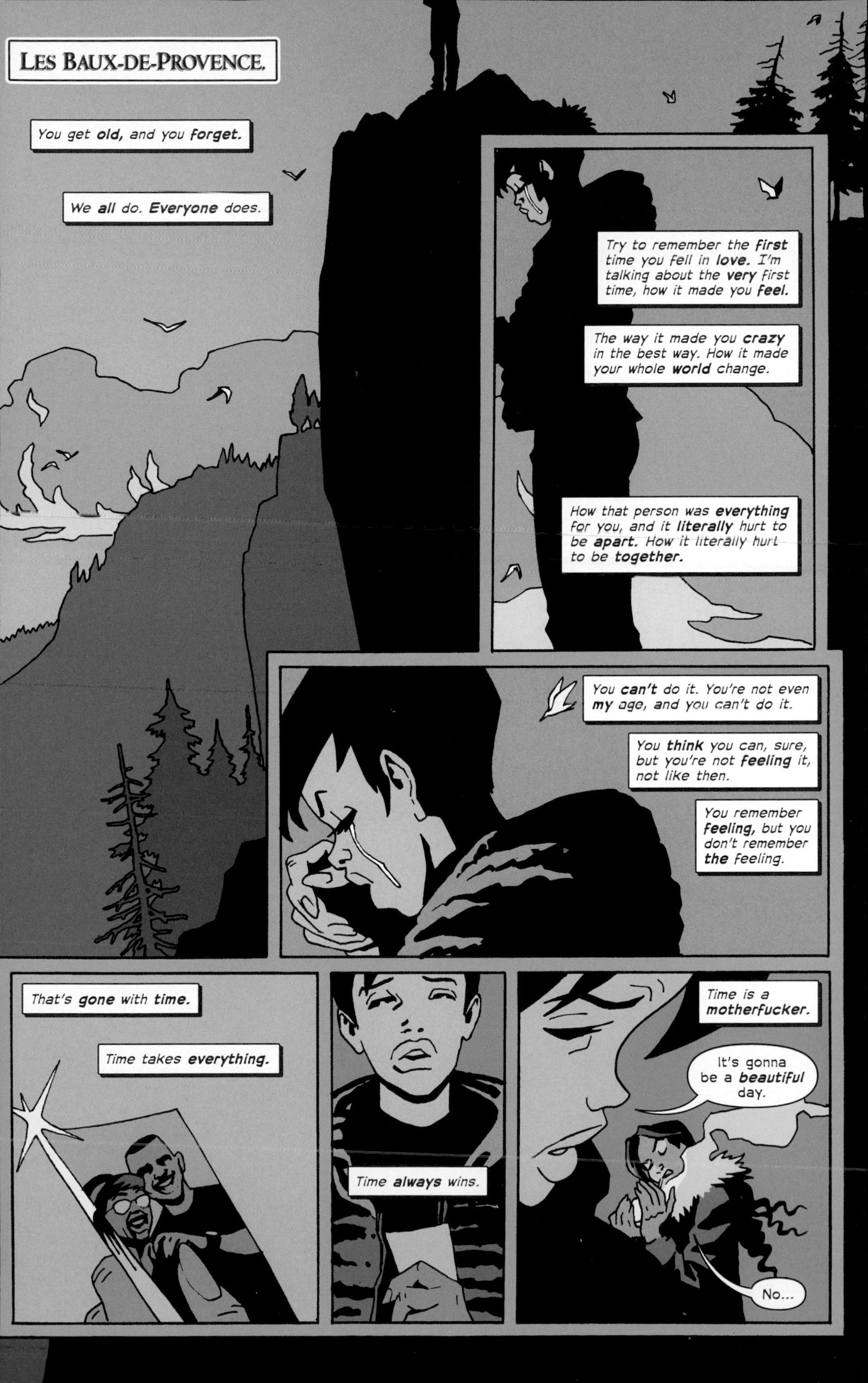
LES BAUX-DE-PROVENCE.
You get old, and you forget.
We all do. Everyone does.
Try to remember the first time you fell in love. I'm talking about the very first time, how it made you feel.
The way it made you crazy in the best way. How it made your whole world change.
How that person was everything for you, and it literally hurt to be apart. How it literally hurt to be together.
You can't do it. You're not even my age, and you can't do it.
You think you can, sure, but you're not feeling it, not like then.
You remember feeling, but you don't remember the feeling.
That's gone with time.
Time takes everything.
Time always wins.
Time is a motherfucker.
It's gonna be a beautiful day.
No...

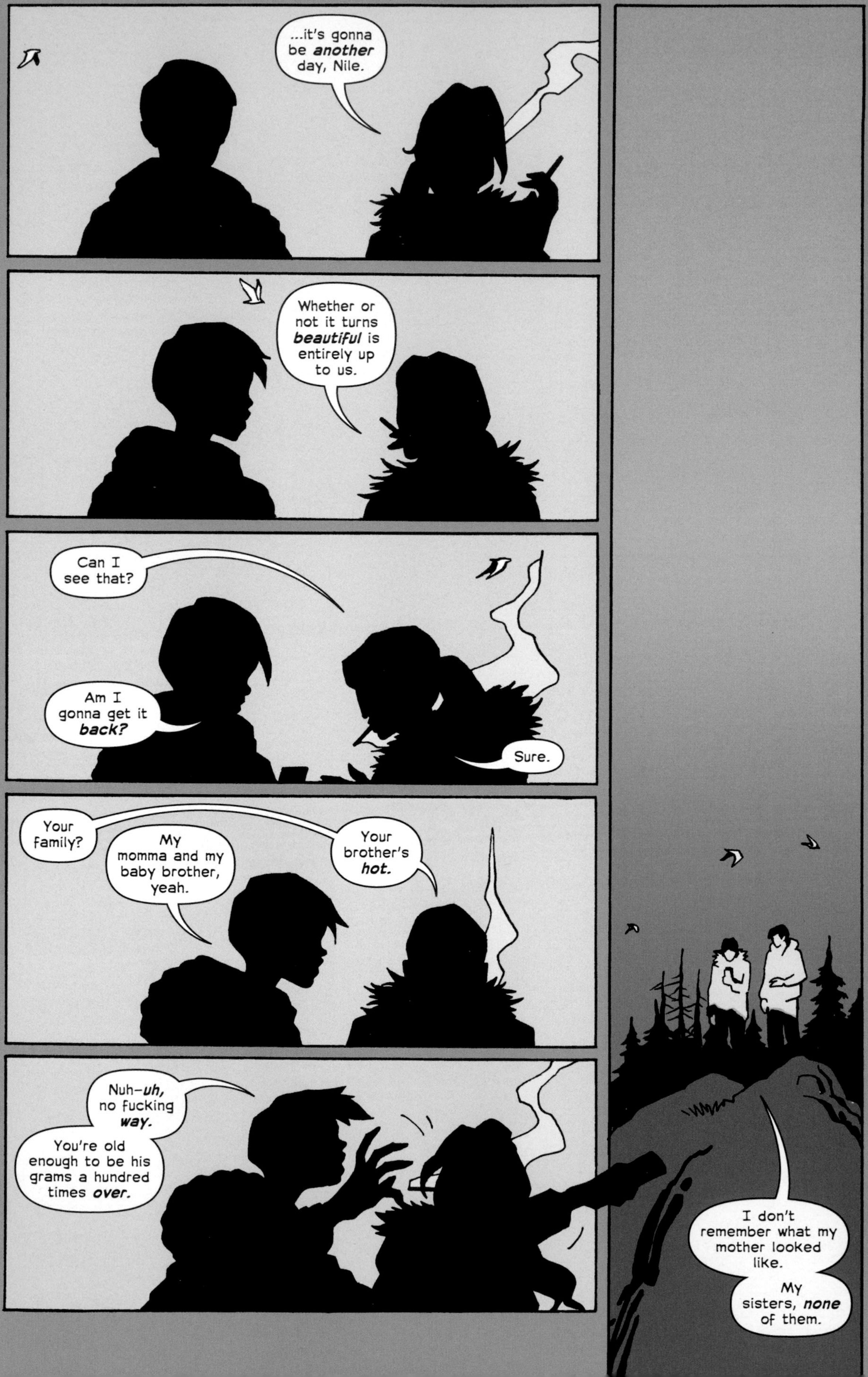

...it's gonna be *another* day, Nile.
Whether or not it turns *beautiful* is entirely up to us.
Can I see that?
Am I gonna get it *back?*
Sure.
Your family?
My momma and my baby brother, yeah.
Your brother's *hot.*
Nuh-*uh,* no fucking *way.*
You're old enough to be his grams a hundred times *over.*
I don't remember what my mother looked like.
My sisters, *none* of them.

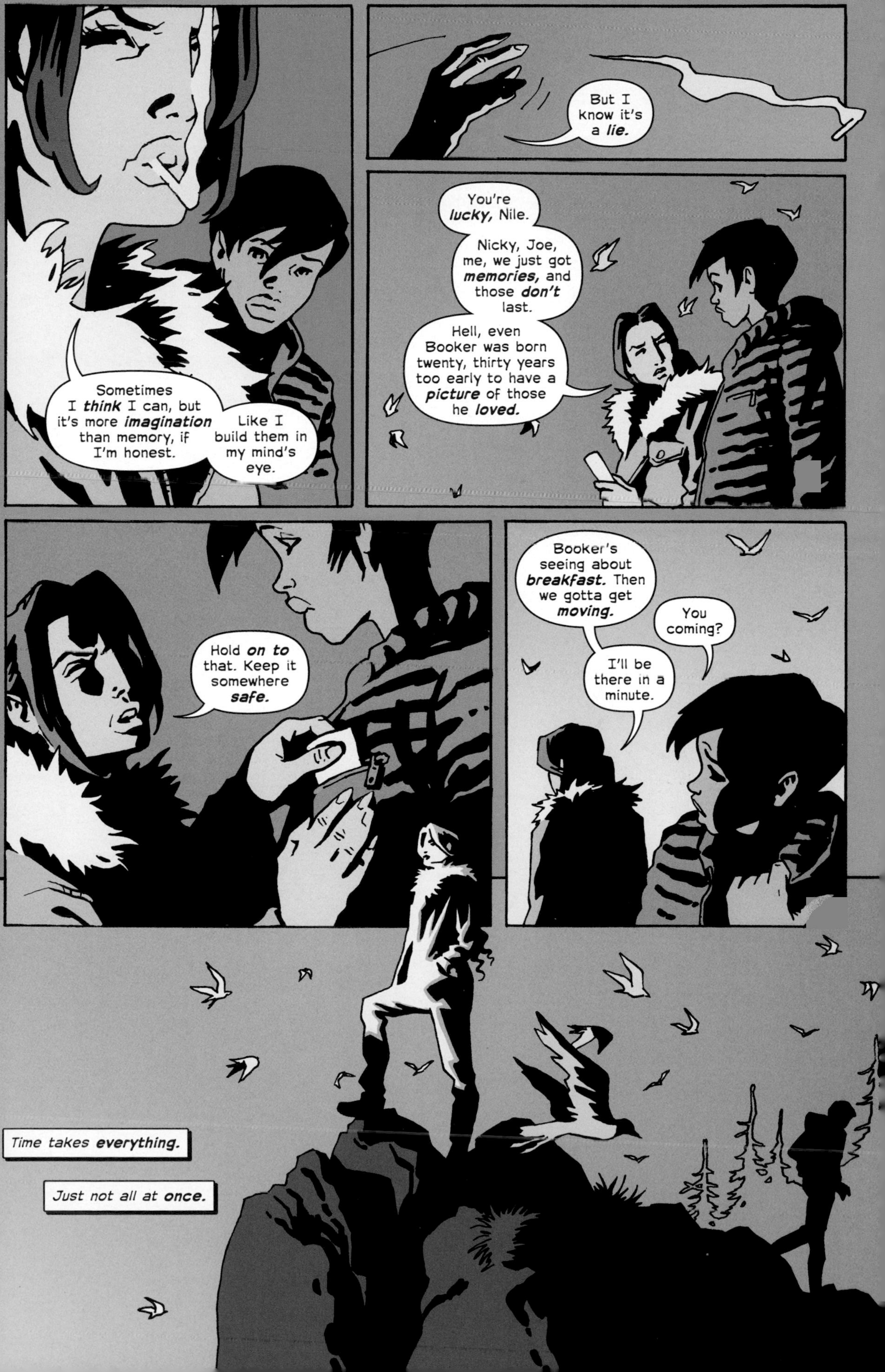
Sometimes I think I can, but it's more imagination than memory, if I'm honest.
Like I build them in my mind's eye.
But I know it's a lie.
You're lucky, Nile.
Nicky, Joe, me, we just got memories, and those don't last.
Hell, even Booker was born twenty, thirty years too early to have a picture of those he loved.
Hold on to that. Keep it somewhere safe.
Booker's seeing about breakfast. Then we gotta get moving.
You coming?
I'll be there in a minute.
Time takes everything.
Just not all at once.

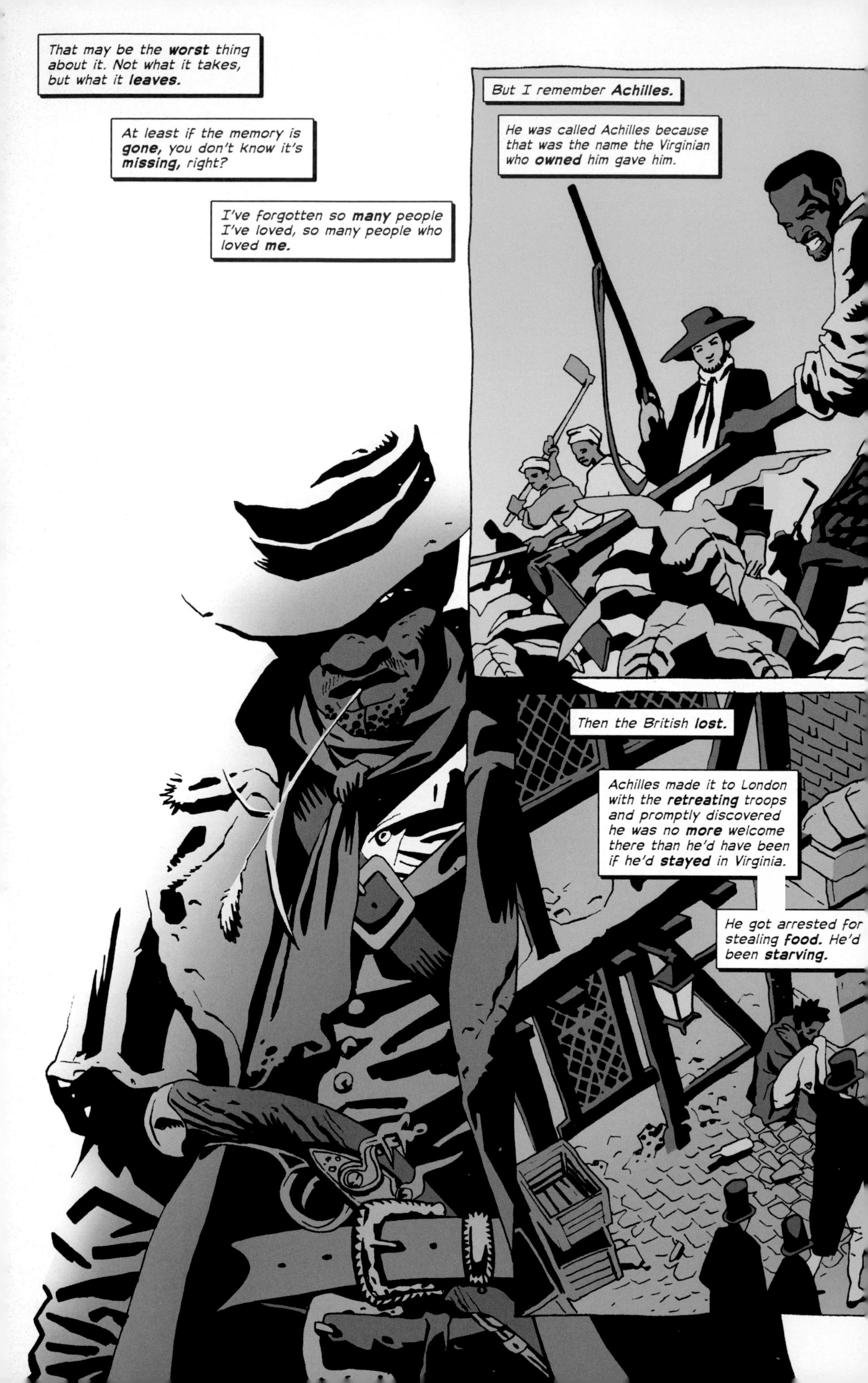
That may be the **worst** thing about it. Not what it takes, but what it **leaves.**
At least if the memory is **gone,** you don't know it's **missing,** right?
I've forgotten so **many** people I've loved, so many people who loved **me.**
But I remember **Achilles.**
He was called Achilles because that was the name the Virginian who **owned** him gave him.
Then the British **lost.**
Achilles made it to London with the **retreating** troops and promptly discovered he was no **more** welcome there than he'd have been if he'd **stayed** in Virginia.
He got arrested for stealing **food.** He'd been **starving.**

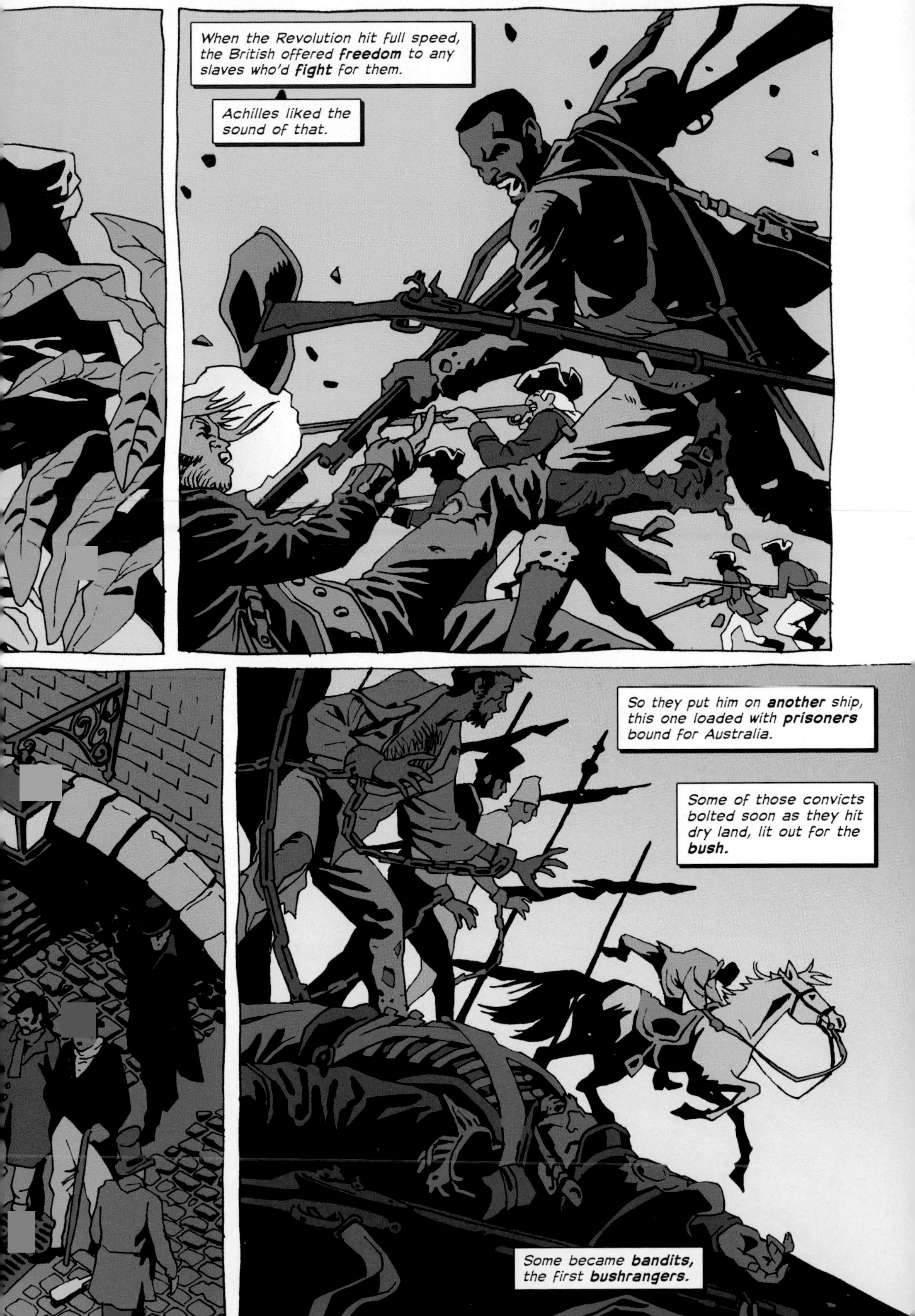
When the Revolution hit full speed, the British offered **freedom** to any slaves who'd **fight** for them.
Achilles liked the sound of that.
So they put him on **another** ship, this one loaded with **prisoners** bound for Australia.
Some of those convicts bolted soon as they hit dry land, lit out for the **bush.**
Some became **bandits,** the first **bushrangers.**

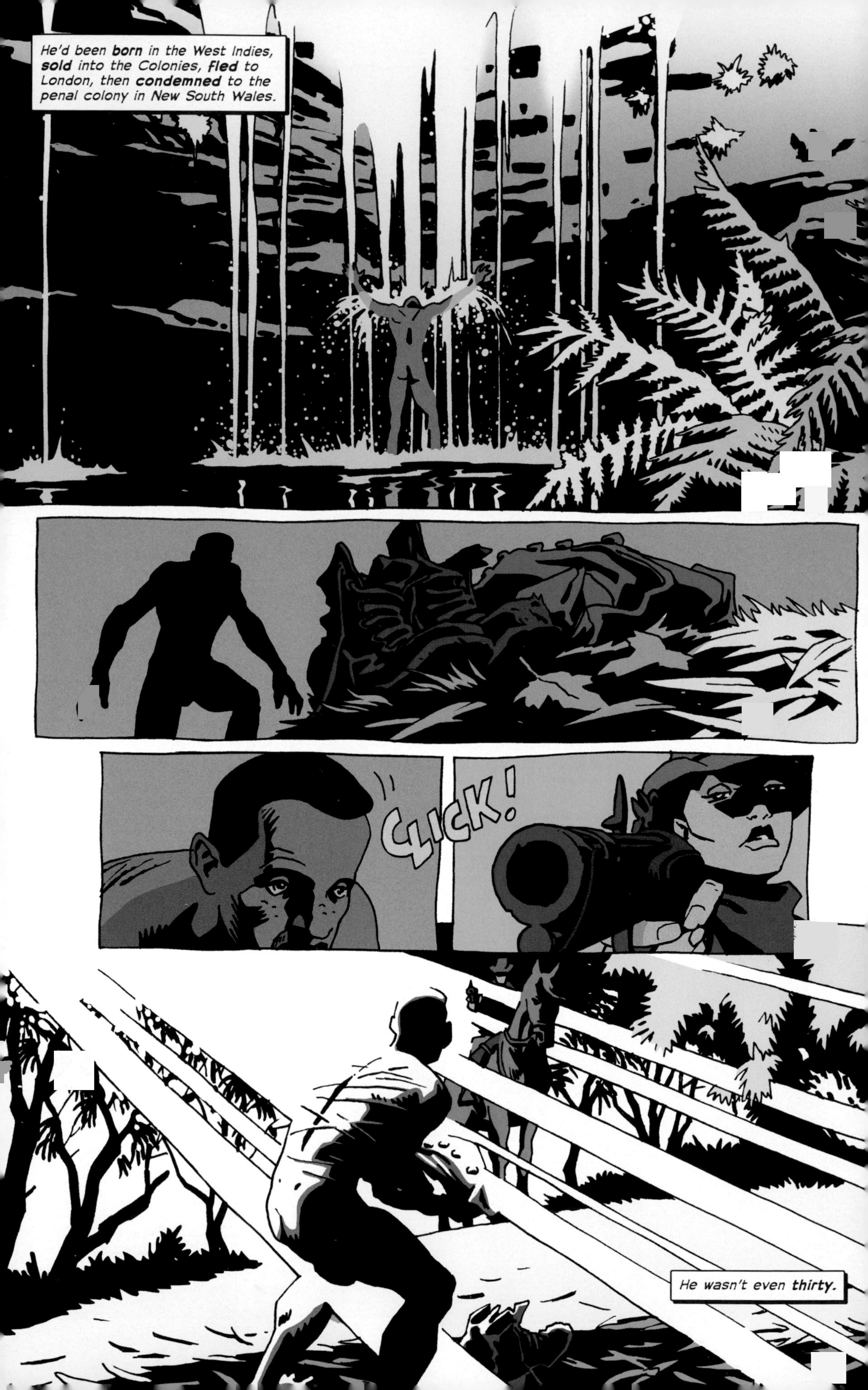
He'd been **born** in the West Indies, **sold** into the Colonies, **fled** to London, then **condemned** to the penal colony in New South Wales.
CLICK!
He wasn't even **thirty**.

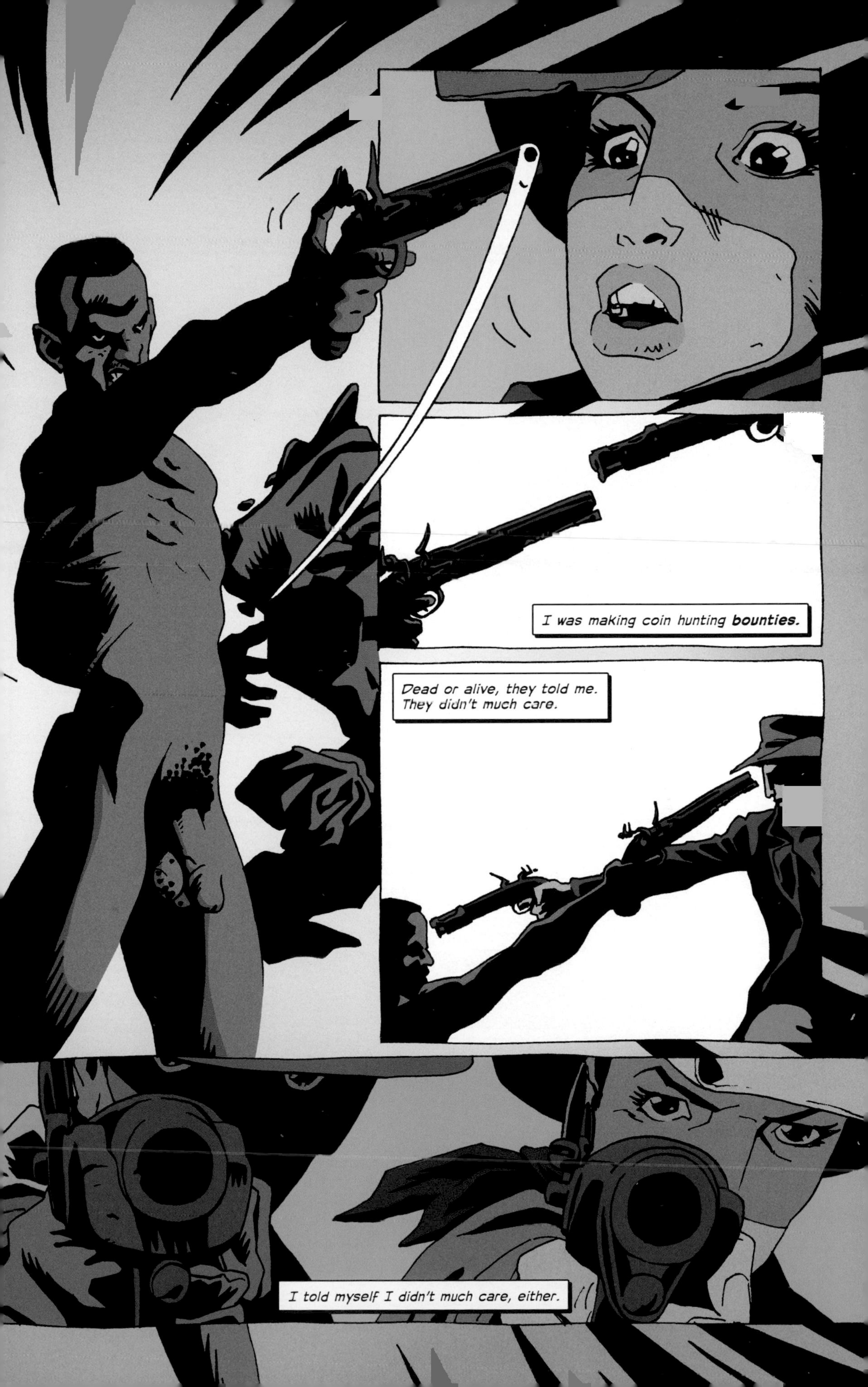
I was making coin hunting **bounties.**
Dead or alive, they told me. They didn't much care.
I told myself I didn't much care, either.

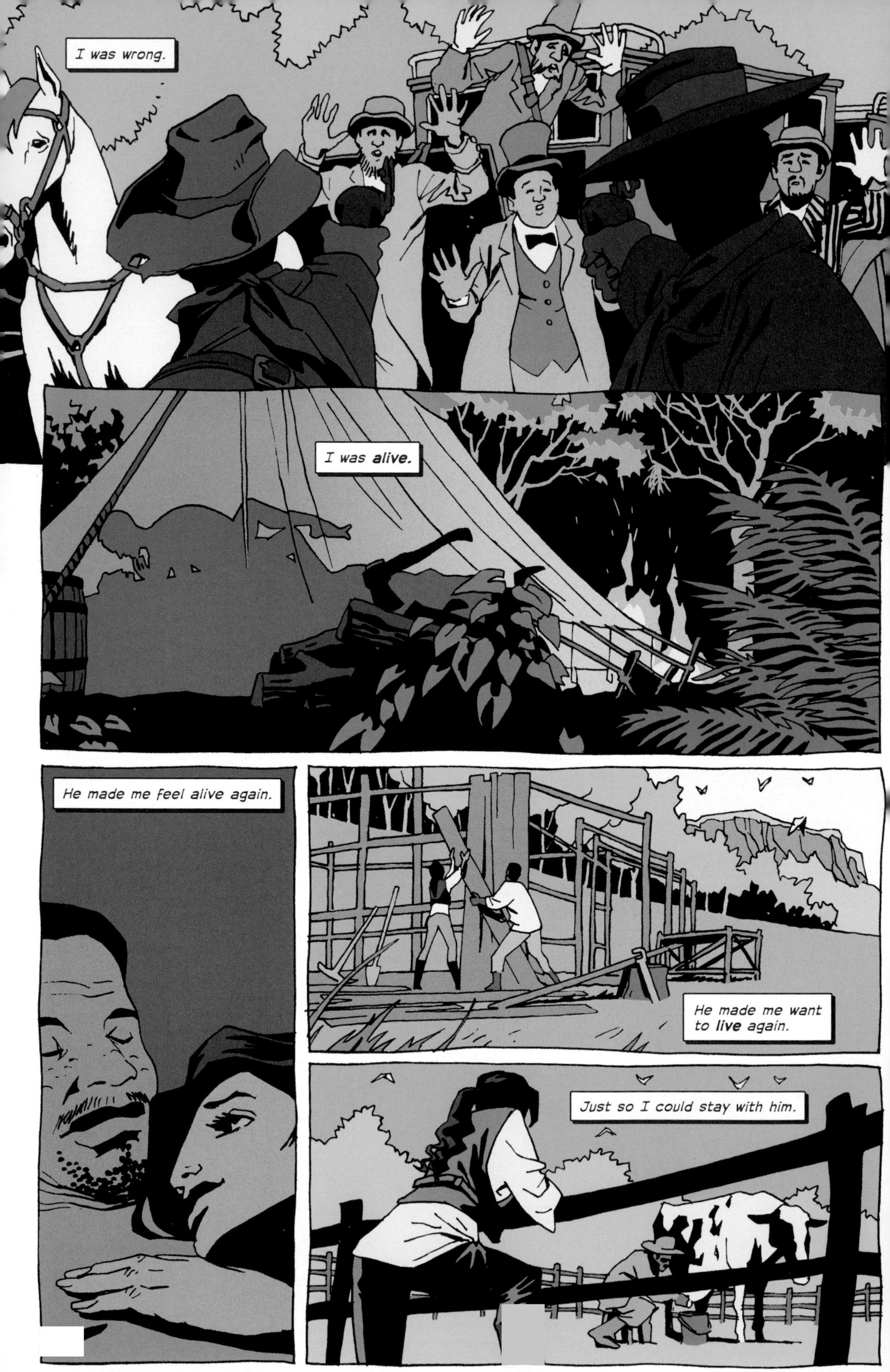
I was wrong.
I was **alive.**
He made me feel alive again.
He made me want to **live** again.
Just so I could stay with him.

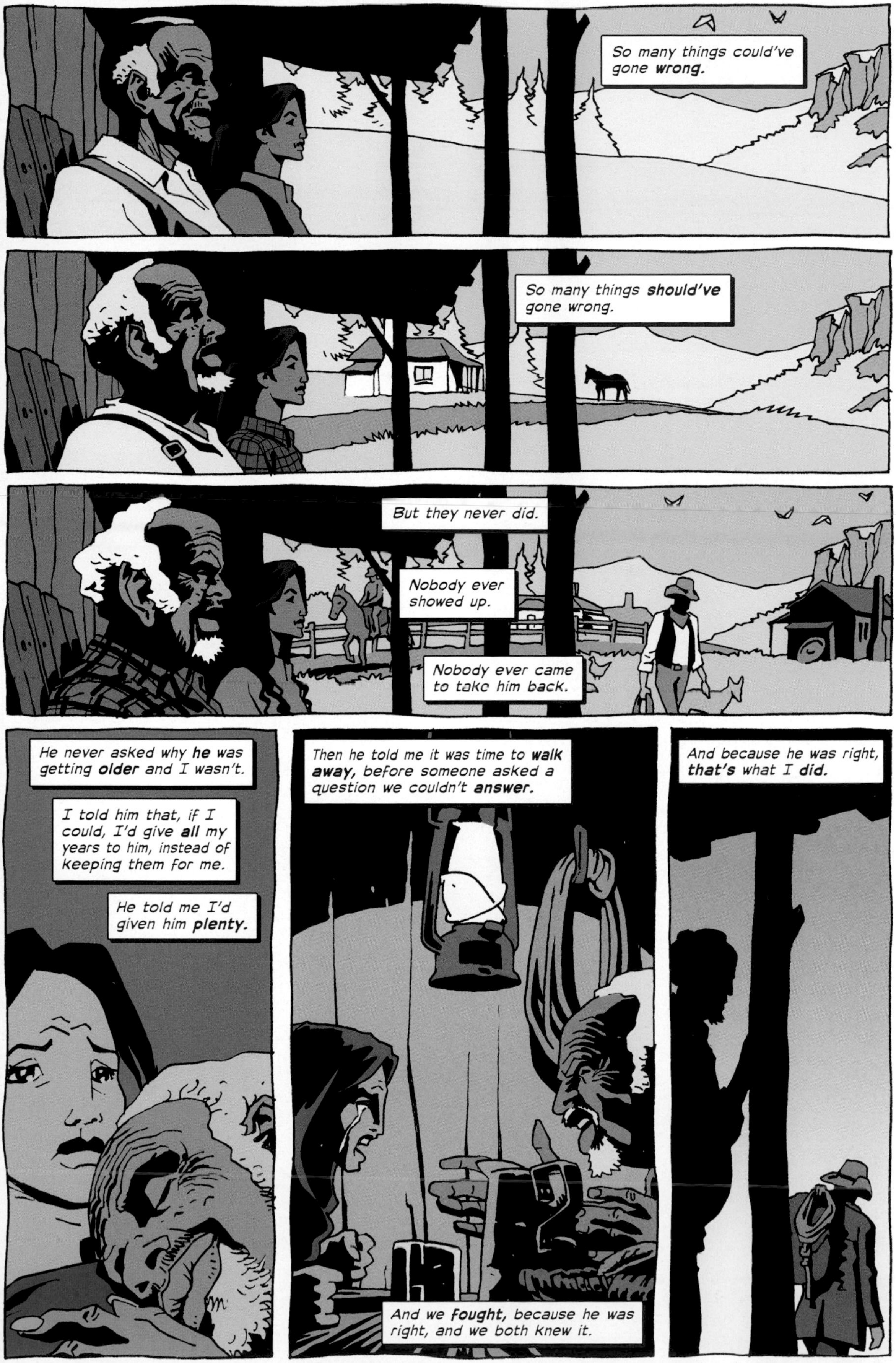
So many things could've gone **wrong.**
So many things **should've** gone wrong.
But they never did.
Nobody ever showed up.
Nobody ever came to take him back.
He never asked why **he** was getting **older** and I wasn't.
I told him that, if I could, I'd give **all** my years to him, instead of keeping them for me.
He told me I'd given him **plenty.**
Then he told me it was time to **walk away,** before someone asked a question we couldn't **answer.**
And we **fought,** because he was right, and we both knew it.
And because he was right, **that's** what I **did.**

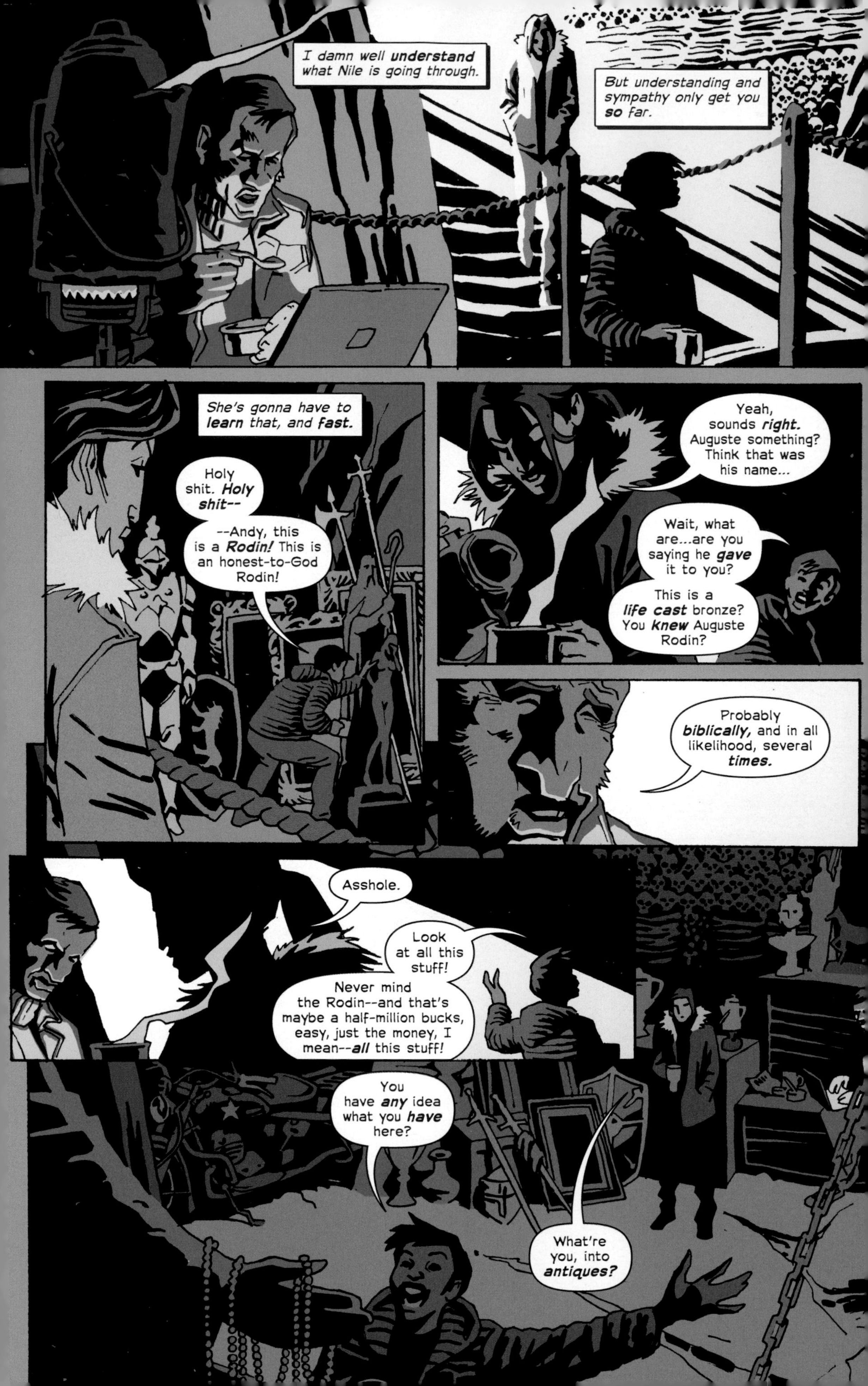

I damn well **understand** what Nile is going through.
But understanding and sympathy only get you **so** far.
She's gonna have to **learn** that, and **fast.**
Holy shit. **Holy shit--**
--Andy, this is a **Rodin!** This is an honest-to-God Rodin!
Yeah, sounds **right.** Auguste something? Think that was his name...
Wait, what are...are you saying he **gave** it to you?
This is a **life cast** bronze? You **knew** Auguste Rodin?
Probably **biblically,** and in all likelihood, several **times.**
Asshole.
Look at all this stuff!
Never mind the Rodin--and that's maybe a half-million bucks, easy, just the money, I mean--**all** this stuff!
You have **any** idea what you **have** here?
What're you, into **antiques?**

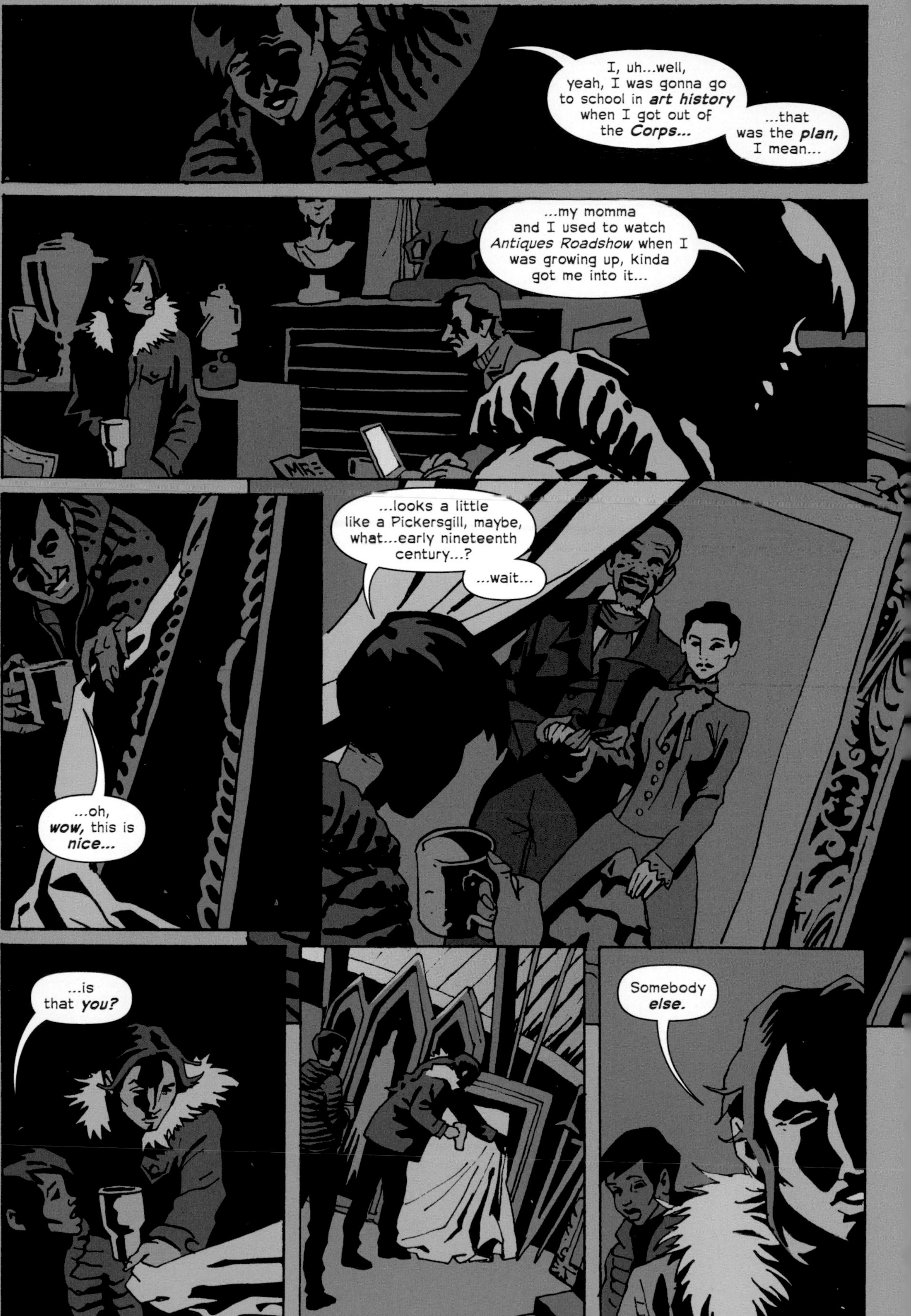
I, uh...well, yeah, I was gonna go to school in *art history* when I got out of the *Corps...*
...that was the *plan,* I mean...
...my momma and I used to watch *Antiques Roadshow* when I was growing up, kinda got me into it...
...oh, *wow,* this is *nice...*
...looks a little like a Pickersgill, maybe, what...early nineteenth century...?
...wait...
...is that *you?*
Somebody *else.*

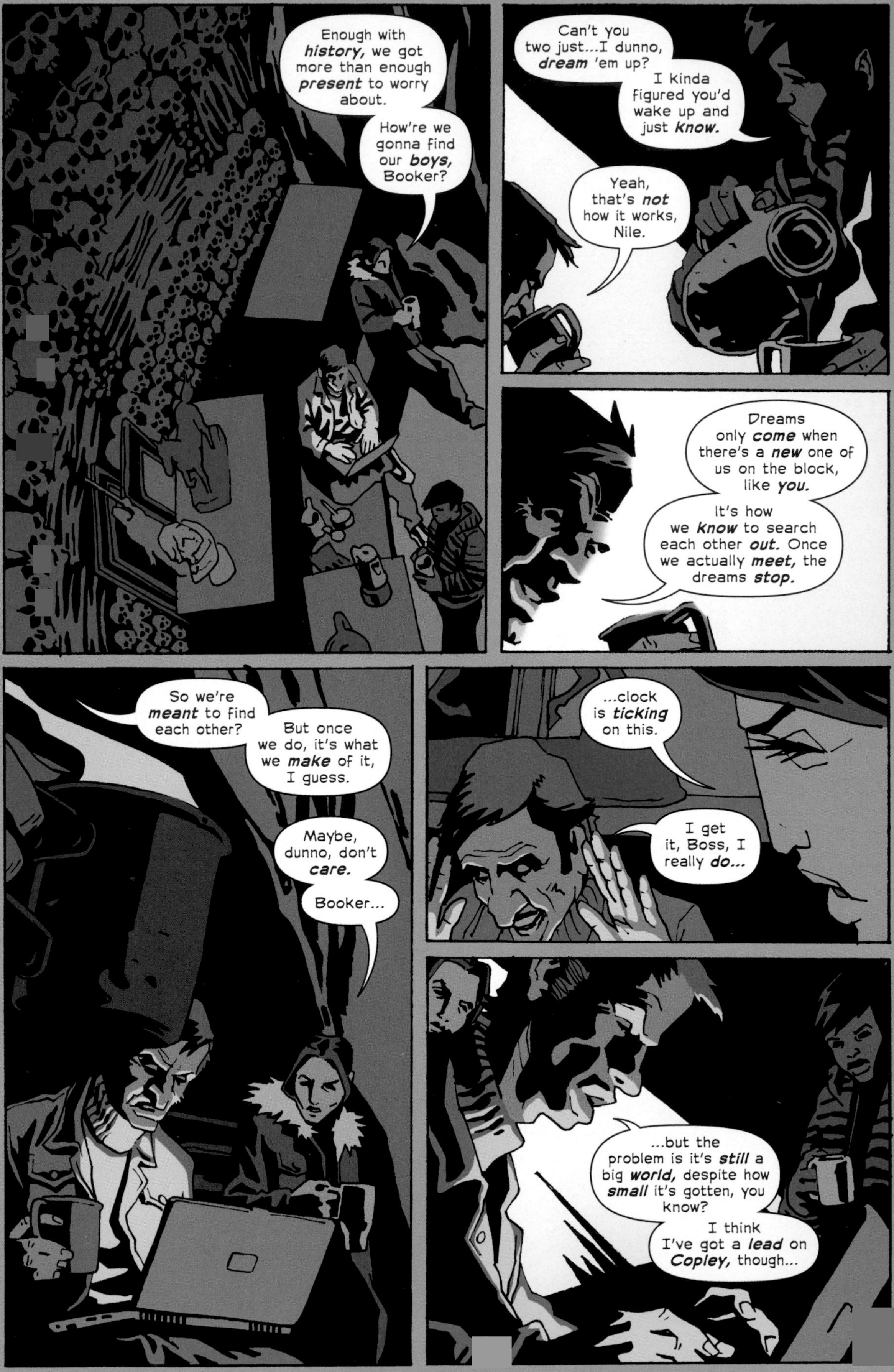
Enough with history, we got more than enough present to worry about.
How're we gonna find our boys, Booker?
Can't you two just...I dunno, dream 'em up?
I kinda figured you'd wake up and just know.
Yeah, that's not how it works, Nile.
Dreams only come when there's a new one of us on the block, like you.
It's how we know to search each other out. Once we actually meet, the dreams stop.
So we're meant to find each other?
But once we do, it's what we make of it, I guess.
Maybe, dunno, don't care.
Booker...
...clock is ticking on this.
I get it, Boss, I really do...
...but the problem is it's still a big world, despite how small it's gotten, you know?
I think I've got a lead on Copley, though...

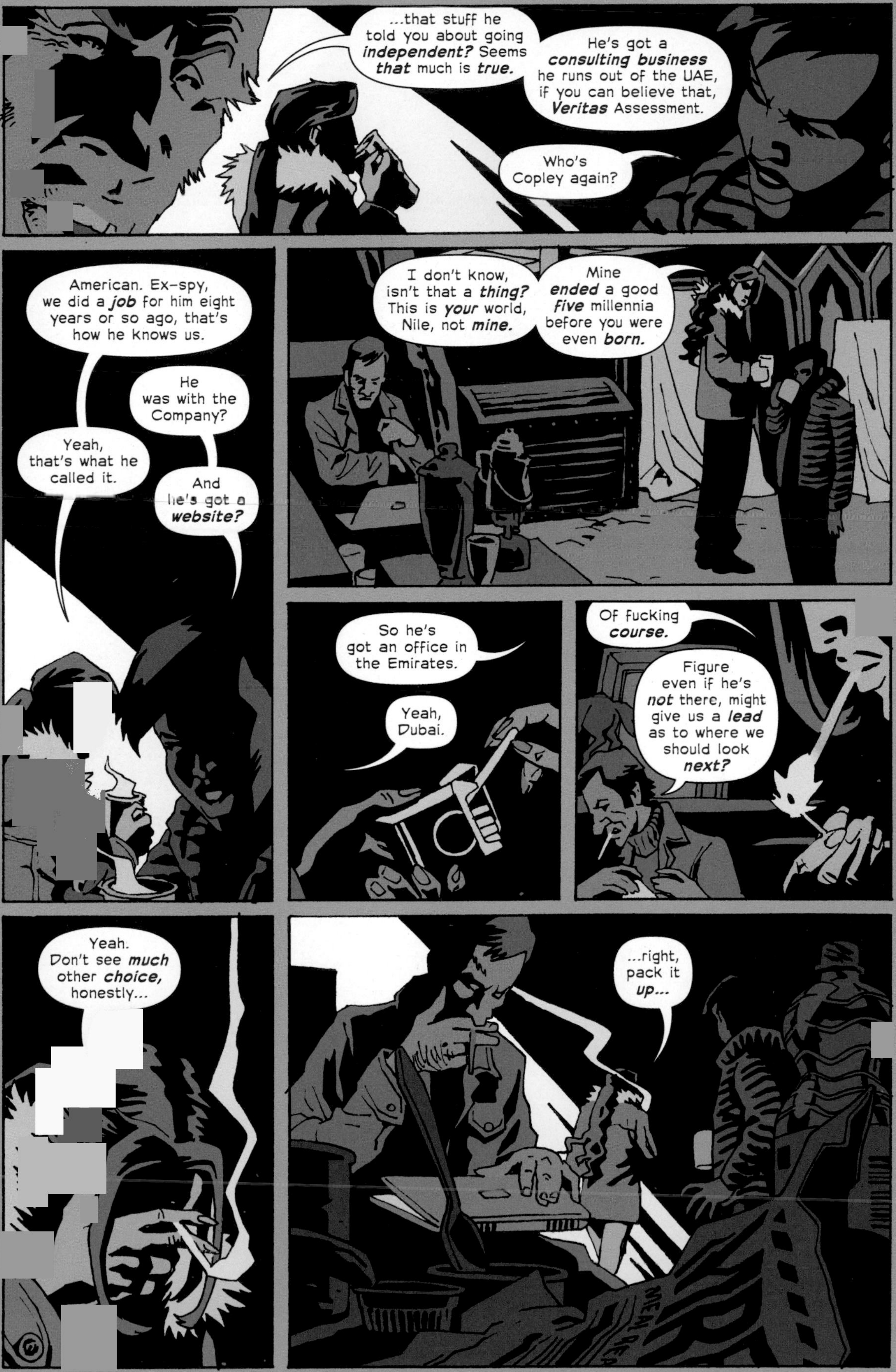
...that stuff he told you about going *independent?* Seems *that* much is *true.*
He's got a *consulting business* he runs out of the UAE, if you can believe that, *Veritas* Assessment.
Who's Copley again?
American. Ex-spy, we did a *job* for him eight years or so ago, that's how he knows us.
He was with the Company?
Yeah, that's what he called it.
And he's got a *website?*
I don't know, isn't that a *thing?* This is *your* world, Nile, not *mine.*
Mine *ended* a good *five* millennia before you were even *born.*
So he's got an office in the Emirates.
Yeah, Dubai.
Of fucking *course.*
Figure even if he's *not* there, might give us a *lead* as to where we should look *next?*
Yeah. Don't see *much* other *choice,* honestly...
...right, pack it *up...*

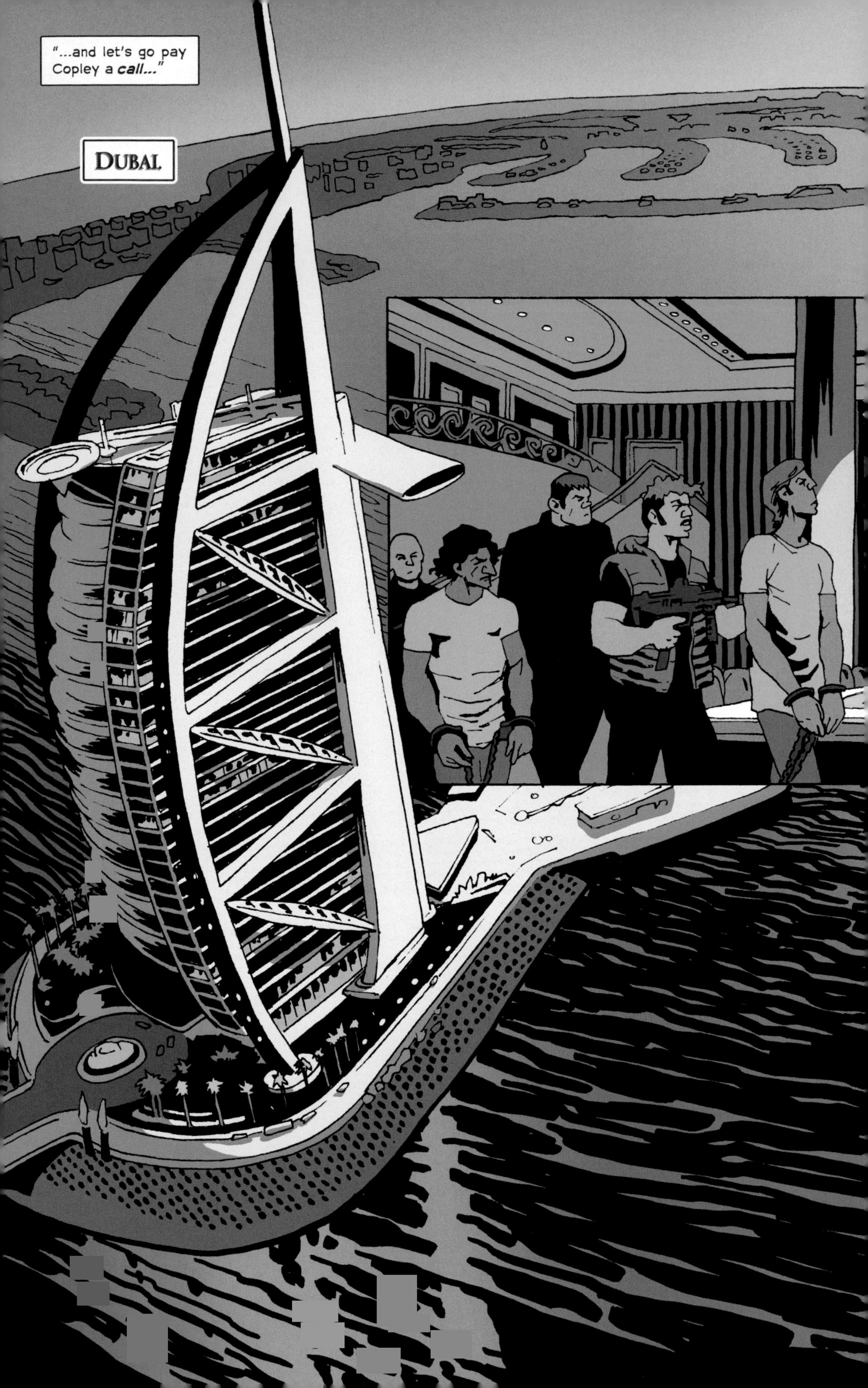
"...and let's go pay Copley a *call...*"
DUBAI.

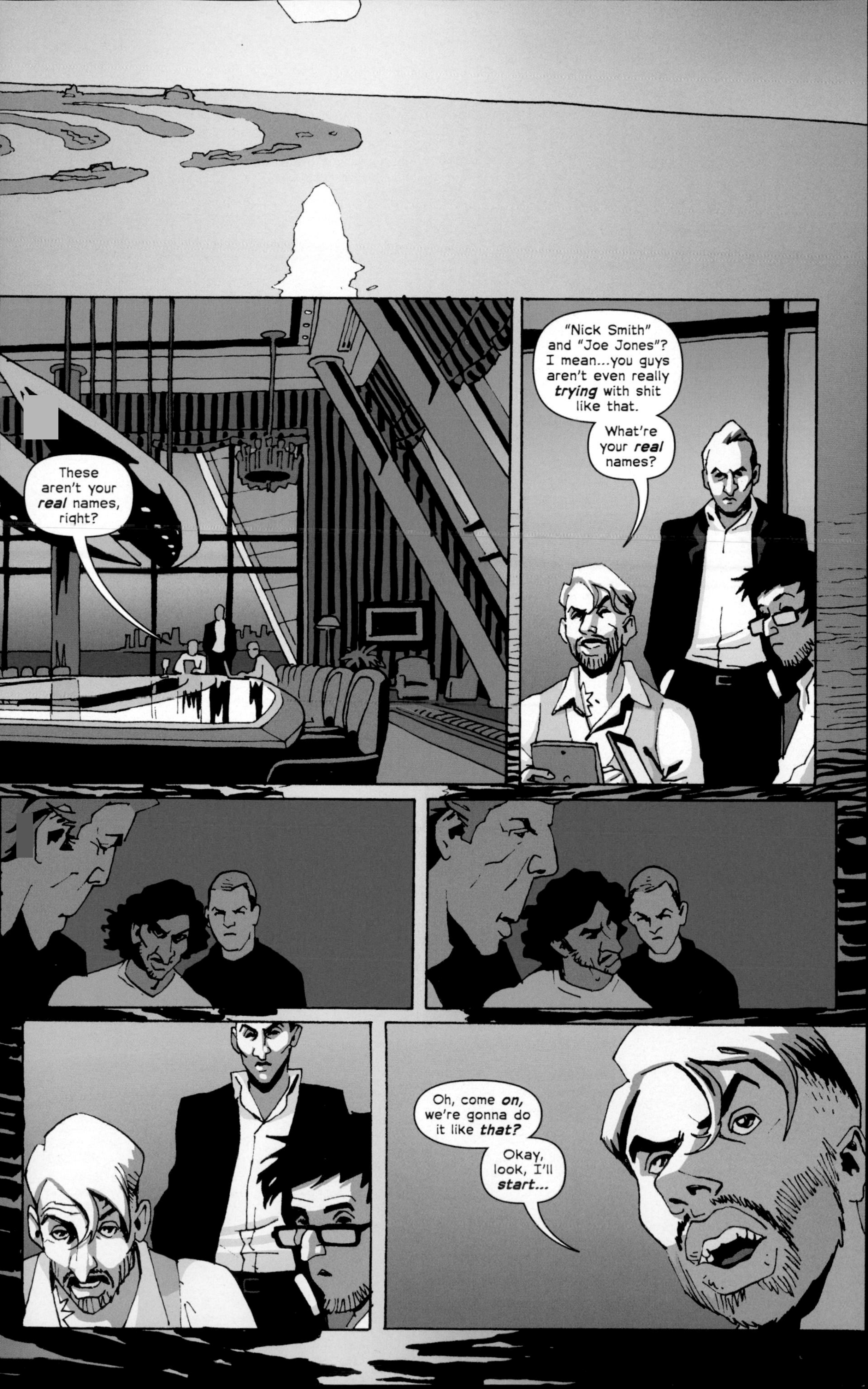
These aren't your real names, right?
"Nick Smith" and "Joe Jones"? I mean...you guys aren't even really trying with shit like that.
What're your real names?
Oh, come on, we're gonna do it like that?
Okay, look, I'll start...

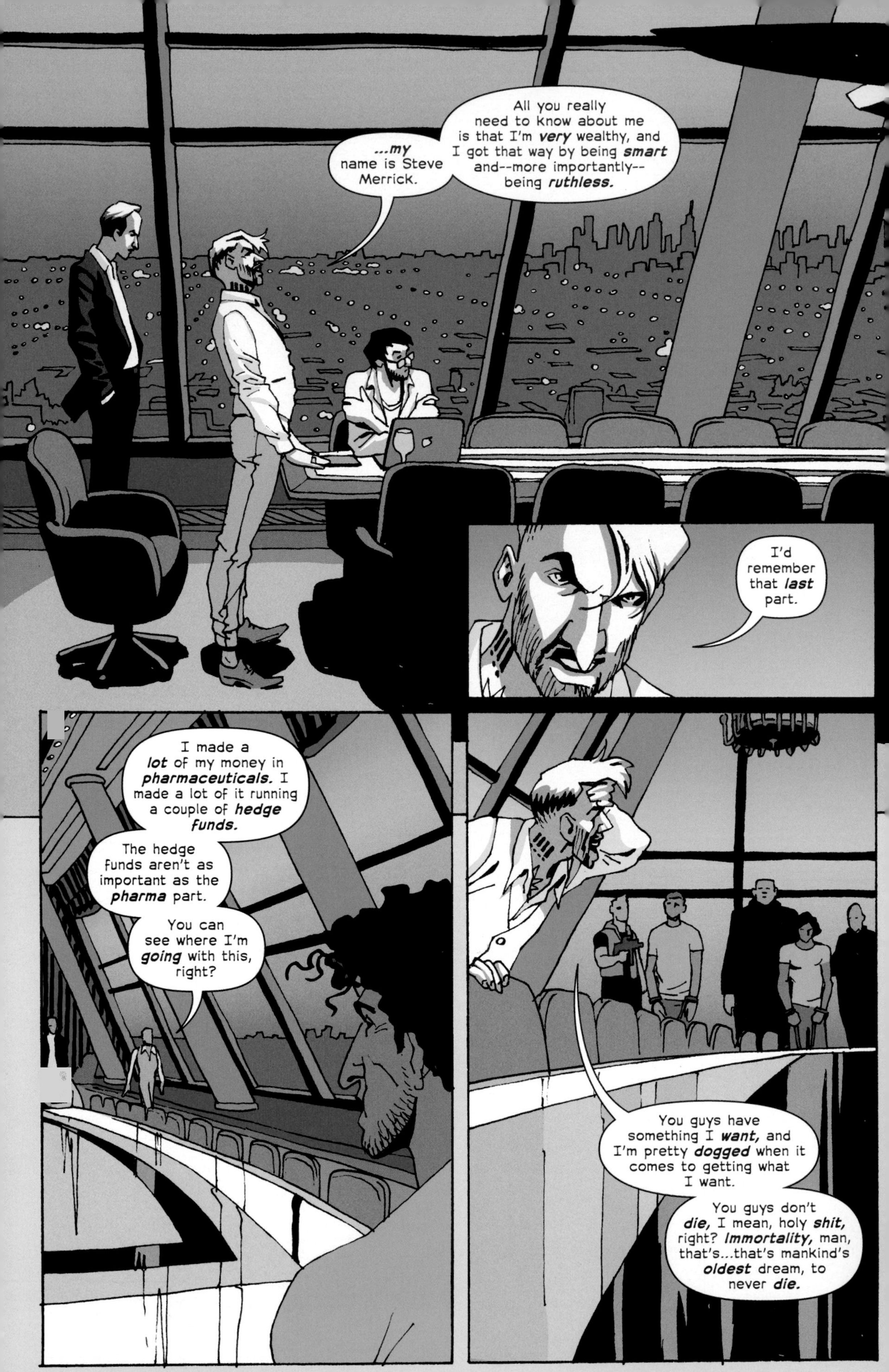
...my name is Steve Merrick.
All you really need to know about me is that I'm very wealthy, and I got that way by being smart and--more importantly--being ruthless.
I'd remember that last part.
I made a lot of my money in pharmaceuticals. I made a lot of it running a couple of hedge funds.
The hedge funds aren't as important as the pharma part.
You can see where I'm going with this, right?
You guys have something I want, and I'm pretty dogged when it comes to getting what I want.
You guys don't die, I mean, holy shit, right? Immortality, man, that's...that's mankind's oldest dream, to never die.

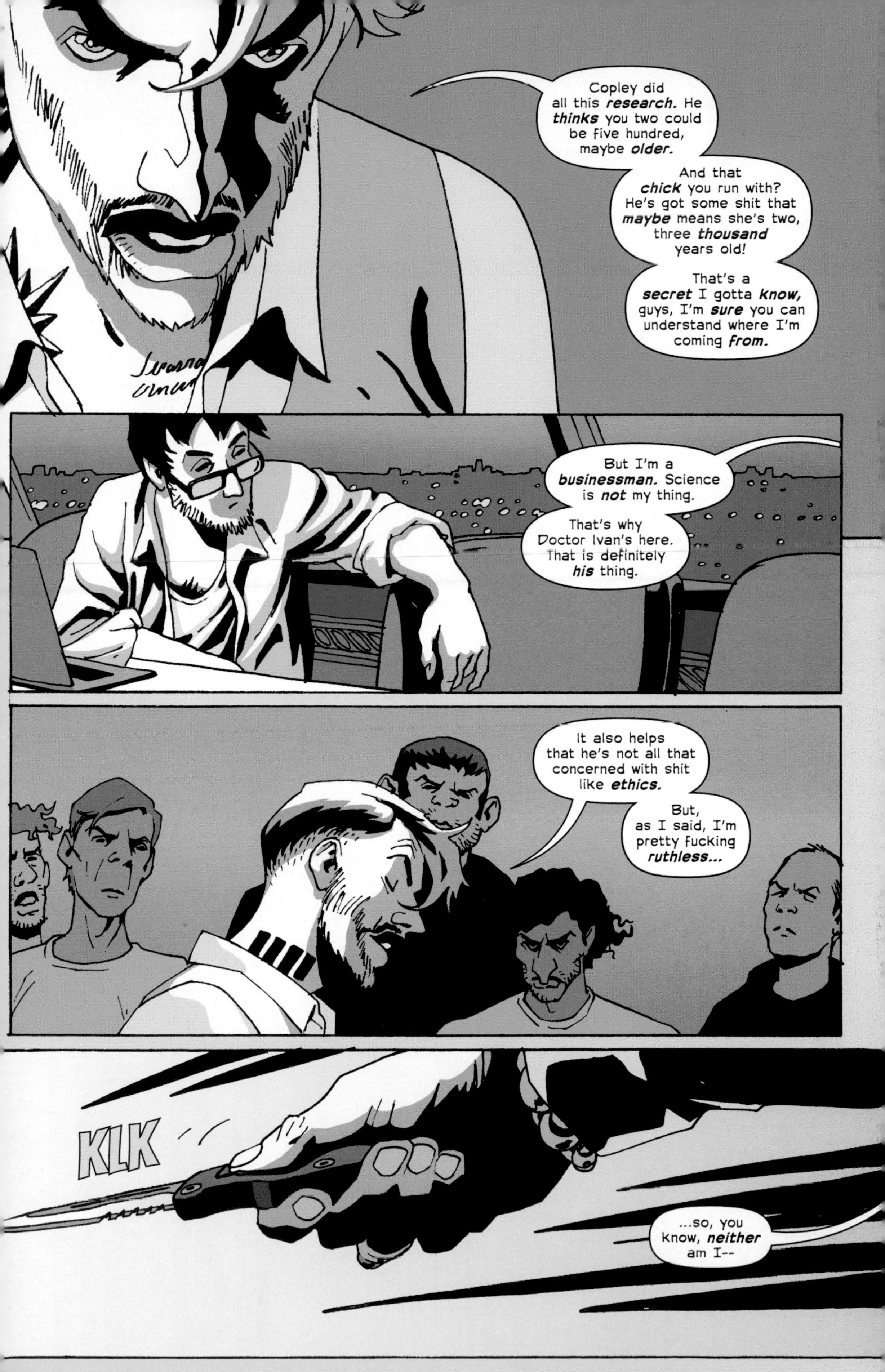
Copley did all this *research.* He *thinks* you two could be five hundred, maybe *older.*
And that *chick* you run with? He's got some shit that *maybe* means she's two, three *thousand* years old!
That's a *secret* I gotta *know,* guys, I'm *sure* you can understand where I'm coming *from.*
But I'm a *businessman.* Science is *not* my thing.
That's why Doctor Ivan's here. That is definitely *his* thing.
It also helps that he's not all that concerned with shit like *ethics.*
But, as I said, I'm pretty fucking *ruthless...*
KLK
...so, you know, *neither* am I--

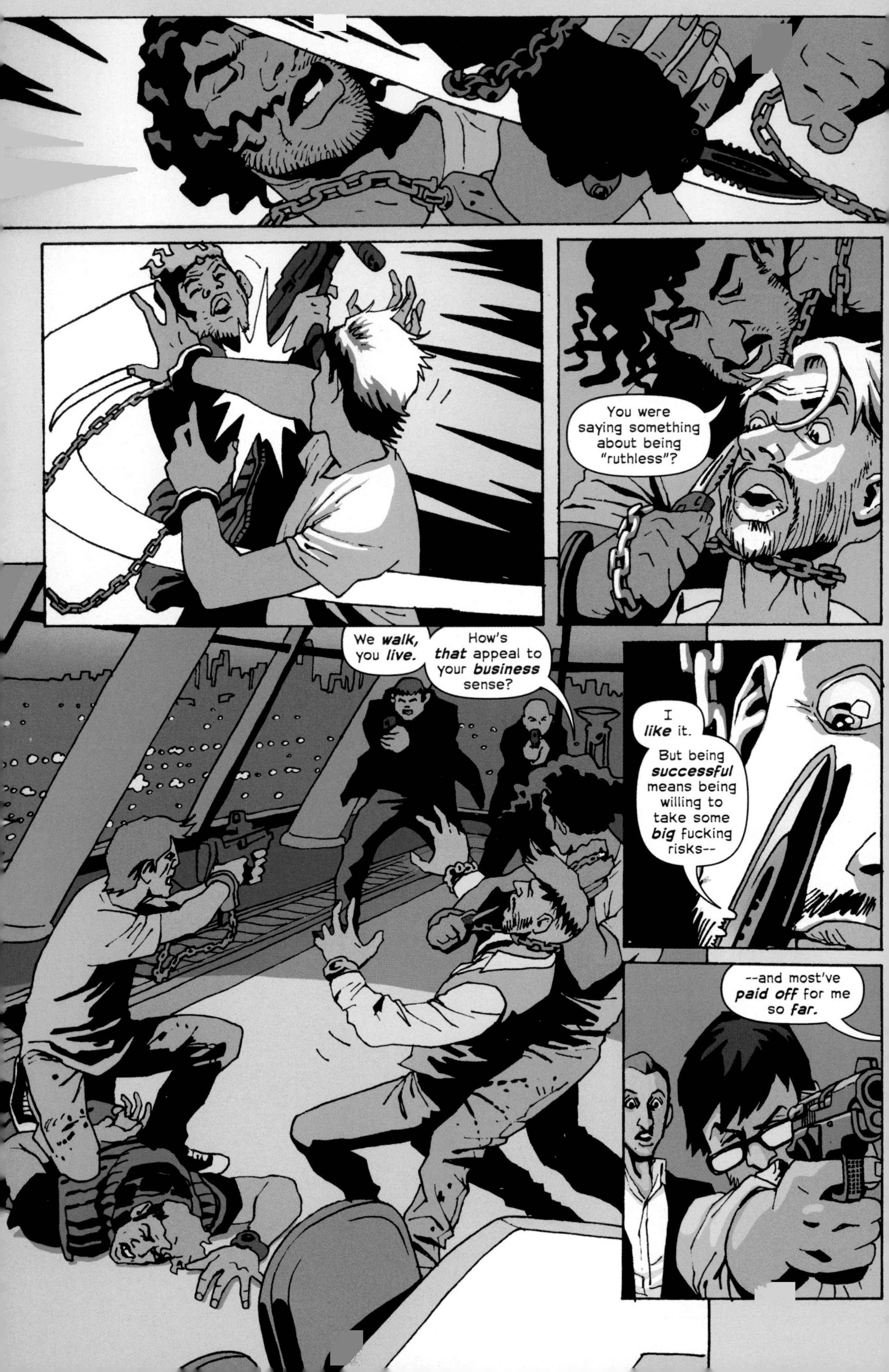
You were saying something about being "ruthless"?
We *walk,* you *live.*
How's *that* appeal to your *business* sense?
I *like* it.
But being *successful* means being willing to take some *big* fucking risks--
--and most've *paid off* for me so *far.*

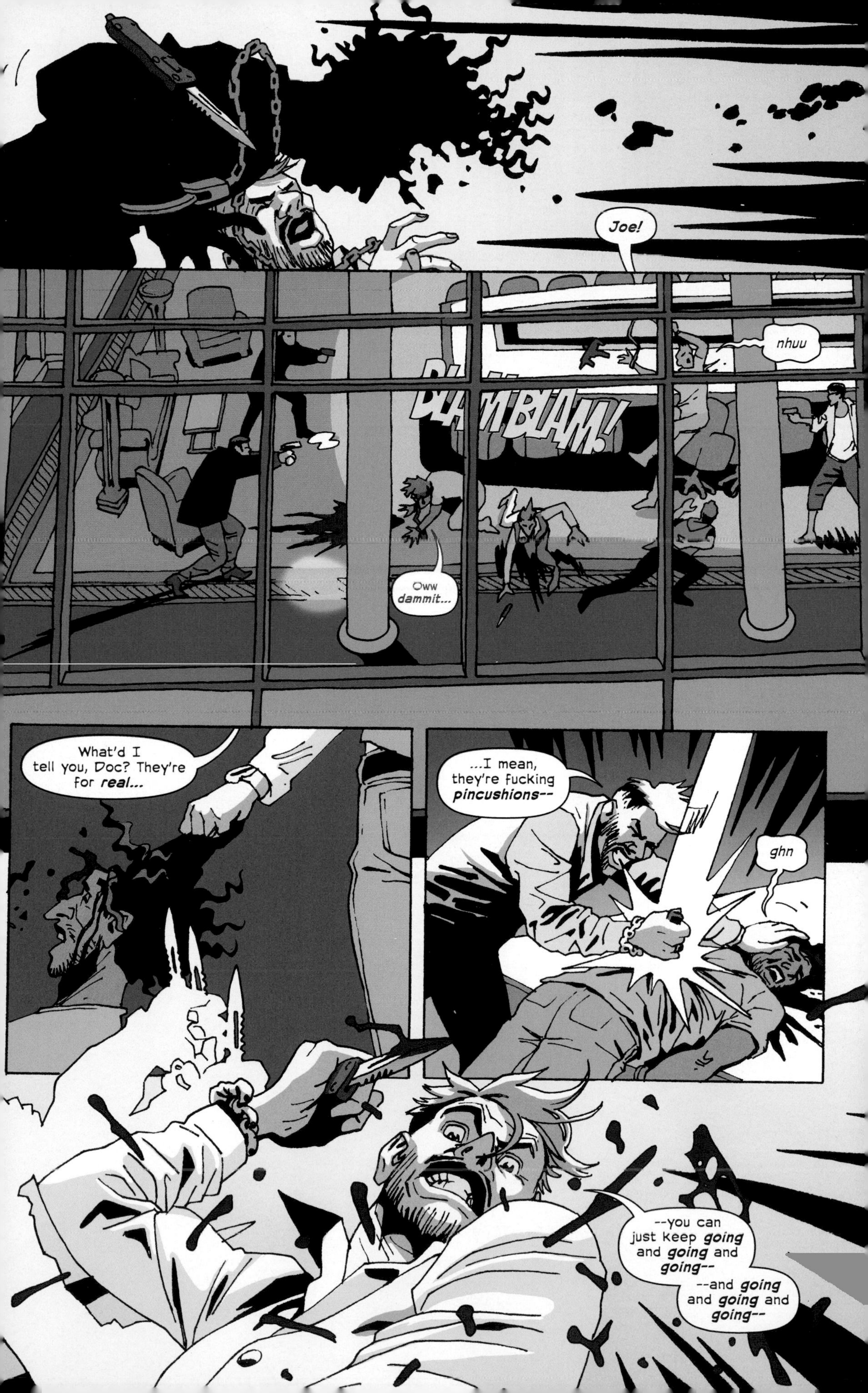
Joe!
nhuu
BLAM BLAM!
Oww dammit...
What'd I tell you, Doc? They're for *real...*
...I mean, they're fucking *pincushions--*
ghn
--you can just keep *going* and *going* and *going--*
--and *going* and *going* and *going--*

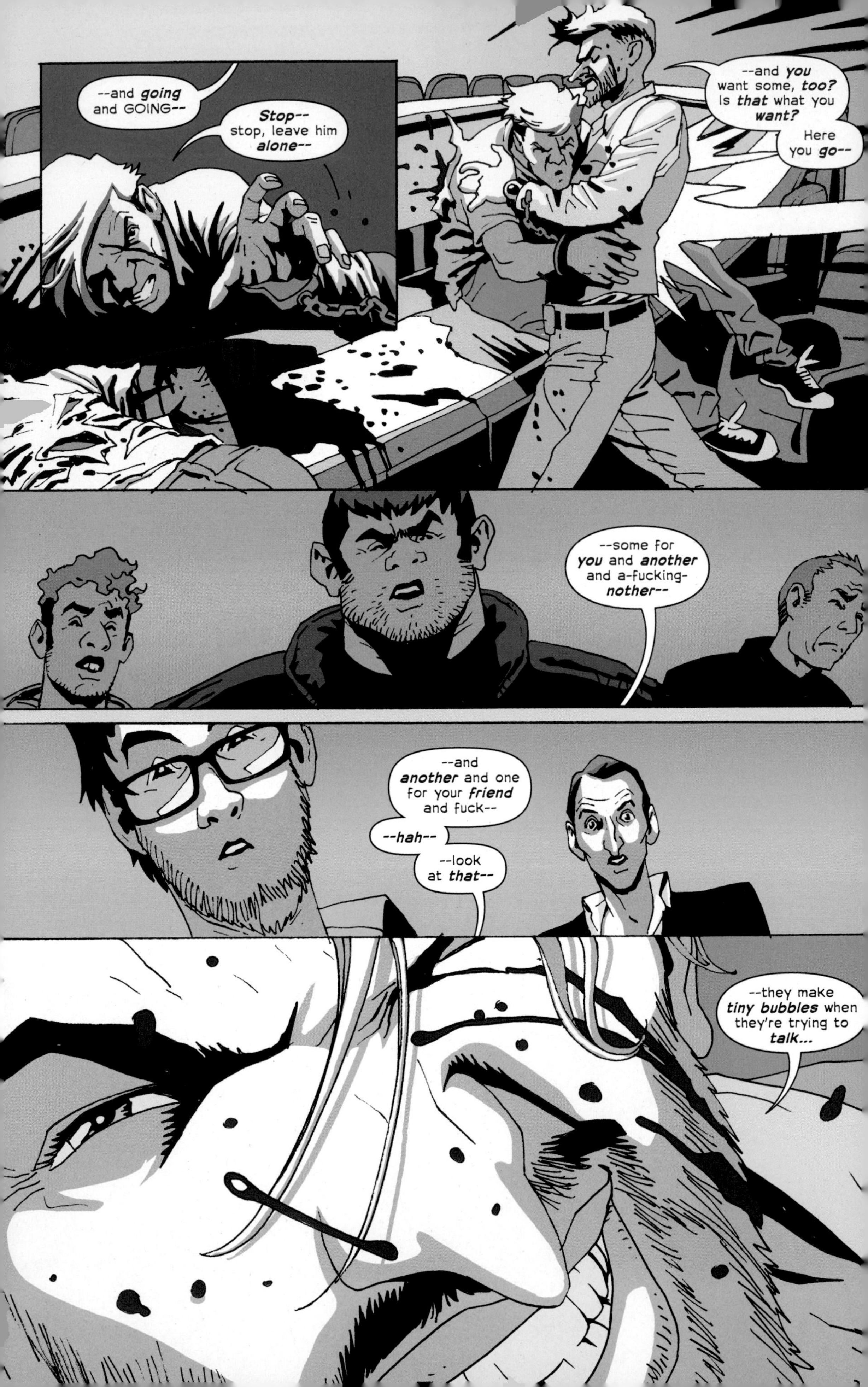
--and *going* and GOING--
Stop-- stop, leave him ***alone***--
--and ***you*** want some, ***too?*** Is ***that*** what you ***want?***
Here you ***go***--
--some for ***you*** and ***another*** and a-fucking-***nother***--
--and ***another*** and one for your ***friend*** and fuck--
--hah--
--look at ***that***--
--they make ***tiny bubbles*** when they're trying to ***talk...***

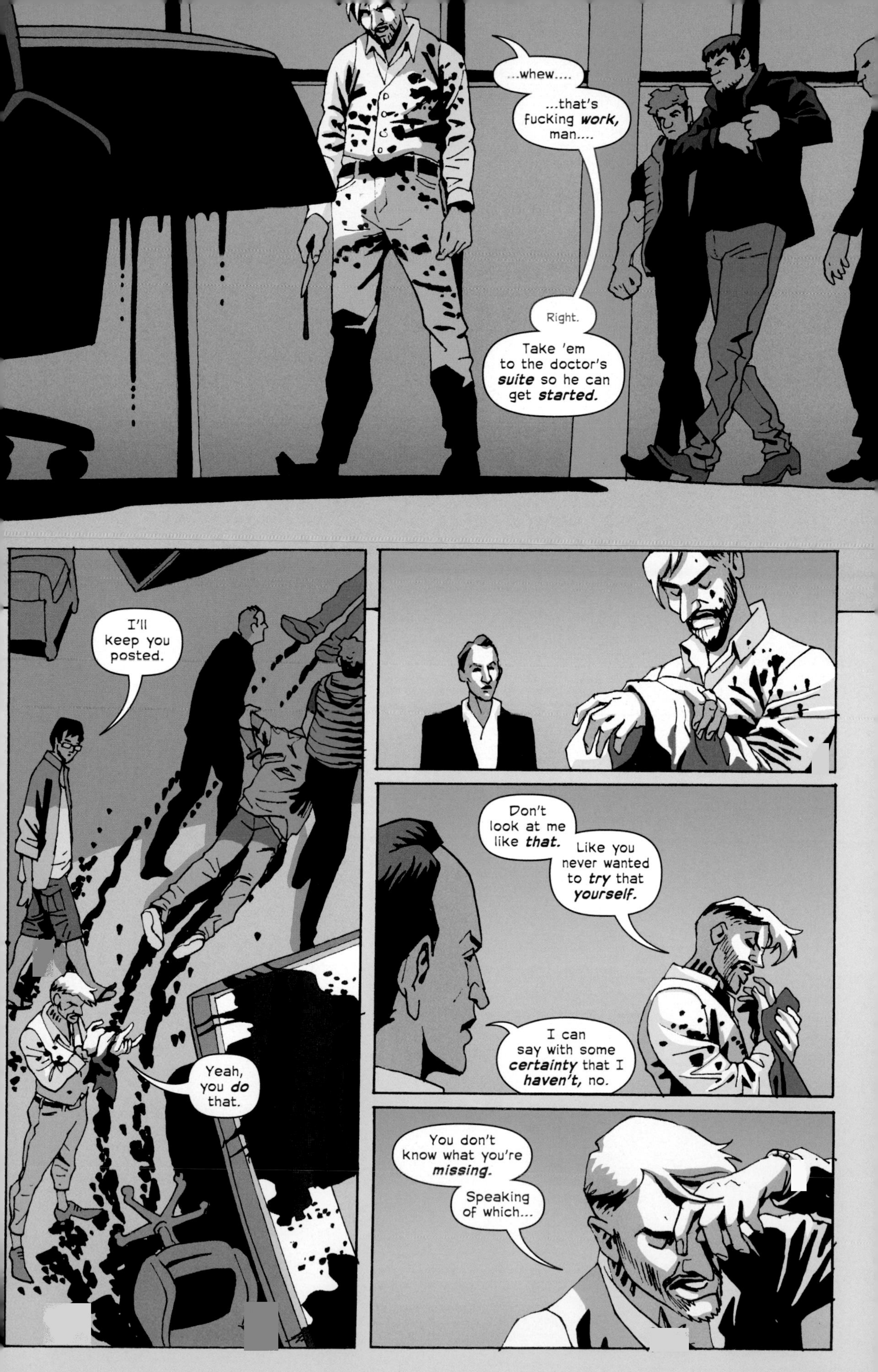
...whew....
...that's fucking work, man....
Right.
Take 'em to the doctor's suite so he can get started.
I'll keep you posted.
Yeah, you do that.
Don't look at me like that.
Like you never wanted to try that yourself.
I can say with some certainty that I haven't, no.
You don't know what you're missing.
Speaking of which...

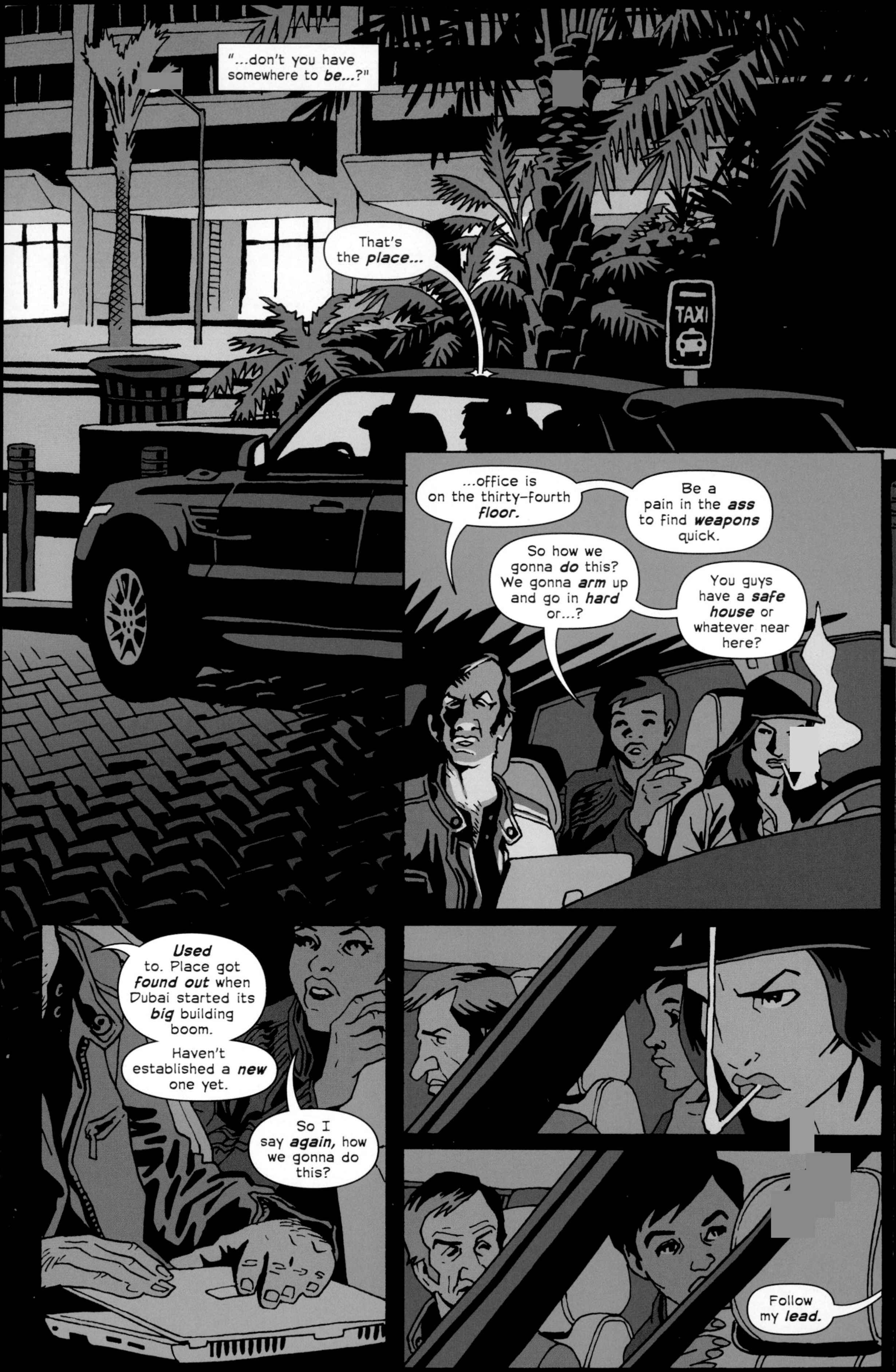
"...don't you have somewhere to be...?"
That's the place...
...office is on the thirty-fourth floor.
Be a pain in the ass to find weapons quick.
So how we gonna do this? We gonna arm up and go in hard or...?
You guys have a safe house or whatever near here?
TAXI
Used to. Place got found out when Dubai started its big building boom.
Haven't established a new one yet.
So I say again, how we gonna do this?
Follow my lead.

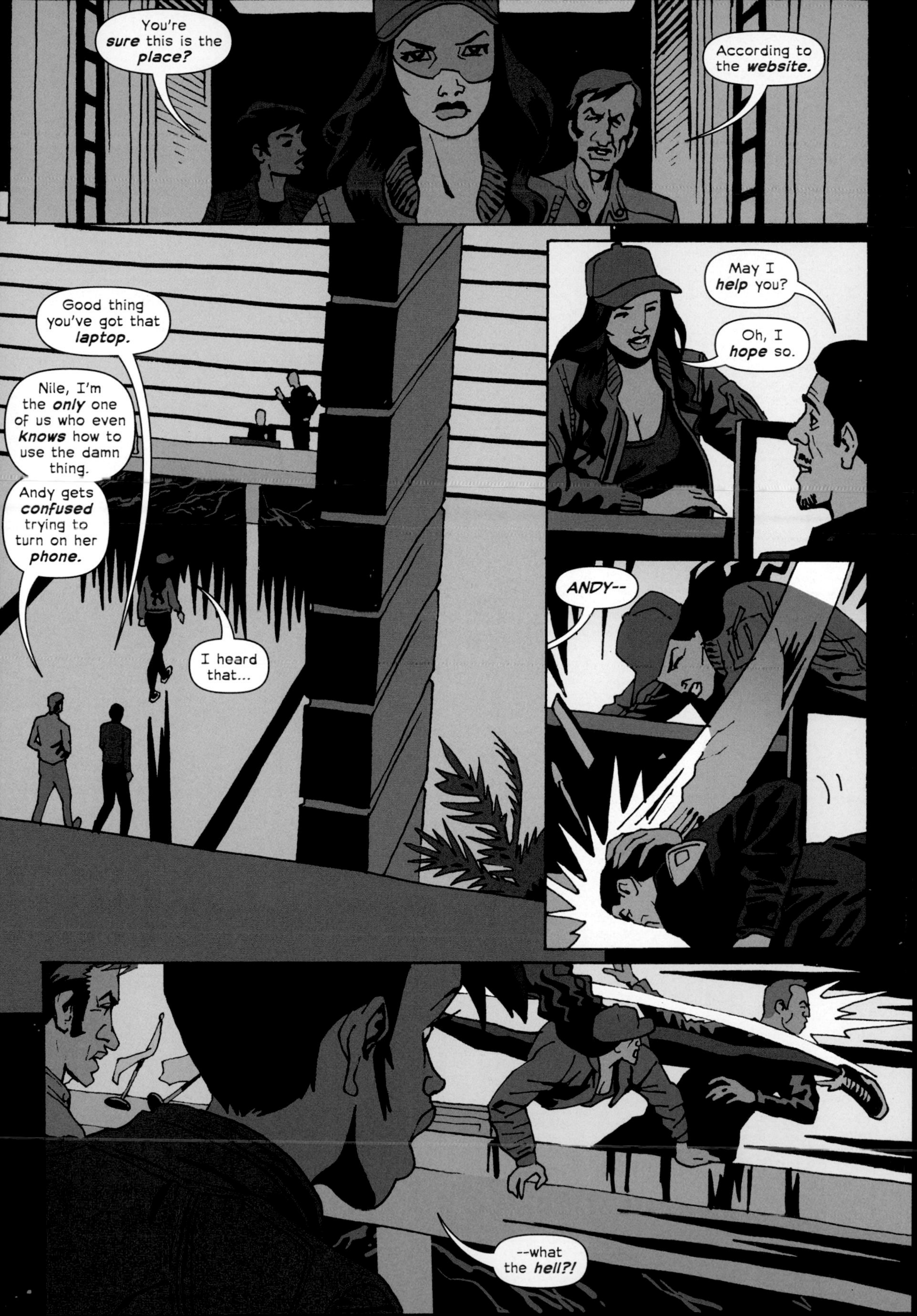
You're sure this is the place?
According to the website.
Good thing you've got that laptop.
Nile, I'm the only one of us who even knows how to use the damn thing.
Andy gets confused trying to turn on her phone.
I heard that...
May I help you?
Oh, I hope so.
ANDY--
--what the hell?!

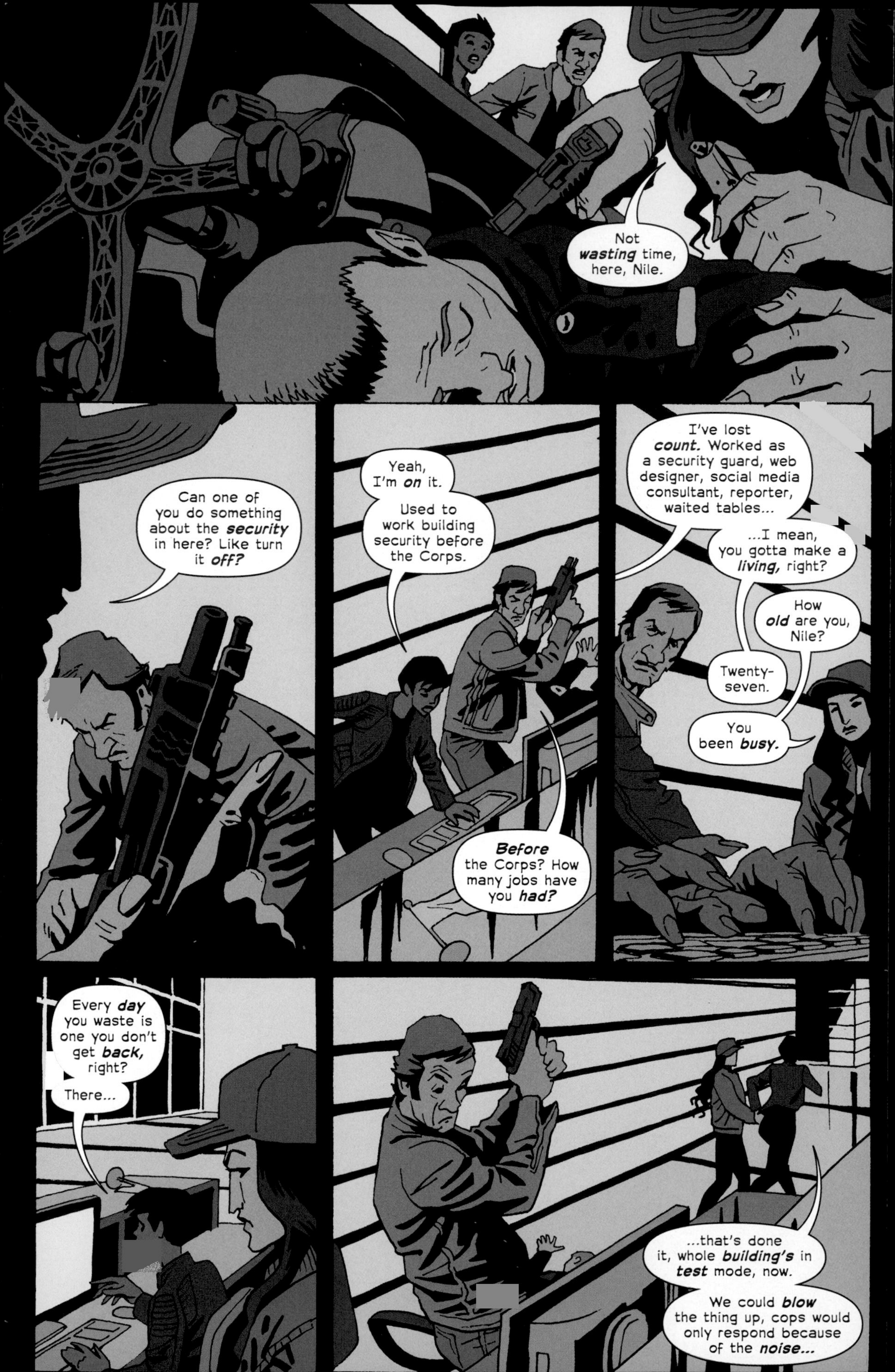
Not *wasting* time, here, Nile.
Can one of you do something about the *security* in here? Like turn it *off?*
Yeah, I'm *on* it.
Used to work building security before the Corps.
Before the Corps? How many jobs have you *had?*
I've lost *count.* Worked as a security guard, web designer, social media consultant, reporter, waited tables...
...I mean, you gotta make a *living,* right?
How *old* are you, Nile?
Twenty-seven.
You been *busy.*
Every *day* you waste is one you don't get *back,* right?
There...
...that's done it, whole *building's* in *test* mode, now.
We could *blow* the thing up, cops would only respond because of the *noise...*

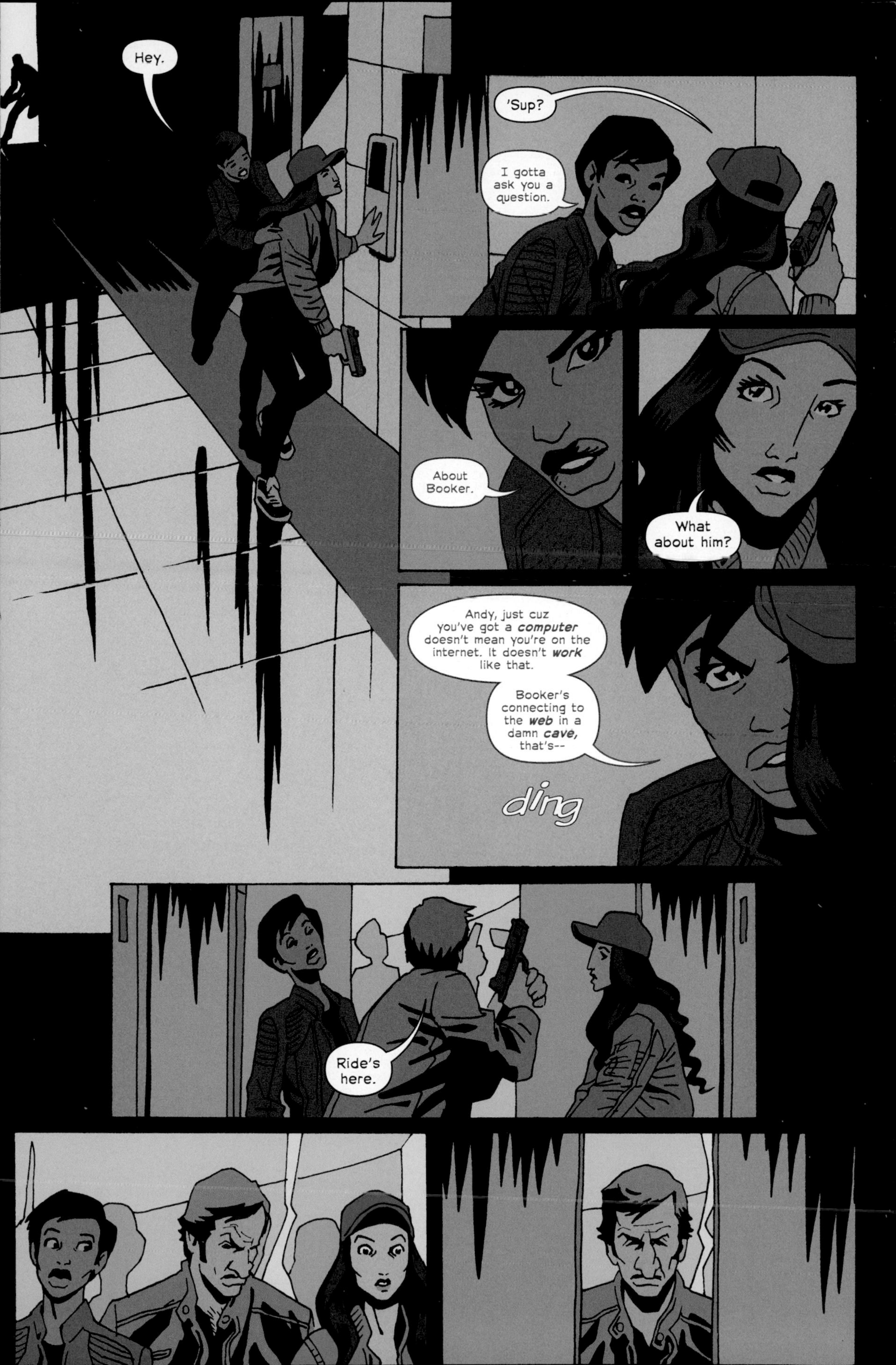
Hey.
'Sup?
I gotta ask you a question.
About Booker.
What about him?
Andy, just cuz you've got a ***computer*** doesn't mean you're on the internet. It doesn't ***work*** like that.
Booker's connecting to the ***web*** in a damn ***cave,*** that's--
ding
Ride's here.

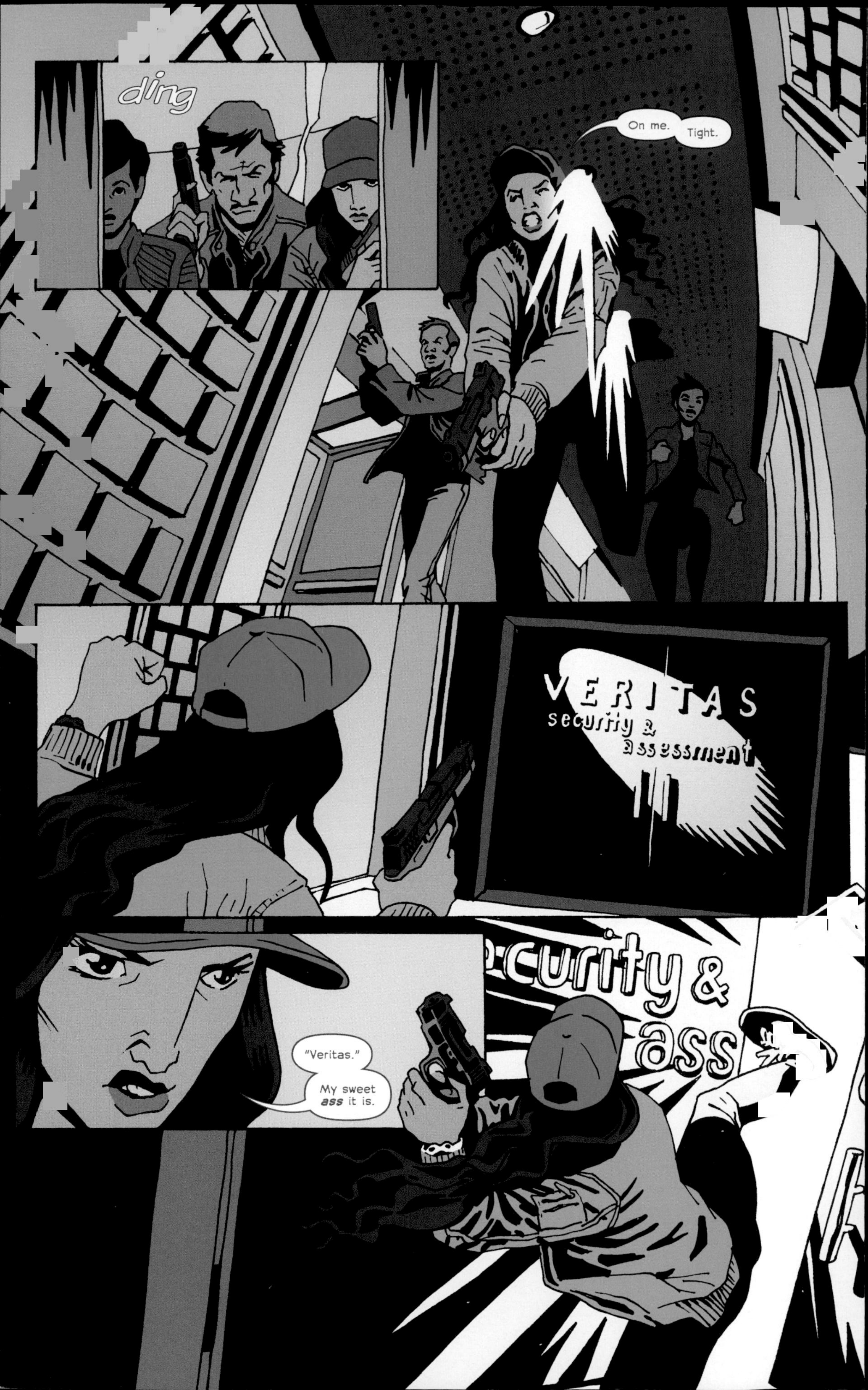
ding
On me.
Tight.
VERITAS
security &
assessment
"Veritas."
My sweet ***ass*** it is.

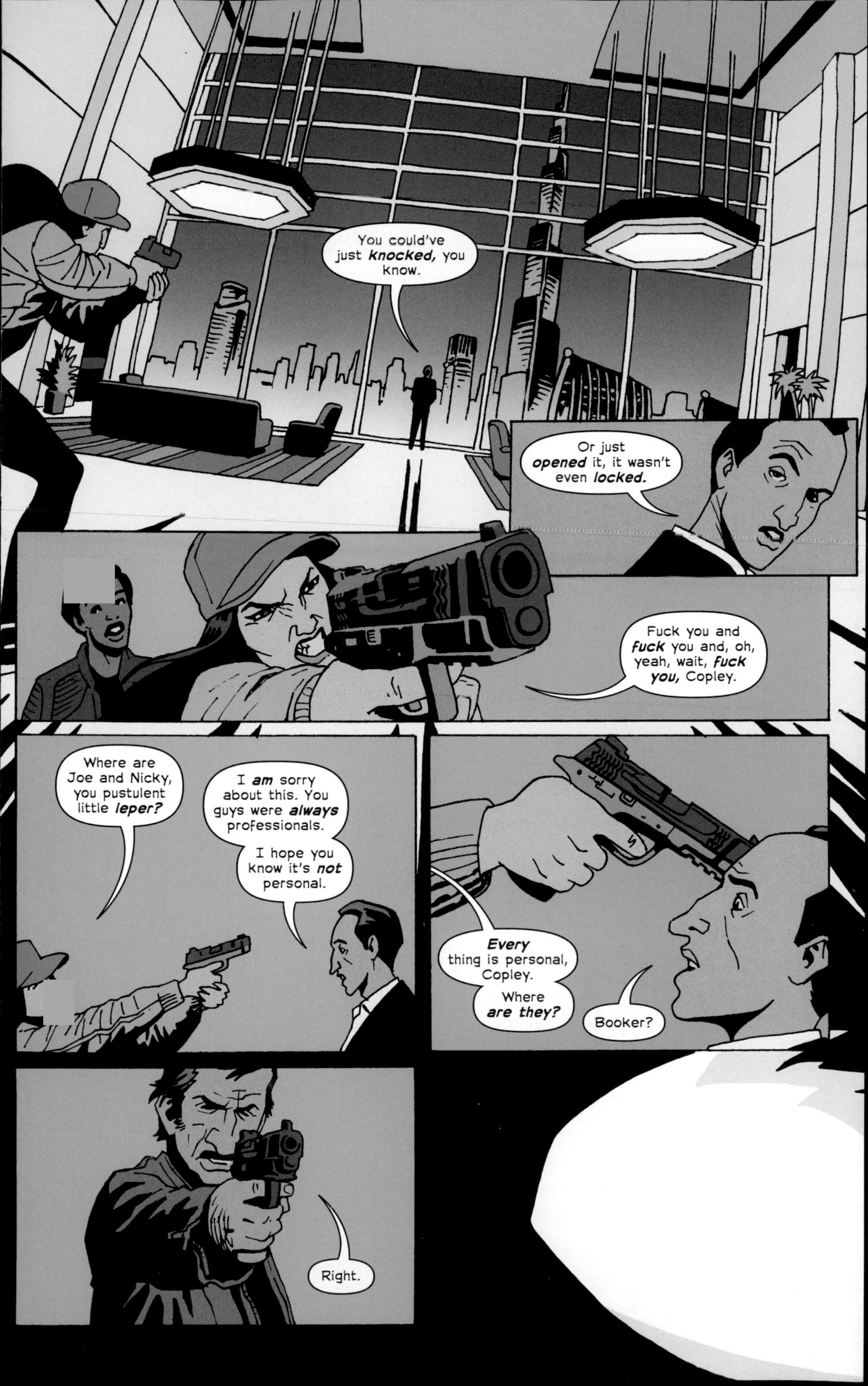
You could've just *knocked,* you know.
Or just *opened* it, it wasn't even *locked.*
Fuck you and *fuck* you and, oh, yeah, wait, *fuck you,* Copley.
Where are Joe and Nicky, you pustulent little *leper?*
I *am* sorry about this. You guys were *always* professionals.
I hope you know it's *not* personal.
Every thing is personal, Copley.
Where *are they?*
Booker?
Right.

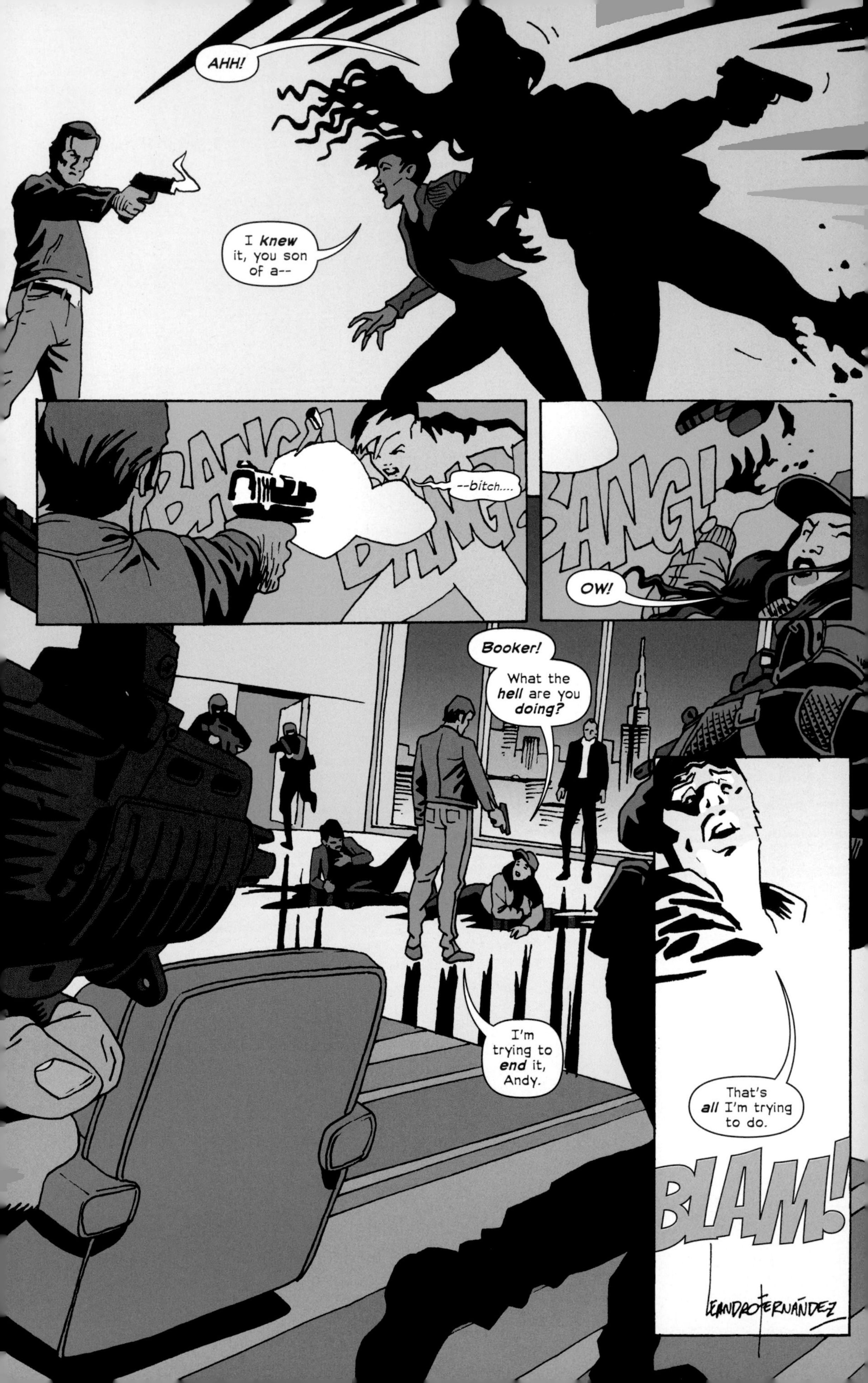
AHH!
I knew it, you son of a--
BANG!
BANG!
--bitch....
BANG!
OW!
Booker!
What the hell are you doing?
I'm trying to end it, Andy.
That's all I'm trying to do.
BLAM!
LEANDRO FERNÁNDEZ

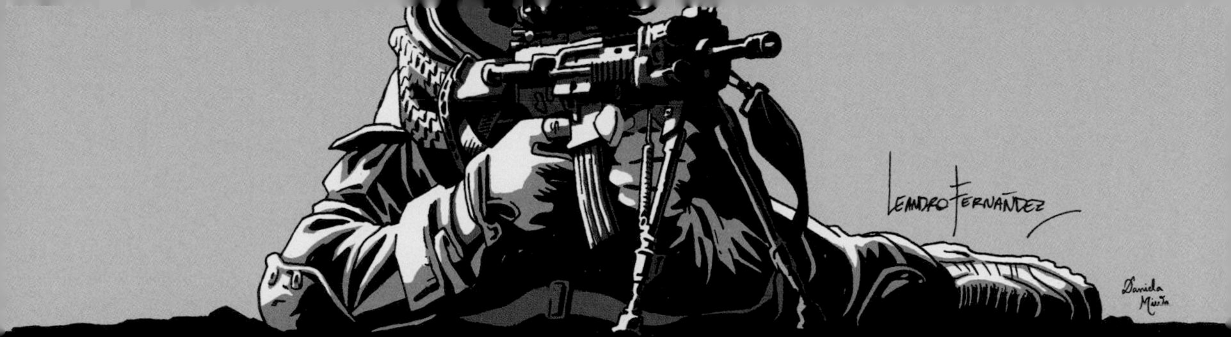
LEANDRO FERNÁNDEZ

CHAPTER FIVE

"IT IS MORE **SHAMEFUL** TO **DISTRUST** OUR FRIENDS THAN TO BE **DECEIVED** BY THEM."

~CONFUCIUS

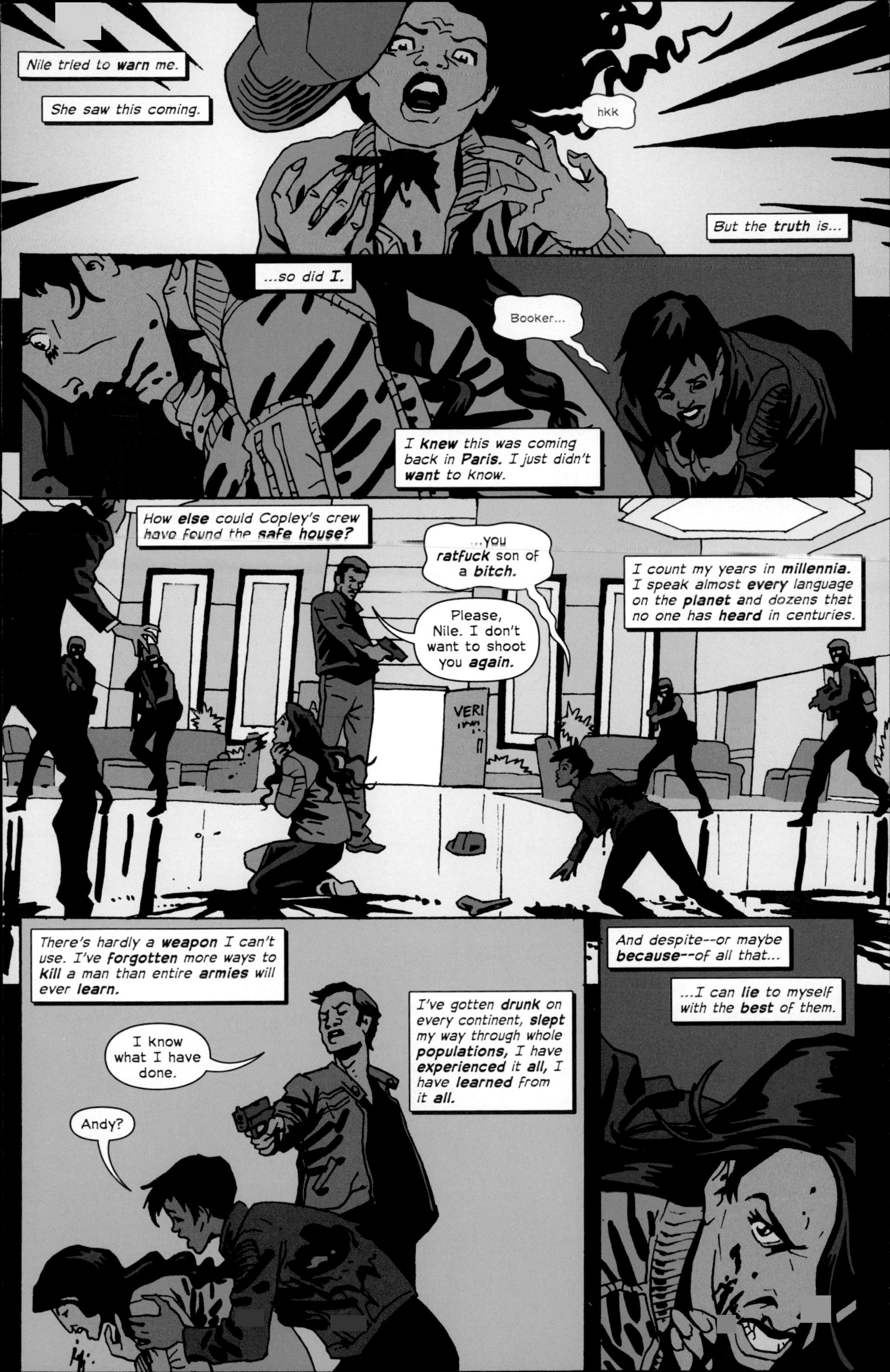

Nile tried to warn me.
She saw this coming.
hkk
But the truth is...
...so did I.
Booker...
I knew this was coming back in Paris. I just didn't want to know.
How else could Copley's crew have found the safe house?
...you ratfuck son of a bitch.
Please, Nile. I don't want to shoot you again.
I count my years in millennia. I speak almost every language on the planet and dozens that no one has heard in centuries.
VERI
There's hardly a weapon I can't use. I've forgotten more ways to kill a man than entire armies will ever learn.
I know what I have done.
I've gotten drunk on every continent, slept my way through whole populations, I have experienced it all, I have learned from it all.
Andy?
And despite--or maybe because--of all that...
...I can lie to myself with the best of them.

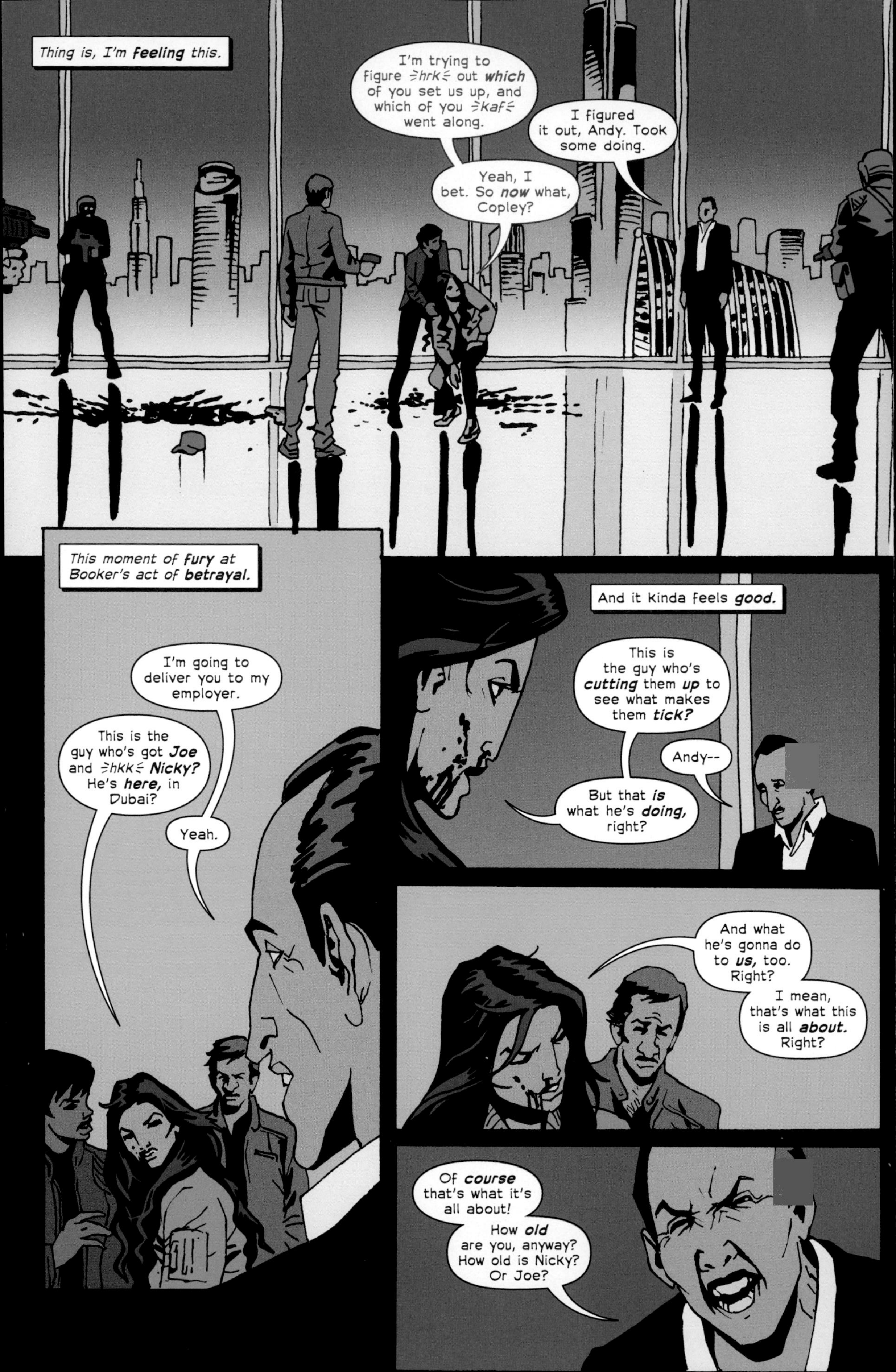

Thing is, I'm **feeling** this.
I'm trying to figure =hrk= out **which** of you set us up, and which of you =kaf= went along.
I figured it out, Andy. Took some doing.
Yeah, I bet. So **now** what, Copley?
This moment of **fury** at Booker's act of **betrayal.**
I'm going to deliver you to my employer.
This is the guy who's got **Joe** and =hkk= **Nicky?** He's **here,** in Dubai?
Yeah.
And it kinda feels **good.**
This is the guy who's **cutting** them **up** to see what makes them **tick?**
Andy--
But that **is** what he's **doing,** right?
And what he's gonna do to **us,** too. Right?
I mean, that's what this is all **about.** Right?
Of **course** that's what it's all about!
How **old** are you, anyway? How old is Nicky? Or Joe?

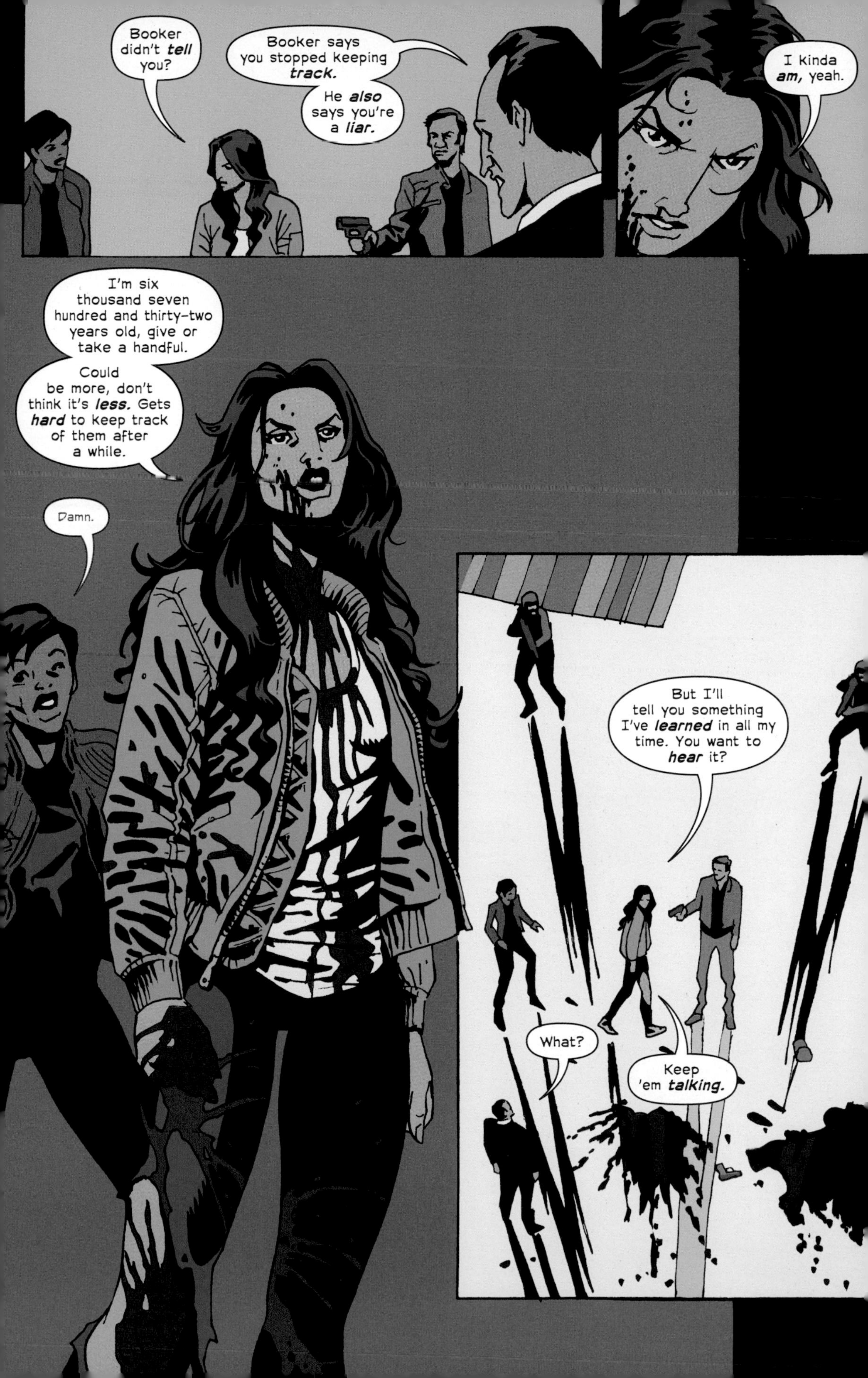
Booker didn't *tell* you?
Booker says you stopped keeping *track.*
He *also* says you're a *liar.*
I kinda *am,* yeah.
I'm six thousand seven hundred and thirty-two years old, give or take a handful.
Could be more, don't think it's *less.* Gets *hard* to keep track of them after a while.
Damn.
But I'll tell you something I've *learned* in all my time. You want to *hear* it?
What?
Keep 'em *talking.*

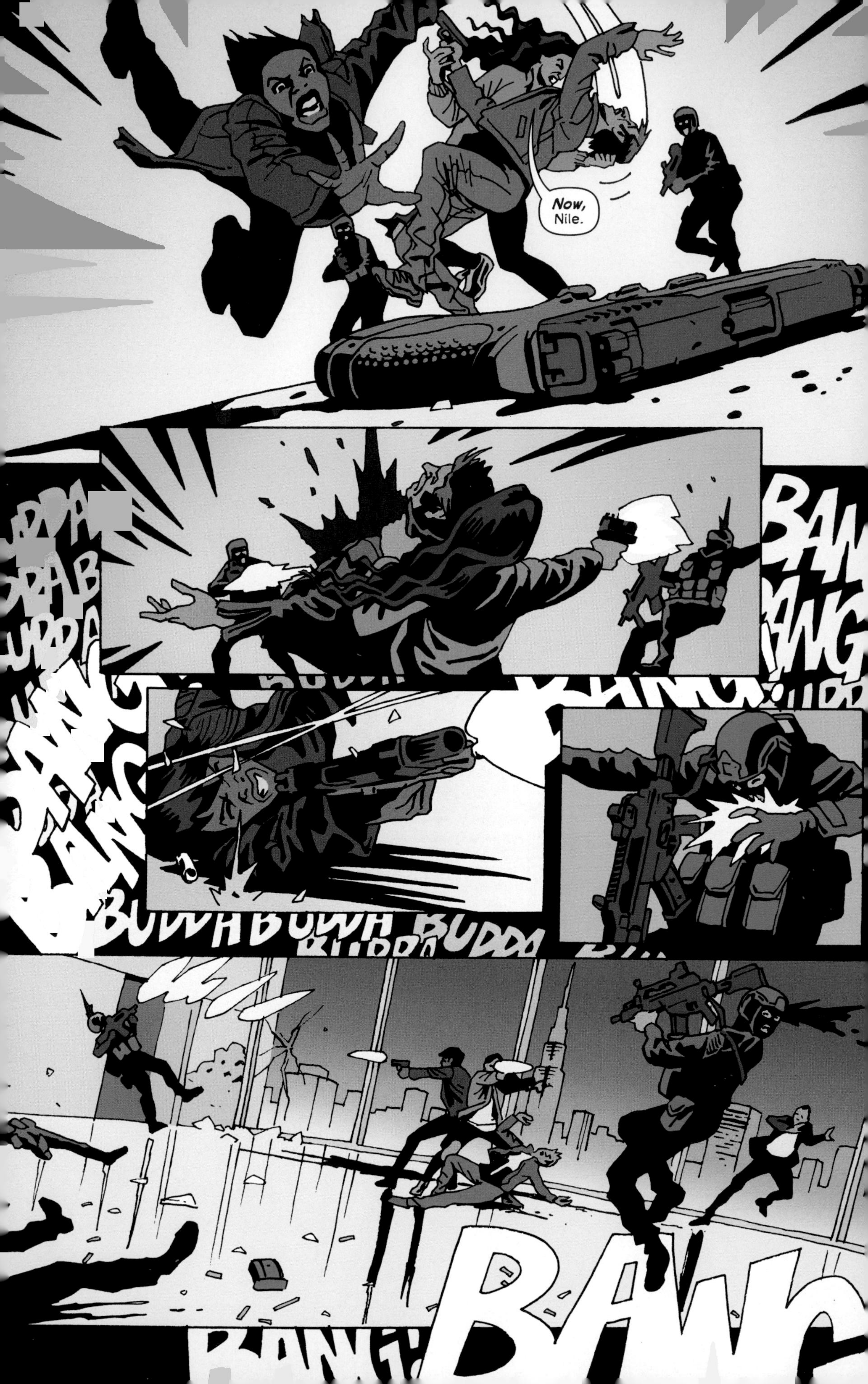
Now, Nile.
BUDDA BUDDA BUDDA

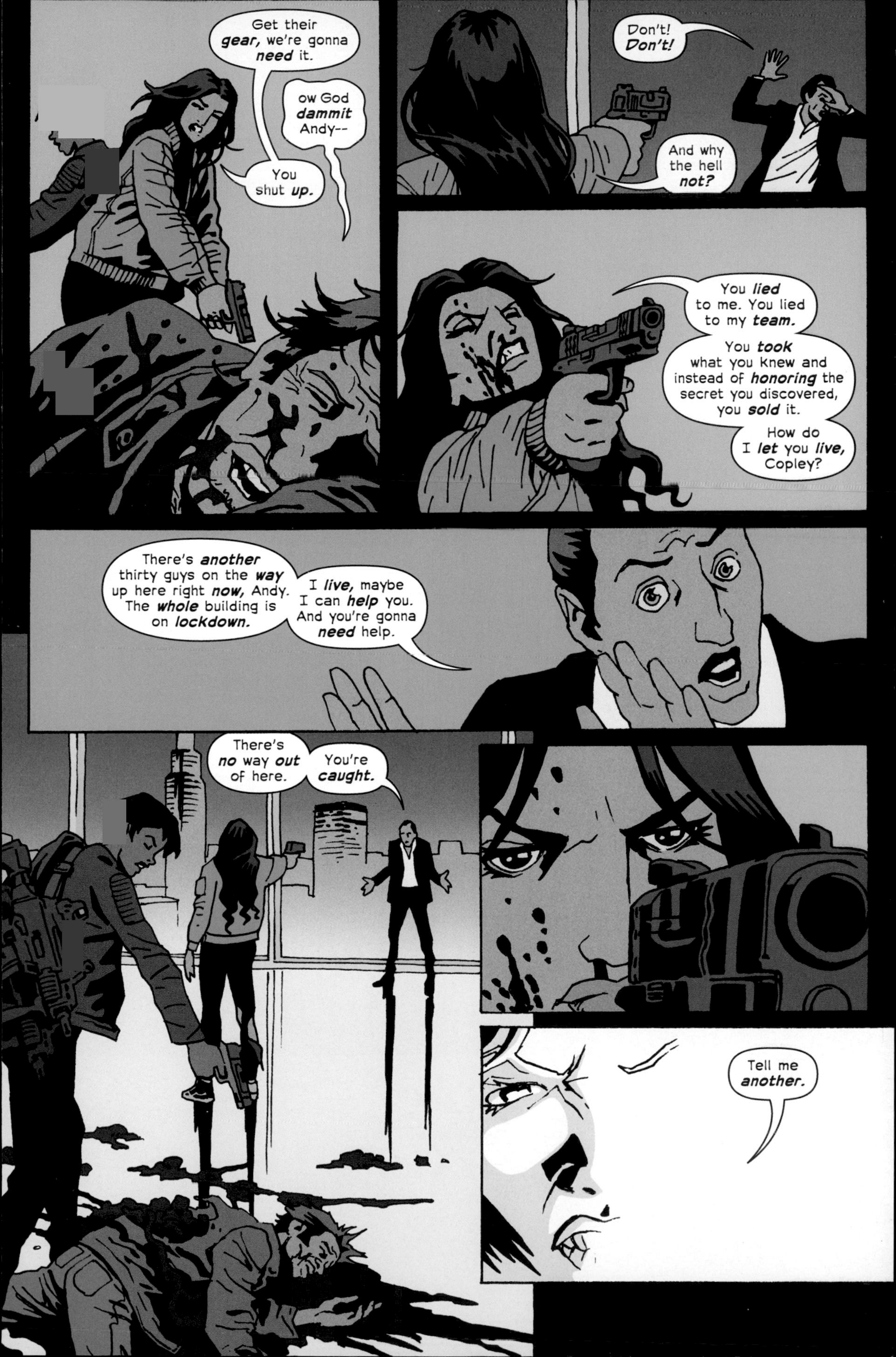
Get their gear, we're gonna need it.
ow God dammit Andy--
You shut up.
Don't! Don't!
And why the hell not?
You lied to me. You lied to my team.
You took what you knew and instead of honoring the secret you discovered, you sold it.
How do I let you live, Copley?
There's another thirty guys on the way up here right now, Andy. The whole building is on lockdown.
I live, maybe I can help you. And you're gonna need help.
There's no way out of here.
You're caught.
Tell me another.

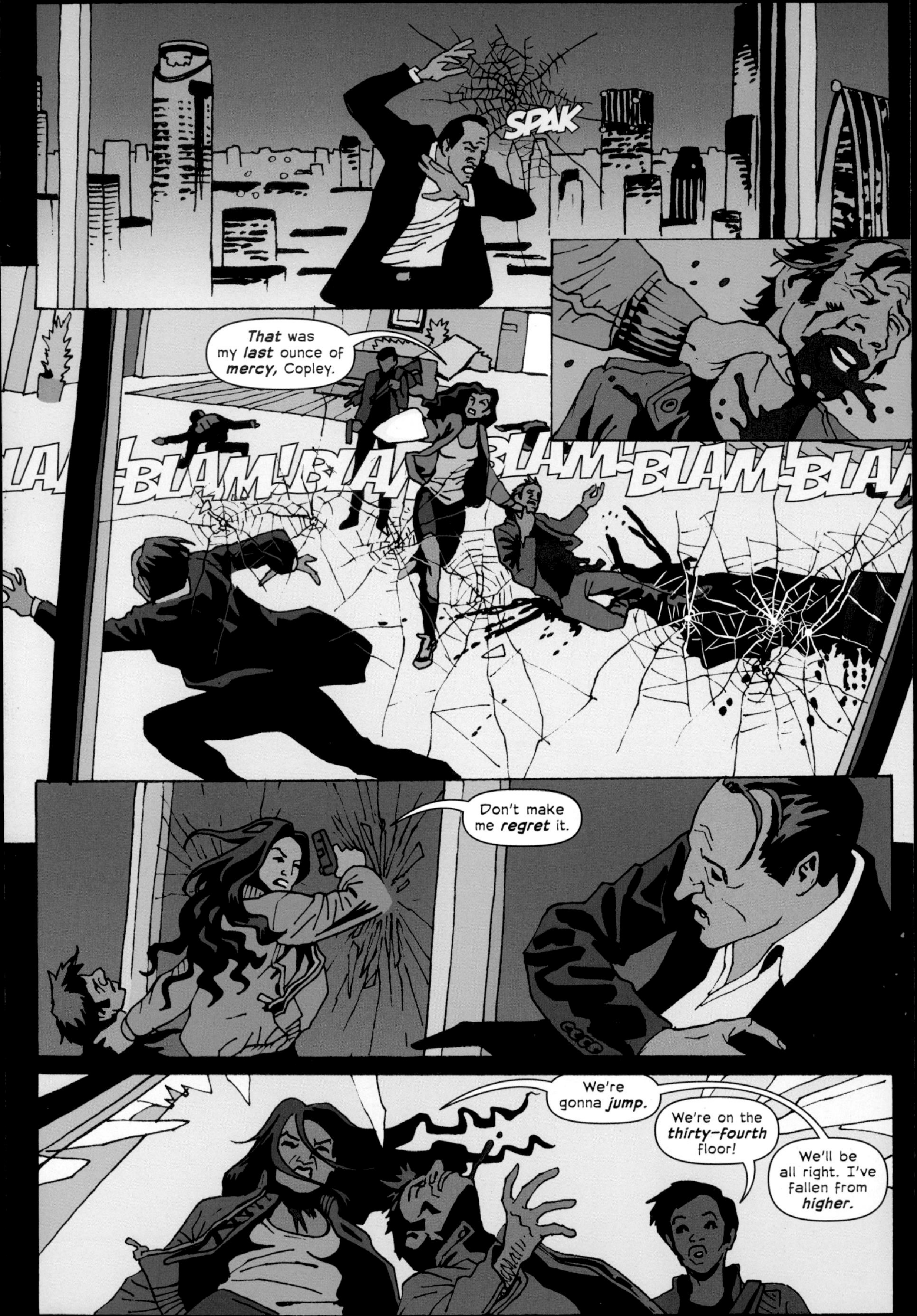

SPAK
That was my last ounce of mercy, Copley.
BLAM! BLAM! BLAM BLAM BLAM
Don't make me regret it.
We're gonna jump.
We're on the thirty-fourth floor!
We'll be all right. I've fallen from higher.

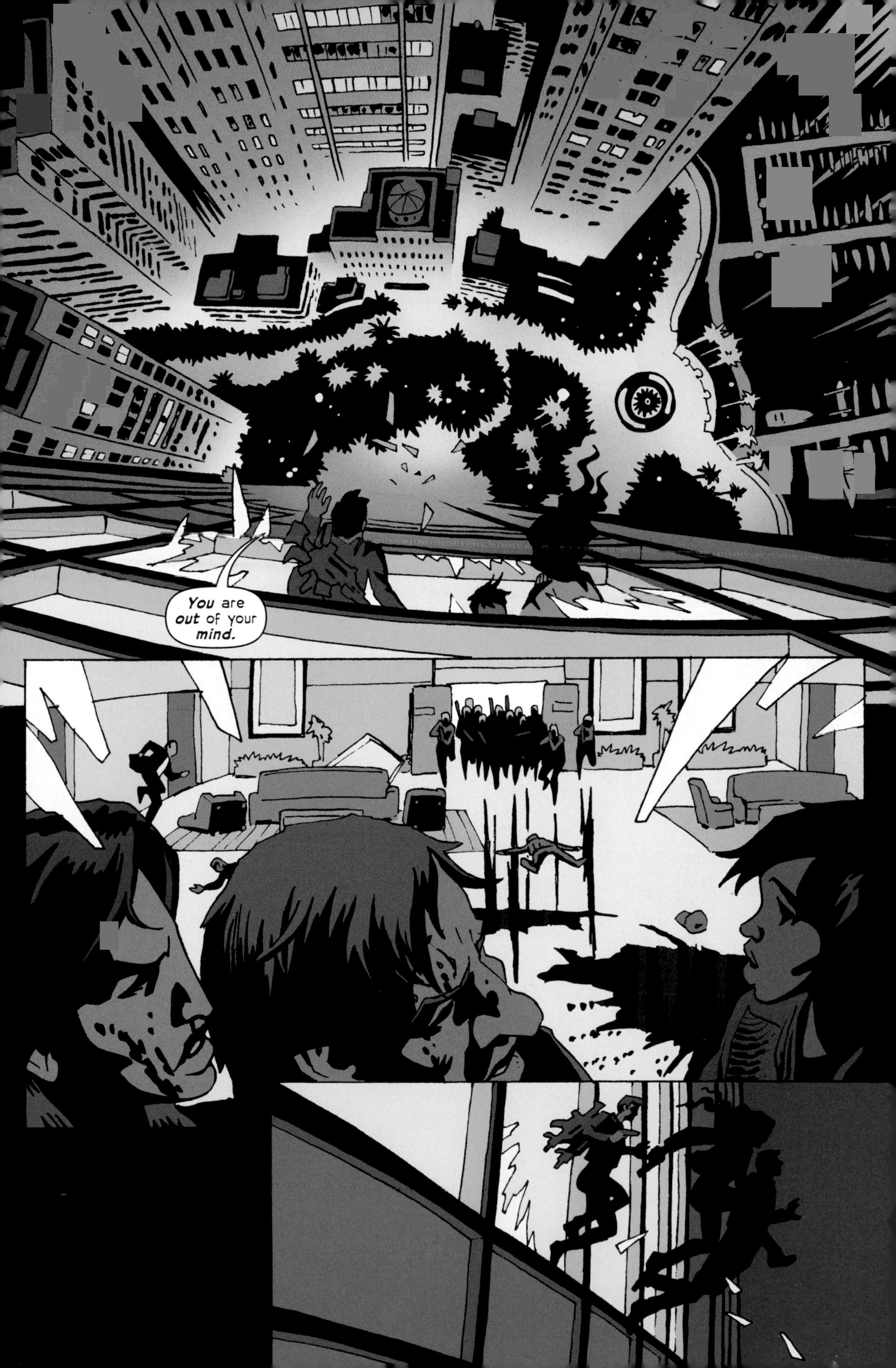
You are out of your mind.

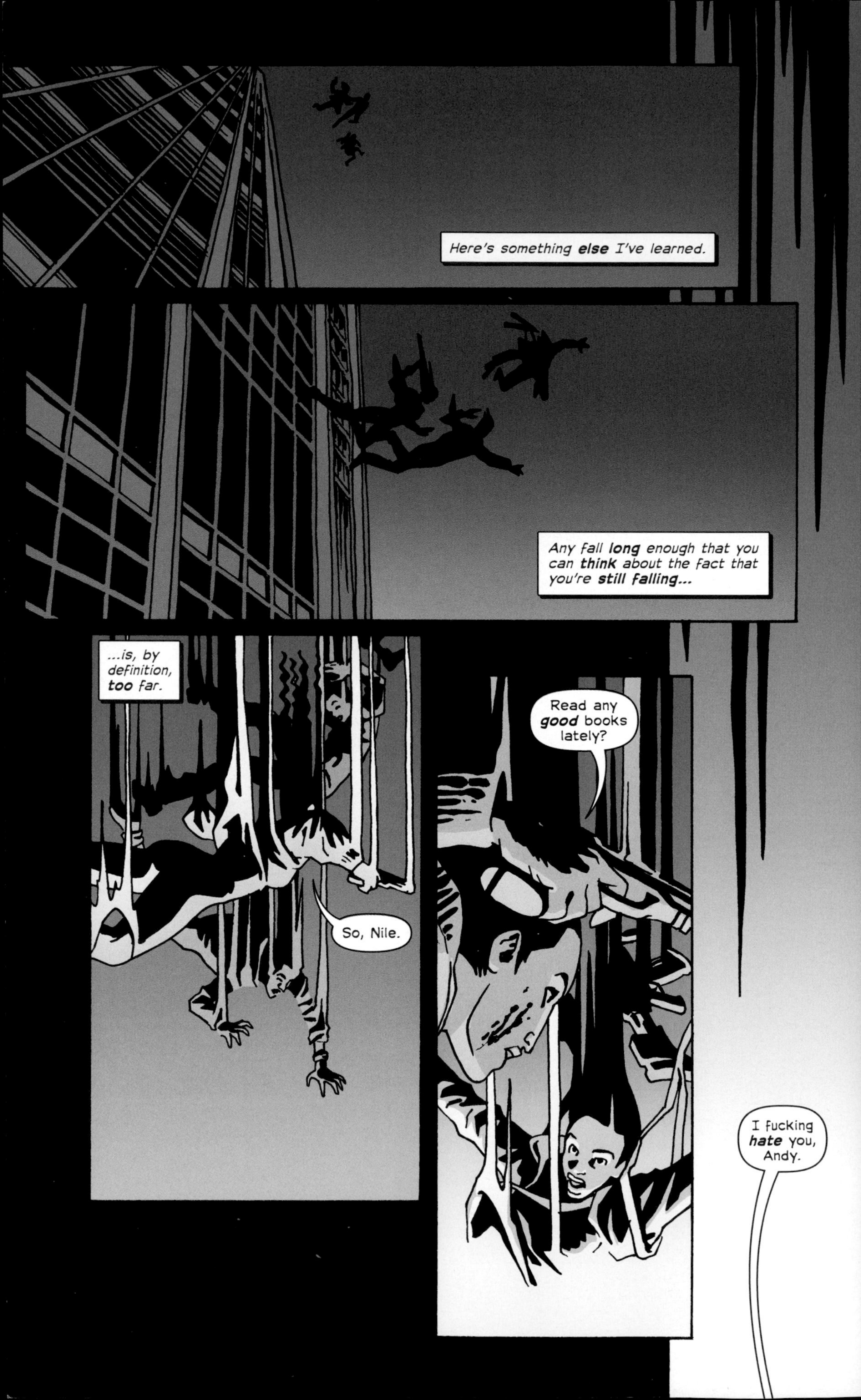
Here's something **else** I've learned.
Any fall **long** enough that you can **think** about the fact that you're **still falling...**
...is, by definition, **too** far.
So, Nile.
Read any **good** books lately?
I fucking **hate** you, Andy.

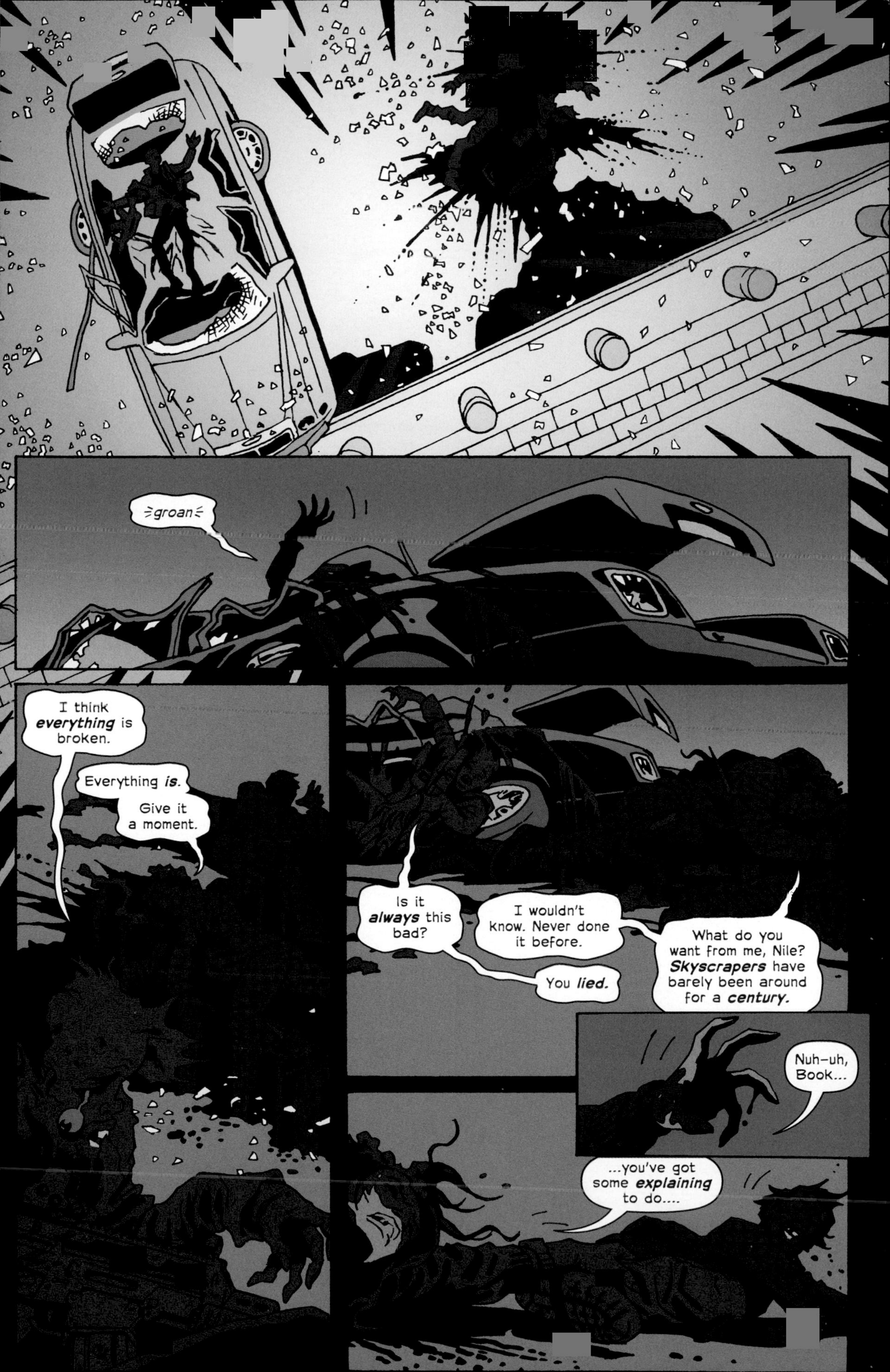
groan
I think everything is broken.
Everything is.
Give it a moment.
Is it always this bad?
I wouldn't know. Never done it before.
You lied.
What do you want from me, Nile? Skyscrapers have barely been around for a century.
Nuh-uh, Book...
...you've got some explaining to do....

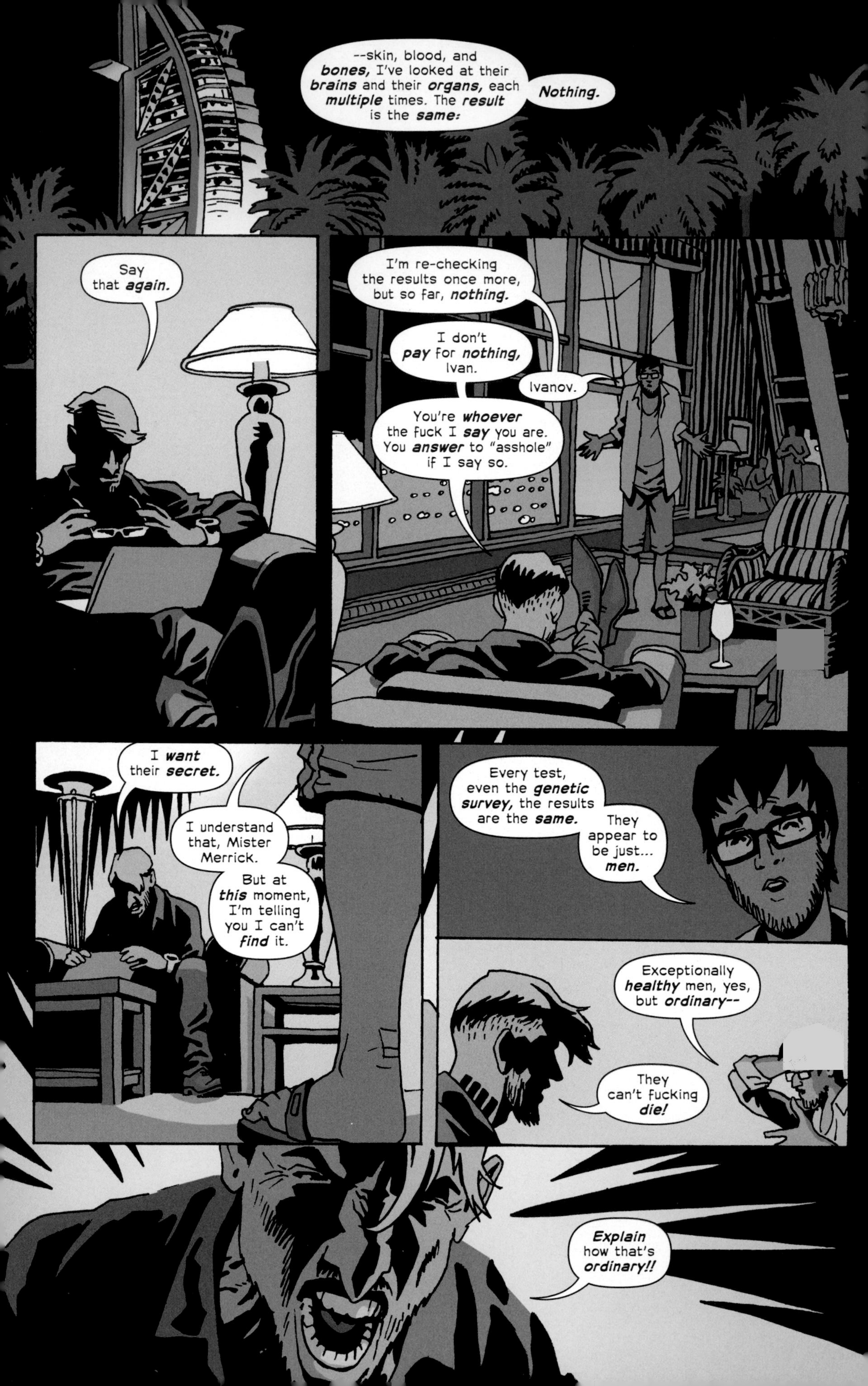
--skin, blood, and bones, I've looked at their brains and their organs, each multiple times. The result is the same:
Nothing.
Say that again.
I'm re-checking the results once more, but so far, nothing.
I don't pay for nothing, Ivan.
Ivanov.
You're whoever the fuck I say you are. You answer to "asshole" if I say so.
I want their secret.
I understand that, Mister Merrick.
But at this moment, I'm telling you I can't find it.
Every test, even the genetic survey, the results are the same.
They appear to be just... men.
Exceptionally healthy men, yes, but ordinary--
They can't fucking die!
Explain how that's ordinary!!

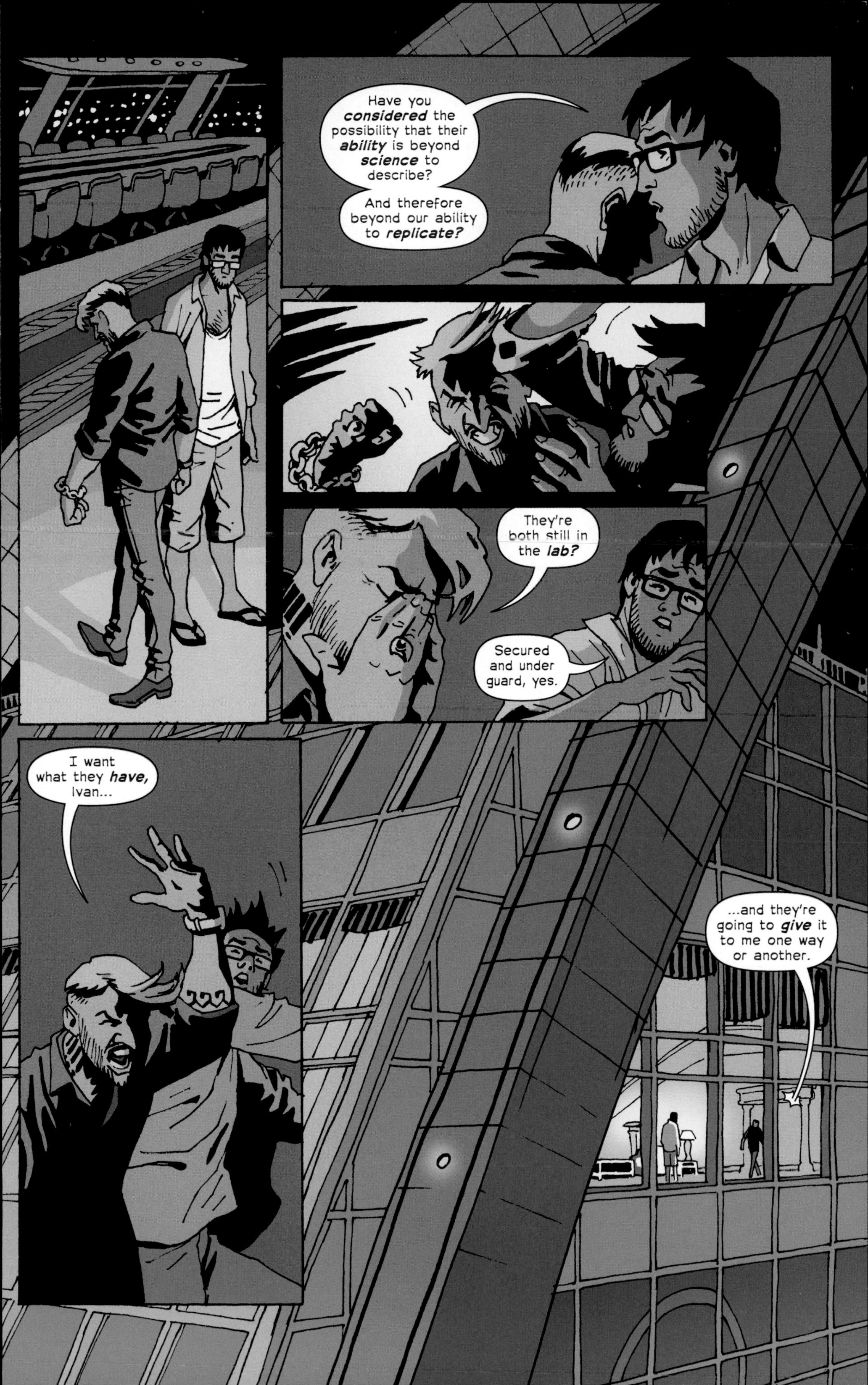

Have you *considered* the possibility that their *ability* is beyond *science* to describe?
And therefore beyond our ability to *replicate?*
They're both still in the *lab?*
Secured and under guard, yes.
I want what they *have,* Ivan...
...and they're going to *give* it to me one way or another.

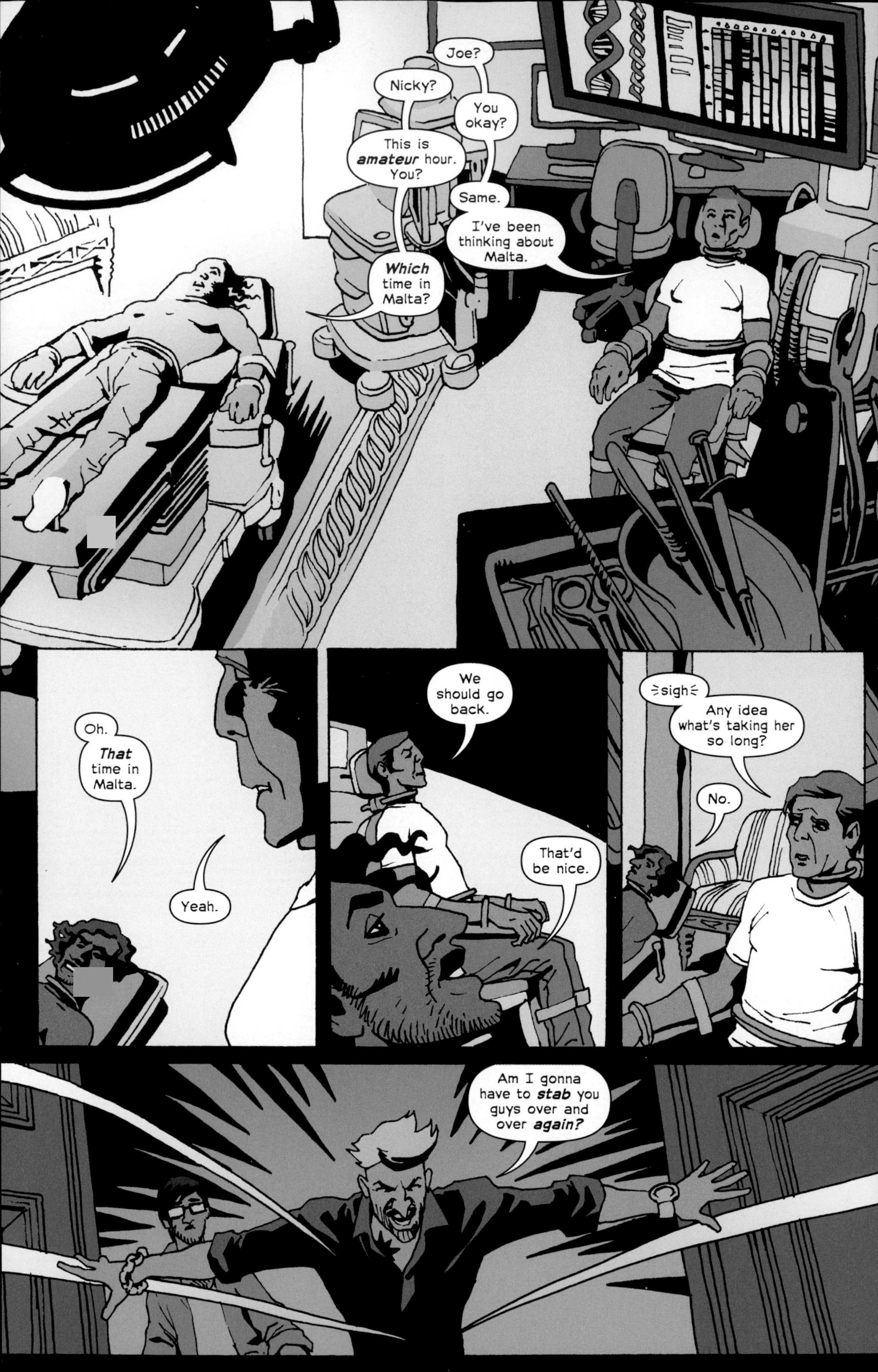
Joe?
Nicky?
You okay?
This is *amateur* hour. You?
Same.
I've been thinking about Malta.
Which time in Malta?
Oh. *That* time in Malta.
Yeah.
We should go back.
That'd be nice.
sigh
Any idea what's taking her so long?
No.
Am I gonna have to *stab* you guys over and over *again?*

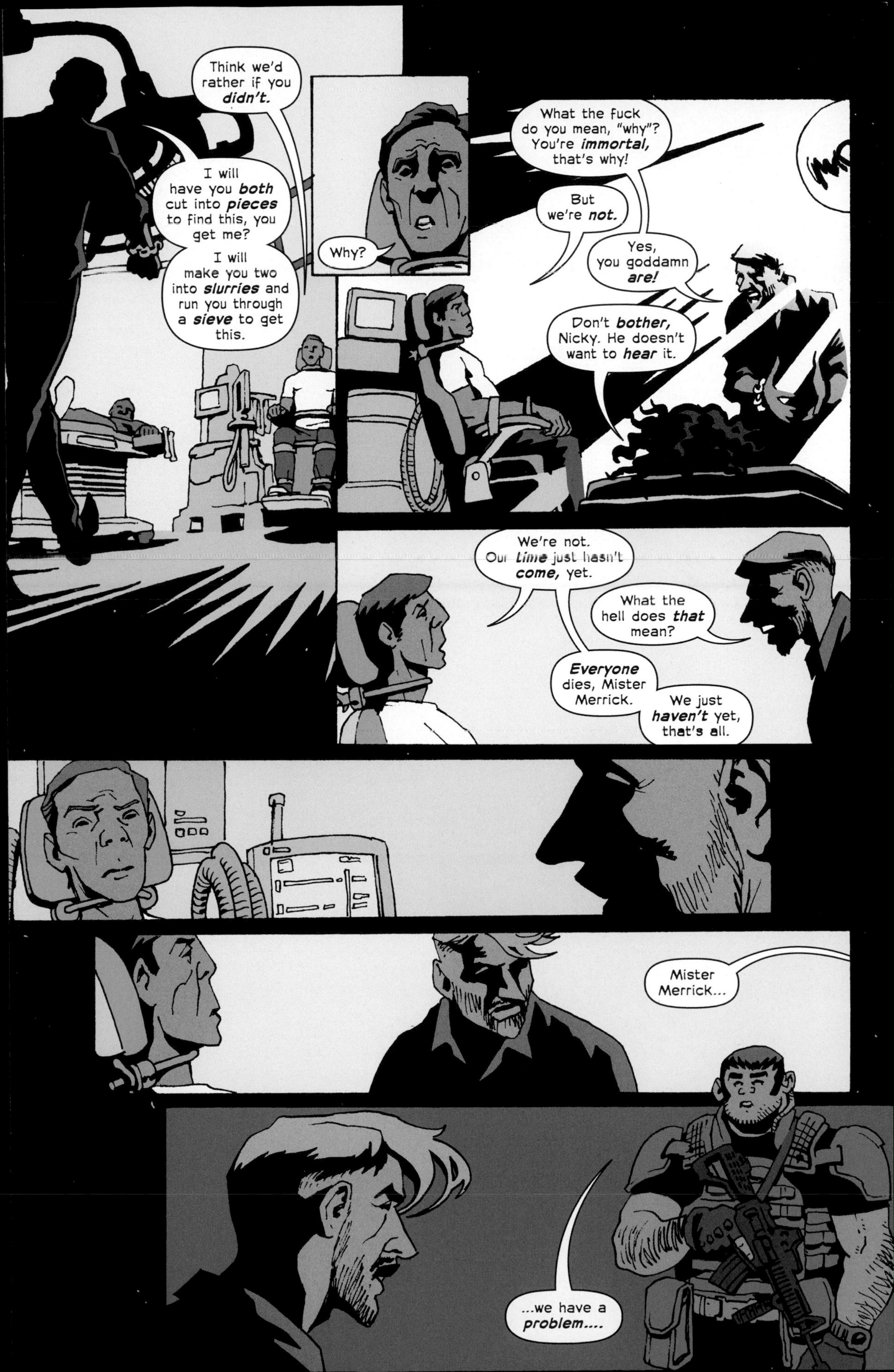
Think we'd rather if you didn't.
I will have you both cut into pieces to find this, you get me?
I will make you two into slurries and run you through a sieve to get this.
Why?
What the fuck do you mean, "why"? You're immortal, that's why!
But we're not.
Yes, you goddamn are!
Don't bother, Nicky. He doesn't want to hear it.
We're not. Our time just hasn't come, yet.
What the hell does that mean?
Everyone dies, Mister Merrick.
We just haven't yet, that's all.
Mister Merrick...
...we have a problem....

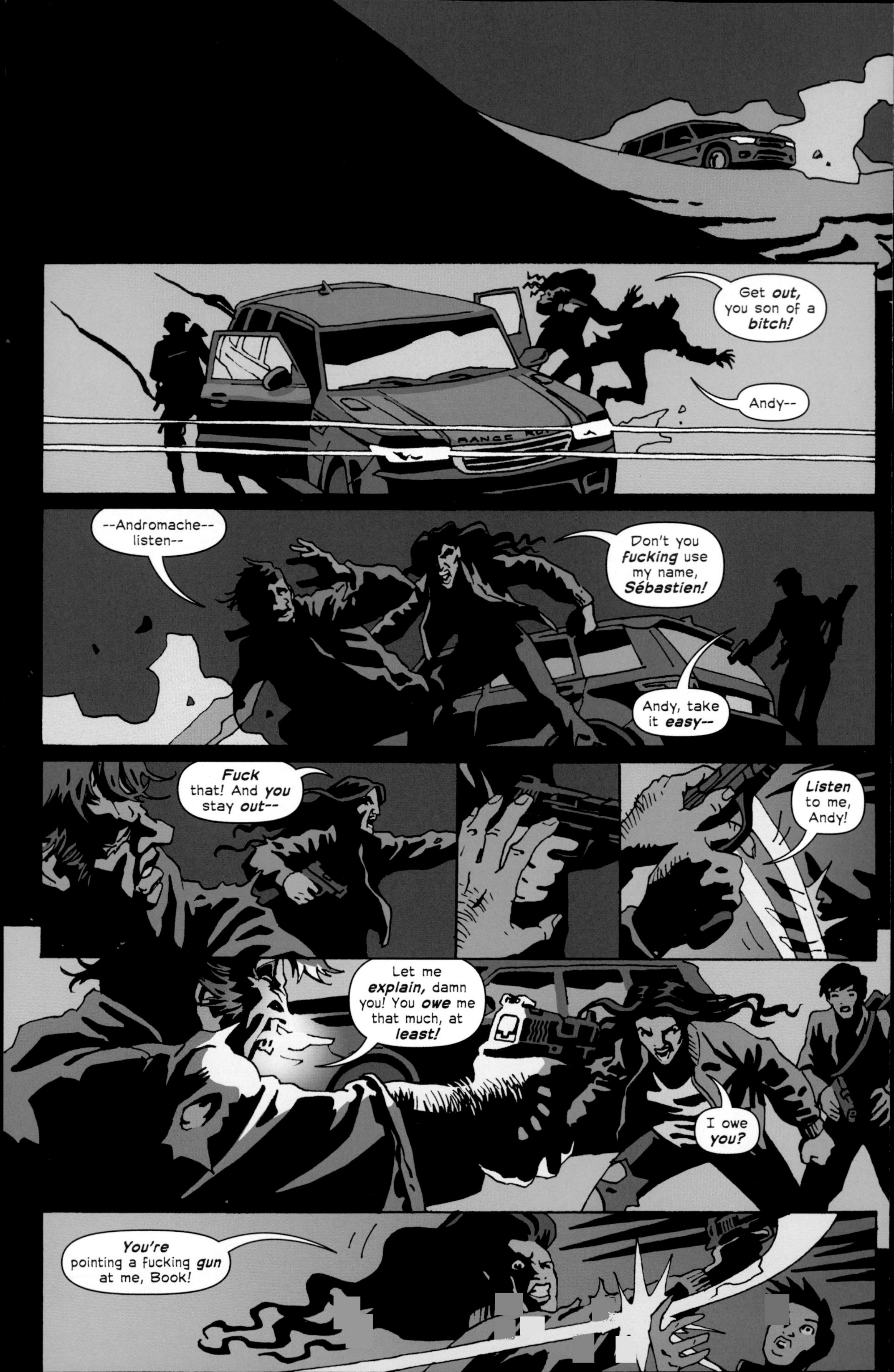
Get out, you son of a bitch!
Andy--
RANGE RO
--Andromache-- listen--
Don't you fucking use my name, Sébastien!
Andy, take it easy--
Fuck that! And you stay out--
Listen to me, Andy!
Let me explain, damn you! You owe me that much, at least!
I owe you?
You're pointing a fucking gun at me, Book!

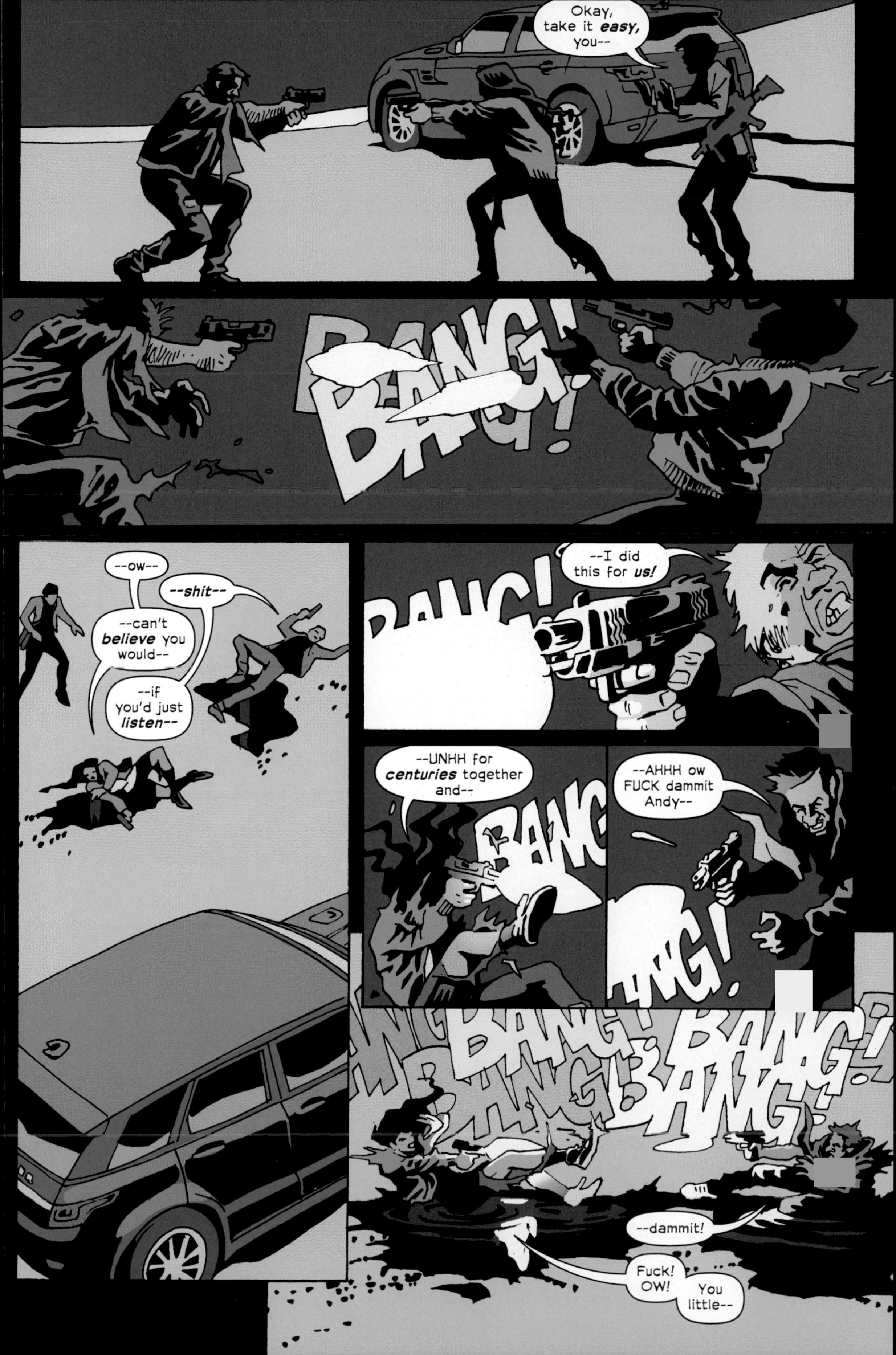
Okay, take it *easy,* you--
BANG! BANG!
--ow--
--shit--
--can't *believe* you would--
--if you'd just *listen--*
--I did this for *us!*
BANG!
--UNHH for *centuries* together and--
BANG
--AHHH ow FUCK dammit Andy--
BANG!
BANG! BANG! BANG! BANG! BANG!
--dammit!
Fuck! OW!
You little--

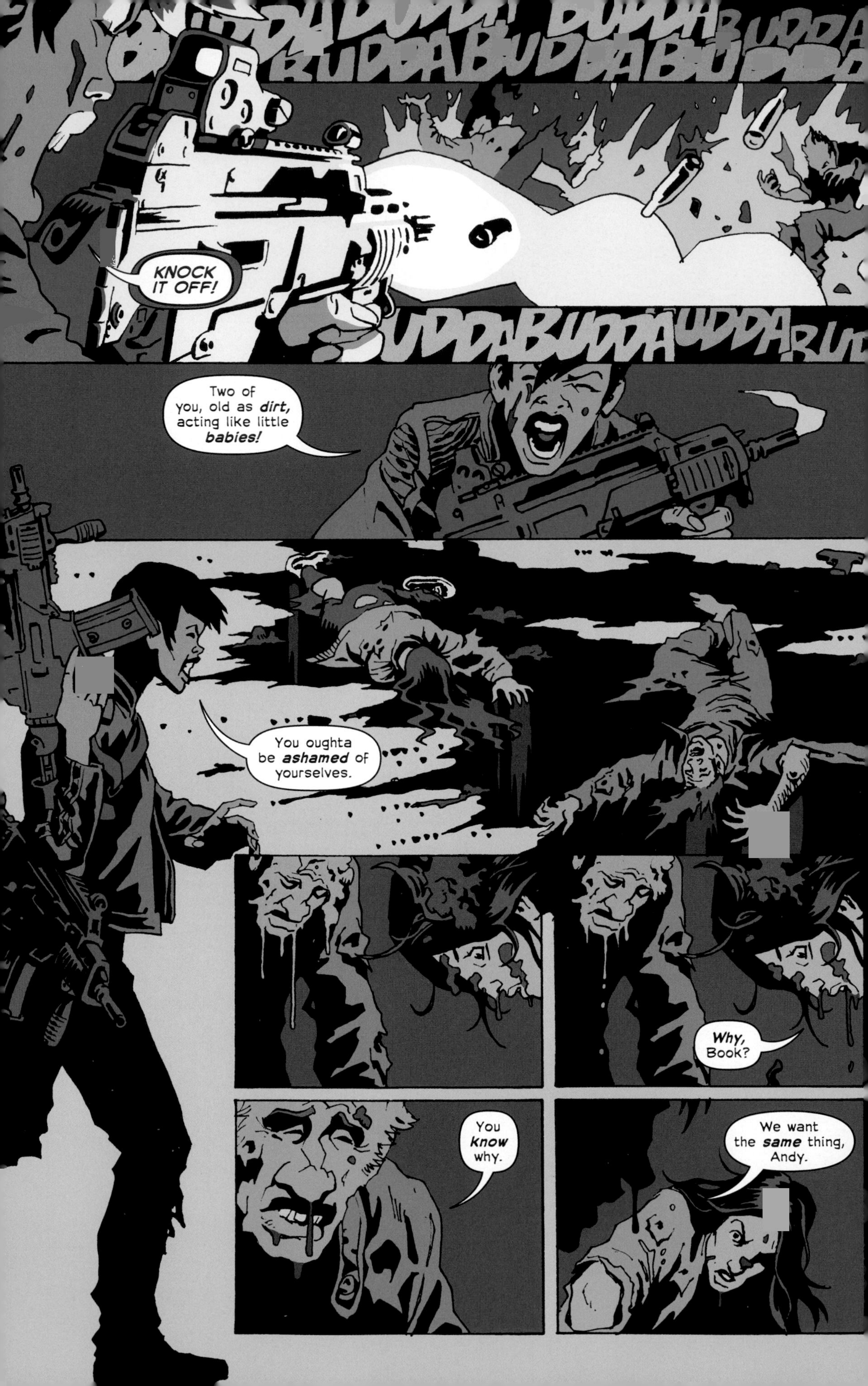
BUDDA
KNOCK IT OFF!
UDDABUDDAUDDA
Two of you, old as *dirt,* acting like little ***babies!***
You oughta be ***ashamed*** of yourselves.
Why, Book?
You ***know*** why.
We want the ***same*** thing, Andy.

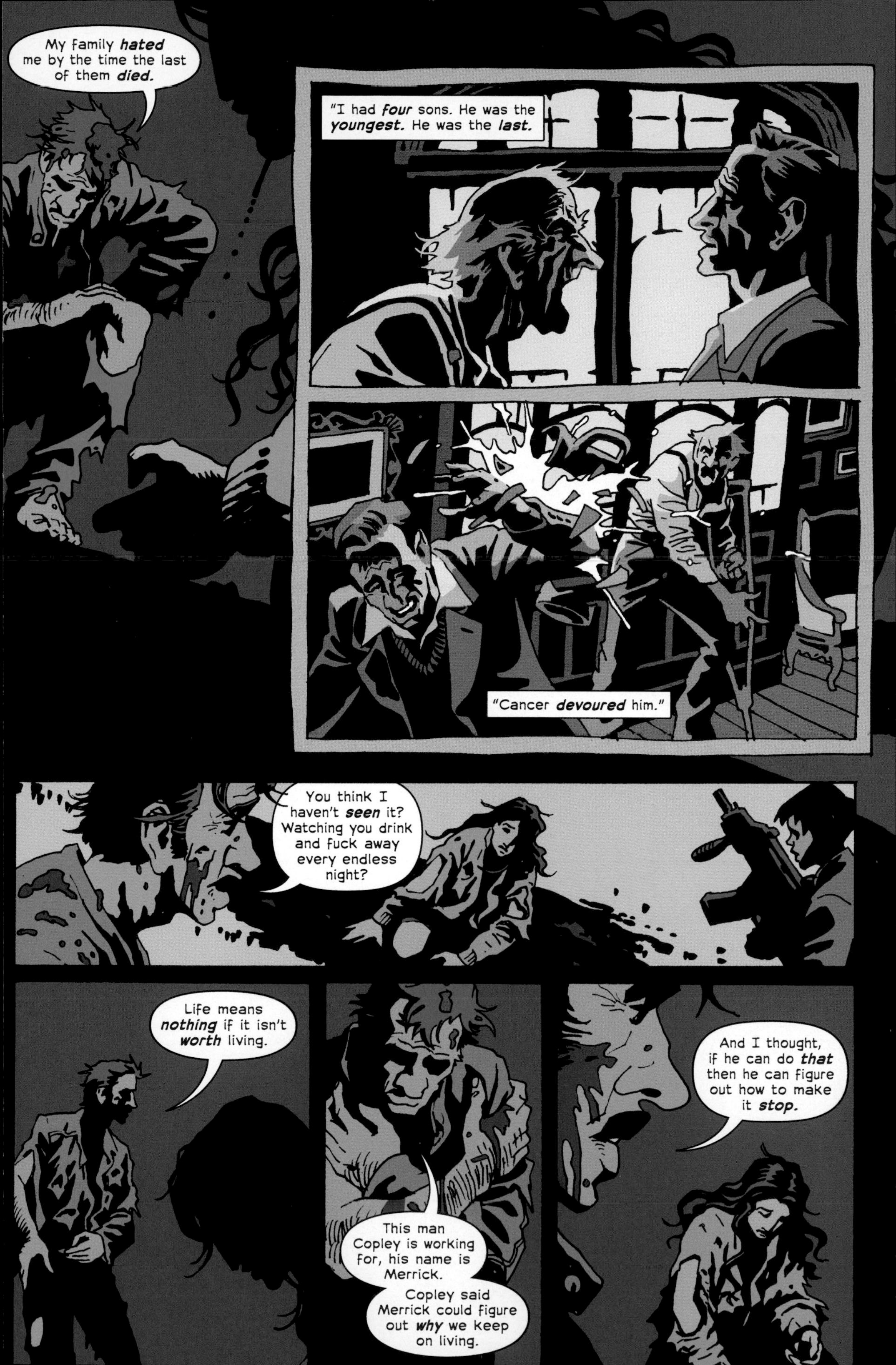
My family *hated* me by the time the last of them *died.*
"I had *four* sons. He was the *youngest.* He was the *last.*
"Cancer *devoured* him."
You think I haven't *seen* it? Watching you drink and fuck away every endless night?
Life means *nothing* if it isn't *worth* living.
This man Copley is working for, his name is Merrick.
Copley said Merrick could figure out *why* we keep on living.
And I thought, if he can do *that* then he can figure out how to make it *stop.*

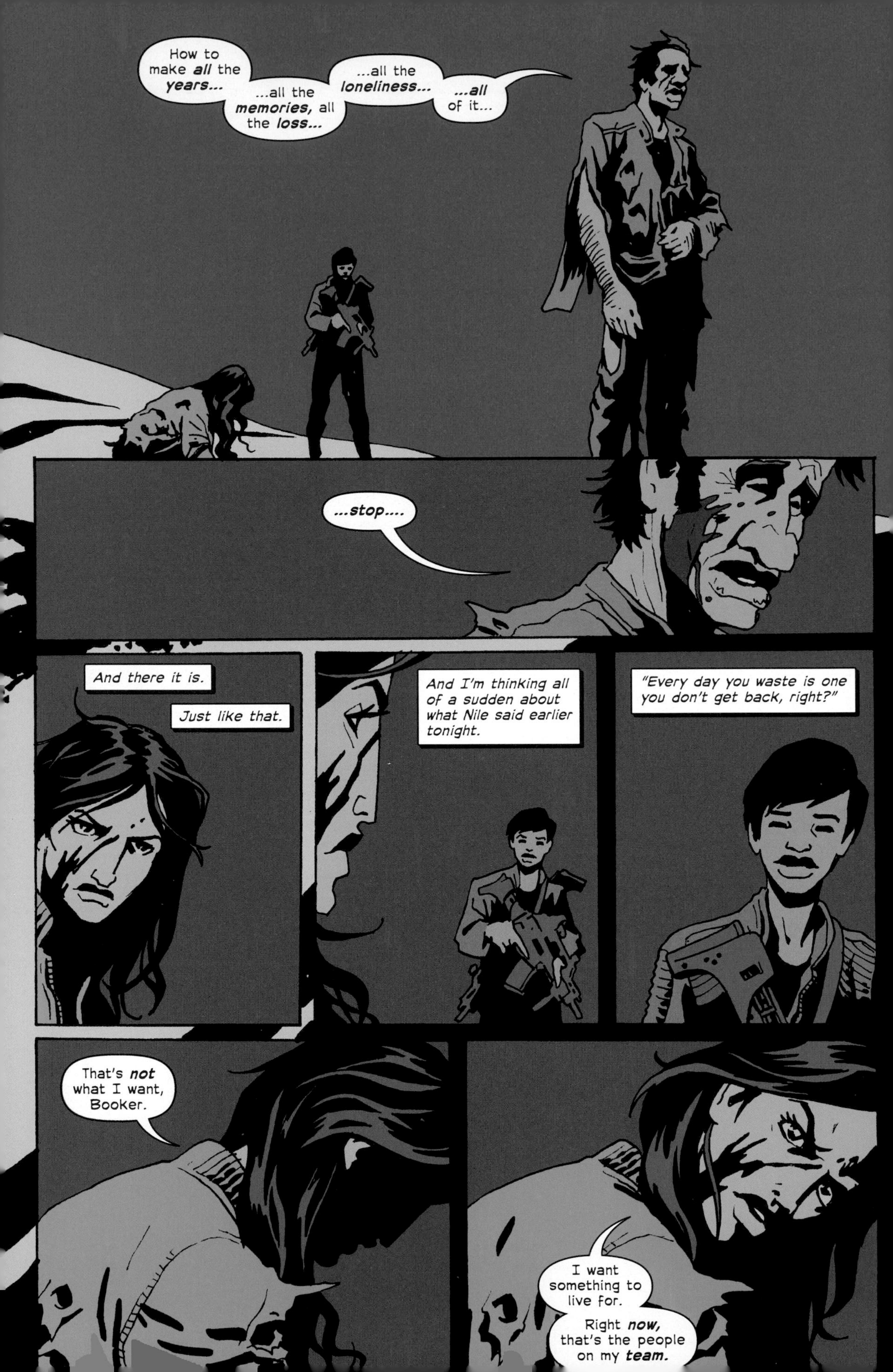
How to make all the years...
...all the memories, all the loss...
...all the loneliness...
...all of it...
...stop....
And there it is.
Just like that.
And I'm thinking all of a sudden about what Nile said earlier tonight.
"Every day you waste is one you don't get back, right?"
That's not what I want, Booker.
I want something to live for.
Right now, that's the people on my team.

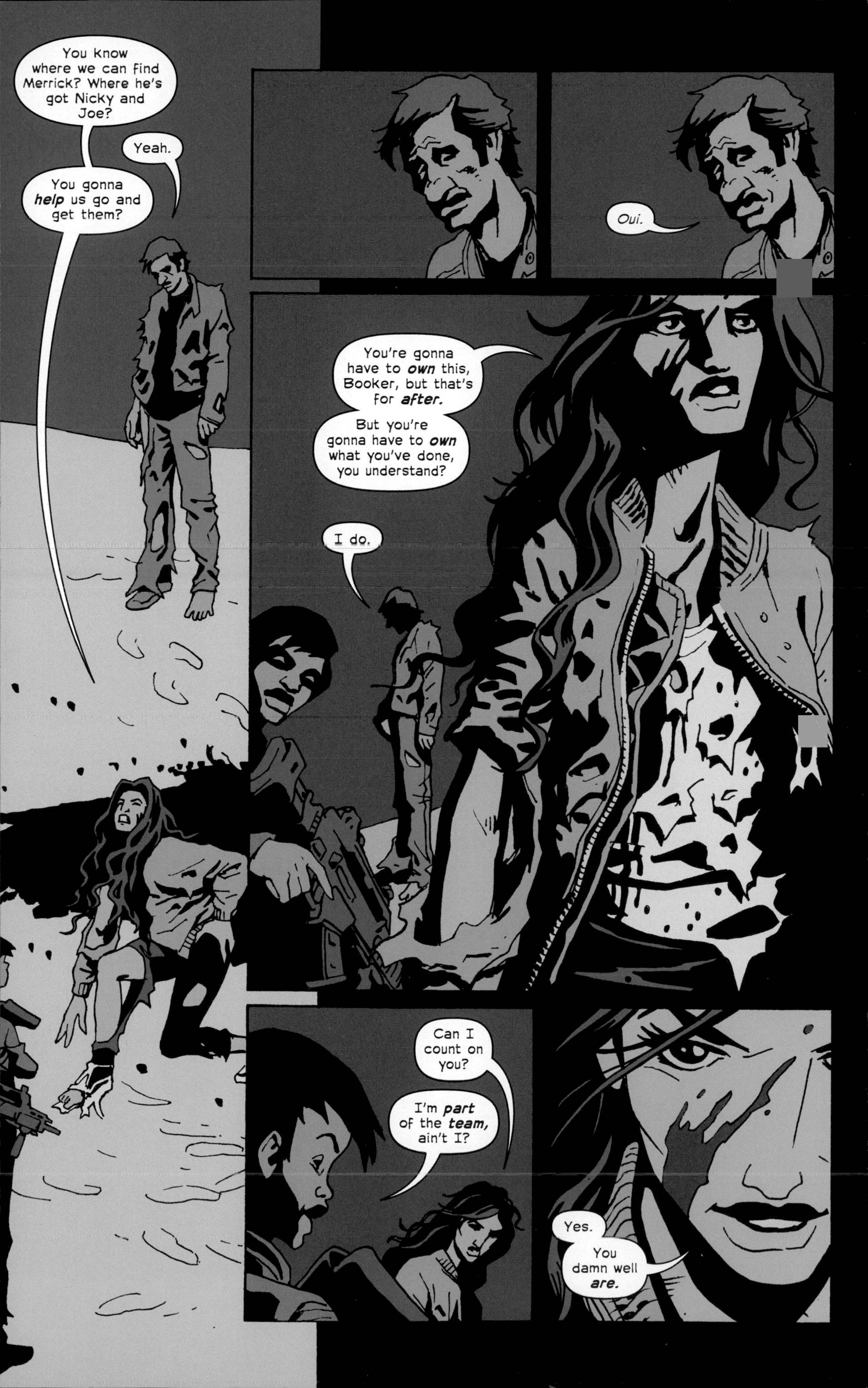
You know where we can find Merrick? Where he's got Nicky and Joe?
Yeah.
You gonna **help** us go and get them?
Oui.
You're gonna have to **own** this, Booker, but that's for **after.**
But you're gonna have to **own** what you've done, you understand?
I do.
Can I count on you?
I'm **part** of the **team,** ain't I?
Yes.
You damn well **are.**

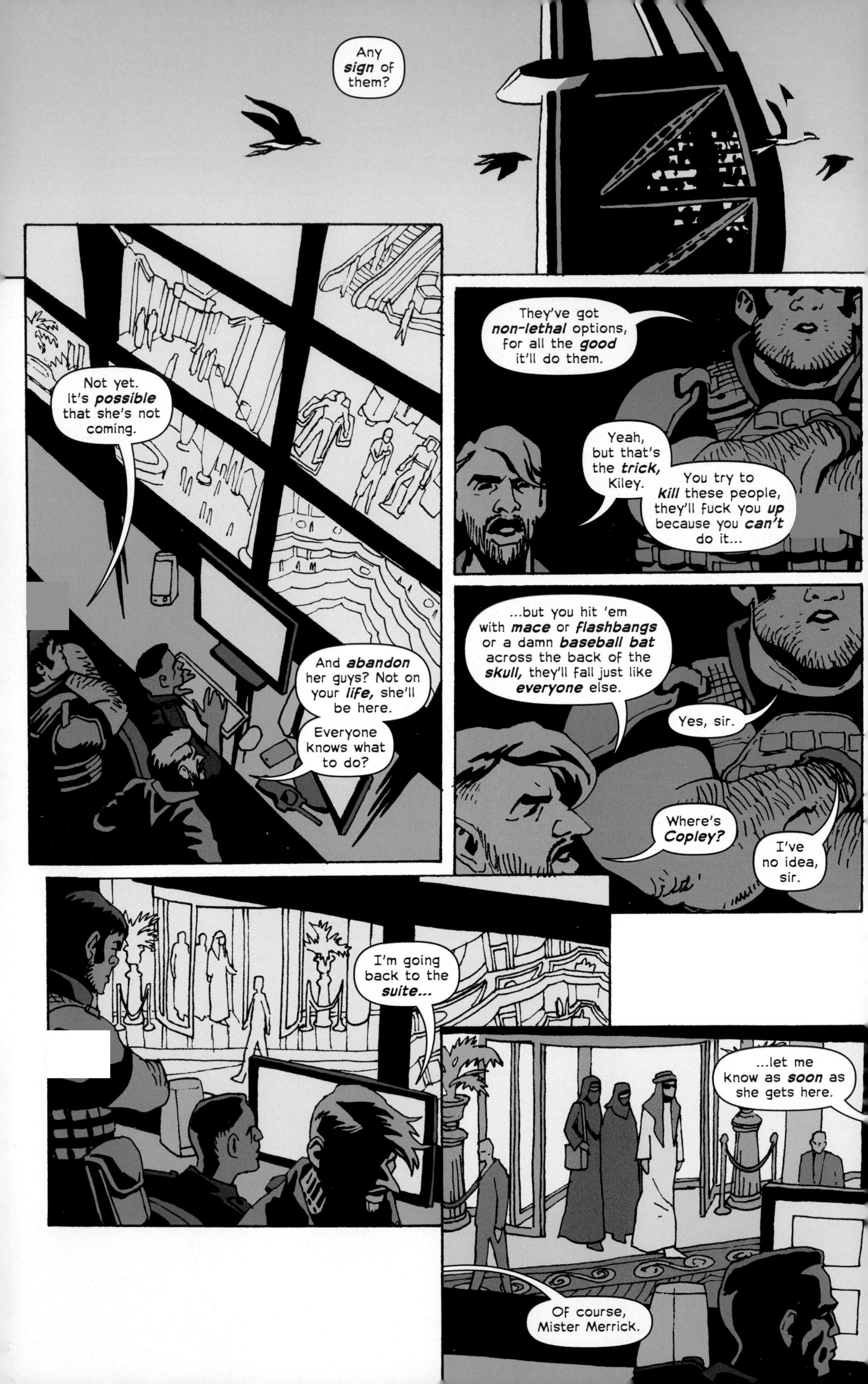
Any *sign* of them?
Not yet. It's *possible* that she's not coming.
And *abandon* her guys? Not on your *life,* she'll be here.
Everyone knows what to do?
They've got *non-lethal* options, for all the *good* it'll do them.
Yeah, but that's the *trick,* Kiley.
You try to *kill* these people, they'll fuck you *up* because you *can't* do it...
...but you hit 'em with *mace* or *flashbangs* or a damn *baseball bat* across the back of the *skull,* they'll fall just like *everyone* else.
Yes, sir.
Where's *Copley?*
I've no idea, sir.
I'm going back to the *suite...*
...let me know as *soon* as she gets here.
Of course, Mister Merrick.

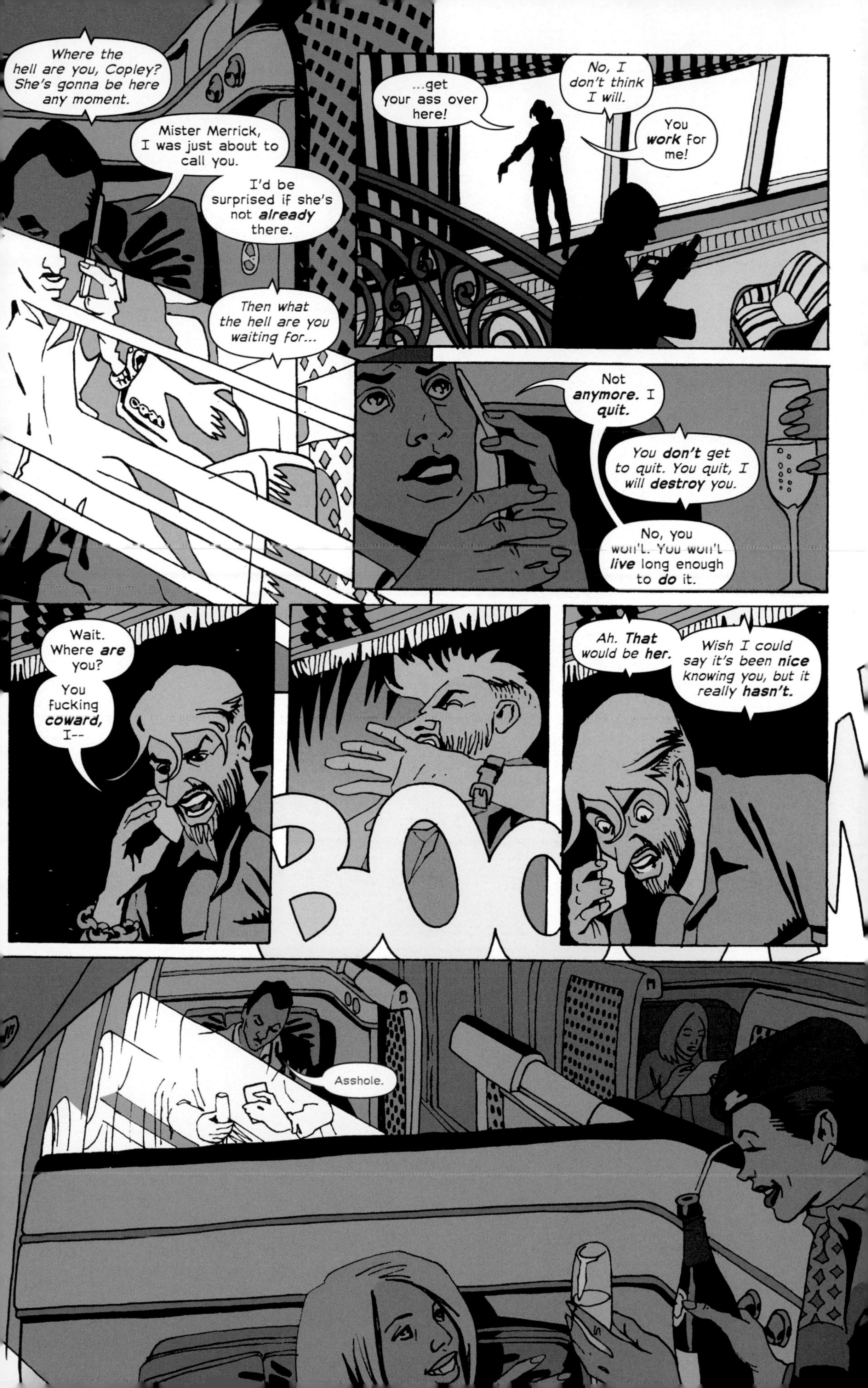
Where the hell are you, Copley? She's gonna be here any moment.
Mister Merrick, I was just about to call you.
I'd be surprised if she's not *already* there.
Then what the hell are you waiting for...
...get your ass over here!
No, I don't think I will.
You **work** for me!
Not **anymore.** I **quit.**
You **don't** get to quit. You quit, I will **destroy** you.
No, you won't. You won't **live** long enough to **do** it.
Wait. Where **are** you?
You fucking **coward,** I--
Ah. **That** would be **her.**
Wish I could say it's been **nice** knowing you, but it really **hasn't.**
Asshole.

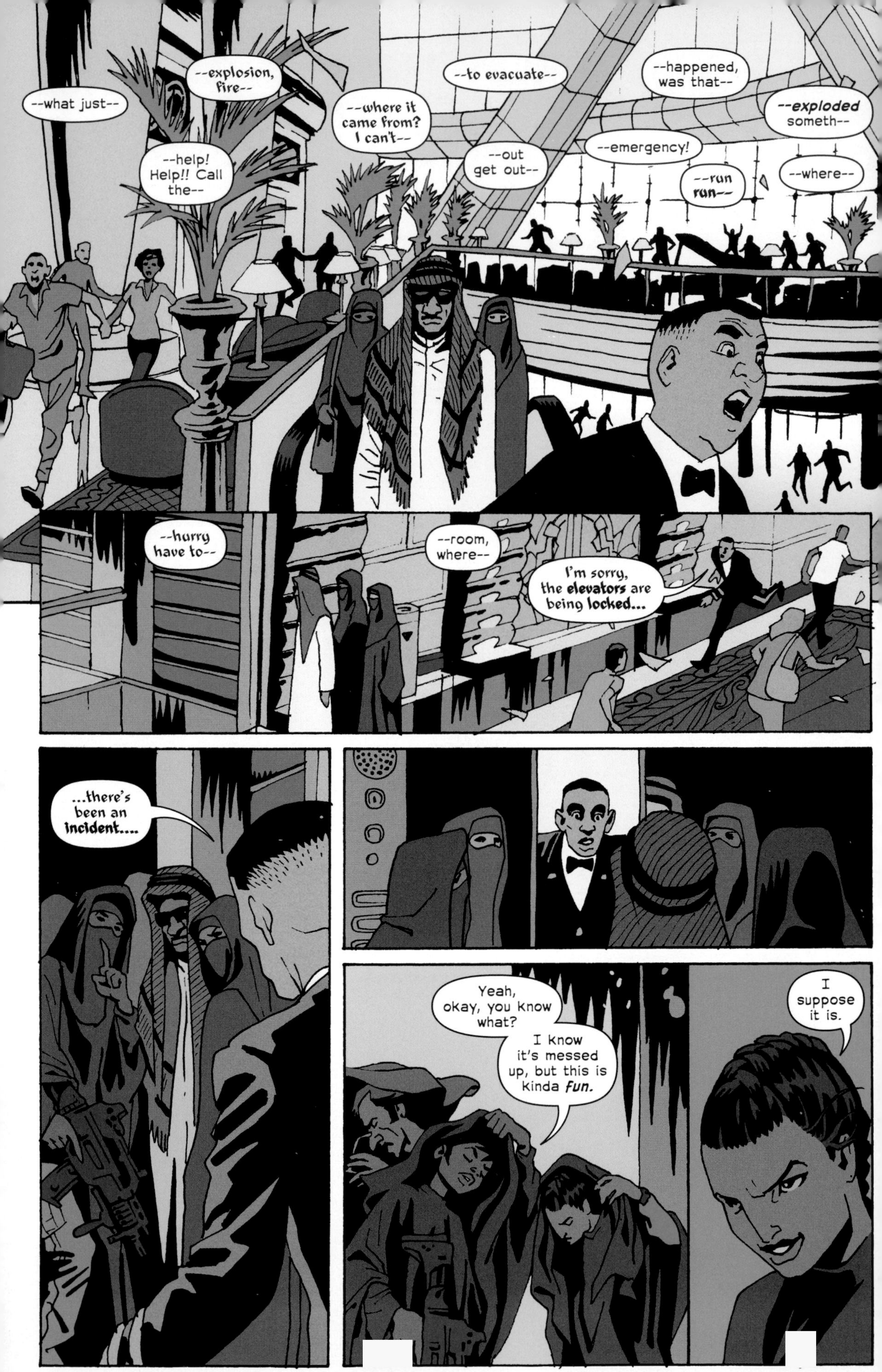
--what just--
--explosion, fire--
--help! Help!! Call the--
--where it came from? I can't--
--to evacuate--
--out get out--
--happened, was that--
--emergency!
--run run--
--exploded someth--
--where--
--hurry have to--
--room, where--
I'm sorry, the elevators are being locked...
...there's been an incident....
Yeah, okay, you know what?
I know it's messed up, but this is kinda fun.
I suppose it is.

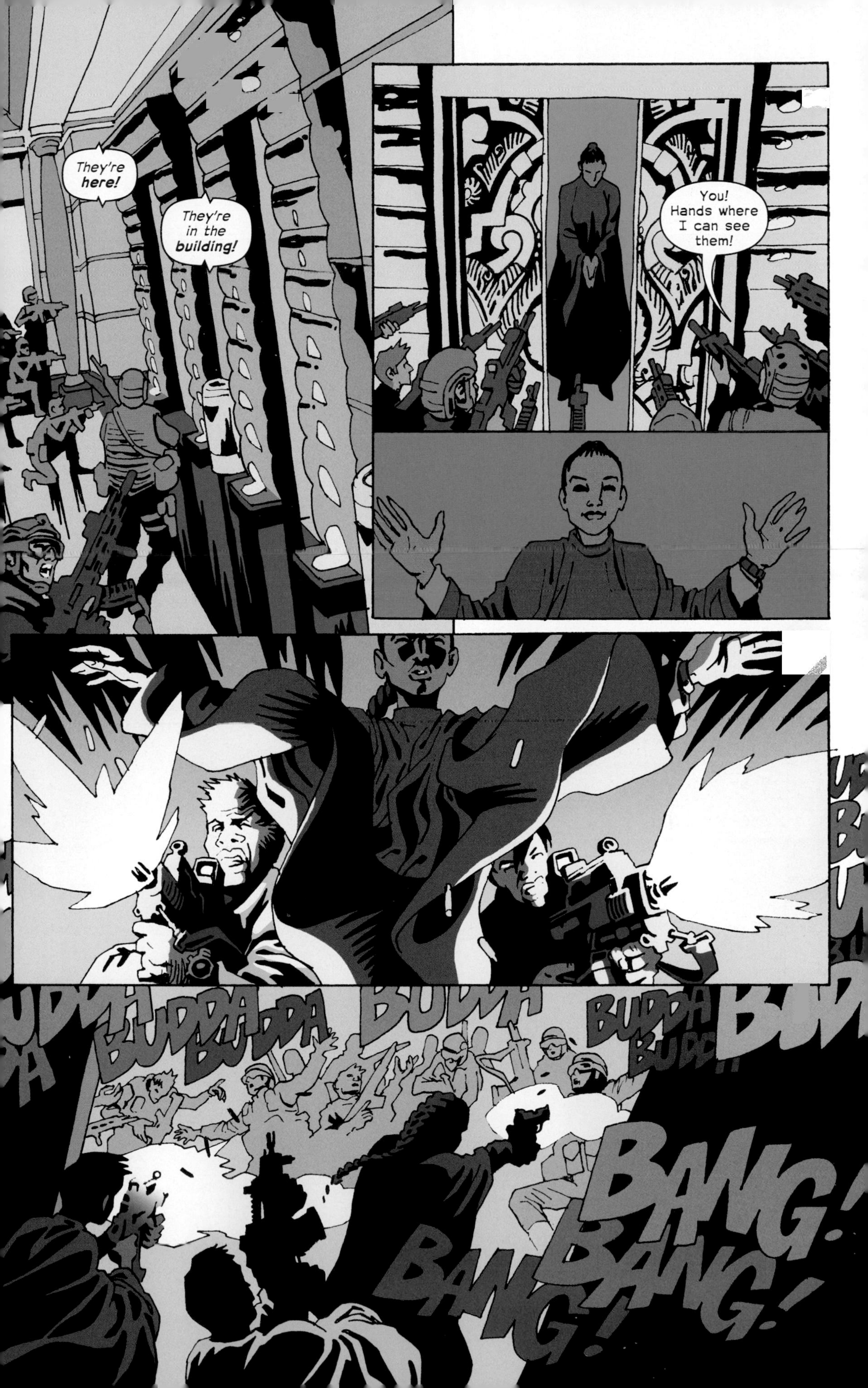
They're here!
They're in the building!
You! Hands where I can see them!
BUDDA BUDDA BUDDA
BUDDA BUDDA
BANG! BANG! BANG!

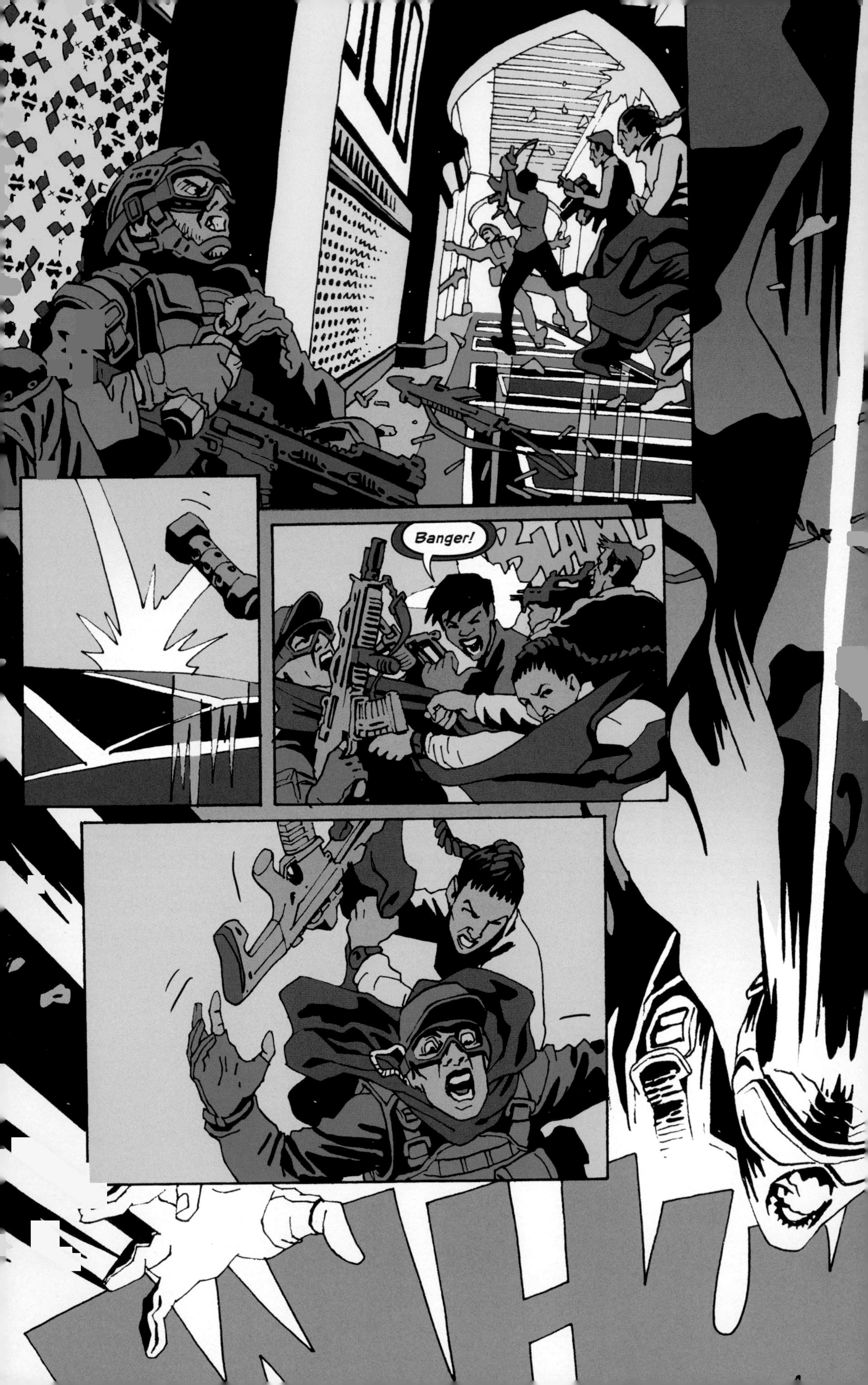
Banger!

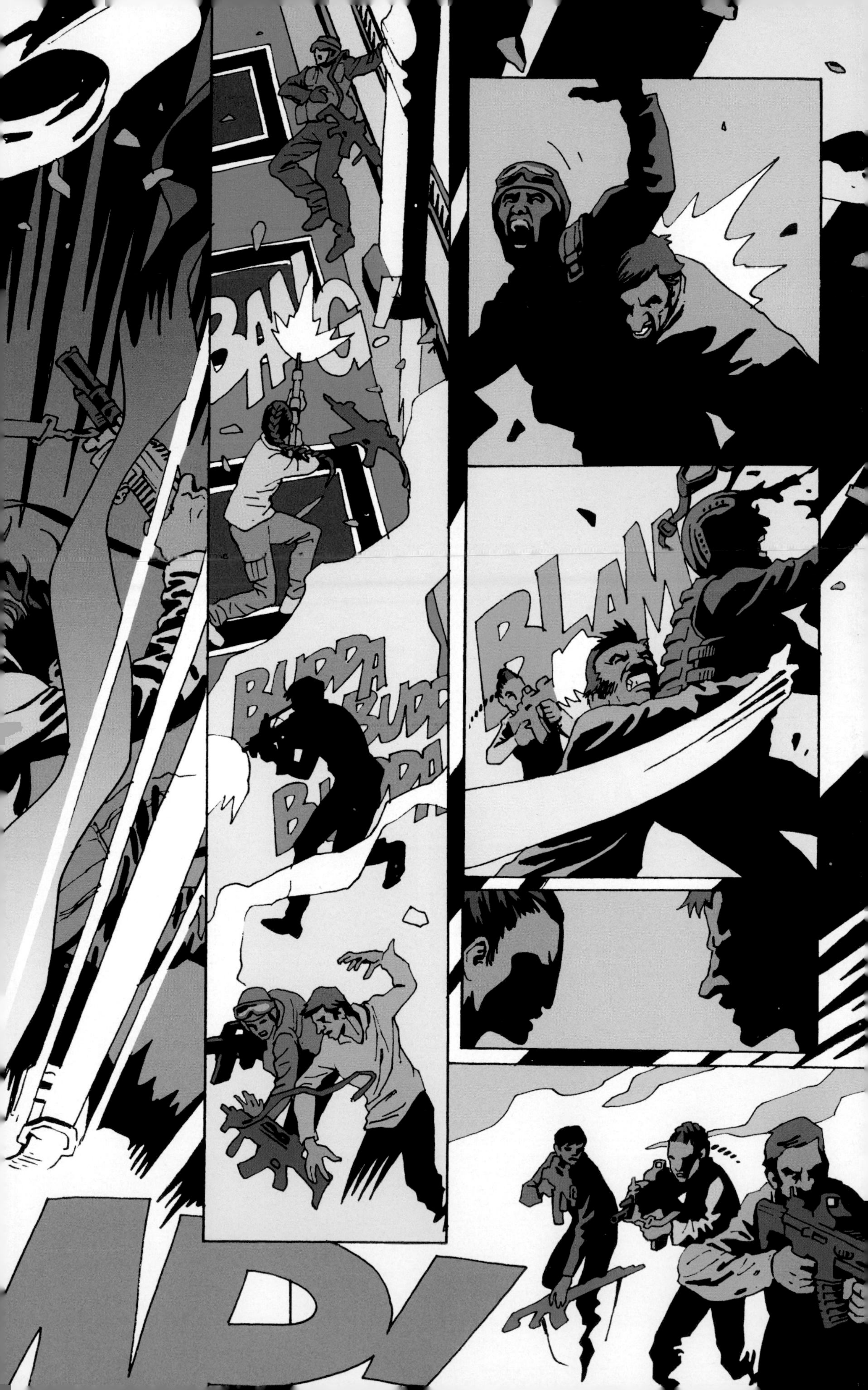
BANG!
BUDDA
BLAM

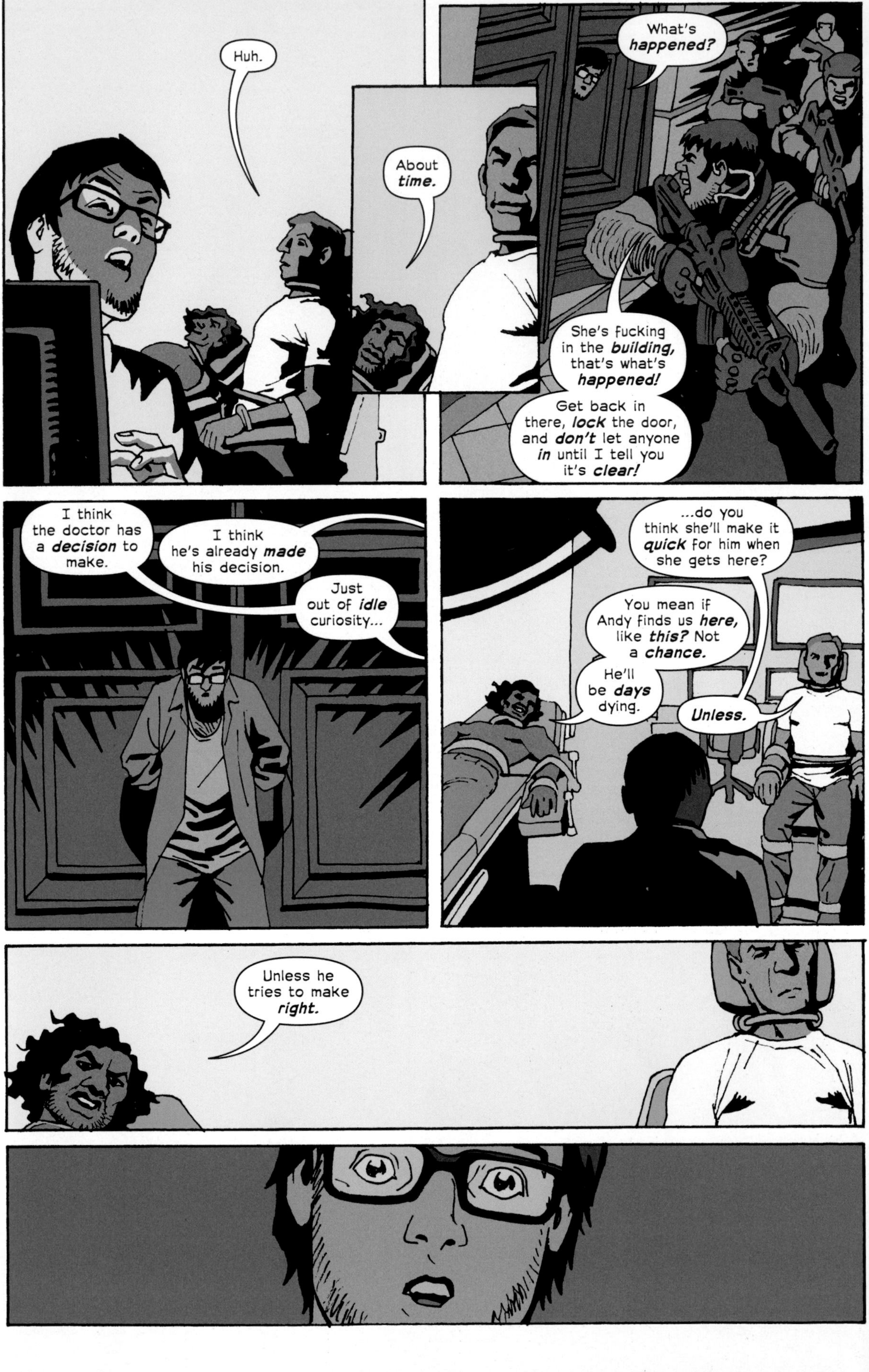
Huh.
About time.
What's happened?
She's fucking in the building, that's what's happened!
Get back in there, lock the door, and don't let anyone in until I tell you it's clear!
I think the doctor has a decision to make.
I think he's already made his decision.
Just out of idle curiosity...
...do you think she'll make it quick for him when she gets here?
You mean if Andy finds us here, like this? Not a chance.
He'll be days dying.
Unless.
Unless he tries to make right.

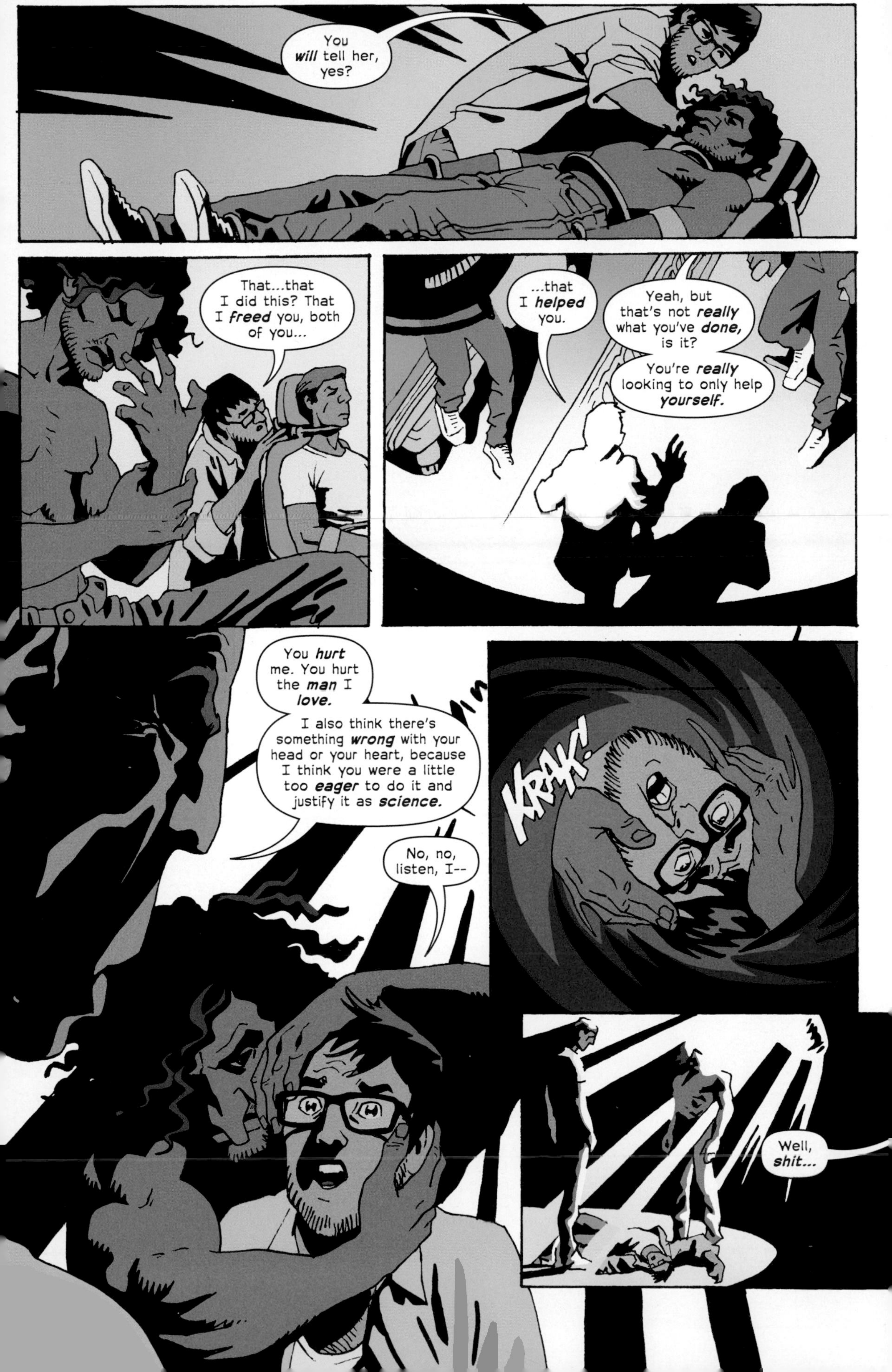
You *will* tell her, yes?
That...that I did this? That I *freed* you, both of you...
...that I *helped* you.
Yeah, but that's not *really* what you've *done,* is it?
You're *really* looking to only help *yourself.*
You *hurt* me. You hurt the *man* I *love.*
I also think there's something *wrong* with your head or your heart, because I think you were a little too *eager* to do it and justify it as *science.*
No, no, listen, I--
KRAK!
Well, *shit...*

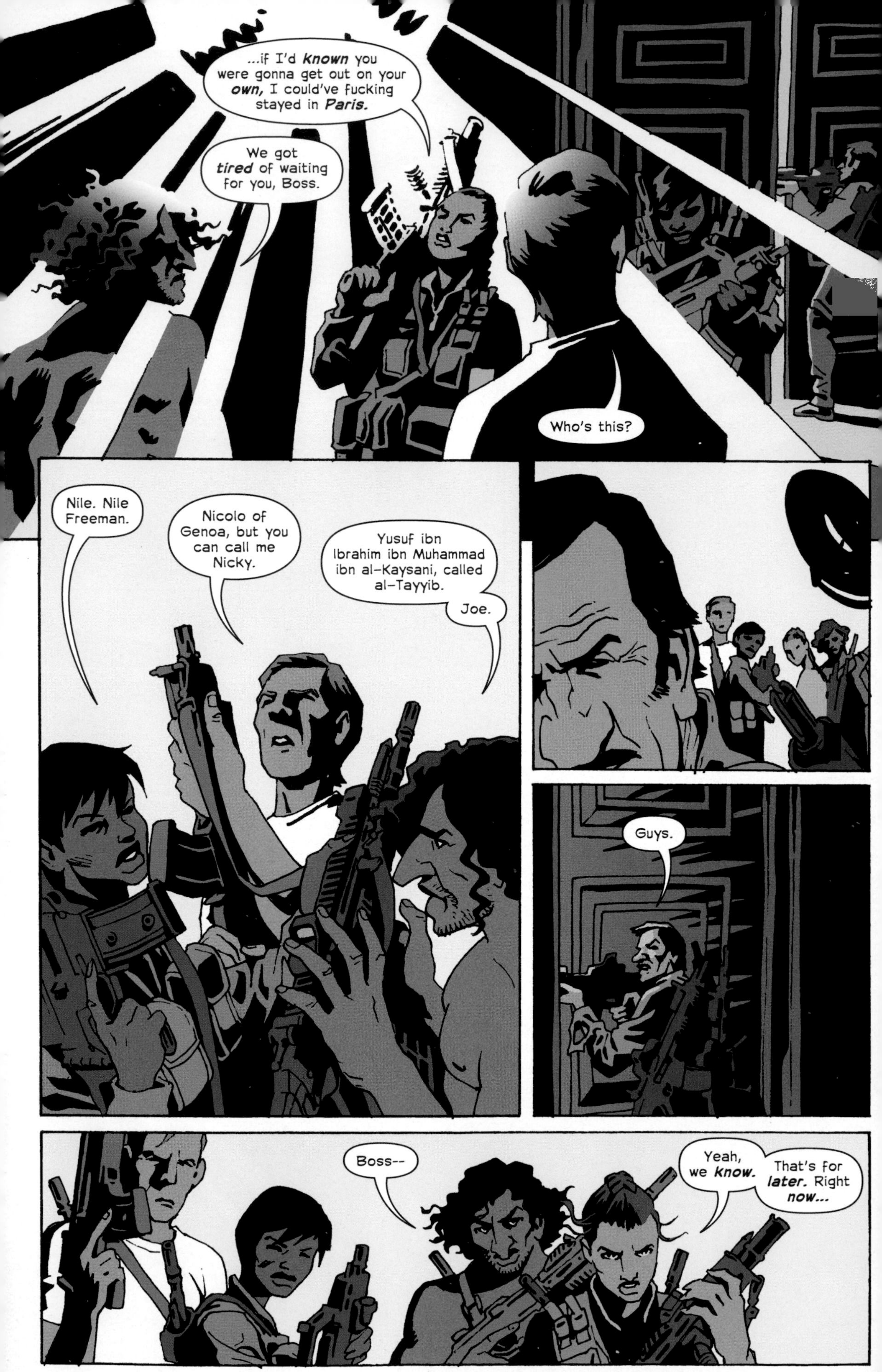
...if I'd *known* you were gonna get out on your *own,* I could've fucking stayed in *Paris.*
We got *tired* of waiting for you, Boss.
Who's this?
Nile. Nile Freeman.
Nicolo of Genoa, but you can call me Nicky.
Yusuf ibn Ibrahim ibn Muhammad ibn al-Kaysani, called al-Tayyib.
Joe.
Guys.
Boss--
Yeah, we *know.*
That's for *later.* Right *now...*

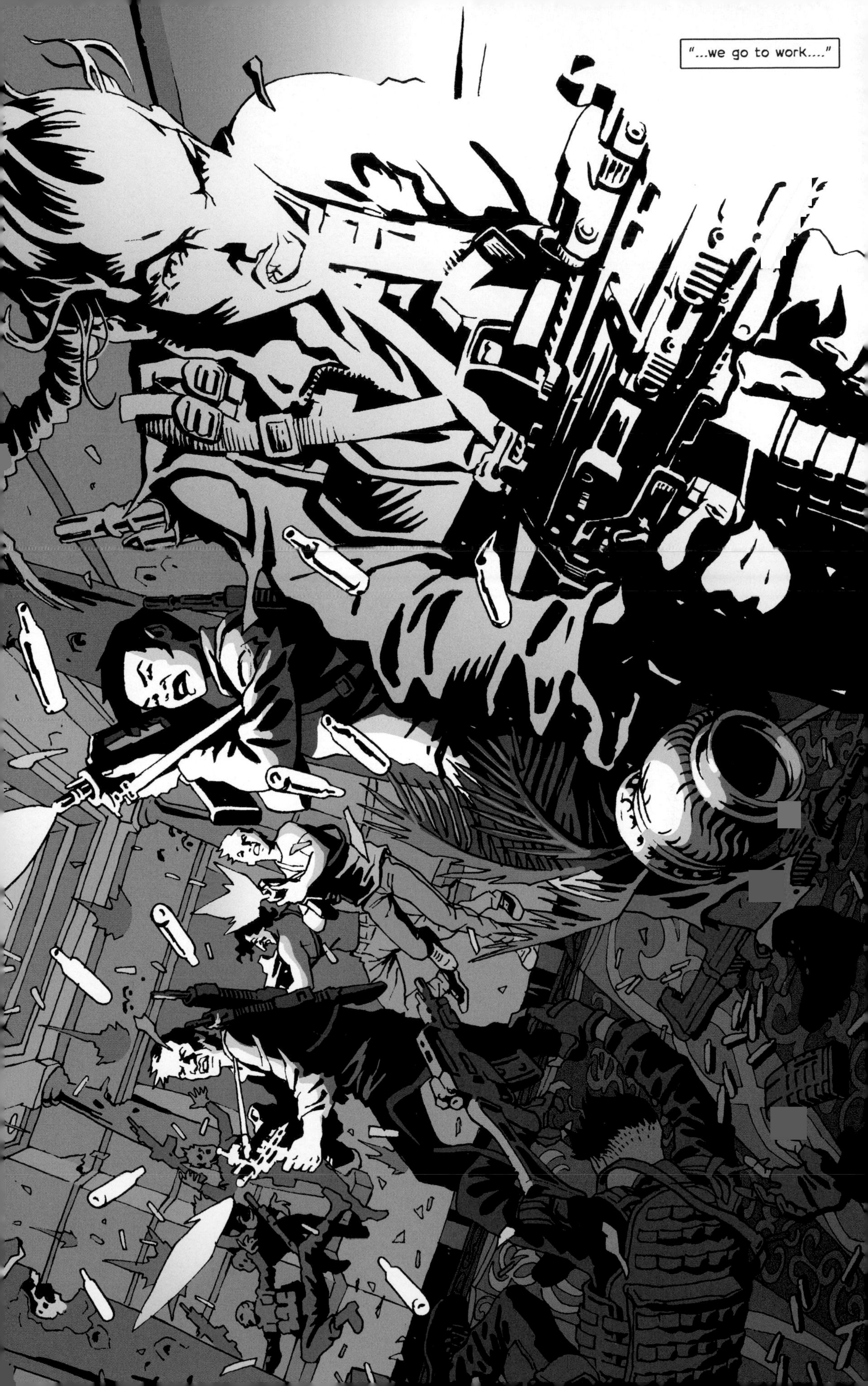
"...we go to work...."

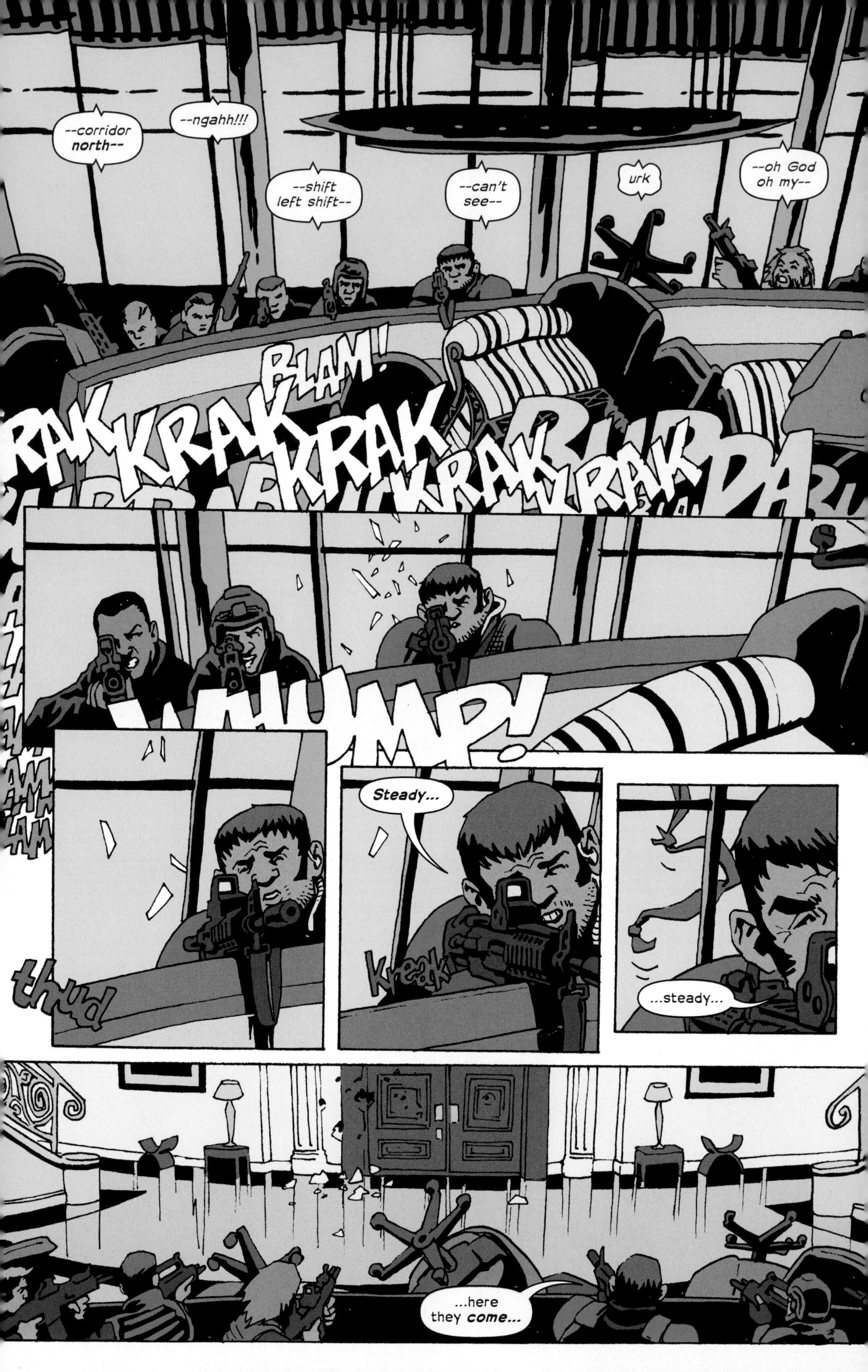
--corridor north--
--ngahh!!!
--shift left shift--
--can't see--
urk
--oh God oh my--
BLAM!
KRAK KRAK KRAK KRAK KRAK KRAK
WHUMP!
thud
Steady...
Kreak
...steady...
...here they come...

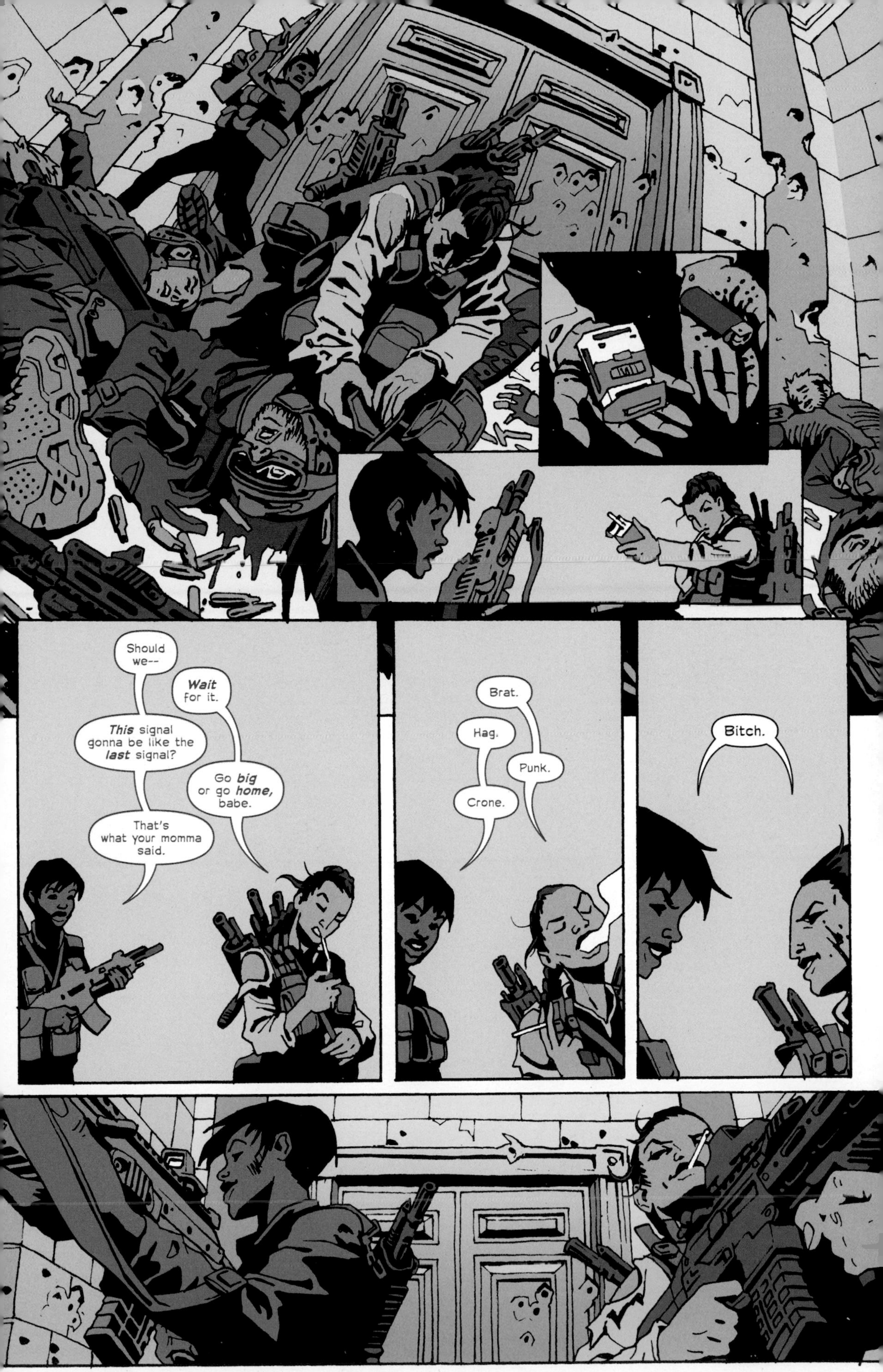
Should we--
Wait for it.
This signal gonna be like the last signal?
Go big or go home, babe.
That's what your momma said.
Brat.
Hag.
Punk.
Crone.
Bitch.

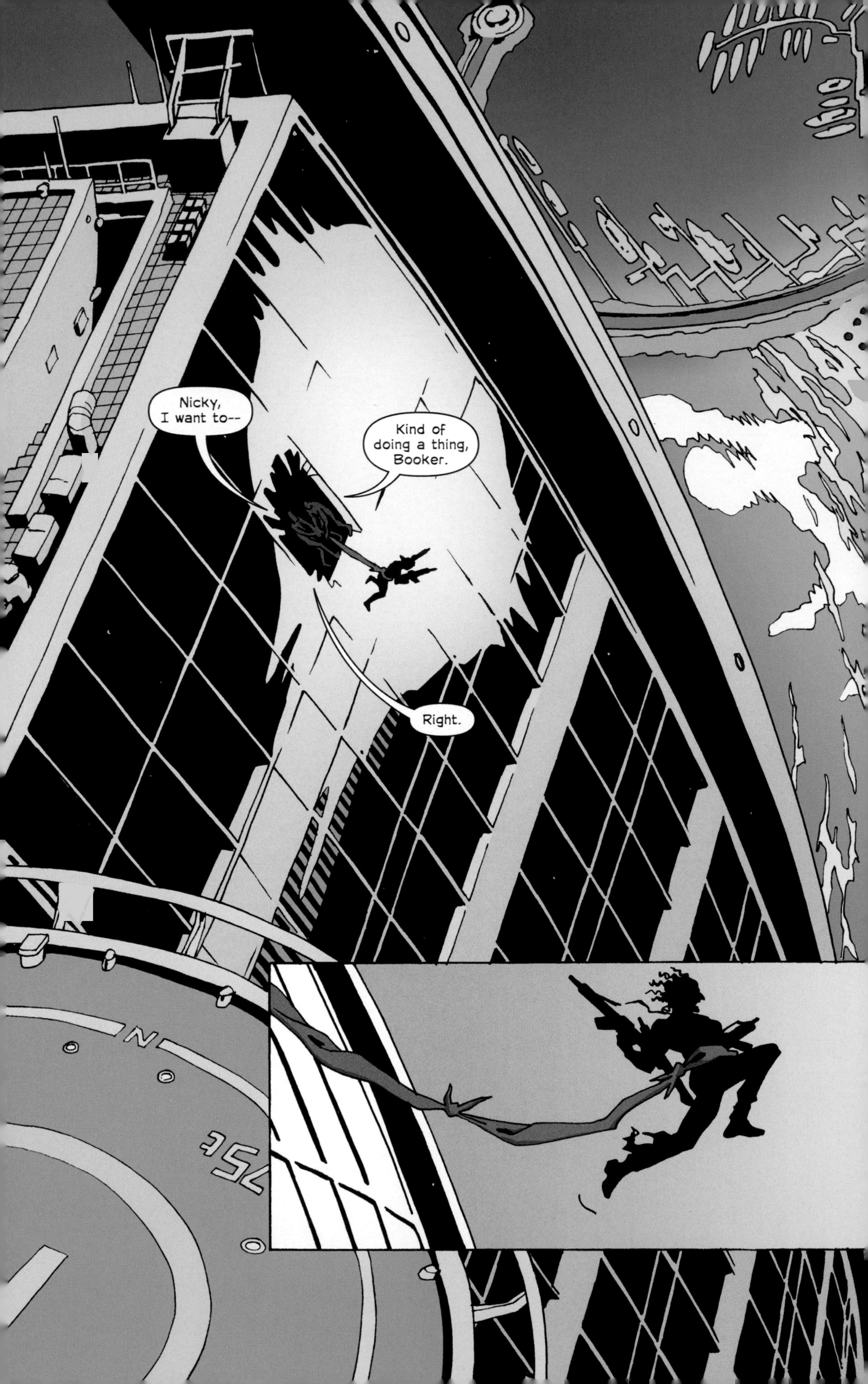
Nicky, I want to--
Kind of doing a thing, Booker.
Right.

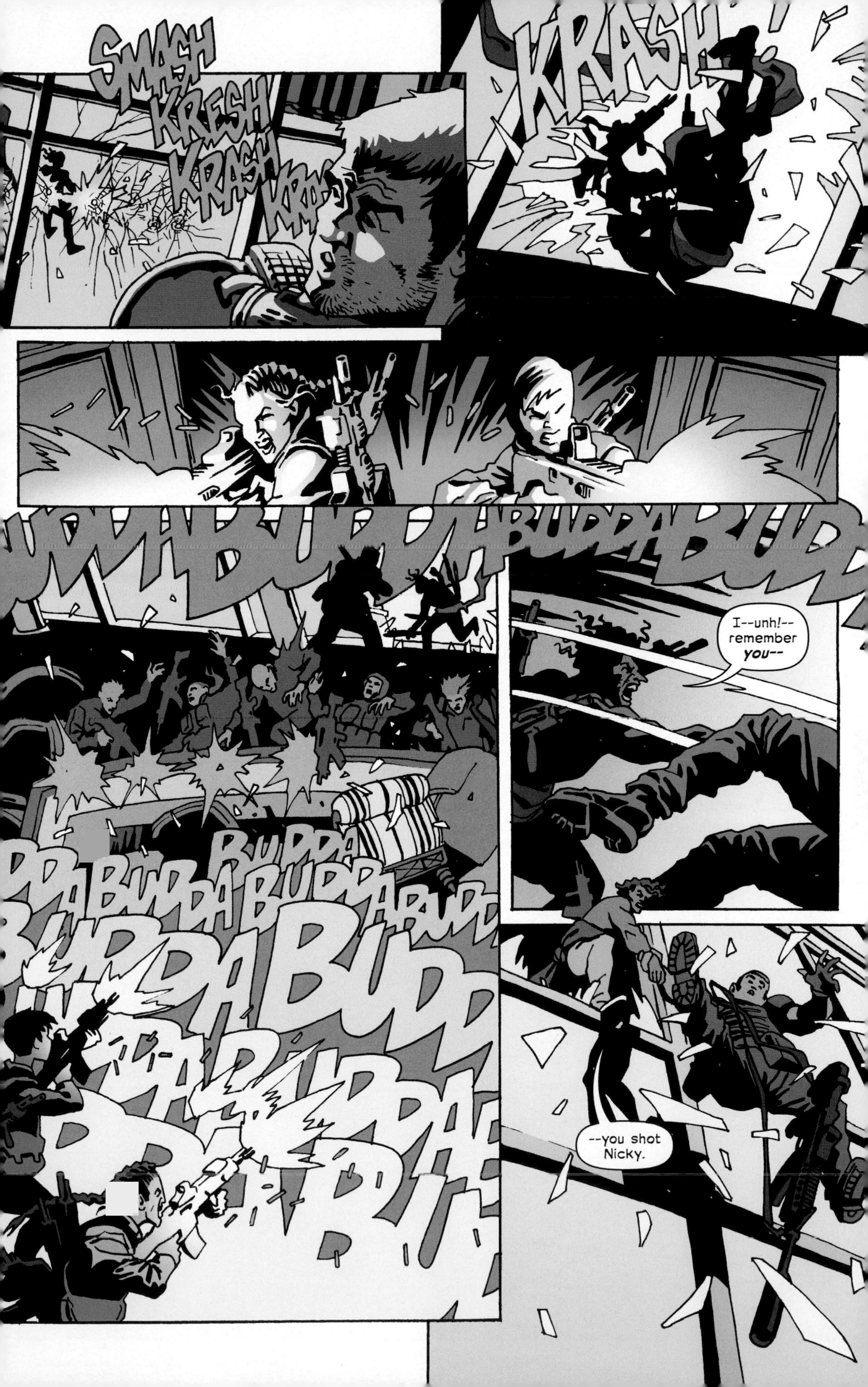
SMASH
KRESH
KRASH
KRASH
BUDDABUDDABUDDABUDD
BUDDA
BUDDA BUDDA BUDD
BUDDA
I--unh!--remember you--
--you shot Nicky.

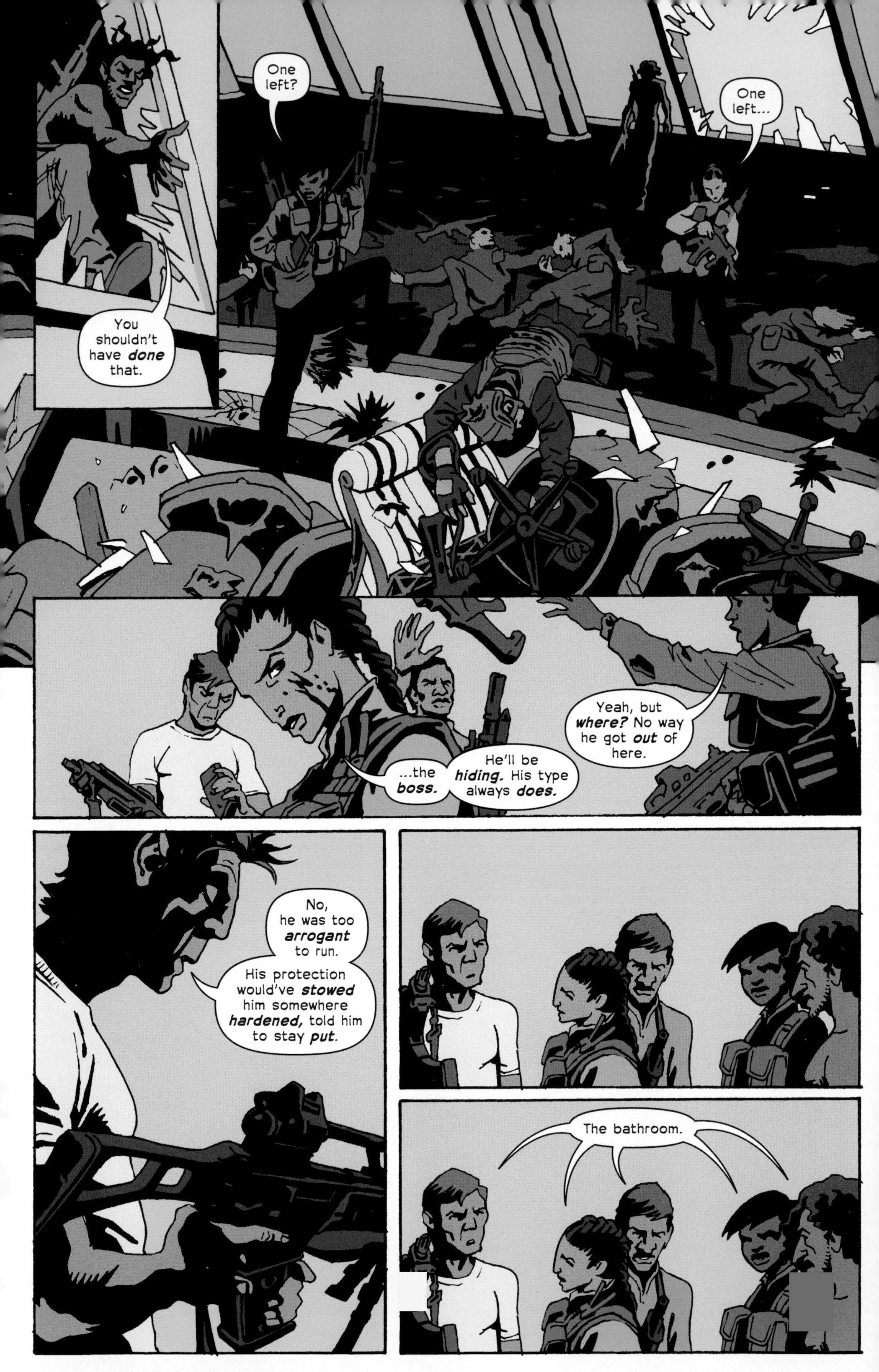
One left?
One left...
You shouldn't have *done* that.
...the *boss.*
He'll be *hiding.* His type always *does.*
Yeah, but *where?* No way he got *out* of here.
No, he was too *arrogant* to run.
His protection would've *stowed* him somewhere *hardened,* told him to stay *put.*
The bathroom.

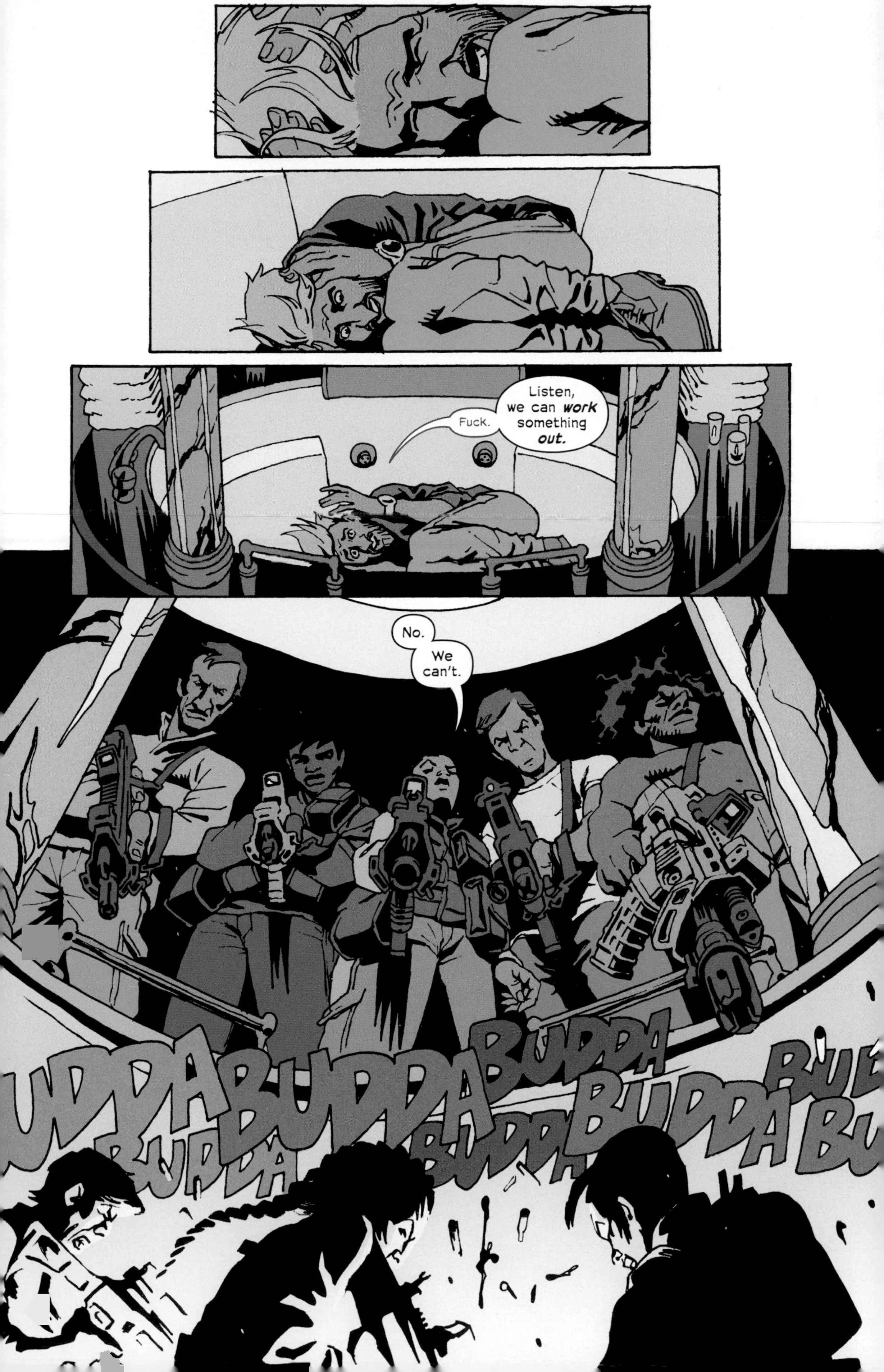

Fuck.
Listen, we can *work* something *out.*
No.
We can't.
BUDDA BUDDA BUDDA BUDDA

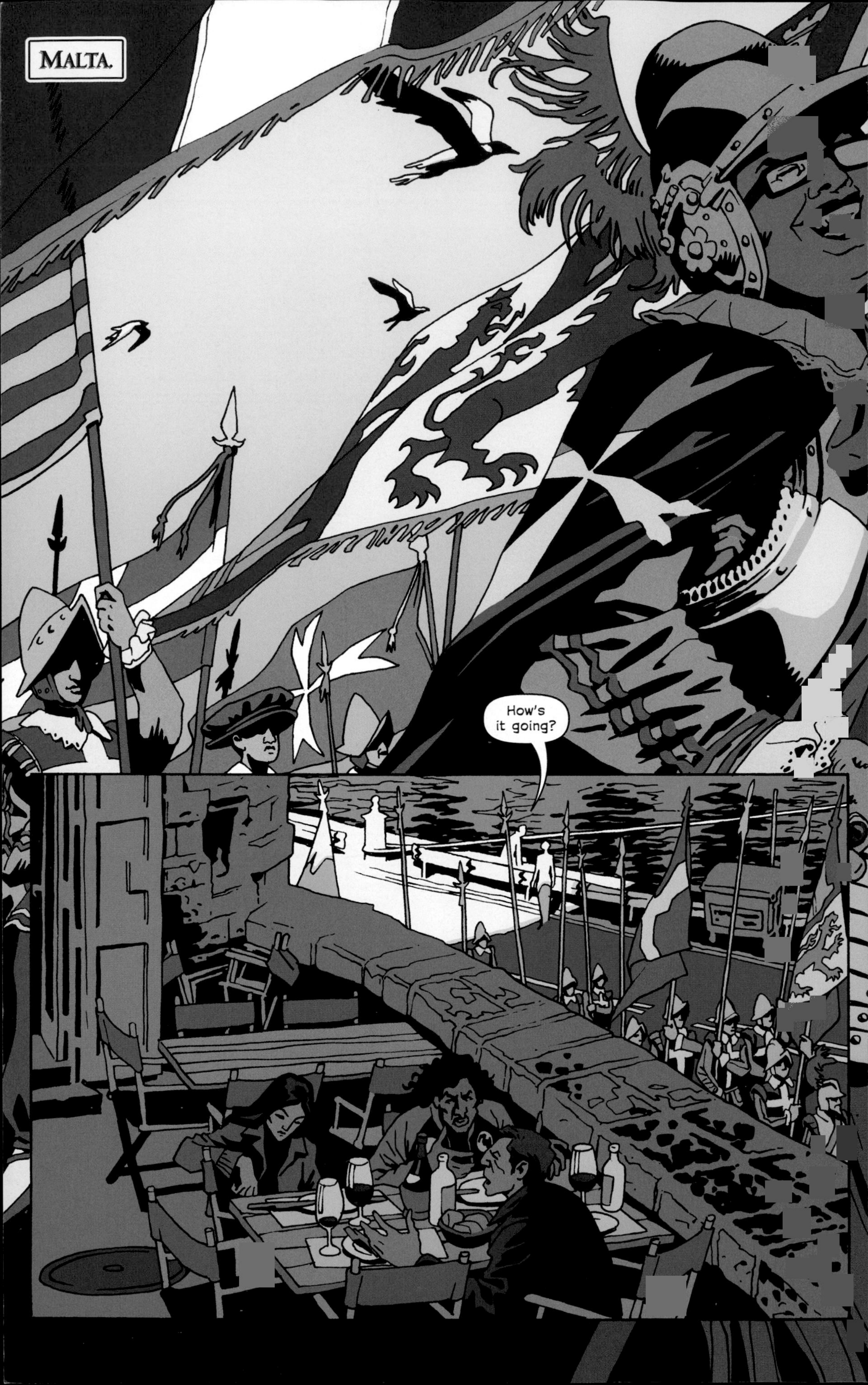
MALTA.
How's it going?

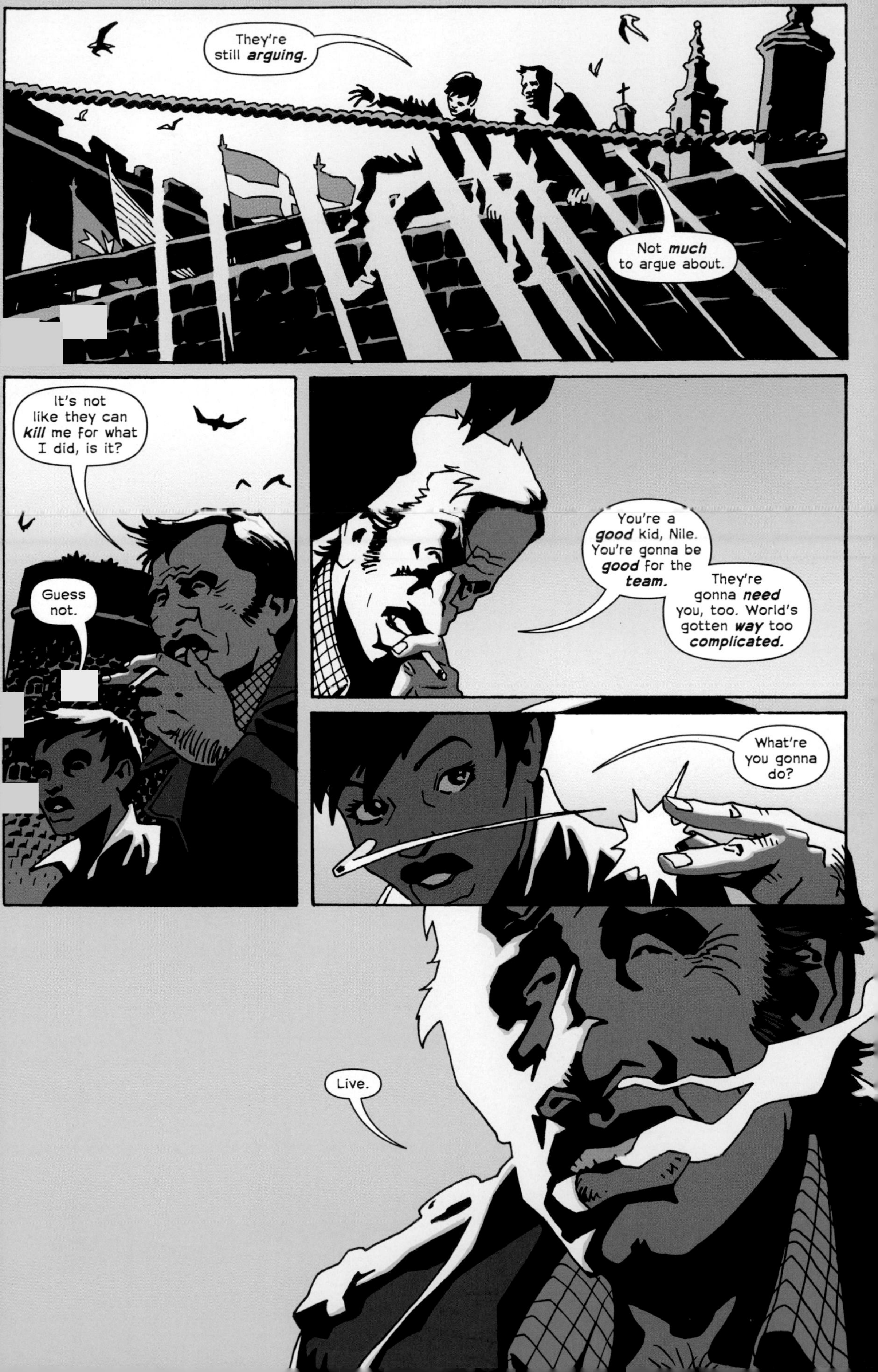
They're still *arguing.*
Not *much* to argue about.
It's not like they can *kill* me for what I did, is it?
Guess not.
You're a *good* kid, Nile. You're gonna be *good* for the *team.*
They're gonna *need* you, too. World's gotten *way* too *complicated.*
What're you gonna do?
Live.

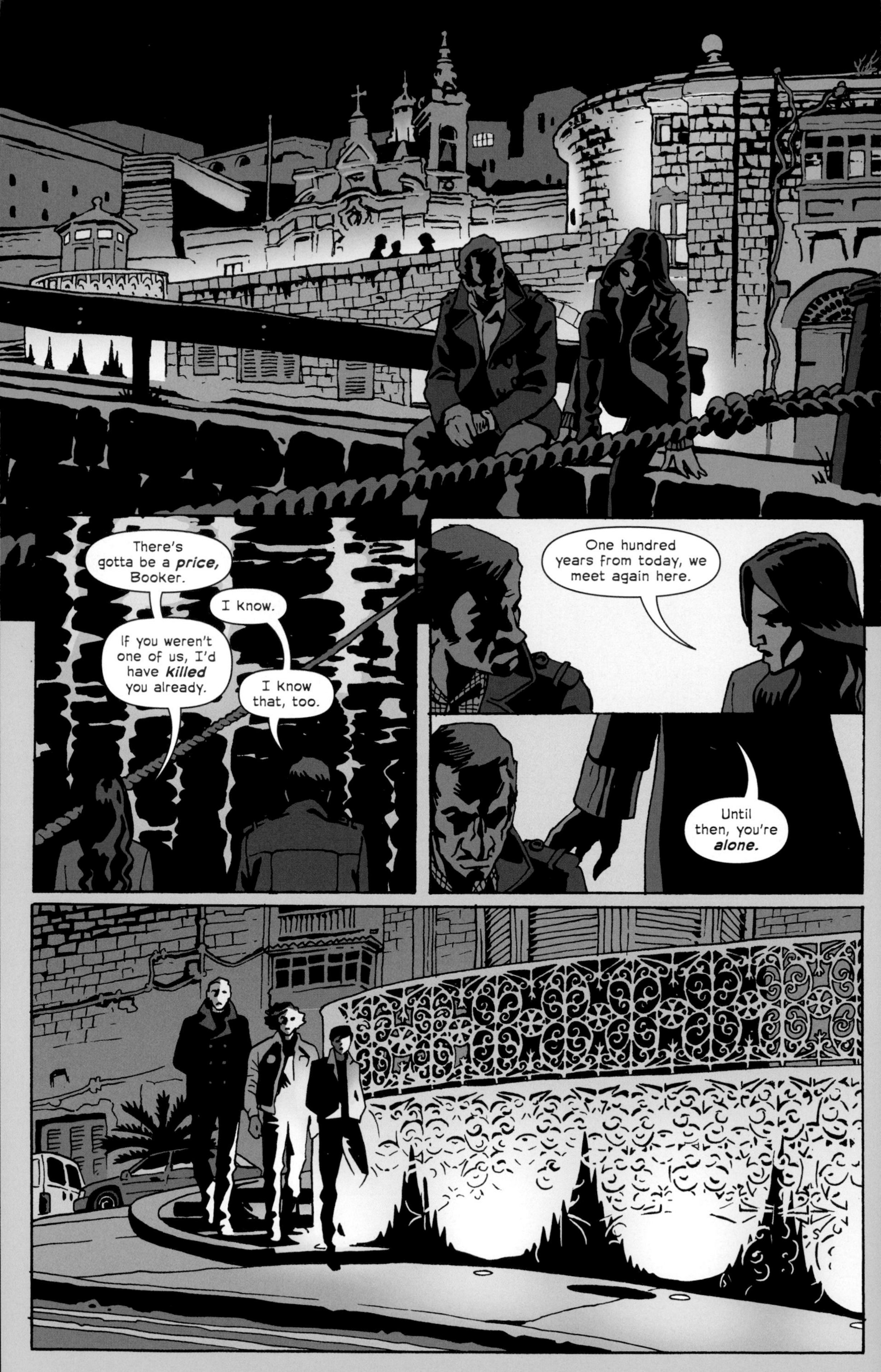
There's gotta be a *price,* Booker.
I know.
If you weren't one of us, I'd have *killed* you already.
I know that, too.
One hundred years from today, we meet again here.
Until then, you're *alone.*

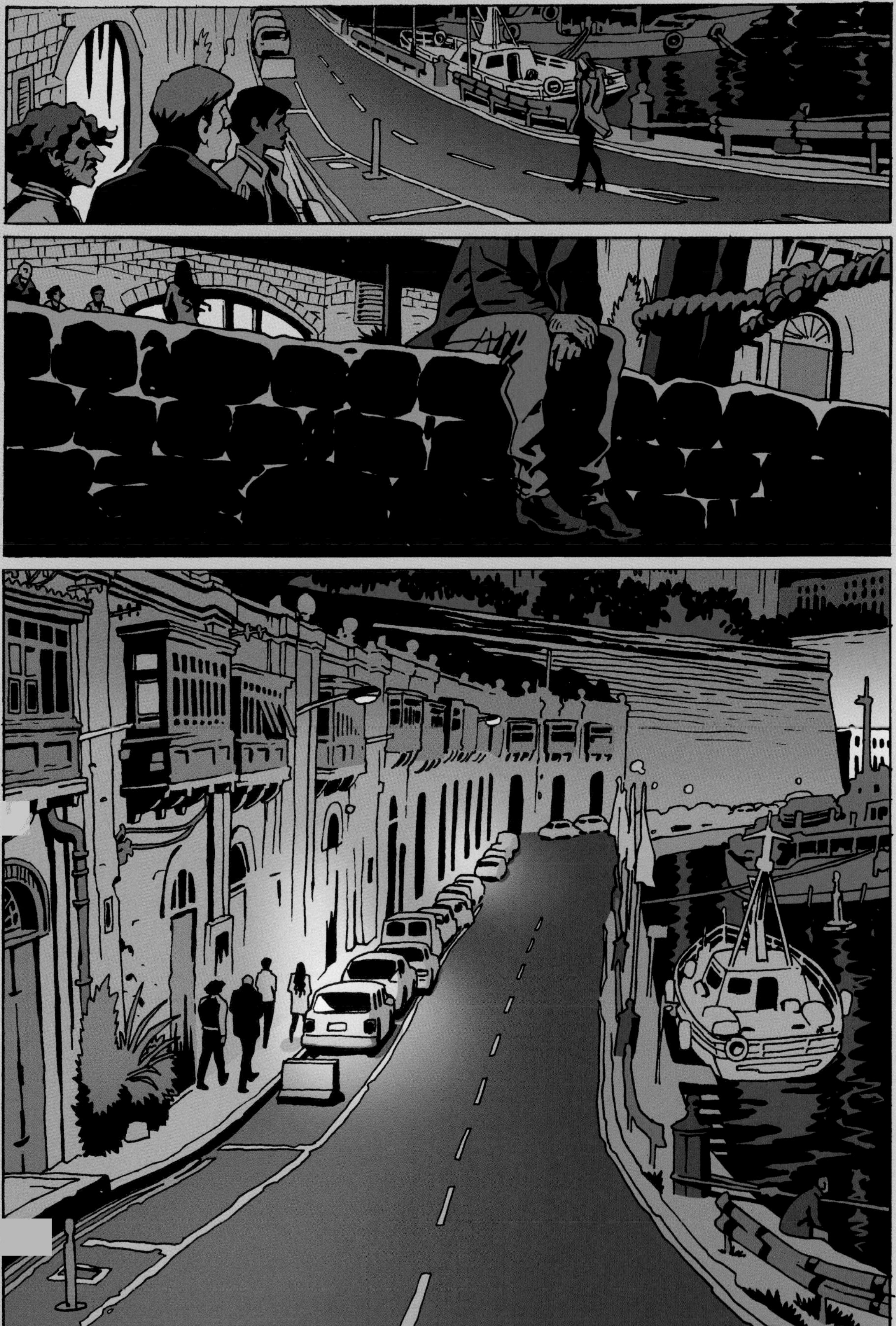
LEANDRO FERNANDEZ

"**SOLDIERS** live.

And wonder **WHY.**"

~Glen Cook

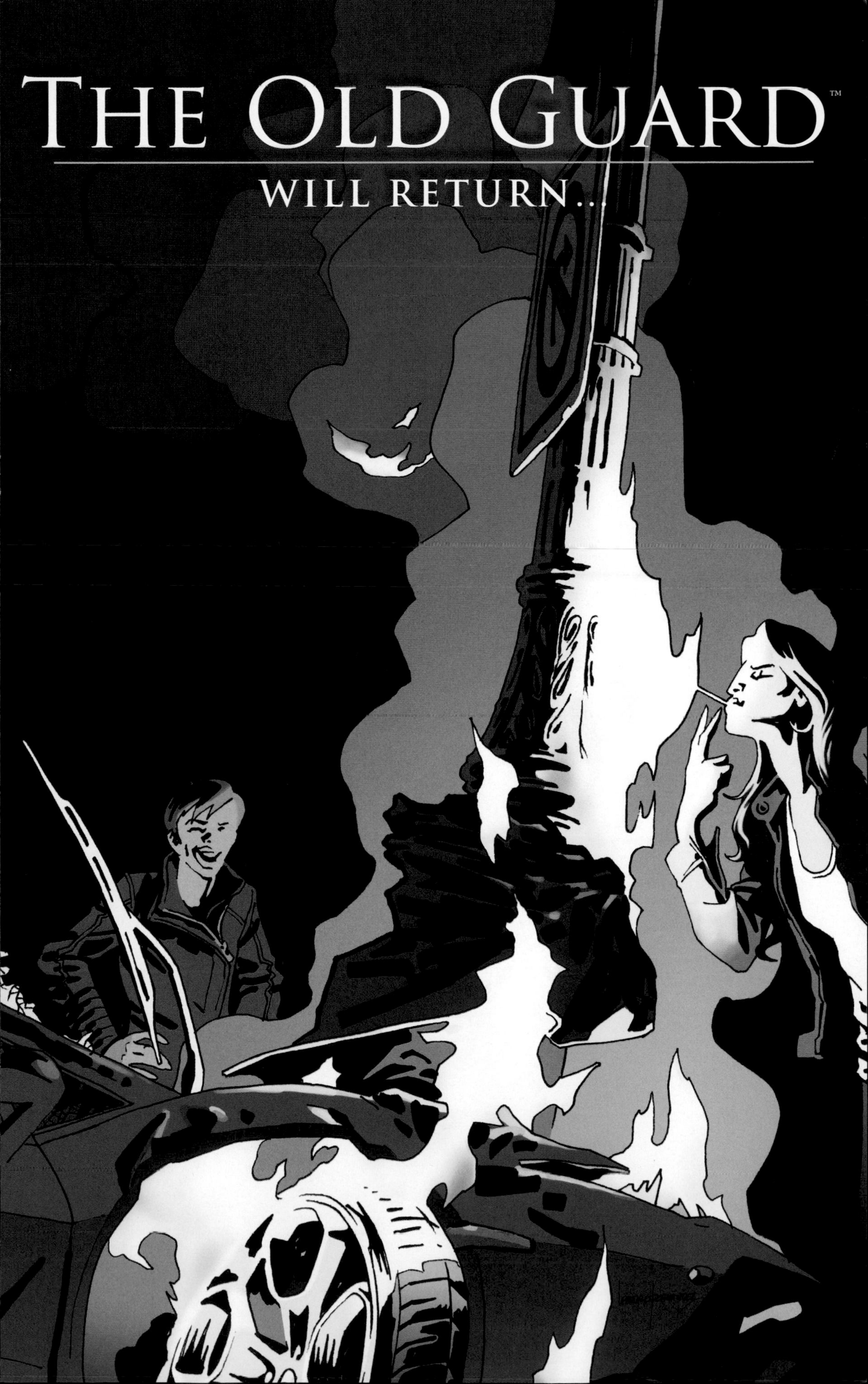
THE OLD GUARD™
WILL RETURN...

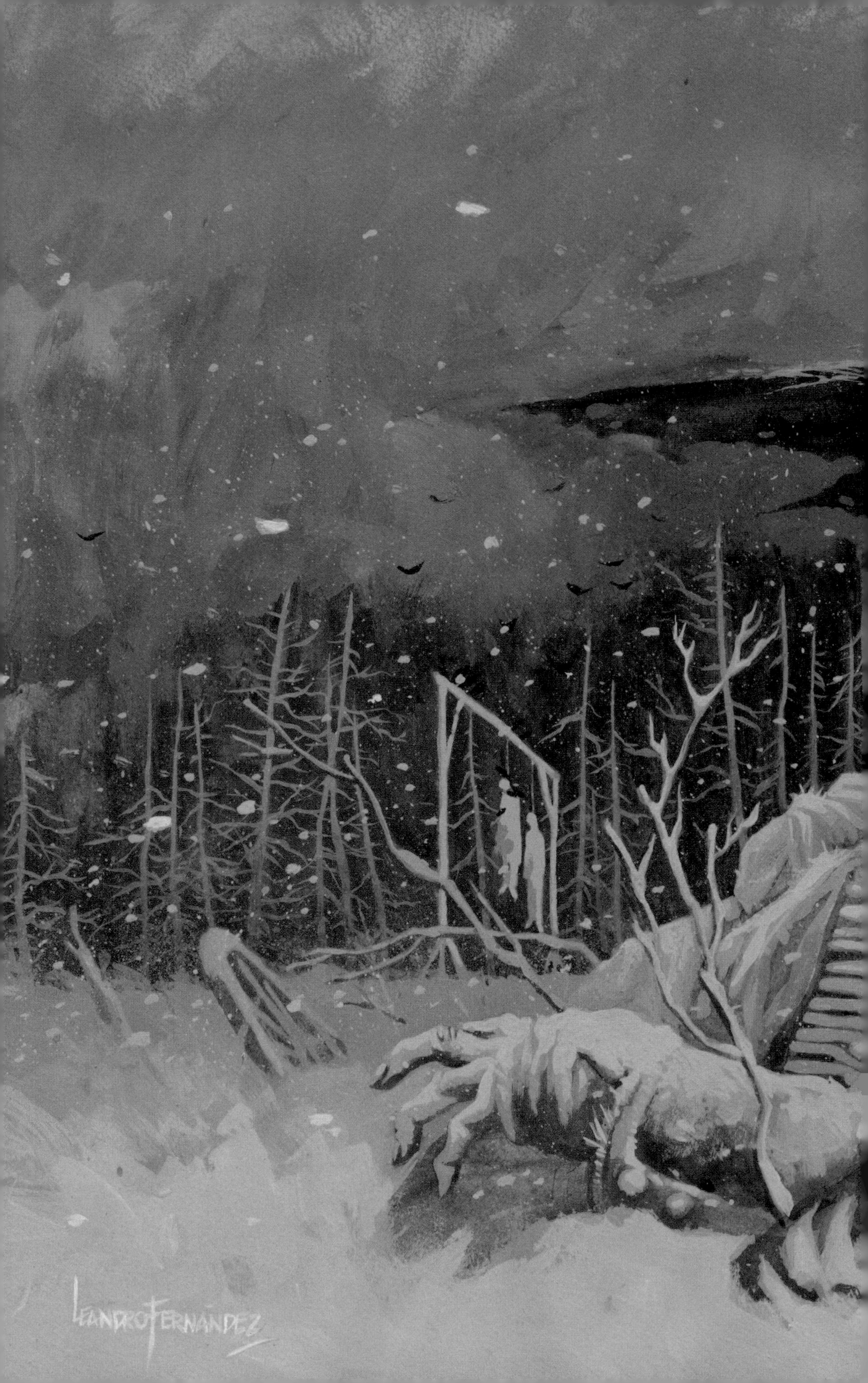
LEANDRO FERNANDEZ

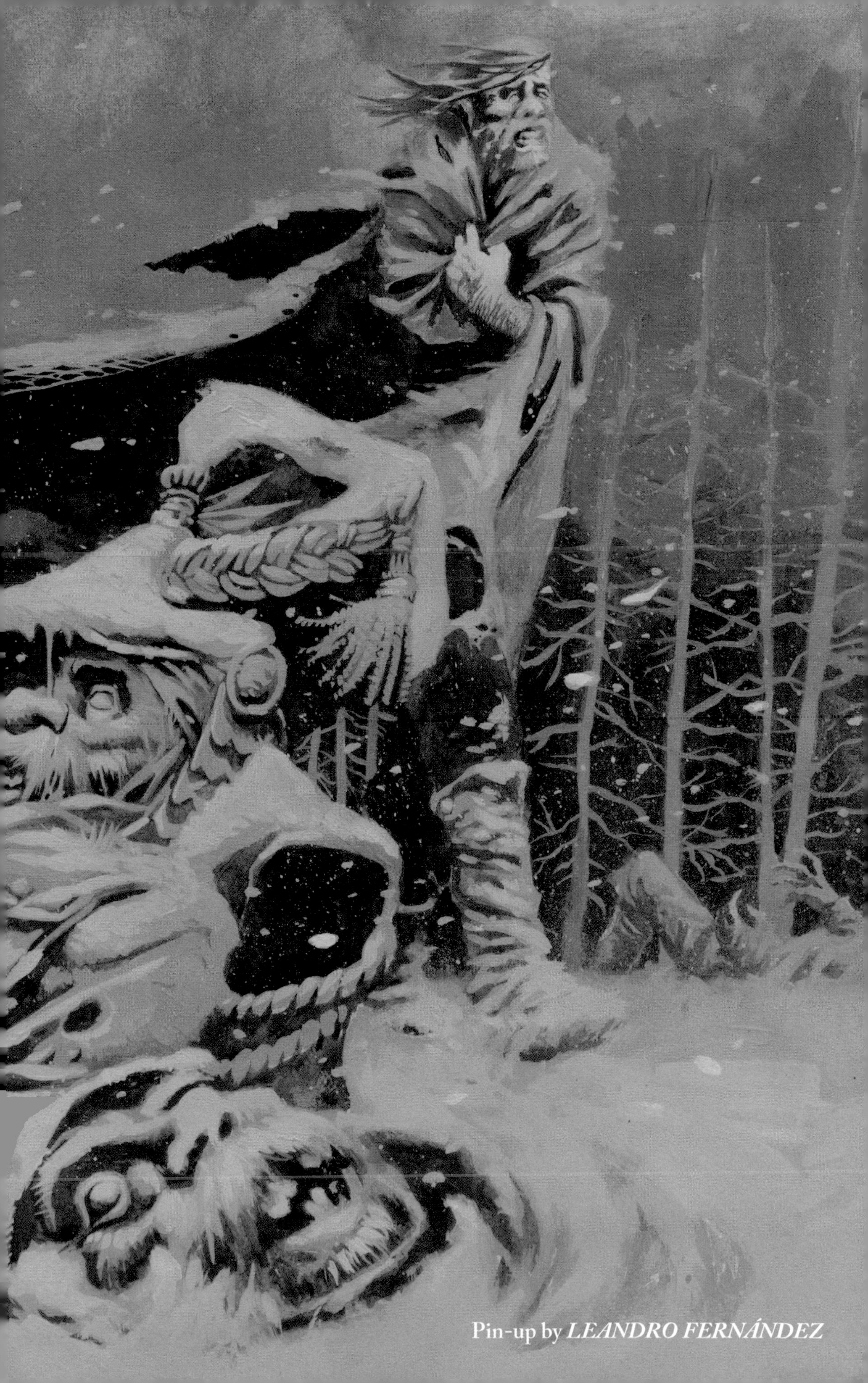

Pin-up by *LEANDRO FERNÁNDEZ*

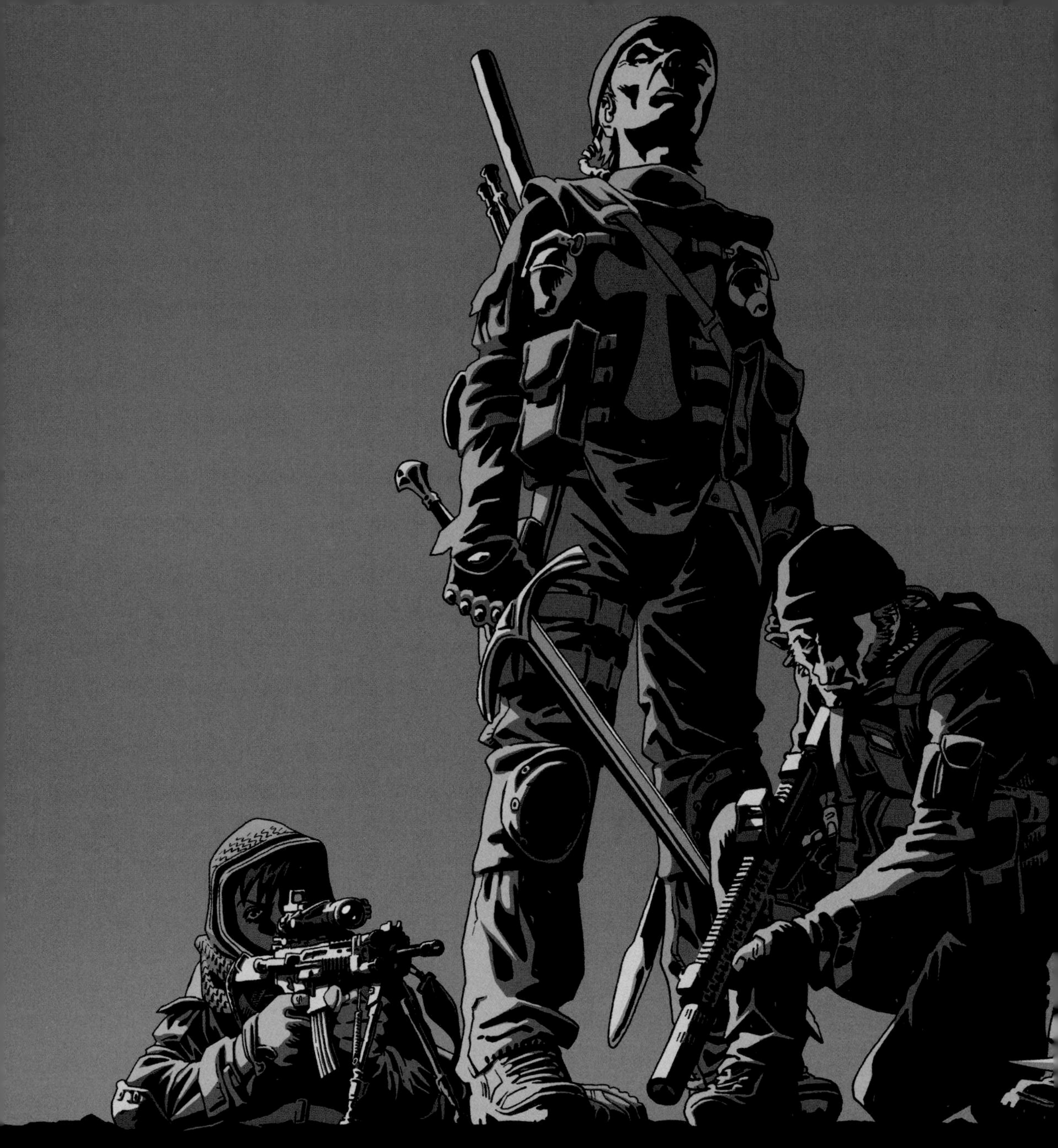

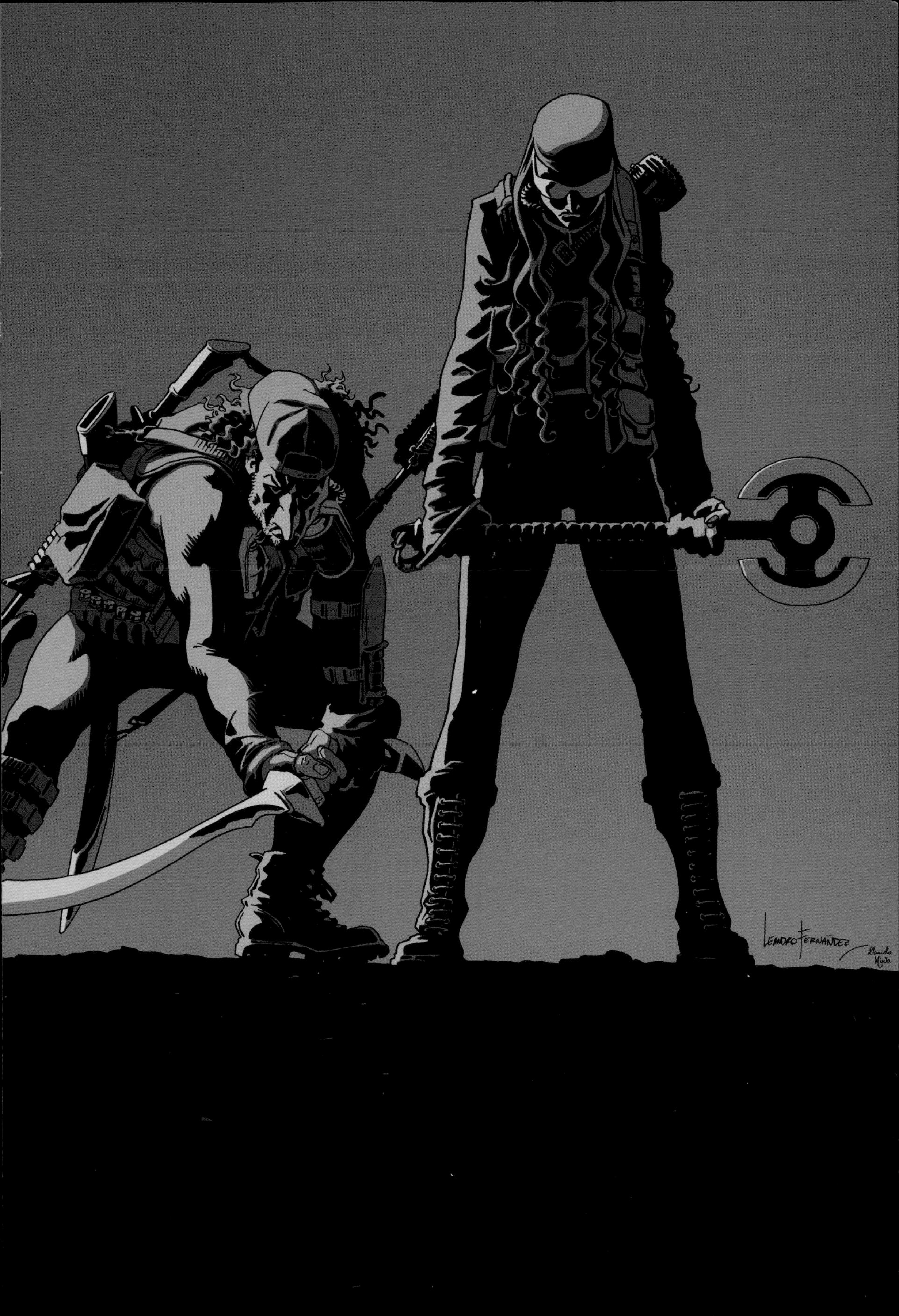
LEANDRO FERNÁNDEZ
Daniela Miwa

Issue One "Wraparound" Variant Cover by *LEANDRO FERNÁNDEZ*
with *DANIELA MIWA*

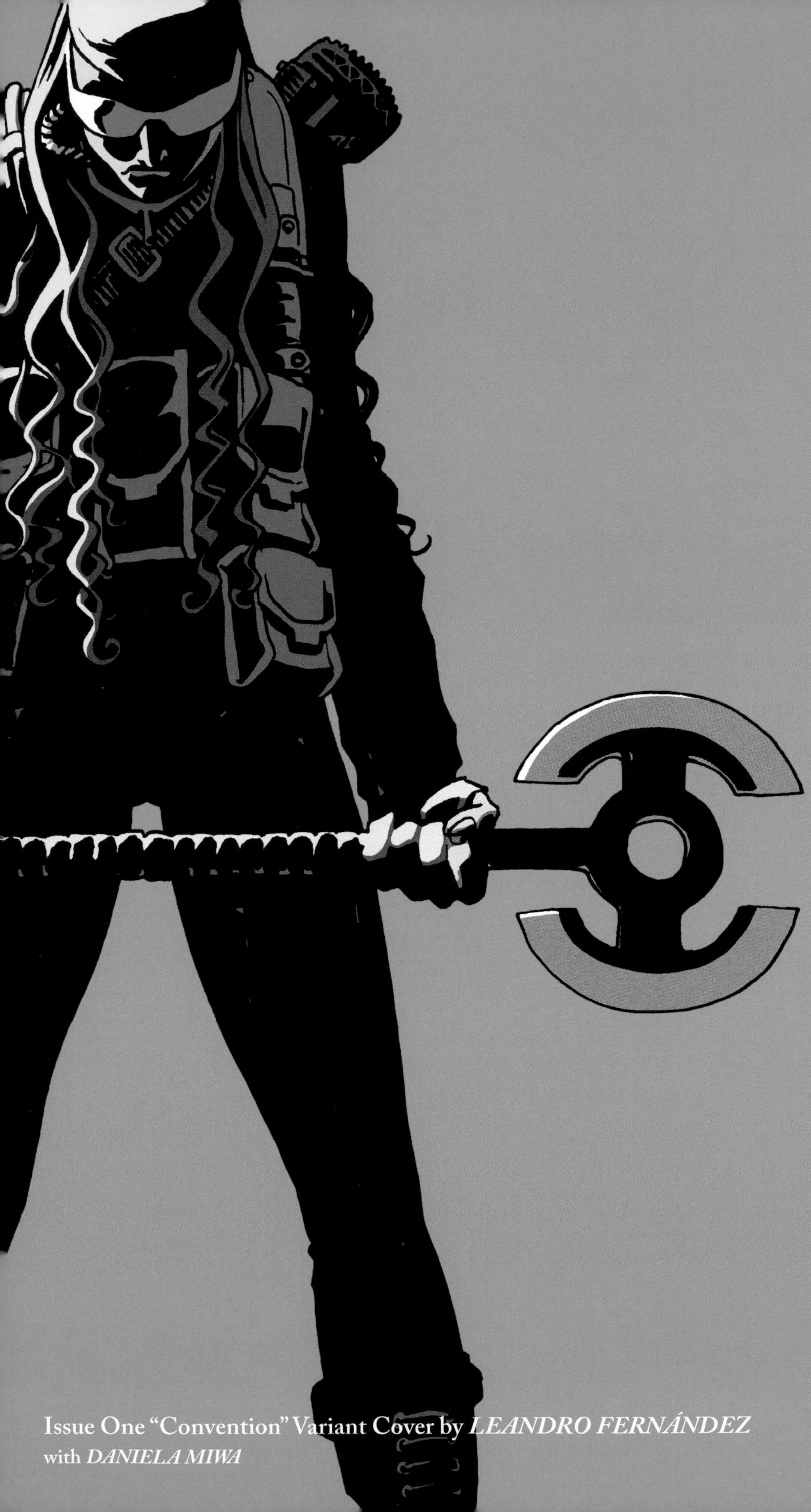

Issue One "Convention" Variant Cover by *LEANDRO FERNÁNDEZ*
with *DANIELA MIWA*

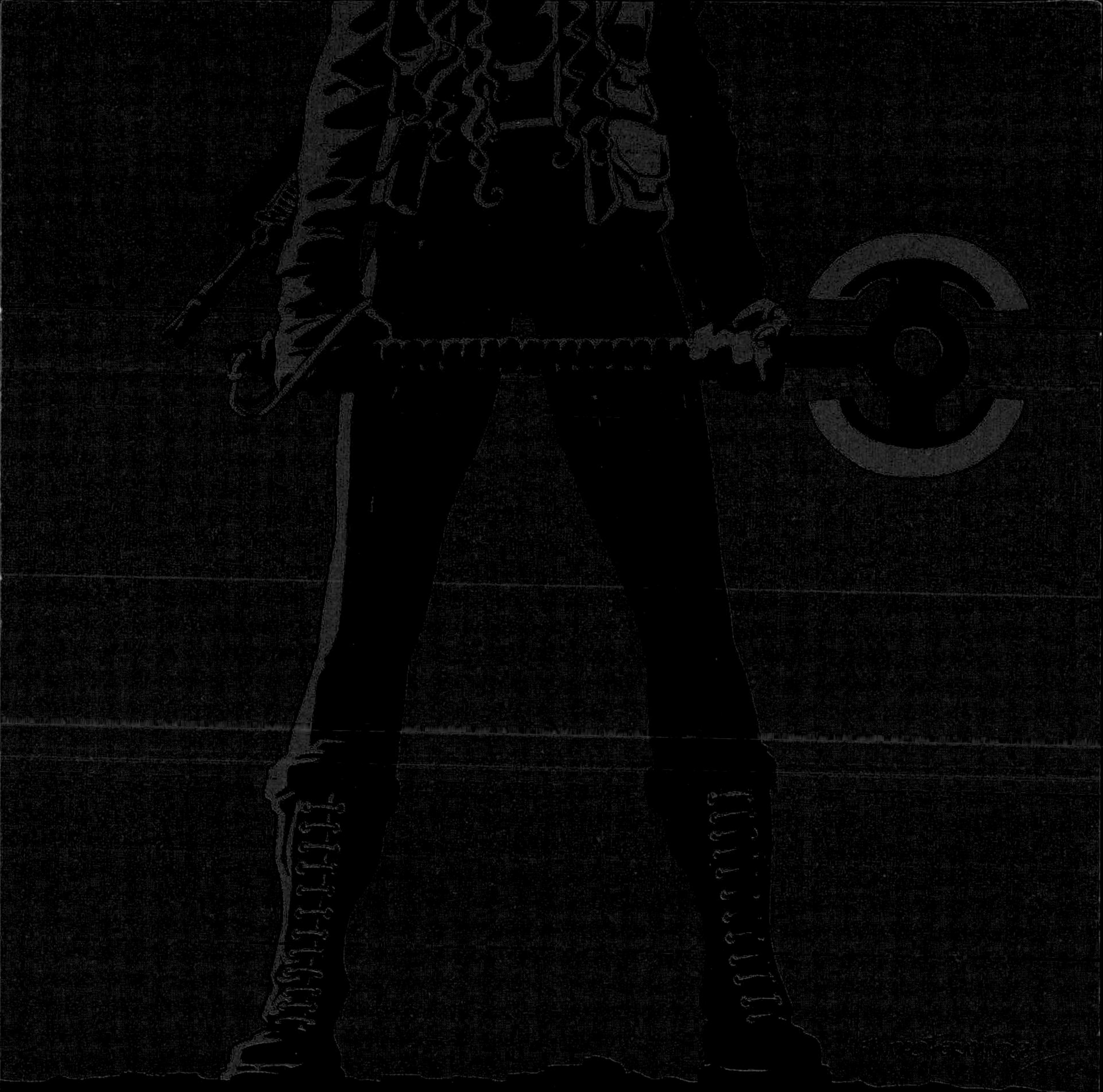

Issue One Second Printing Cover by *LEANDRO FERNÁNDEZ*
with *ALEJANDRO ARBONA*

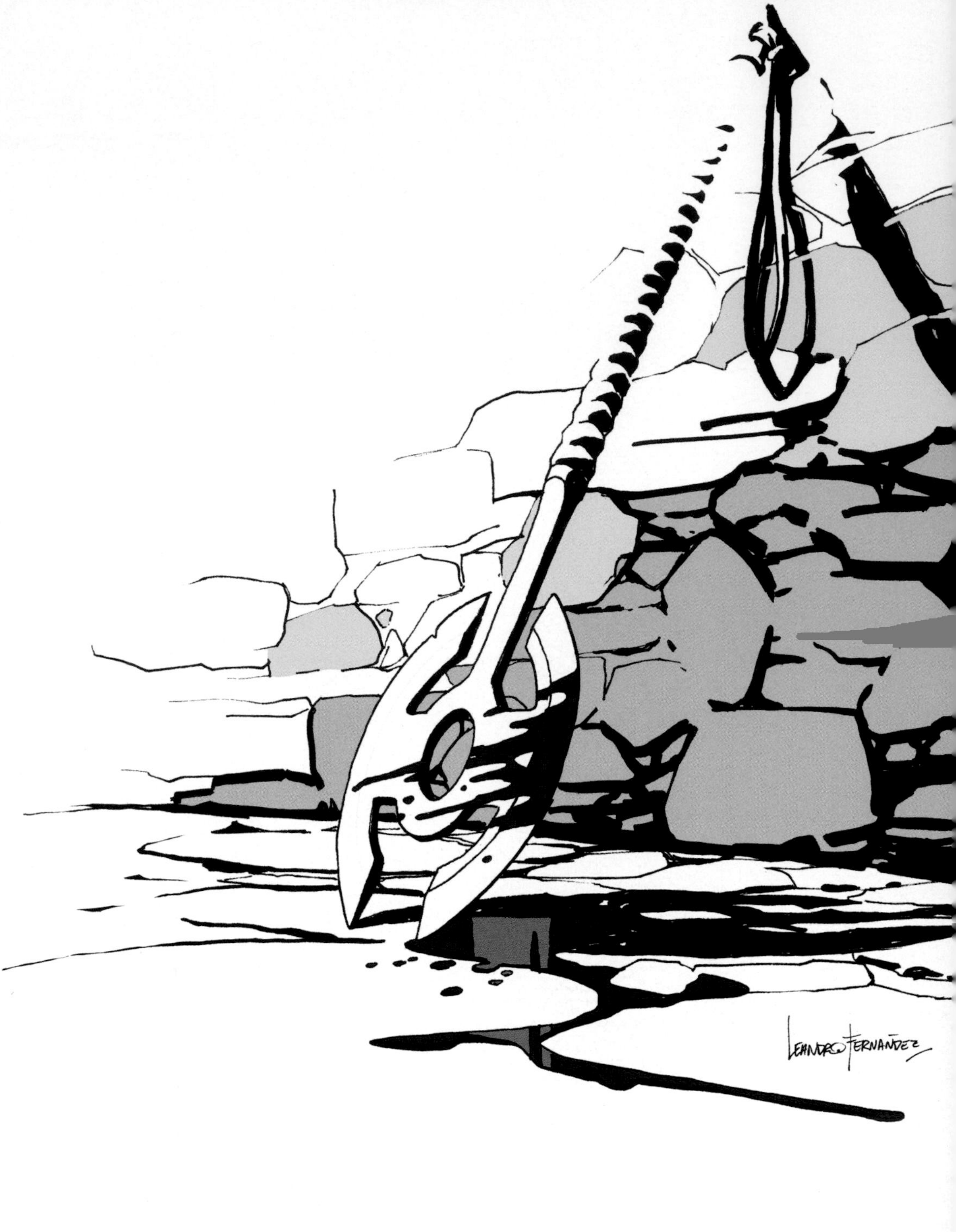
LEANDRO FERNANDEZ

Issue One Third Printing Cover by *LEANDRO FERNÁNDEZ*

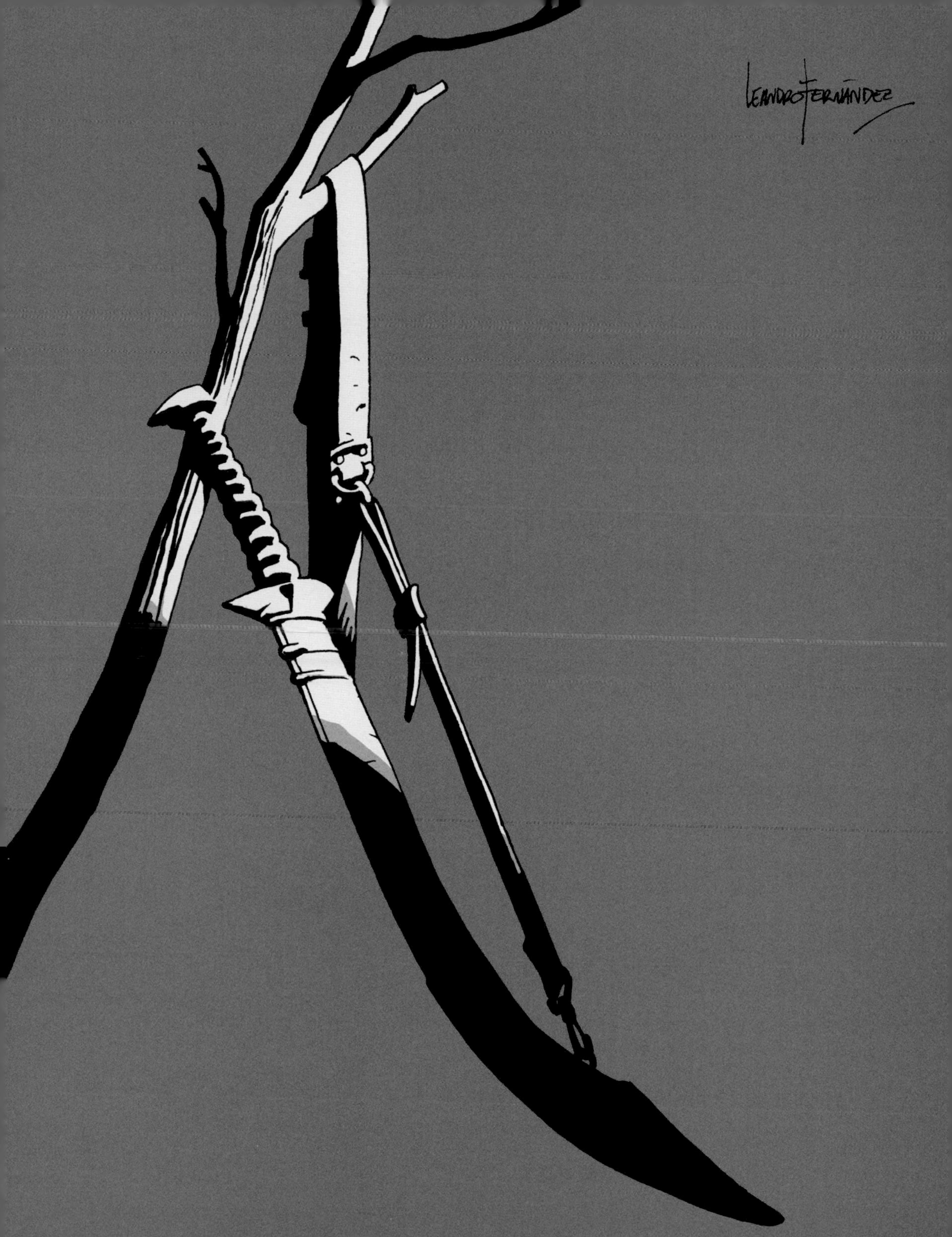
LEANDRO FERNÁNDEZ

Issue Two Second Printing Cover by *LEANDRO FERNÁNDEZ*

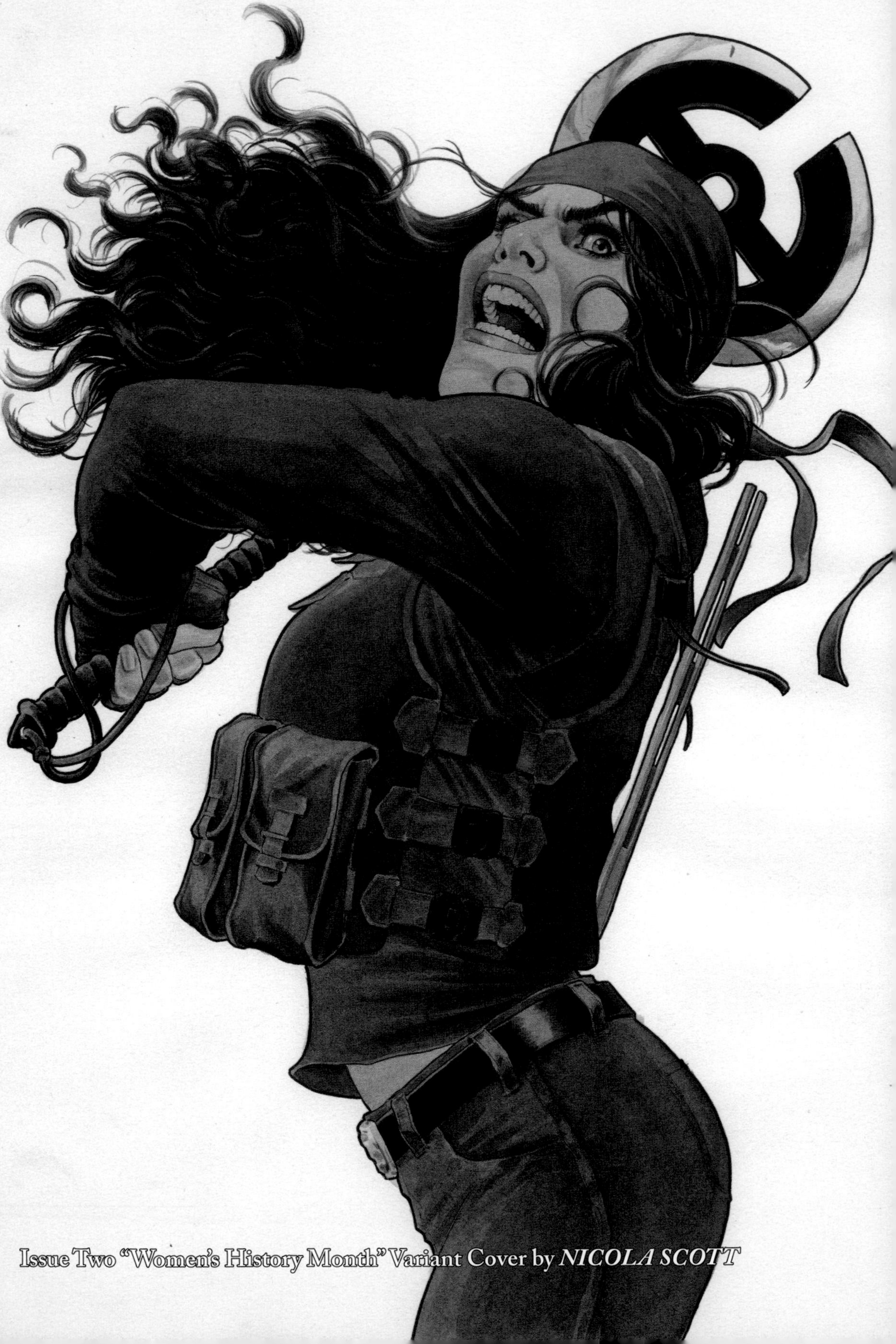

Issue Two "Women's History Month" Variant Cover by *NICOLA SCOTT*

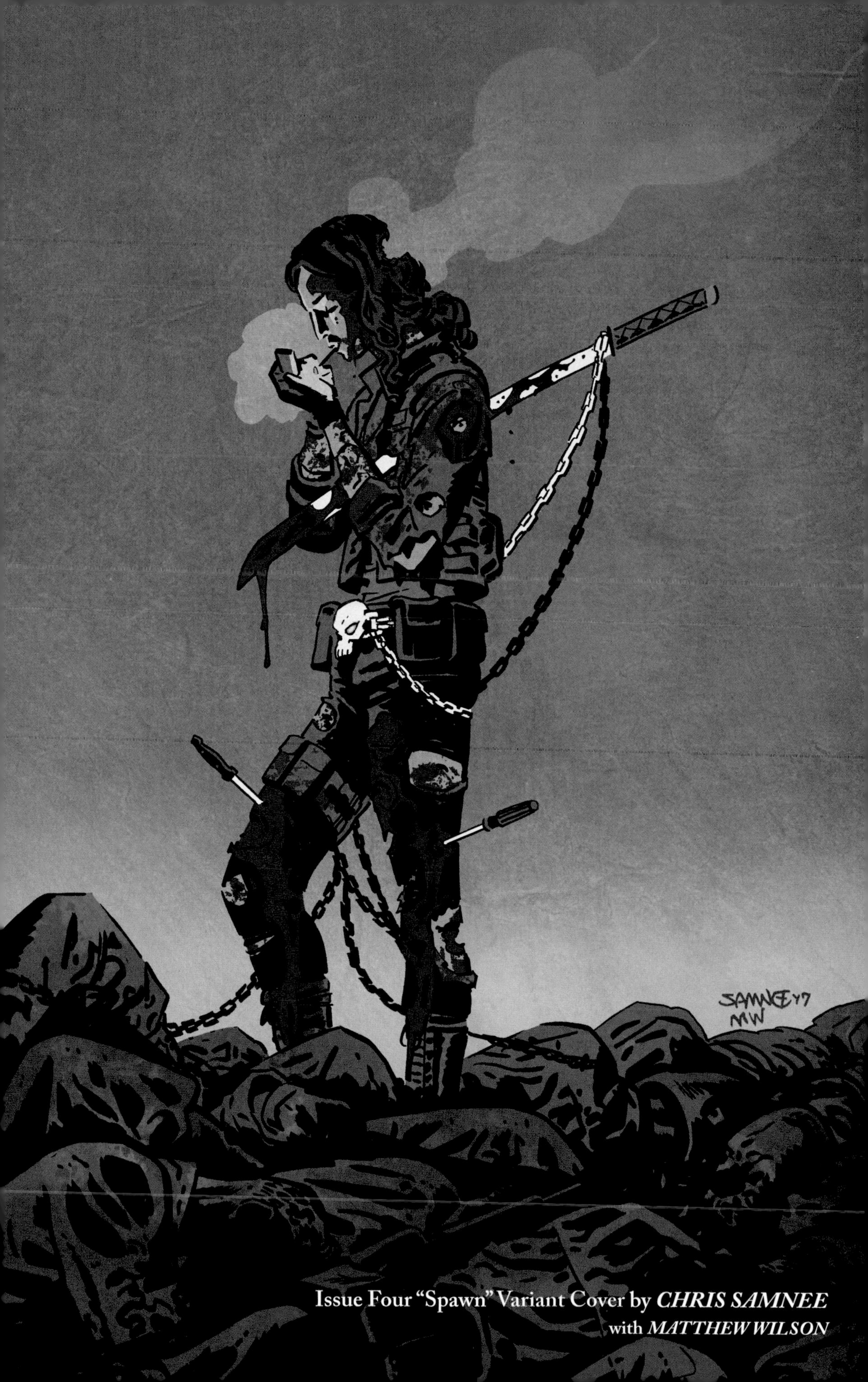
SAMNEE '17
MW

Issue Four "Spawn" Variant Cover by *CHRIS SAMNEE*
with *MATTHEW WILSON*

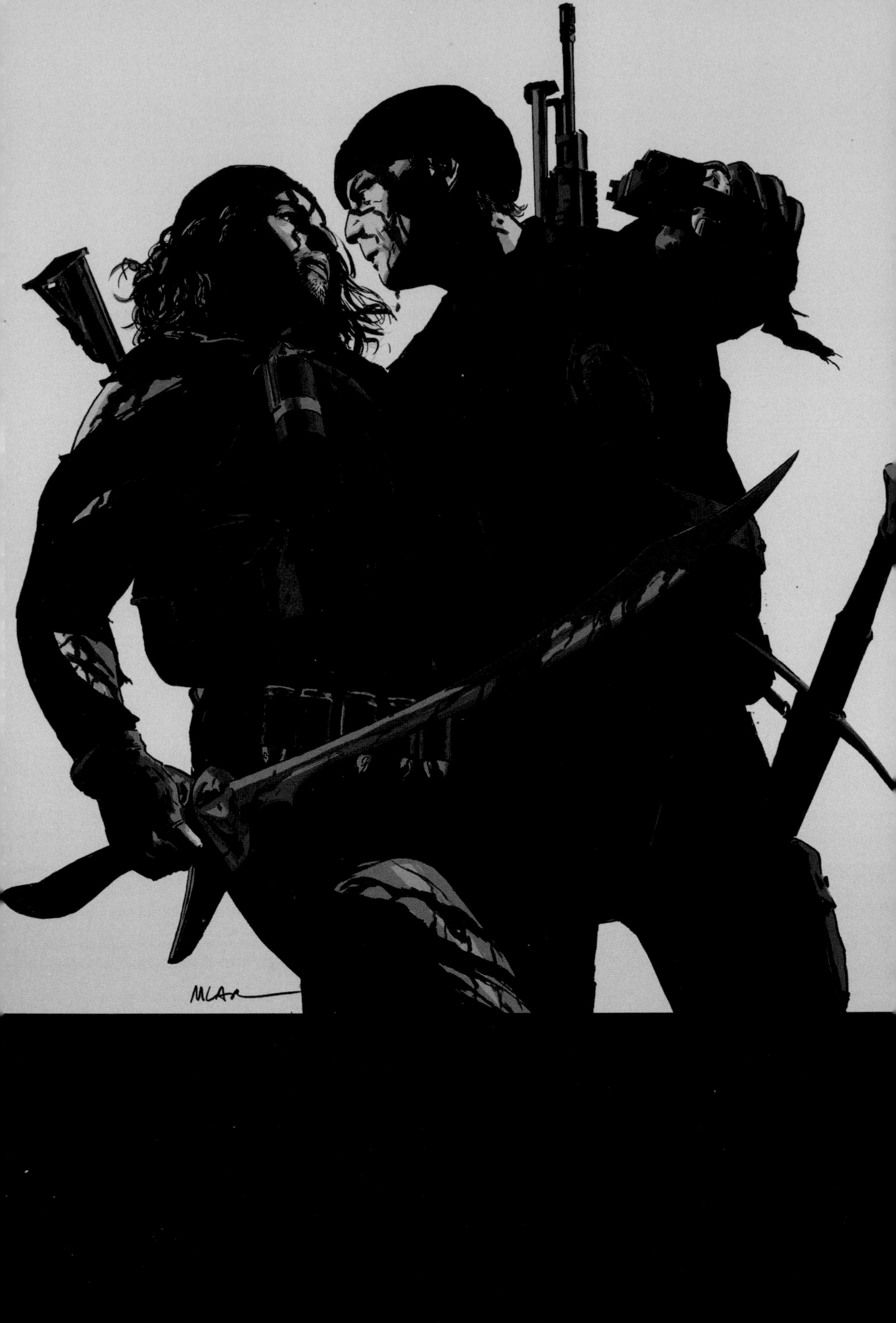

Issue Five "Pride" Variant Cover by *MICHAEL LARK*